**RECEIVED**

AUG 2 0 2019

Douglass-~~~~~ Library

|||||||||||||||||||||||||||||
D0744169

NO LONGER P,  ~~ERTY OF
SEATTLE PUBLIC LIBRARY

# ARTURO'S
# ISLAND

# ARTURO'S ISLAND

## A Novel

ELSA MORANTE

Translated by Ann Goldstein

LIVERIGHT PUBLISHING CORPORATION
A Division of W. W. Norton & Company
*Independent Publishers Since 1923*
NEW YORK • LONDON

Copyright © Elsa Morante Estate
Published by arrangement with The Italian Literary Agency
Translation copyright © 2019 by Ann Goldstein

Originally published in Italian as *L'isola di Arturo*

All rights reserved
Printed in the United States of America

For information about permission to reproduce selections from this book, write to
Permissions, Liveright Publishing Corporation, a division of
W. W. Norton & Company, Inc., 500 Fifth Avenue, New York, NY 10110

For information about special discounts for bulk purchases, please contact
W. W. Norton Special Sales at specialsales@wwnorton.com or 800-233-4830

Manufacturing by Worzalla
Book design by Ellen Cipriano
Production manager: Lauren Abbate

Library of Congress Cataloging-in-Publication Data

Names: Morante, Elsa, approximately 1912–1985, author. | Goldstein, Ann, translator.
Title: Arturo's island : a novel / Elsa Morante ; translated by Ann Goldstein.
Other titles: Isola di Arturo. English
Description: New York : Liveright Publishing Corporation, 2019.
Identifiers: LCCN 2018046181 | ISBN 9781631493294 (hardcover)
Classification: LCC PQ4829.O615 I813 2019 | DDC 853/.912—dc23
LC record available at https://lccn.loc.gov/2018046181

Liveright Publishing Corporation, 500 Fifth Avenue, New York, N.Y. 10110
www.wwnorton.com

W. W. Norton & Company Ltd., 15 Carlisle Street, London W1D 3BS

1 2 3 4 5 6 7 8 9 0

*for Remo N.*

What you thought was a tiny point on earth
was all.
And no one can ever steal that matchless treasure from your
jealous sleeping eyes.
Your first love will never be violated.

Virgin, she is wrapped in night
like a gypsy in her black shawl,
star suspended in the northern sky
for eternity: no danger can touch her.

Young friends, handsomer than Alexander and Euryalos,
forever handsome, protect the sleep of my boy.
The fearful emblem will never cross the threshold
of that blessed little island.

                    And you'll never know the law
that I, like so many, have learned—
and that has broken my heart:

*Outside Limbo there is no Elysium.*

If I see myself in him, it seems clear to me . . .

—Umberto Saba, *Il Canzoniere*

# CONTENTS

# ARTURO'S ISLAND

# CHAPTER 1

# King and Star of the Sky

*. . . Paradise*

*lofty and chaotic . . .*

—SANDRO PENNA, *POESIE*

## King and Star of the Sky

One of my first glories was my name. I had learned early (*he*, it seems to me, was the first to inform me) that Arturo—Arcturus—is a star: the swiftest and brightest light in the constellation of Boötes, the Herdsman, in the northern sky! And that this name was also borne by a king in ancient times, the commander of a band of faithful followers: all heroes, like the king himself, and treated by the king as equals, as brothers.

Unfortunately, I later discovered that that famous Arthur, King of Britain, was not a true story, only a legend; and so I abandoned him for other, more historical kings (in my opinion legends were childish). Still, another reason was enough in itself for me to give a noble value to the name Arturo: and that is, that it was my mother, I learned, who, although I think ignorant of the aristocratic symbolism, decided on that name. Who was herself simply an illiterate young woman but for me more than a sovereign.

In reality, I knew almost nothing about her, for she wasn't even eighteen when she died, at the moment that I, her only child, was born. And the sole image of her I ever knew was a portrait on a postcard. A faded, ordinary, almost ghostlike figure, but the object of fantastic adoration for my entire childhood.

The poor itinerant photographer to whom we owe this unique image portrayed her in the first months of her pregnancy. You can tell from her body, even amid the folds of the loose-fitting dress, that she's pregnant; and she holds her little hands clasped in front of her, as if to hide herself, in a timid, modest pose. She's very serious, and in her black eyes you can read not only submissiveness, which is usual in most of our girls and young village brides, but a stunned and slightly fearful questioning. As if, among the common illusions of maternity, she already suspected that her destiny would be death and eternal ignorance.


## The Island


All the islands of our archipelago, here in the Bay of Naples, are beautiful.

For the most part, the land is of volcanic origin, and, especially near the ancient craters, thousands of flowers grow wild: I've never seen anything like it on the mainland. In spring, the hills are covered with broom: traveling on the sea in the month of June you recognize its wild, caressing odor as soon as you approach our harbors.

Up in the hills in the countryside, my island has solitary narrow roads enclosed between ancient walls, behind which orchards and vineyards extend, like imperial gardens. It has several beaches with pale, fine sand, and other, smaller shores, covered with pebbles and shells, hidden amid high cliffs. In those towering rocks, which loom over the water, seagulls and turtledoves make their nests, and you can hear their voices, especially in the early morning, sometimes lamenting, sometimes gay. There, on quiet days, the sea is gentle and cool, and lies on the shore like dew. Ah, I wouldn't ask to be a seagull or a dolphin; I'd be content to be a scorpion fish, the ugliest fish in the sea, just to be down there, playing in that water.

Around the port, the streets are all sunless alleys, lined with plain, centuries-old houses, which, although painted in beautiful pink or grayish shell colors, look severe and melancholy. On the sills of the small windows, which are almost as narrow as loopholes, you sometimes see a carnation growing in a tin can, or a little cage that seems fit for a cricket but holds a captured turtledove. The shops are as deep and dark as brigands' dens. In the café at the port, there's a coal stove on which the owner boils Turkish coffee, in a deep blue enameled coffeepot. She's been a widow for many years, and always wears the black of mourning, the black shawl, the black earrings. A photograph of the deceased, on the wall beside the cash register, is festooned with dusty leaves.

The innkeeper, in his tavern, which is opposite the monument of Christ the Fisherman, is raising an owl, chained to a plank high up against the wall. The owl has delicate black and gray feathers, an elegant tuft on his head, blue eyelids, and big eyes of a red-gold color, circled with black; he always has a bleeding wing, because he constantly pecks at it with his beak. If you stretch out a hand to give him a little tickle on the chest, he bends his small head toward you, with an expression of wonder.

When evening descends, he starts to struggle, tries to take off, and falls back, and sometimes ends up hanging head down, flapping on his chain.

In the church at the port, the oldest on the island, there are some wax saints, less than three palms high, locked in glass cases. They have skirts of real lace, yellowed, faded cloaks of brocatelle, real hair, and from their wrists hang tiny rosaries of real pearls. On their small fingers, which have a deathly pallor, the nails are sketched with a threadlike red line.

Those elegant pleasure boats and cruise ships that in greater and greater numbers crowd the other ports of the archipelago hardly ever dock at ours; here you'll see some barges or merchant ships, besides the fishing boats of the islanders. For many hours of the day the square at the port seems almost deserted; on the left, near the statue of Christ the Fisherman, a single carriage for hire awaits the arrival of the regularly scheduled steamers, which stop here for a few minutes and disembark three or four passengers altogether, mostly people from the island. Never, not even in summer, do our solitary beaches experience the commotion of the bathers from Naples and other cities, and all parts of the world, who throng the beaches of the surrounding areas. And if a stranger happens to get off at Procida, he marvels at not finding here that open and happy life, of celebrations and conversations on the street, of song and the strains of guitars or mandolins, for which the region of Naples is known throughout the world. The Procidans are surly, taciturn. All the doors are closed, almost no one looks out the window, every family lives within its four walls and doesn't mingle with the others. Friendship, among us, isn't welcomed. And the arrival of a stranger arouses not curiosity but, rather, distrust. If he asks questions, they are answered reluctantly, because the people of my island don't like their privacy spied on.

They are a small dark race, with elongated black eyes, like Orientals. And they so closely resemble one another you might say they're all related. The women, following ancient custom, live cloistered like nuns. Many of them still wear their hair coiled, shawls over their heads, long dresses, and, in winter, clogs over thick black cotton stockings; in summer some go barefoot. When they pass barefoot, rapid and noiseless, avoiding encounters, they might be feral cats or weasels.

They never go to the beach; for women it's a sin to swim in the sea, and a sin even to watch others swimming.

In books, the houses of ancient feudal cities, grouped together or scattered through the valley and across the hillsides, all in sight of the castle that dominates them from the highest peak, are often compared to a flock around the shepherd. Thus, too, on Procida, the houses—from those densely crowded at the port, to the ones spread out on the hills, and the isolated country farmhouses—appear, from a distance, exactly like a herd scattered at the foot of the castle. This castle rises on the highest hill (which among the other, smaller hills is like a mountain); and, enlarged by structures superimposed and added over the centuries, has acquired the mass of a gigantic citadel. To passing ships, especially at night, all that appears of Procida is this dark mass, which makes our island seem like a fortress in the middle of the sea.

For around two hundred years, the castle has been used as a penitentiary: one of the biggest, I believe, in the whole country. For many people who live far away the name of my island means the name of a prison.

On the western side, which faces the sea, my house is in sight of the castle, but at a distance of several hundred meters as the crow flies, and over numerous small inlets from which, at night, the fishermen set out in their boats with lanterns lighted. At that distance you can't distinguish the bars on the windows, or the circuit of the guards around the walls; so that, especially in winter, when the air is misty and the moving clouds pass in front of it, the penitentiary might seem the kind of abandoned castle you find in many old cities. A fantastic ruin, inhabited only by snakes, owls, and swallows.

## The Story of Romeo the Amalfitano

My house rises alone at the top of a steep hill, in the middle of an uncultivated terrain scattered with lava pebbles. The façade looks toward the town, and on that side the hill is buttressed by an old wall made of pieces of rock; here lives the deep blue lizard (which is found nowhere else, nowhere else in the world). On the right, a stairway of stones and earth descends toward the level ground where vehicles can go.

Behind the house there is a broad open space, beyond which the land becomes steep and impassable. And by means of a long rockslide you reach a small, triangular, black-sand beach. No path leads to this beach; but, if you're barefoot, it's easy to descend precipitously amid the rocks. At the bottom a single boat was moored: it was mine, and was called *Torpedo Boat of the Antilles*.

My house isn't far from a small, almost urban square (boasting, among other things, a marble monument) or from the densely built dwellings of the town. But in my memory it has become an isolated place, and its solitude makes an enormous space around it. There it sits, malign and marvelous, like a golden spider that has woven its iridescent web over the whole island.

It's a two-story palazzo, plus the cellar and the attic (in Procida houses that have around twenty rooms, which in Naples might seem small, are called palazzi), and, as with most of the inhabited area of Procida, which is very old, it was built at least three centuries ago.

It's a pale pink color, square, rough, and constructed without elegance; it would look like a large farmhouse if not for the majestic central entrance and the Baroque-style grilles that protect all the windows on the outside. The façade's only ornaments are two iron balconies, suspended on either side of the entrance, in front of two blind windows. These balconies, and also the grilles, were once painted white, but now they're all stained and corroded by rust.

A smaller door is cut into one panel of the central entrance door, and this is the way we usually go in: the two panels are, instead, never opened, and the enormous locks that bolt them from the inside have been eaten by rust and are unusable. Through the small door you enter a long, windowless hall, paved with slate, at the end of which, in the style of Procida's grand houses, a gate opens to an internal garden. This gate is guarded by two statues of very faded painted terra-cotta, portraying two hooded figures, which could be either monks or Saracens, you can't tell. And, beyond the gate, the garden, enclosed by the walls of the house like a courtyard, appears a triumph of wild greenery.

There, under the beautiful carob tree, my dog Immacolatella is buried.

From the roof of the house, one can see the full shape of the island, which resembles a dolphin; its small inlets, the penitentiary, and not far away, on the sea, the bluish purple form of the island of Ischia. The silvery shadows of more distant islands. And, at night, the firmament, where Boötes the Herdsman walks, with his star Arturo.

From the day it was built, for more than two centuries, the house was a monastery: this fact is common among us, and there's nothing romantic about it. Procida was always a place of poor fishermen and farmers, and its rare grand buildings were all, inevitably, either convents, or churches, or fortresses, or prisons.

Later, those religious men moved elsewhere, and the house ceased to belong to the Church. For a certain period, during and after the wars of the past century, it housed regiments of soldiers; then it was abandoned and uninhabited for a long time; and finally, about half a century ago, it was bought by a private citizen, a wealthy shipping agent from Amalfi, who, passing through Procida, made it his home, and lived there in idleness for thirty years.

He transformed part of the interior, especially the upper floor, where he knocked down the dividing walls between numerous cells of the former monastery and covered the walls with wallpaper. Even in my time, although the house was run-down and in constant disrepair, it preserved the arrangement and the furnishings as he had left them. The furniture, which had been collected by a picturesque but ignorant imagination from the small antique and secondhand dealers of Naples, gave the rooms a certain romantic-country aspect. Entering, you had the illusion of a past of grandmothers and great-grandmothers, of ancient female secrets.

And yet from the time those walls were erected until the year our family arrived, they had never seen a woman.

When, a little more than twenty years ago, my paternal grandfather, Antonio Gerace, who had emigrated from Procida, returned with a modest fortune from America, the Amalfitano, who by then was an old man, still lived in the ancient palazzo. In old age, he had become blind; and it was said that this was a punishment from Santa Lucia, because he hated women. He had hated them since youth, to the point that he wouldn't receive even his own sisters, and when the Sisters of the Consolation came to beg he left them outside the door. For that reason, he had never married; and he was never seen in church, or in the shops, where women are more readily encountered.

He wasn't hostile to society; in fact, he had quite a splendid character, and often gave banquets, and even masked parties, and on such occasions he proved to be generous to the point of madness, so that he had become a legend on the island. However, no woman was admitted to his entertainments; and the girls of Procida, envious of their boyfriends and brothers who took part in those mysterious evenings, spitefully nicknamed the Amalfitano's abode the Casa dei Guaglioni, or Boys' House (*guaglione*, in Neapolitan dialect, means boy or youth).

My grandfather Antonio, disembarking in his homeland after some decades of absence, did not think that destiny had reserved the Casa dei Guaglioni for his family. He scarcely recalled the Amalfitano, with whom he had never had a friendly relationship; and that old monastery-barracks among the thorns and prickly pears did not in the least resemble the dwelling he had dreamed of for himself during his exile. He bought a house in the country, with a farm, in the southern part of the island, and went to live there, alone with his tenant farmers, being a bachelor with no close relatives.

Actually, there existed on the earth *one* close relative of Antonio Gerace, whom he had never seen. This was a son, born during his early life as an emigrant, from a relationship with a young German schoolteacher, whom he soon abandoned. For several years after the abandonment (the emigrant had moved to America following a short stint in Germany), the girl-mother had continued to write to him, begging him for material help, because she found herself without work, and seeking to move him with marvelous descriptions of the child. But the emigrant was himself so wretched at the time that he stopped answering the letters, until the young woman, discouraged, stopped writing. And when, returning to Procida aged and without heirs, Antonio tried to find her, he learned that she had died, leaving the child, now around sixteen, in Germany.

Antonio Gerace then summoned that son to Procida, to finally give him his own name and his own inheritance. And so he who was to become my father disembarked on the island of Procida, dressed in rags like a gypsy (I learned later).

He must have had a hard life. And his childish heart must have been nourished on rancor not only toward his unknown father but also toward all the other innocent Procidans. Maybe, too, by some act or behavior, they affronted his irascible pride from the start, and forever. Certainly, on the island, his indifferent and offensive manner made him universally hated. With his father, who tried to win his affection, the boy was aloof to the point of cruelty.

The only person on the island he saw was the Amalfitano. It was some time since the latter had given entertainments or parties, and he lived isolated in his blindness, surly and proud, refusing to receive those who sought him out and pushing away with his stick those who approached him on the street. His tall, melancholy figure had become detested by everyone.

His house opened again to only one person: the son of Antonio Gerace, who formed such a close friendship with him that he spent every day in his company, as if the Amalfitano, and not Antonio Gerace, were his real father. And the Amalfitano devoted to him an exclusive and tyrannical affection: it seemed that he couldn't live a day without him. If the son was late in his daily visit, the Amalfitano went out to meet him, sitting at the end of the street to wait. And, unable to see if he was finally coming, in his blind man's anxiety he would every so often call out his name, in a hoarse voice that seemed already to come from the grave. If passersby answered that Gerace's son wasn't there, he would throw some coins and banknotes on the ground, haphazardly and with contempt, so that, thus paid, they would go and summon him. And if they returned later to say that they hadn't found him at home, he had them search the entire island, even unleashing his dogs in the hunt. In his life now there was nothing else: either being with his only friend or waiting for him. Two years later, when he died, he left him the house on Procida.

Not long afterward, Antonio Gerace died: and the son, who some months earlier had married an orphan from Massa, moved to the Amalfitano's house with his young, pregnant bride. He was then about nineteen, and the wife not yet eighteen. It was the first time, in almost three centuries since the palazzo was built, that a woman had lived within its walls.

The farmers remained in my grandfather's house and on his land, and are still tenants there today.

## The Boys' House

The premature death of my mother, at eighteen, giving birth to her first child, was certainly a confirmation, if not the origin, of a popular rumor according to which the deceased owner's hatred meant that it was forever fatal for a woman to live in the Casa dei Guaglioni, the Boys' House, or even simply to enter it.

My father had barely a faint smile of scorn for that country tale, so that I, too, from the start learned to consider it with the proper contempt, as the superstitious nonsense it was. But it had acquired such authority on the island that no woman would ever agree to be our servant. During my childhood a boy from Naples worked for us; his name was Silvestro, and at the time he entered our house (shortly before my birth) he was fourteen or fifteen. He returned to Naples at the time of his military service, and was replaced by one of our tenant farmers, who came only a couple of hours a day, to do the cooking. No one gave any thought to the dirt and disorder of the rooms, which to us seemed natural, like the vegetation of the uncultivated garden within the walls of the house.

It's impossible to give an accurate picture of this garden (today the cemetery of my dog Immacolatella). Around the adult carob could be found, among other things, the rotting frames of old furniture covered with mosses, broken dishes, demijohns, oars, wheels, and so on. And amid the rocks and the debris grew plants with distended, thorny leaves, sometimes beautiful and mysterious, like exotic specimens. After the rains, hundreds of flowers of more noble stock bloomed, from seeds and bulbs planted there long ago. And in the summer drought everything blackened, as if burned.

In spite of our affluence, we lived like savages. A couple of months after my birth, my father had departed from the island for an absence of almost half a year: leaving me in the arms of our first boy, who was very serious for his age and raised me on goat's milk. It was the same boy who taught me to speak, to read and write; and then, reading the books I found in the house, I educated myself. My father never cared to make me go to school: I was always on vacation, and my days of wandering, especially during his long absences, ignored any rule or schedule. Only hunger and sleep signaled the time to return home.

No one thought to give me money, and I didn't ask for it; besides, I didn't feel a need for it. I don't remember ever possessing a cent, in all my infancy and childhood.

The farm inherited from my grandfather Gerace provided the foods necessary for our cook: who didn't depart too far from the primitive and the barbarian in the arts of the kitchen. His name was Costante; and he was as taciturn and rough as his predecessor, Silvestro (the one I could, in a certain sense, call my nurse), had been gentle.

Winter evenings and rainy days I occupied with reading. After the sea and roaming around the island, I liked reading best. Usually I read in my room, lying on the bed, or on the sofa, with Immacolatella at my feet.

Our rooms gave onto a narrow hall, along which, at one time, the brothers' cells (perhaps twenty in all) had opened. The former owner had knocked down most of the walls between the cells in order to make the rooms more spacious; but (perhaps charmed by their decorations and carvings) had left some of the old doors intact. So, for example, my father's room had three doors, all in a row along the hall, and five windows, similarly in a line. Between my room and my father's, one cell had been preserved in its original dimensions, and there, during my childhood, the boy Silvestro slept. His sofa bed (or, to be clearer, a sort of cot) was still there, together with the empty chest for storing pasta where he put his clothes.

As for my father and me, we didn't put our clothes anywhere. Our rooms had dressers and wardrobes available, which, if you opened them, threatened to collapse, and emitted the odors of some extinct Bourbon bourgeoisie. But these pieces of furniture were of no use to us, except, sometimes, for tossing no longer serviceable objects that cluttered the rooms—for example, old shoes, broken fishing rods, shirts reduced to rags, and so on. Or storing booty: fossil shells, from the time when the island was still a submarine volcano; cartridge cases; bottoms of bottles mottled by the sand; pieces of rusted engines. And subaqeous plants, and starfish, which later dried out or rotted in the musty drawers. Maybe that's partly why I've never recognized the smell of our rooms anywhere else, in any human space or even in the dens of earthly animals; maybe, rather, I've found something similar in the bottom of a boat, or in a cave.

Those enormous dressers and wardrobes, occupying a large part of the free wall space, barely left a place for the beds, which were the usual iron bedsteads, with decorations of mother-of-pearl or painted landscapes, such as are found in all the bedrooms of Procida and Naples. Our winter blankets, in which I slept wrapped up, as if in a sack, were full of moth holes; and the mattresses, which were never plumped or carded, were flattened with use, like sheets of dough.

I recall that every so often, using a pillow or an old leather jacket that had belonged to Silvestro as a broom, my father, with my help, swept up from around his bed the old cigarette butts, which we piled in a corner of the room and later threw out the window. It was impossible to say in our house what material or color the floor was, because it was hidden under a layer of hardened dust. Similarly, the windowpanes were all blackened and opaque; suspended high up in the corners and between the window grilles the iridescence of spider webs was visible, shining in the light.

I think that the spiders, the lizards, the birds, and in general all non-human beings must have considered our house an uninhabited tower from the time of Barbarossa, or even a rocky protrusion rising from the sea. Along the outside walls, lizards emerged from cracks and secret furrows as from the earth; countless swallows and wasps made nests there. Birds of foreign species, passing over the island on their migrations, stopped to rest on the windowsills. And even the seagulls came to dry their feathers on the roof after their dives, as if on the mast of a ship or the top of a cliff.

At least one pair of owls lived in our house, although it was impossible for me to discover where; but it's a fact that, as soon as evening descended, you could see them flying out of the walls, with their entire family. Other owls, of different species, came from far away to hunt in our land, as in a forest. One night, an immense owl, an eagle owl, came to rest on my window. From its size I thought for a moment that it was an eagle; but it had much paler feathers, and later I recognized it from its small upright ears.

In some of the uninhabited rooms of the house, the windows, forgotten, stayed open in all seasons. And, entering those rooms unexpectedly, at an interval of months, you might encounter a bat, or hear the cries of mysterious broods hidden in a chest or among the rafters.

Certain curious creatures turned up, species never seen on the island. One morning, I was sitting on the ground behind the house, pounding almonds with a stone, when I saw emerge, up from the rockslide, a small, very pretty animal, of a species between a cat and a squirrel. It had a large tail and a triangular snout with white whiskers, and it observed me attentively. I threw it a shelled almond, hoping to ingratiate myself. But my gesture frightened it, and it fled.

Another time, at night, looking out over the edge of the slope, I saw a bright white quadruped, the size of a medium tuna, advancing up from the sea toward our house; it had curved horns, which looked like crescent moons. As soon as it became aware of me it turned back and disappeared amid the cliffs. I suspected that it was a dugong, a rare species of amphibious ruminant, which some say never existed, others that it is extinct. Many sailors, however, are sure they've often seen one of these dugongs, which lives in the neighborhood of the Grotta Azzurra of Capri. It lives in the sea like a fish, but is greedy for vegetables, and during the night comes out of the water to steal from the farms.

As for visits from humans, Procidans or foreigners, the Casa dei Guaglioni had not received any for years.

On the first floor was the brothers' former refectory, transformed by the Amalfitano into a reception room. It was an enormous space, with a high ceiling, almost twice the height of the other rooms, and windows that were high off the ground and looked toward the sea. The walls, unlike those of the other rooms, were not covered with wallpaper but decorated all around by a fresco, which imitated a columned loggia, with vine shoots and bunches of grapes. Against the back wall there was a table more than six meters long, and scattered everywhere were broken-down sofas and chairs, seats of every style, and faded cushions. One corner was occupied by a large fireplace, which we never used. And from the ceiling hung an immense chandelier of colored glass, caked with dust: only a few blackened bulbs were left, so that it gave off the same light as a candle.

It was here that in the days of the Amalfitano, amid music and singing, the groups of youths had their gatherings. The room still bore traces of their celebrations, and faintly recalled the great halls of villas occupied by the conquerors in war or, in some respects, the assembly halls in prisons—and in general all the places where youths and boys gather together without women. The worn, dirty fabrics covering the sofas showed cigarette burns. And on the walls, as well as on the tables, there were inscriptions and drawings: names, signatures, jokes, and expressions of melancholy or of love, and lines from songs. Then a pierced heart, a ship, the figure of a soccer player balancing the ball on his toes. And some humorous drawings: a skull smoking a pipe, a mermaid sheltering under an umbrella, and so on.

Numerous other drawings and inscriptions had been scratched off, I don't know by whom; the scars of the erasures remained visible on the plaster and on the wooden tables.

In other rooms, too, similar traces of past guests could be found. For example, in a small unused room, you could still read on the wallpaper above an alabaster stoup (left from the time of the monastery) a faded ink signature surrounded by flourishes: "Taniello." But, apart from these unknown signatures and worthless drawings, nothing else could be found, in the house, to bear witness to the time of parties and banquets. I learned that after the death of the shipping agent many Procidans who had taken part in those celebrations in their youth showed up at the Casa dei Guaglioni to demand objects and souvenirs. They claimed, vouching for one another, that the Amalfitano had promised them as gifts for the day of his death. So there was a kind of sack; and perhaps it was then that the costumes and masks were carried off, which are even now much talked about on the island; and the guitars, and mandolins, and glasses with toasts written in gold on the crystal. Maybe some of these spoils have been saved, in the cottages of peasants or fishermen. And the women of the family, now old, look with a sigh at such mementos, feeling again the jealousy they felt as girls of the mysterious revels from which they were excluded. They're almost afraid to touch those dead objects, which might contain in themselves the hostile influence of the Casa dei Guaglioni!

Another mystery was what became of the Amalfitano's dogs. It's known that he had several, and loved them; but at his death they disappeared from the house without a trace. Some assert that, after their master was carried to the cemetery, they grew sad, refusing food, and were all left to die. Others say that they began to roam the island like wild beasts, growling at anyone who approached, until they all became rabid, and the wardens captured them one by one, and killed them, throwing them off a cliff.

Thus the things that had happened in the Casa dei Guaglioni before my birth came down to me indistinctly, like adventures from long-ago centuries. Even of my mother's brief stay (aside from the photograph that Silvestro had saved for me) I could find no sign in the house. From Silvestro himself I learned that one day when I was around two months old, and my father had recently departed on his travels, some relatives from Massa arrived, apparently peasants, who carried off everything that had belonged to my mother, as if it were their lawful inheritance: her trousseau, brought as a dowry, her clothes, and even her clogs and her mother-of-pearl rosary. They certainly took advantage of the fact that there was no adult in the house to resist: and Silvestro at a certain point was afraid that they wanted to carry me off, too. So, on some pretext, he hurried to his cell, where he had put me to sleep on the bed, and quickly hid me in the old pasta crate where he kept his clothes (and whose battered cover let in air). Next to me he put the bottle of goat's milk, so that if I woke up I would be quiet and give no sign of my presence. But I didn't wake up, staying silent during the entire visit of the relatives, who, besides, weren't much concerned to have news of me. Only on the point of leaving with their bundle of things, one of them, more out of politeness than anything else, asked if I was growing well and where I was: and Silvestro answered that I had been put out to nurse. They were satisfied with that and, returning forever to Massa, were not heard from again.

And so passed my solitary childhood, in the house denied to women.

In my father's room there is a large photograph of the Amalfitano. It portrays a slender old man, enveloped in a long jacket, with unfashionable pants that allow a glimpse of white stockings. His white hair falls behind his ears like a horse's mane, and his high, smooth forehead, struck by the light, has an unnatural whiteness. His lifeless, open eyes have the clear, enraptured expression of certain animal eyes.

The Amalfitano chose a calculated, bold pose for the photographer. He is taking a step, and hints at a gallant smile, as if in greeting. With his right hand, he raises an iron-tipped black stick, which he is in the act of twirling; and with the left he holds two large dogs on a leash. Under the portrait, in the shaky hand of a semiliterate blind old man, he has written a dedication to my father:

*TO WILHELM*

*ROMEO*

This photograph of the Amalfitano reminded me of the figure of Boötes, Arturo's constellation, as it was drawn on a big map of the northern hemisphere in an astronomy atlas that we had in the house.

## Beauty

What I know about my father's origins I learned when I was already grown. Since I was a boy, I'd occasionally heard the people of the island call him "bastard," but that word sounded to me like a title of authority and mysterious prestige: such as "margrave," or some similar title. For many years, no one ever told me anything about the past of my father and grandfather: the Procidans are not loquacious, and, at the same time, following my father's example, I kept my distance from the island's inhabitants, and had no friends among them. Costante, our cook, was a presence more animal than human. In the many years that he worked for us, I don't remember ever exchanging with him two words of conversation; and, besides, I very rarely saw him. When his work in the kitchen was done, he returned to the farm; and I, coming home when I felt like it, found his simple dishes waiting for me, now cold, in the empty kitchen.

Most of the time, my father lived far away. He would come to Procida for a few days, and then leave again, sometimes remaining absent for entire seasons. If at the end of the year you made a summary of his rare, brief sojourns on the island, you would find that, out of twelve months, he had been on Procida, with me, for perhaps two. Thus I spent almost all my days in absolute solitude; and this solitude, which began in early childhood (with the departure of my nurse Silvestro), seemed to me my natural condition. I considered my father's every sojourn on the island an extraordinary favor on his part, a special concession that I was proud of.

I believe I had barely learned to walk when he bought me a boat. And one day when I was about six, he brought me to the farm, where the farmer's shepherd bitch was nursing her month-old puppies, so that I could choose one. I chose the one that seemed to me the most high-spirited, with the friendliest eyes. It turned out to be a female; and since she was white, like the moon, she was called Immacolatella.

As for providing me with shoes, or clothes, my father seldom remembered. In the summer, I wore no other garment than a pair of trousers, in which I also dove into the water, letting the air dry them on me. Only occasionally did I add to the trousers a cotton shirt that was too short, and all torn and loose. Unlike me, my father possessed a pair of khaki bathing trunks; but, apart from that, he, too, in summer, wore nothing but some old faded trousers and a shirt that no longer had a single button, and fell open over his chest. Sometimes he knotted around his neck a flower-patterned kerchief, of the type that peasant women buy at the market for Sunday Mass. And that cotton rag, on him, seemed to me the mark of a leader, a wreath of flowers that declared the glorious conqueror!

Neither he nor I owned a coat. In winter, I wore two sweaters, one over the other, and he a sweater underneath and, on top, a threadbare, shapeless checked wool jacket, with excessively padded shoulders that increased the authority of his height. The use of underwear was almost completely unknown to us.

He had a wristwatch (with a steel case and a heavy steel-link wristband), which also marked the seconds and could even be worn in the water. He had a mask for looking underwater when you were swimming, a speargun, and naval binoculars with which you could distinguish the ships traveling on the high sea, along with the figures of sailors on the bridge.

My childhood is like a happy land, and he is the absolute ruler! He was always passing through, always leaving; but in the brief intervals that he spent on Procida I followed him like a dog. We must have been a comical pair, for anyone who met us! He advancing with determination, like a sail in the wind, with his fair-haired foreigner's head, his lips in a pout and his eyes hard, looking no one in the face. And I behind, turning proudly to right and left with my dark eyes, as if to say: "Procidans, my father is passing by!" My height, at that time, was not much beyond a meter, and my black hair, curly as a gypsy's, had never known a barber. (When it got too long, I shortened it energetically with the scissors, in order not to be taken for a girl; only on rare occasions did I remember to comb it, and in the summer it was always encrusted with sea salt.)

Our pair was almost always preceded by Immacolatella, who ran ahead, turned back, sniffed all the walls, stuck her muzzle in all the doors, greeted everyone. Her friendliness toward our fellow citizens often made me impatient, and with imperious whistles I recalled her to the rank of the Geraces. I thus had occasion to practice whistling. Since I'd lost my baby teeth, I'd become a master of the art. Putting index and middle fingers in my mouth, I could draw out martial sounds.

I could also sing reasonably well; and from my nurse I had learned various songs. Sometimes, while I walked behind my father or was out in the boat with him, I sang over and over again "Women of Havana," "Tabarin," "The Mysterious Sierra," or Neapolitan songs, for example the one that goes: *Tu si' 'a canaria! Tu si' ll'amore!* (You're the canary! You're love!), hoping that in his heart my father would admire my voice. He gave no sign even of hearing it. He was always silent, brusque, touchy, and reluctantly conceded me a glance or two. But it was already a great privilege for me that the only company tolerated by him on the island was mine.

In the boat, he rowed, and I monitored the route, sitting in the stern or astride the prow. Sometimes, intoxicated by that divine happiness, I let go, and with enormous presumption began to give orders: Go, right oar! Go, with the left! Back-oar! But if he raised his eyes to look at me his silent splendor reminded me how small I was. And it seemed to me that I was a minnow in the presence of a great dolphin.

The primary reason for his supremacy over all others lay in his difference, which was his greatest mystery. He was different from all the men of Procida, that is to say from all the people I knew in the world, and also (O bitterness) from me. Mainly he stood out from the islanders because of his height. (But that height revealed itself only in comparison, if you saw him near others. When he was alone, isolated, he seemed almost small, his proportions were so graceful.)

Besides his height, his coloring distinguished him. His body in summer acquired a gentle brown radiance, drinking in the sun, it seemed, like an oil; but in winter he became as pale as a pearl. And I, who was dark in every season, saw in that something like the sign of a race not of the earth: as if he were the brother of the sun and the moon.

His hair was soft and smooth, of an opaque blond, which in certain lights glinted with gem-like highlights; and on the nape, where it was shorter, almost shaved, it was truly gold. Finally, his eyes were a blue-violet that resembled the color of certain expanses of the sea darkened by clouds.

∽⊙⊚∾

That beautiful hair of his, always dusty and disheveled, fell in locks over his wrinkled brow, as if to hide his thoughts with their shadow. And his face, which preserved, through the years, the energetic forms of adolescence, had a closed and arrogant expression.

Sometimes a flash of the jealous secrets that his thoughts seemed always intent on passed over his face: for example, a rapid, wild, and almost gratified smile; or a slightly devious and insulting grimace; or an unexpected ill humor, without apparent cause. For me, who could not attribute to him any human whim, his brooding was grand, like the darkening of the day, a sure sign of mysterious events, as important as universal history.

His motives belonged to him alone. For his silences, his celebrations, his contempt, his sufferings I did not seek an explanation. They were, for me, like sacraments: great and grave, beyond any earthly measure and any frivolity.

If, let's say, he had shown up one day drunk, or delirious, I would surely have been unable to imagine, even with that, that he was subject to the common weaknesses of mortals! Like me, he never got sick, as far as I remember; however, if I had seen him sick, his illness would not have seemed to me one of the usual accidents of nature. It would have assumed, in my eyes, almost the sense of a ritual mystery, in which Wilhelm Gerace was the hero, and the priests summoned to be present received the privilege of a consecration! And certainly I would not have doubted, I believe, that some upheaval of the cosmos, from the earthly lands to the stars, was bound to accompany that paternal mystery.

There is, on the island, a stretch of level ground surrounded by tall rocks where there's an echo. Sometimes, if we happened to go there, my father amused himself by shouting phrases in German. Although I didn't know their meaning, I understood, from his arrogant expression, that they must be terrible, rash words: he flung them out in a tone of defiance and almost profanation, as if he were violating a law, or breaking a magic spell. When the echo came back to him, he laughed, and let out more brutal words. Out of respect for his authority, I didn't dare to second him, and although I trembled with warlike anxiety, I listened to those enigmas in silence. It seemed to me that I was present not at the usual game of echoes, common among boys, but at an epic duel. We're at Roncesvalles, and suddenly Orlando will erupt onto the plain with his horn. We're at Thermopylae and behind the rocks the Persian knights are hiding, in their pointed caps.

When, on our rounds through the countryside, we came to an upward slope, he would be seized by impatience and take off at a run, with the determination of a wonderful task, as if he were climbing the mast of a sailboat. And he didn't care to know if I was behind him or not; but I followed at breakneck speed, with the disadvantage of my shorter legs, and joy kindled my blood. That was not one of the usual runs I did, countless times a day, competing with Immacolatella. It was a famous tournament. Up there a cheering finish line awaited us, and all *thirty million gods!*

His vulnerabilities were as mysterious as his indifference. I remember that once, while we were swimming, he collided with a jellyfish. Everyone knows the result of such an accident: a brief, inconsequential reddening of the skin. He, too, surely knew that; but, seeing his chest marked by those bloody stripes, he was stricken by a horror that made him go pale to his lips. He fled immediately to the shore and threw himself faceup on the ground, arms spread, like one already overwhelmed by the nausea of the death agony! I sat beside him: I myself had more than once been the victim of sea urchins, jellyfish, and other marine creatures, giving no importance to their injuries. But that day, when he was the victim, a solemn sense of tragedy invaded me. A vast silence fell over the beach and the whole sea, and in it the cry of a passing seagull seemed to me a female lament, a Fury.

## The Absolute Certainties

He scorned to win my heart. He left me in ignorance of German, his native tongue; with me, he always used Italian, but it was an Italian different from mine, which Silvestro had taught me. All the words he spoke seemed to be just invented, and still undomesticated; and even my Neapolitan words, which he often used, became, uttered by him, bolder and new, as in poems. That strange language gave him, for me, the charm of the Sibyls.

How old was he? Around nineteen years older than me! His age seemed serious and respectable, like the holiness of the Prophets or of King Solomon. Every act of his, every speech, had a dramatic fatality for me. In fact, he was the image of certainty, and everything he said or did was the verdict of a universal law from which I deduced the first commandments of my life. Here was the greatest seduction of his company.

By birth he was a Protestant; but he professed no faith, displaying a sullen indifference toward Eternity and its problems. I've been a Catholic, on the other hand, since I was a month old, on the initiative of my nurse Silvestro, who took care, at the time, to have me baptized in the parish church at the port.

That was, I think, the first and last time I visited a church as a Christian subject. I liked at times to linger in a church, as in a beautiful aristocratic room, in a garden, on a ship. But I would have been ashamed to kneel, or perform other ceremonies, or pray, even only in thought: as if I could truly believe that that was the house of God, and that God is in communication with us, or even exists!

My father had received some education, thanks to the teacher, his girl-mother; and he possessed (in large part inherited from her) some books, including some in Italian. To this small family library were added, in the Casa dei Guaglioni, numerous volumes left there by a young literature student who for many summers had been a guest of Romeo the Amalfitano. Not to mention various novels suitable for youthful taste, mysteries and adventure stories of differing provenance. And so I had available a respectable library, even if it was made up of battered old volumes.

They were, for the most part, classics, or scholastic or educational texts: atlases and dictionaries, history books, narrative poems, novels, tragedies, and poetry collections, and translations of famous works. Apart from the texts incomprehensible to me (written in German or Latin or Greek), I read and studied all these books; and some, my favorites, I reread many times, so that even today I remember them almost by heart.

Among the many teachings, then, that I got from my readings, I chose on my own the most fascinating, and those were the teachings that best corresponded to my natural feeling about life. With those and, in addition, the early certainties that the person of my father had already inspired in me, a kind of Code of Absolute Truth took shape in my consciousness, or imagination, whose most important laws could be listed like this:

I. THE AUTHORITY OF THE FATHER IS SACRED!

II. TRUE MANLY GREATNESS CONSISTS IN THE COURAGE TO ACT, IN DISDAIN FOR DANGER, AND IN VALOR DISPLAYED IN COMBAT.

III. THE BASEST ACT IS BETRAYAL. THUS ONE WHO BETRAYS HIS OWN FATHER OR LEADER, OR A FRIEND, ETC., HAS REACHED THE LOWEST POINT OF DEPRAVITY!

IV. NO LIVING CITIZEN ON THE ISLAND OF PROCIDA IS WORTHY OF WILHELM GERACE AND HIS SON ARTURO. FOR A GERACE TO BE FRIENDLY TOWARD A FELLOW CITIZEN WOULD BE TO DEBASE HIMSELF.

V. NO AFFECTION IN LIFE EQUALS A MOTHER'S.

VI. THE CLEAREST PROOFS AND ALL HUMAN EXPERIENCES DEMONSTRATE THAT GOD DOES NOT EXIST.

## The Second Law

These boyhood certainties of mine were for a long time not only what I honored and loved but the substance of the only possible reality for me! In those years, to live outside my great certainties would have appeared to me not only dishonorable but impossible.

However, lacking a suitable interlocutor with whom to discuss them intimately, I had never said a word about them to anyone in the world. My Code had remained my jealous secret: and this, certainly, out of superiority and pride, was a good quality; but it was also a difficult quality. Another difficult quality of my Code was a reticence. None of my laws, I mean, named the thing I hated most: that is, death. That reticence was, on my part, a sign of elegance and of contempt for that hated thing, which could only insinuate itself into the words of my laws in a devious manner, like a pariah or a spy.

In my natural happiness, I avoided all thoughts of death, as of an impossible figure with horrendous vices: hybrid, abstruse, full of evil and shame. But, at the same time, the more I hated death, the more fun I had and the more pleasure I got from attempting proofs of daring: in fact, I disliked any game that didn't include the fascination of risk. And so I had grown up in that contradiction: loving valor, hating death. It may be, though, that it wasn't a contradiction.

All reality appeared to me clear and distinct: only the abstruse stain of death muddied it; and so my thoughts, as I said, retreated with horror at that point. On the other hand, with a similar horror I thought I recognized a perhaps fatal sign of my immaturity, like fear of the dark in ignorant girls (immaturity was my shame). And I waited, as for a sign of marvelous maturity, for that unique muddiness—death—to dissolve into the clarity of reality, like smoke into transparent air.

Until that day, I could consider myself only, in essence, an inferior, a boy; and meanwhile, as if drawn in by the insidious pull of a mirage, I ran wild, *a little hooligan* (as my father said), in every kind of childish exploit . . . But such bold acts, naturally, could not suffice, in my judgment, to promote me to the envied rank (maturity) or free me from an inner and supreme doubt of myself.

In fact, it was in essence always a matter of games; death, there, was still a stranger to me, almost an unreal fantasy. How would I behave at the true test, in war, for example, when I really saw that murky, monstrous stain advancing, growing larger, before me?

Thus, a skeptic in my games of childish daring, from the start I always waited at the ultimate challenge, like a provocateur and rival of myself. Maybe, was it because I was only a vain kid and no more (as W.G. once accused me of being)? Maybe, was my precocious bitterness toward death, which shadowed me and tempted me to redemption, nothing but the anxiety to be pleasing to myself to the point of perdition—the same anxiety that destroyed Narcissus?

Or maybe, instead, was it only a pretext? There is no answer. And, besides, it's my business. In conclusion: in my Code, the Second Law (where the famous reticence huddled more naturally, as in its den) counted most of all for me.

## The Fourth Law

The Fourth Law, suggested to me by my father's attitude, was, perhaps along with my natural inclination, evidently the original cause of my Procidan solitude. I seem to see again my small figure of the time wandering around at the port, amid the traffic and the movement of people, with an expression of mistrustful and surly superiority, like a stranger who finds himself in the middle of a hostile population. The most demeaning feature I noted, in that population, was a permanent dependence on practical necessity; and that feature made the glorious and different species of my father stand out even more! There not only the poor but the rich as well seemed constantly preoccupied by their present interests or earnings: all of them, from the ragged kids who scuffled for a coin, or a crust of bread, or a colored pebble, to the owners of fishing boats, who discussed the price of fish as if that were the most important value of their existence. No one among them, evidently, was interested in books, or in great actions! Sometimes the schoolboys were lined up in an open space by the teacher for pre-military exercises. But the teacher was fat and sluggish, the boys displayed neither ability nor enthusiasm, and the whole spectacle, from the uniforms to the actions and the methods, appeared so unmartial, in my judgment, that I immediately looked away with a sense of pain. I would have blushed with shame if my father, turning up at that moment, had surprised me looking at certain scenes and certain characters!

## The Prison Fortress

The only inhabitants of the island who did not seem to arouse my father's contempt and antipathy were the invisible, unnamed inmates of the prison. In fact, certain of his romantic and terrible habits might let me suppose that a kind of brotherhood, or code of silence, bound him not only to them but to all the life convicts and imprisoned of the earth. And I, too, of course, was on their side, not only in imitation of my father but from a natural inclination, which made prison seem an unjust, absurd monstrosity, like death.

The prison fortress was a kind of grim and sacred domain, and thus forbidden; and I don't remember that, during all my childhood and adolescence, I ever entered alone. Sometimes, as if enthralled, I started up the ascent that led to it, and then, as soon as I saw those gates, I fled.

I recall that, during walks with my father in those days, I had perhaps once or twice passed through the gates of the fortress and traversed its solitary spaces. And in my childhood memory those rare excursions were like journeys through a region far from my island. Following my father, I looked furtively from the deserted roadway toward those barred slits of windows like air vents, or glimpsed, behind an infirmary grille, the mournful white color of a prisoner's uniform . . . and immediately turned away my gaze. Curiosity, or even mere interest, on the part of free and happy people seemed to me insulting to the prisoners. The sun, on those streets, was an insult, and up there the roosters crowing on the balconies of the cottages, the doves cooing along the cornices irritated me, with their tactless insolence. Only my father's freedom did not seem offensive, but, on the contrary, comforting, like an assurance of happiness, the only one on that sad height. With his rapid, graceful gait, slightly swaying like a sailor's, and his blue shirt swelling in the wind, he seemed to me the messenger of a victorious adventure, of an enchanting power. In the depths of my feelings, I was almost convinced that only a mysterious contempt, or carelessness, kept him from exercising his heroic will, beating down the gates of the prison and freeing the prisoners. Truly, I could imagine no limits to his dominion. If I had believed in miracles, I would surely have considered him capable of performing them. But, as I've already revealed, I didn't believe in miracles or in occult powers, to which some people entrust their fate, the way shepherd girls entrust it to the witches or the fairies!

## Pointless Acts of Bravado

The books I liked most, needless to say, were those which celebrated, with real or imagined examples, my ideal of human greatness, whose living incarnation I recognized in my father.

If I had been a painter, and had had to illustrate epic poems, history books, and so on, I think that in the vestments of their leading heroes I would always have painted a portrait of my father, again and again. And to begin the work I would have had to dissolve a quantity of gold dust on my palette, so as to color the locks of those protagonists in a worthy fashion.

As girls imagine fair-haired fairies, fair-haired saints, and fair-haired queens, I imagined great captains and warriors all as fair, and resembling my father like brothers. If a hero I liked in a book turned out to be, from the descriptions, dark and of medium height, I preferred to believe it was the historian's mistake. But if the description was documented, and unquestionable, I liked that hero less, and he could no longer be my ideal champion.

When Wilhelm Gerace set out again on his travels, I was convinced that he was leaving to carry out adventurous and heroic deeds: I would certainly have believed him if he had told me that he was going to conquer the Poles, or Persia, like Alexander the Great; that he had waiting for him, beyond the sea, companies of gallant men under his command; that he was a scourge of pirates or bandits, or, on the contrary, that he himself was a great pirate, or a bandit. He never said a word about his life outside the island; and my imagination pined for that mysterious, fascinating existence, in which, naturally, he considered me unworthy to participate. My respect for his will was such that I didn't allow myself, even in thought, the intention to secretly spy on him, or follow him; and I didn't dare even to question him. I wanted to win his respect, and maybe his admiration, hoping that one day, finally, he would choose me as a companion on his journeys.

Meanwhile, when we were together, I was always looking for occasions to appear bold and fearless in his eyes. Barefoot, almost flying on my toes, I crossed cliffs that were burning hot from the sun; I dove into the sea from the highest rocks; I performed extraordinary aquatic acrobatics, wild, flashy exercises, and demonstrated my expertise in every kind of swimming, like a champion. I swam underwater until I lost my breath, and resurfacing brought back underwater prey: sea urchins, starfish, shells. But, peering at him from afar, I sought admiration in his gaze, or at least attention, in vain. He sat on the shore taking no notice of me; and when, pretending that I was indifferent to my feats, I casually ran to join him, and collapsed on the sand next to him, he rose capriciously, negligently, eyes distracted and brow wrinkled, as if a mysterious invitation had been murmured in his ear. He raised his arms lazily; he slipped sideways into the sea. And he went off, swimming very slowly, as if embraced by the sea, by the sea as if by a bride.

## The Story of Algerian Dagger

Finally one day I believed that the occasion I had always been waiting for to prove myself had arrived! We were swimming together, and, as we swam, he inexplicably lost in the sea the famous amphibious watch he was so proud of and wore in the water. We were both saddened by the loss; he looked at the sea with an expression of rage, then looked again at his bare wrist; and he answered me with a shrug when I offered to go and look for the watch in the underwater depths. Yet he gave me his scuba mask, and I left, trembling with ambition and honor. He stayed on the shore, waiting for me.

◦◦◉◦◦

I explored the whole seafloor, in the area that we had passed through earlier on our swim: the water there was not very deep, and was broken by shoals and reefs. My search continued, the high cliffs hid me from his view; and resurfacing every so often to get my breath I heard his whistles calling me back. At first I didn't answer, because I was ashamed of not being able to announce a victory; but finally, to reassure him that I hadn't disappeared into the sea like the watch, I answered him, from the top of a cliff, with a long whistle. He looked at me in silence, without any gesture; and I, looking at his body, gilded by summer, and marked at the wrist by a whiter circle, decided: "Either return to him with the watch or die!"

⋅⊙⊙⋅

I put on the mask again, and resumed my exploration. By now, finding the watch did not mean only the recovery of a treasure: it was no longer only a question of honor. The search had assumed a strange sense of fatality, the time already passed seemed immeasurable, and its end was like a milestone of my fate! I wandered through those varied and fantastic depths, outside of human realms, burning, minute by minute, with that unparalleled hope: of shining, like a prodigy, in the eyes of Him! It was this, the grandiose stake that was in play! And no one to help me, neither angels nor saints to pray to. The sea is an indifferent splendor, like Him.

⋅⊙⊙⋅

My search remained futile; exhausted, I took off the mask and, with my hands, gripped a rock sticking out of the water to rest. The rock hid from me the view of the shore, and hid from my father the scene of my defeat. I was alone on a field without directions, worse than a maze.

Then, at a movement I made as I gripped the rock, dejectedly keeping myself afloat, I spied a metallic glint in the sun! Planting my hands, I jumped up and discovered the lost watch, sparkling in a dry hollow in the rock. It was unharmed, and bringing it to my ear I heard it ticking.

I held it in my fist and, with the mask hanging around my neck, in a few seconds reached the beach. My father's eyes lighted up at seeing me arrive victorious. "You found it!" he exclaimed, almost incredulous. And in the act of possession, and affirmation of a right, he tore the watch from my hands, as if it were some booty that I could compete for. He brought it to his ear, and looked at it with satisfaction.

"It was there, on that rock there!" I cried, still panting. I was beside myself, I would have liked to skip and dance, but I proudly restrained myself, so as not to show how much importance I gave my undertaking. My father looked at the rock frowning, lost in thought:

"Ah," he said after a moment, "now I remember. I took it off while we were searching for shellfish, to get some limpets that were wedged in at the tip of the rock. Then you called to show me a sea urchin you'd found, and made me forget. If you hadn't been so bullying, you with your sea urchin, I wouldn't have forgotten it!

"Lost!" he added then, shrugging his shoulders, in a sarcastic tone. "I knew it, I knew it couldn't be lost. It has a very secure clasp, guaranteed." And, with satisfaction, he carefully fastened the watch around his wrist.

So fate had played a trick, my action lost almost any splendor. The disappointment, mounting like a fever, made the muscles of my face tremble and burned my eyes. I thought, "If I cry, I'm dishonored," and to protect myself, with violence, from my weakness, I angrily took the useless mask off my neck, and angrily gave it to my father.

My father, taking it back, gave me an arrogant glance as if to say, "Hey, kid!" and I, unable to look at him after I'd been so disrespectful, wanted to flee. But quickly, with a playful expression, he placed his bare foot firmly on my bare foot, to hold me in check; and I saw his face bending over me, smiling, with a marvelous look that, for an instant, made him resemble a goat. He put his wrist with the watch under my eyes and said harshly:

"You know the maker of this watch? Read it, it's printed on the face."

On the face, in almost imperceptible letters, was printed the word "Amicus."

"It's a Latin word," my father explained. "You know what it means?"

"Friend!" I answered, pleased with my quickness.

"*Friend!*" he repeated. "And this watch, with this name, has a meaning of great importance. An importance of life and death. Guess."

I smiled, imagining for a moment that my father, with that symbol of the watch, wanted to proclaim our friendship: in life and in death.

"You can't guess!" he exclaimed, with a slight grimace of contempt. "You want to know? This watch is a present that a friend of mine gave me, maybe the dearest friend I have: you know the phrase 'two bodies and one soul'? For example, one New Year's Eve long ago, I was in a town where I didn't know anyone. I was alone, I had used up all my money, and I had to spend the night under a bridge in the cold. That night, my friend was in a different city, and hadn't heard from me for a long time, so he couldn't know where or in what condition I was. In fact, since it was New Year's, he had wondered all evening: 'I wonder where he is? I wonder who he's celebrating with tonight?' And he went to bed early, but around midnight he began shivering, with a chill that he couldn't explain. He didn't have a fever, he was in a heated room, in bed, with warm covers, and all night he continued to shiver, unable to get warm, as if he had gone to bed on the icy earth, with no shelter.

"Another time, joking with him, I unluckily fell, injuring my knee on a piece of glass. And he, by himself, with an Algerian dagger I'd given him, made a wound in his knee, in the same place.

"When he gave me the watch he said: 'Here, I've locked up my heart in this watch. Take it, I give you my heart. Wherever you are, near or far from me, the day this watch stops ticking, my heart, too, will have stopped beating!' "

It was unusual for my father to make me a speech so long and intimate. But he didn't tell me the name of his great friend, and immediately a name flashed in my mind: Romeo! Romeo-Boötes, in fact, was the only friend of my father I'd heard about; but he was dead, and so it was another my father was speaking of today. This other, who in my mind had the name Algerian Dagger, lived in the glorious Orients that my father always returned to: foremost among the satellites who, in those fugitive southern zones, followed the light of Wilhelm Gerace. The favorite! For a moment I glimpsed him: abandoned, in who knows what magnificent, tragic rooms, perhaps in the Great Urals, alone, waiting for my father; his face rapt, Semitic-looking, his knee bleeding, and a void in place of his heart.

## Departures

That day, my father left. As usual, Immacolatella and I watched him as he randomly put back in his suitcase the shirts without buttons, the sweater, the heavy jacket, and so on. Every time he left, he put his entire wardrobe in the suitcase, since he could never predict how long he would be away: he might return in two or three days, or he might be absent for months, until winter and beyond.

He always made his preparations for departure at the last minute, with a mechanical haste in his gestures, while his face was distracted, as if in his mind he had already left the island. Suddenly, when I saw him close the suitcase, I felt my heart whirl with an unexpected resolve and I said to him:

"Couldn't I go with you?"

I hadn't planned to ask the question that day, and it was immediately clear that he didn't even consider it. His gaze darkened slightly, and his lips made an almost imperceptible frown, as if he were thinking of something else.

"With me!" he replied then, studying me. "To do what? You're a little kid. Wait till you grow up, to go with me."

He rapidly tied a rope around his suitcase (which was an ordinary one, and beat-up) and secured it with a strong, skillful sailor's knot. Then, with Immacolatella and me on his heels, he hurried downstairs. Thus he left the Casa dei Guaglioni at a swift pace, holding the suitcase by one end of the rope, his cheeks alight, his eyes clouded by impatience. Now already he was mythical, unreachable, like a gaucho crossing the Argentine pampas with a lassoed bull; or a captain of the Greek armies flying in a chariot over the plain of Troy, with the corpse of the conquered Trojan dragging behind; or a horse tamer on the steppes, running beside his horse, ready to jump onto its back. And to think that he had still on his skin the salt of the Procidan sea, where he had been swimming with me that morning!

Down in the street the carriage that would take him to the port was waiting, and I sat beside him on the red damask seat while, as usual, Immacolatella followed us happily on foot, to race against the horse. From the start of the route, she easily outpaced us by a good distance, and came back from the end of the street with her ears in the wind, barking as if to greet us and provoke the horse. But he proceeded at his usual old trot, and didn't take the trouble to compete, surely considering her a fanatic.

My father was silent and kept looking at his watch: then he looked at the driver's back, and the horse, with a stubborn impatience, as if to incite the driver to crack the whip harder, and the horse to run. And meanwhile my imagination rose, like a flame, toward another departure, which today had been promised. Then, I would sit in the carriage beside my father; but not to accompany him to the port and say goodbye from the pier while he departs on the steamer, no! to board the ship with him and depart with him! Maybe for Venice, or Palermo, maybe as far as Scotland, or the mouth of the Nile, or Colorado! To find again Algerian Dagger and our other followers, who will be waiting for us there.

*Wait till you grow up, to go with me.* I had a thought of rebellion against the absoluteness of life, which condemned me to pass an endless Siberia of days and nights before taking me away from this bitter situation: of being a boy. Out of impatience, at that moment, I would even have subjected myself to a very long lethargy, which would let me get through my lesser ages without being aware of it, to find myself suddenly a man, equal to my father. *Equal to my father!* "Unfortunately," I thought, looking at him, "even when I'm a man I can never be his equal. I'll never have blond hair, or violet-blue eyes, nor will I ever be so handsome!"

The steamer that came from Ischia and was to carry my father to Naples had not yet entered the harbor. There were still a few minutes to wait. My father and I sat nearby on the suitcase, and Immacolatella, tired out from her races, lay at our feet. She seemed convinced that that sojourn on the pier meant the end of the journey for our family. And that, having now reached our destination and settled down, we could all three rest as long as we liked, without ever having to be separated.

But when the gangplank had been lowered, and my father and I got up, she, too, quickly rose, wagging her tail, without showing any surprise. When my father was separated from the two of us, on the ship that was moving away from the pier, she barked loudly, with an accusing expression; but she didn't make a fuss. She wasn't too sad that my father had left. For her I was the master. If I had left, she certainly would have jumped into the sea and tried to swim to the ship; then, returning to land, desperate, she would have remained on the pier weeping and calling me, until death.

## Immacolatella

From the moment my father left Procida, he again became a legend for me! The interval we had spent together—almost still present, almost still my domain, all alight—hovered before me, to fascinate me bitterly with its spectral grace; then, like the Flying Dutchman, it vanished, spinning with dizzying speed. A kind of sparkling mist and some echoes of fractured voices, full of manly arrogance and mockery, were all that remained to me. It already seemed an event outside of time, and outside of the history of Procida: perhaps not *lost* but *nonexistent*! Every sign of my father's sojourn in our house—the hollow left by his head on the pillow, a toothless comb, an empty packet of cigarettes—seemed to me miraculous. Like the Prince on finding Cinderella's glass slipper, I repeated to myself: "So he exists!"

After my father's departures, Immacolatella circled around me constantly in the Casa dei Guaglioni, worried about my listlessness, inciting me to play and forget the past. How many shows that wild dog put on! She leaped into the air and dropped to the ground like a ballerina. She even became a jester: I was her king. And, seeing that I wasn't interested in her, she approached me impatiently, asking with her brown eyes: "What are you thinking right now? Will you tell me what's wrong?" Like women, who often when a man is serious think he's sick, or get jealous, because his serious thoughts seem a betrayal of their frivolity.

As one would with a woman, I avoided her, saying: "Leave me in peace for a while. I want to think. Some things you can't understand. Go and play on your own: we'll see each other later." But she was obstinate, and wouldn't be persuaded; and finally, confronted by her frenzied games, I regained the desire to play and to be frenzied with her. She would have had the right to boast; but she had a happy heart, without vanity. She welcomed me in marvelous triumph, like a final gallop, thinking that I had pretended my earlier seriousness in order to make a good *impression*, as in the tarantella.

Someone will say: So much talk about a dog! But as a boy I had no other companion, and it can't be denied that she was extraordinary. To converse with me, she had invented a kind of deaf-mute language: using her tail, her eyes, her positions, and many different notes of her voice, she could tell me all her thoughts; and I understood her. Although she was a girl, she loved boldness and adventure: she swam with me, and was my helmsman in the boat, barking when obstacles came into view. She followed me everywhere when I roamed the island, and every day, returning with me along lanes in a countryside already passed through countless times, she would get excited, as if we were pioneers in unexplored lands. When, crossing the narrow strait, we disembarked on the uninhabited little island of Vivara, a few meters from Procida, the wild hares fled at our arrival, thinking that I was a hunter with a hunting dog. And she chased them a little, for the pleasure of running, and then came back to me, content to be a shepherd.

She had many loves, but until the age of eight she never got pregnant.

## Grandson of an Ogress?

One could say that in all my youth I knew no female being other than Immacolatella. In my famous Code of Absolute Certainties no law concerned women and love, because I had no certainties (apart from maternal affection) with regard to women. My father's greatest friend, Romeo-Boötes, detested them; but had my mother, as a woman, also been rejected by him? That question was a reason for distrust between me and the shade of the Amalfitano. And it had no answer—since I had never heard from my father any talk about the Amalfitano or about women, and his smile (when the terror of the Casa dei Guaglioni on the part of all women was mentioned) wasn't an explanation but, rather, an enigma.

As for my mother, maybe no more than a couple of times in all our life did I hear him name her; but it was only in passing, and by chance. The memory remains of how his voice seemed to focus almost tenderly for a moment on that name, and immediately moved on, with sharp, evasive haste. He had the expression, on those occasions, of a handsome exotic cat that, walking impudently at night, stops for a moment to look at the cold fur of a lifeless female, touching it with a velvet paw.

Certainly I would have dearly wished him to tell me something about my beloved mother; but I respected his silence, understanding that it must be too painful for him to return to the memory of his wife's death.

And about another death, too, he remained stubbornly silent: I mean about my grandmother, the German. Against her, however, his silence must have fostered some terrible reproach: or at least so I deduced from a single brief episode.

One day, rummaging through some books in the wardrobe in his room while he was smoking absentmindedly nearby, I found in my hands a photograph I'd never seen before: it portrayed a group of girls about the same age, one of whom was marked with an ink cross. Naturally, my gaze rested with greater interest on her, who seemed to me, in the brief minute that I could look, a fairly ordinary girl, dressed in a skirt and blouse and wearing a ribbon in her hair. She had an ample, womanly bosom confined under the white shirt, which was buttoned up to the throat; but otherwise her figure, like the features of her face, was too big, heavy, and solid to be called beautiful. But her romantic pose betrayed an almost pitiful need to feel weak and pretty.

Under the photograph some words were written in German; in addition, I could distinguish a vague resemblance, especially in her gaze and in her mouth, in spite of her ordinary looks, which let me guess at once who she was. A natural curiosity drove me to ask my father for confirmation of my discovery. And I rushed to show him the photograph and ask if that fair-haired woman was my grandmother from Germany.

At which, rousing himself from his absent thoughts, he hastily and rudely observed the card, which I brought him in triumph, and abruptly took it out of my hands. "What sort of relics are you finding?" he said. "It's your grandmother, yes, it's my mother," he then admitted, in a surly tone, emphasizing *it's my mother* with an almost vulgar expression of ostentatious rejection. And he said softly, through clenched teeth, "Rather, luckily, *was*."

He added no other words; but going to the chest of drawers he threw the photograph in the bottom drawer, which he closed brutally with his foot. And in that act, his face disgusted by irritation, like a grim executioner, he seemed to say: "Stay there, evil, terrible, and intolerable woman. And don't ever show up again, from now on!"

That was all; but it was enough to instill in me a confused suspicion that my paternal grandmother had been, in life, an ogress, or some other similar scourge. I happened to glance inside that drawer later, but the photograph had disappeared. My father must have put it in some even darker hiding place.

ﺨﻮﻮ

In conclusion, my father's knowledge did not at all illuminate my ignorance regarding women.

## Women

Besides, apart from the maternity of my mother, nothing, in the obscure population of women, seemed important to me, and it didn't much interest me to investigate their mysteries. All the great actions that enthralled me in books were carried out by men, never by women. Adventure, war, and glory were men's privileges. Women, instead, were love; and books told stories of royal, splendid females. But I suspected that such women, and even that marvelous feeling love, were only an invention of books, not a reality. The perfect hero existed—I saw the proof in my father. But I knew no glorious women, sovereigns of love, like those in books. And so love, passion, that famous great fire, was perhaps a fantastic impossibility.

Although I was ignorant about real women, I had only to catch a glimpse of them to conclude that they had nothing in common with the women of books. According to my judgment, real women possessed no splendor and no magnificence. They were small beings, who could never grow as tall as a man, and they spent their lives shut up in kitchens and other rooms: that explained their pallor. Bundled into aprons, skirts, and petticoats, in which they must always keep hidden, by law, their mysterious body, they appeared to me clumsy, almost shapeless figures. They were always busy, and elusive; they were ashamed of themselves, maybe because they were so ugly; and they went around like sad animals, different in every way from men, without elegance or daring. Often they gathered in a group, and discussed with passionate gestures, glancing around in fear that someone might surprise their secrets. They must share many secrets, what could they possibly be? Surely all childish things! No absolute certainty could interest them.

Their eyes were all the same color: black! Their hair, all of it, was dark, rough, wild. Truly, as far as I was concerned, they could stay as far away as they wanted from the Casa dei Guaglioni: I would never fall in love with one, and didn't want to marry one.

Very occasionally, a foreign woman happened onto the island, who went down to the beach and took off her clothes to swim, without any respect or shame, as if she were a man. Like the other Procidans, I felt no curiosity about foreign swimmers; my father seemed to consider them ridiculous and hateful people, and, with me, fled from the places where they swam. We would happily have chased them away, because we were jealous of our beaches. And no one looked at those women. For the Procidans, and also for me, they were not women but like crazy animals, who had descended from the moon. It didn't even occur to me that their shameless figures might have some beauty.

And so I think I've related almost all the ideas I had at the time about women!

When a girl was born on Procida, the family was displeased. And I thought of the fate of women. As children, they seemed no uglier than boys, nor very different; but they had no hope of growing up to become a handsome, great hero. Their only hope was to become the wife of a hero: to serve him, to wear his name like a coat of arms, to be his undivided property, respected by all; and to bear a handsome son, resembling his father.

My mother missed that satisfaction: she had barely had time to see this dark son, with dark eyes, completely the opposite of her husband, Wilhelm. And if by chance that son, although dark, was destined to become a hero, she couldn't know it, because she was dead.

## The Oriental Tent

In the snapshot that is the only image of her known to me, my mother doesn't appear any more beautiful than other women. But as a boy, looking at that picture, contemplating it, I never wondered if she was ugly or beautiful, and didn't even think of comparing her to others. She was *my mother*! And I can no longer say how many enchanting things her lost maternity meant for me at that time.

She had died because of me: as if I had killed her. I had been the power and violence of her fate; but her consolation cured me of my cruelty. In fact, that was the first blessing, between us: that my remorse merged with her forgiveness.

Examining her portrait in memory, I note that she is just a girl. In fact, she isn't even eighteen. She has a serious and concentrated manner, like an adult, but her curious face is a child's; and the outline of youth is even more recognizable in her disfigured body, clumsily bundled in the clothes of a pregnant woman.

At that time, however, I saw in her portrait a mother, I couldn't see a childlike creature. The age that I gave her was, if I think about it, perhaps a maturity, as great as the sand and summer on the sea, but perhaps also an eternity, virginal, gentle, and unchanging, like a star. She was a person invented by my regrets, and so she had, for me, every wished-for kindness, and different expressions, different voices. But, above all, in the impossible longing I had for her, I thought of her as faithfulness, intimacy, conversation: in other words, all that fathers were not, in my experience.

The mother was someone who would have waited at home for my return, thinking of me day and night. She would have admired all my words, praised all my undertakings, and boasted of the superior beauty of a dark child, with black hair, of average height or maybe even less.

Woe to anyone who dared, in her presence, to speak ill of me! In her opinion, indisputably, I was the greatest personage in the world. The name *Arturo* for her was a gold standard! And in her view it would be enough to say that name for everyone to know that she was speaking of me. The other Arturos existing in the world were all imitators, inferior.

Even hens, or cats, have certain special delicate modulations of their voice when they call their offspring. Therefore one can imagine in what a delightful voice she would have called Arturo. And certainly she would have loaded that name with every sort of female adulation, which I would graciously spurn, as Julius Caesar spurned the crown. In fact, it's noble to show disdain for all kinds of adulation and pampering; but since one can't be pampered by oneself, in life a mother is necessary.

I lived completely ignorant not only of adulation but also of kisses and caresses: and this was a proud honor. But sometimes, especially in the evenings, when I was alone between the walls of a room, and began to miss my mother, *mother* for me signified precisely: *caresses*. I sighed for her large holy body, her hands of silk, her breath. My bed, on winter nights, was freezing cold: and to get warm I had to fall asleep entwined with Immacolatella.

As I didn't believe in God and religions, neither did I believe in a future life and the spirits of the dead. Listening to reason, I knew that all that remained of my mother was underground, in the cemetery of Procida. But reason retreated before her, and, without realizing it, I actually believed in a paradise for her. What else could that sort of Oriental tent be, raised between sky and earth and carried by the breeze, in which she dwelt alone, idle and contemplative, with her eyes on Heaven, like one transfigured? Whenever I turned to my mother, that was where she appeared naturally in my thoughts. Later, the day came when I no longer looked for her, and she disappeared; someone folded up the magnificent Oriental tent and carried it away.

But, while I was a boy, I addressed her at the times when others pray, like a sentimentalist. My mother was always wandering around the island, and was so present, suspended there in the air, that I seemed to be talking to her, the way one talks to a girl looking out from a balcony. She was one of the enchantments of the island. I never went to her grave, because I've always hated cemeteries and all the signs of death; but still one of the spells that bound me to Procida was that small tomb. Since my mother was buried in that place, it almost seemed to me that her fantastic person was a prisoner there, in the blue air of the island, like a canary in its gilded cage. Maybe that was why when I went out in the boat I never got very far before the bitterness of solitude seized me, and made me turn back. It was she who recalled me, like the sirens.

## Waits and Returns

But in truth there was another, even stronger reason that, when I went out on the water, soon made me turn the prow back toward Procida: the suspicion that in my absence my father might return. It seemed to me intolerable not to be on the island when he was; and so, although I was free and dearly loved great enterprises, I never left the sea of Procida for other lands. Often I was tempted to flee in my boat in search of him; but then I would realize how absurd the hope of finding him was, among so many islands and continents. If I left Procida, I might lose him forever, since one certainty existed only on Procida: always, sooner or later, he would return. It wasn't possible to guess when he would return. Sometimes he would reappear suddenly a few hours after his departure; and sometimes he wasn't seen again for many months. And, always, every day, at the arrivals of the steamer, and every evening, returning to the Casa dei Guaglioni, I had a hope of seeing him. This eternal hope was another of Procida's spells.

One morning, Immacolatella and I, in the *Torpedo Boat of the Antilles*, decided to go as far as Ischia. I rowed for almost an hour; but when I turned and saw that Procida had grown distant, such a bitter homesickness gripped me that I couldn't bear it. I reversed course, and we went back.

My father never wrote letters, he never sent news of himself, or any greeting. And for me the certainty that he still existed was miraculous, and that every moment lived by me on Procida he, too, was living in some land or other, in some room, among foreign companions whom I considered glorious and blessed for the sole reason that they were with him. (I didn't doubt, in fact, that being with my father was the most desired form of aristocracy in all human societies.)

As soon as I thought "At this very moment he . . ." I immediately felt a sharp tug inside me, as if, in my mind, a black screen had been torn, and flashes of marvelous stories passed by. In these apparitions of my imagination he was almost never alone: around him were the indistinct persons of his followers; and nearby, always at his side like a shadow, the elect of that aristocracy, Algerian Dagger. My father, waving his pistol in an act of challenge, jumps onto the prow of an immense armed ship, and Algerian Dagger, exhausted, perhaps mortally wounded, drags behind, handing him the last cartridges. My father advances through a dense jungle along with Algerian Dagger, who, armed with a knife, helps him open a path through the lianas. My father is resting in his war tent, lying on a camp bed; and Algerian Dagger, kneeling on the ground at his feet, plays Spanish music on a guitar for him . . .

*Wait till you grow up, to go with me.*

Occasionally during my days of solitude, some trick of the senses gave me the sudden illusion that he had returned! Looking at the sea, on a stormy day, I seemed to hear, in the din of the breakers, his voice calling me. I turned toward the beach: it was empty. One afternoon, reaching the pier after the arrival of the steamer, I spied from a distance a fair-haired man sitting at the café on the square. I hurried to the café, convinced that I would find him, just off the boat, stopping to have a glass of Ischian wine—and found myself facing a dark foreigner, wearing a straw hat . . . One evening, having dinner in the kitchen, I saw Immacolatella go on the alert and leap at the window; I rushed over, hoping to see him outside, arriving as a surprise, and I was in time to see a cat that, having peered in at our dinner, jumped down from the window grate and fled.

Every day, Immacolatella and I were present at almost all the arrivals of the steamer from Naples. The passengers who got off were usually people we knew, for the most part Procidans who had left in the morning and returned in the evening: the shipping agent, the wife of the tailor, the midwife, the owner of the Hotel Savoia. Then, on certain days, you could see disembark, after the ordinary passengers, the prisoners destined for the penitentiary. In civilian clothes, but handcuffed and accompanied by guards, they were immediately loaded onto a police truck, which brought them to the castle. During their brief passage on foot, I avoided looking at them: not out of contempt but out of respect.

Meanwhile, the sailors pulled up the gangplank, the steamer departed for Ischia: this time, too, the fair-haired man I was waiting for hadn't arrived.

But, some time or other, he did arrive. Maybe precisely on a day that, for some reason, I hadn't been on the pier when the steamer docked. And then, coming home, I actually found what I always pictured as a chimera: him, sitting on the bed in his room, smoking a cigarette, the suitcase at his feet, still closed.

Seeing me, he'd say:

"Hello. You're here?"

But at that instant Immacolatella, who had lingered on the street, would enter the room like the wind: and my father began his usual struggle with the dog, who was always exaggerated in her greetings. I would intervene, yelling at her: "Pup. Enough!" That besotted behavior seemed to me a sign of poor judgment on her part. How could she presume? Who could say how many better dogs my father might have met, in all that time! Besides, in my view that wild greeting for my father was only a pretext for making noise. It didn't really matter much to her that my father had returned: for her, I was the master.

Finally, she'd calm down. And my father, smoking his cigarette, would say to me:

"What news?"

But he didn't pay much attention to the news I recounted. Maybe he'd interrupt irrelevantly to ask: "Is the boat in order?" Or begin listening to the time tolled by the bell and, comparing it to his watch, protest: "What does it say, quarter to six? But no, it's almost six! That clock over there is always going crazy." Then, followed by the two of us, silent, aggressive, he'd pace up and down throughout the Casa dei Guaglioni, opening doors and windows, retaking possession. And already the Casa dei Guaglioni seemed like a great ship filled with ocean wind, embarked on stupendous journeys.

Finally, my captain would return to his room and collapse on the bed, faceup, with an unhappy and distracted expression: maybe he was already thinking of leaving again? He'd look at the sky outside the window and observe, "New moon," but with an air of saying: "Always the same moon. The usual moon of Procida!"

## More about the Amalfitano

Meanwhile, observing him, I noticed some wrinkles under his eyes, between his eyebrows, near his lips. I thought, with envy: "They're signs of age. When I have wrinkles, too, it will be a sign that I'm grown up, and then he and I can be together always."

As I waited for that mythological epoch, I cherished another hope for the present, which I never dared confess to my father, because it seemed to me too ambitious. Finally one night I made up my mind and asked him boldly: "Couldn't you, some time or other, bring one of your friends with you here to Procida?" I said *one of your friends*, but I was thinking of one in particular (A.D.).

At first my father gave me no answer except a glance so forbidding that I felt a chill in my heart; and I also felt humiliated, so much that I had the impulse to go to my room, to console myself with the friendship of Immacolatella. But, meanwhile, I saw my father's eyes grow lustrous and animated, as if, looking at me, he had changed his mind. He smiled, and I recognized the fabulous goat-like smile that another time had been the first signal of confidences.

I, too, smiled, although I was still rather vexed. And he, frowning, came out with this extraordinary declaration:

"What friends? Know that here on Procida I have one friend alone and there must be only him. I want no other. And that ban is eternal!"

At that speech, I felt almost transfigured. Who was his only friend, here on Procida? Was it possible that my father really meant to speak of me?

Staring at me severely, he resumed:

"Look there! You know who that is in the photograph?"

And he pointed to the photograph of the Amalfitano that was always in his room.

So I murmured, "Romeo," and he exclaimed, in a tone of cutting superiority:

"Very good, kid."

⁂

"When I came here to Procida for the first time," he began, scowling at the memory, "I immediately realized (and, besides, I knew it even before getting off the boat) that this, for me, was a desert island! I agreed to call myself Gerace, because one name is the same as another. There's even a poem that says so, the type that girls write in autograph albums:

> *What does the name matter? Call the rose*
> *by any other name: will it smell less sweet?*

⁂

"For me *Gerace* meant: future owner of farms and income. And so I bore that Procidan surname. But in this deserted crater, I had only one friend: him! And if Procida became my country, it wasn't because of the Geraces but because of him!

"I recall that when I disembarked here (when everyone looked at me suspiciously, as if at an exotic beast), the only ones who honored me as I deserved were his dogs. There were eight, all mean, and usually they attacked anyone who approached. Instead, when I climbed up here to get a closer look at them (I had had a glimpse from down below, and they interested me, because they were of diverse and handsome breeds), all eight came around to greet me, as if they recognized me and I were already master of the house. That was also when I made his acquaintance; and from then on, you could say, not a day passed that I wasn't here. To tell the truth, I kept coming back more to play with the dogs than for him, since although he made an effort to be brilliant, it wasn't much fun to sit listening to the chat of an old man, who on top of that was blind. But even if I valued the dogs' company more than his, he was content: provided I didn't fail!

"Every so often he said to me: 'I was always fortunate and now, before I die, I've had the greatest good fortune. The only reason I regretted not having married was this: not to have a son of my own, to love as much as myself. And now I've found him, my angel, my son: it's you!'

"He also declared that, the night before he met me, he had gone from one dream to another, and all these dreams were prophetic. He had dreamed, for example, of returning to the time when he was a shipping agent, and of receiving, anonymously, a fragrant wooden chest that contained magnificent colored stones and Oriental spices that gave off a perfume like a garden. Then he had dreamed that, still healthy and spry, he had gone hunting on the island of Vivara; and that his dogs flushed out a family of hares (but without wounding them), among them a young hare as handsome as an angel, which had a ray of gold in its black fur. Then he had dreamed that an enchanted bitter-orange tree was growing in his room, all silvered by the moon . . . and other visions of this type.

"I sneered, skeptical, hearing him tell these stories, because I knew very well that they were all nonsense. He expected me to believe that,

ever since he'd been blind, he'd had fantastic dreams, much more col-
orful than reality, and that even going to sleep had become a gala party,
an adventure from a novel, in other words—a second life. But I knew
a thing or two, on his account, and right away I recognized the trade-
mark of all those boasts. I understood perfectly well that they were his
inventions that he wanted me to believe, to show off, not to make a poor
impression with his miserable old age. But the truth was that for him it
was too late even for the consolation of dreams. Like most old people
diminished at the end, he suffered from insomnia, and was also ill with
stupid manias, frenzies, obsessions, which disturbed him day and night.
These things were known about him, here on Procida. But he didn't
want to confess them to me: first of all, out of vanity; and then because
he guessed that if he got in the habit of crying about his troubles, I
would soon leave him. I'm made like that, I don't have the vocation of
a sister of charity. My mother, too, scolded me all the time: *You're one
of those of whom the Gospel says: if a friend asks them for bread, they give
him a stone.*

"Well, in the midst of all his boasts, the reality was that for him
the only wonderful dream was my company—it didn't take much to
grasp that. And as for me, even though I would have liked some vari-
ation, I didn't have a lot of choice in the matter of pastimes, here on
Procida. I had no other friend, no place to go, and, besides, I never
had a cent in my pocket. In fact your grandfather, before letting me
inherit, didn't fork out any money, nor did I ask for any. Rather, I
preferred to ask the Amalfitano, but he gave it to me reluctantly, and
only a little, for cigarettes; because he was afraid that if I had money
available I could run away from the island.

"So, one way or another, I ended up here every day.

"Sometimes he'd say to me: 'Think, in the past I saw so many landscapes, so many people: I could populate a nation with the people I've
seen. And the dearest friend of my entire existence, which is you, I only

met now that I'm blind. To say that I knew all the beauty of life, I'd have to see one person alone: you. And yet it is precisely you I haven't been able to see. Now, at the thought of dying, of leaving this life and this beautiful island of Procida, where I've known all happiness and freedom from care, I console myself with one hope: Some believe that the dead are spirits and see everything. Who can say that it's not true? And if it's true I'll be able to see you after I die. That consoles me for death. What do you think?' I answered him: 'Hope, hope, Amalfi'—that's what I usually called him—'if the dead really can see, you can be content to die. To see me it's worth the trouble. Too bad the facts are different: do you want to know what difference there is between a blind man, like you, and a dead man?' 'What difference? Tell me.' 'A blind man like you still has eyes, but no longer has sight; and a dead man doesn't have sight and doesn't have eyes, either. You can be sure, Amalfi, you, you've never seen me in person and you never will, forever and ever.'

"He was constantly asking me to describe what I looked like: my features, and the colors of my face and my eyes, and if I had streaks in my irises, a halo around the pupils, and so on. And, in order not to satisfy his curiosity too completely, I answered sometimes one way, sometimes another, capriciously. Once I told him that I had bloodshot eyes, like a tiger; and once that I had one blue eye and one black. Or I said that I had a scar on my cheek and immediately contracted the muscles of my face so that when, to make sure, he touched my cheek, he found there a deep hollow, and was almost in doubt.

"Then he said to me: 'But on the other hand it's better for me not to see you when I'm dead. What could I expect from it, except a bitter sorrow, since I'd see that you had made other friends, and were together with them, as before you were with me? I'd see you in the company of other friends, maybe on this very island where our friendship is written even in the rocks, even in the air!' 'Ah, of that,' I answered, 'you can be sure. The company of the dead is fine for the beyond, but I am ALIVE, and I will find my companions among the living. Of course I'll have better things to do, during my days, than cultivate chrysanthemums on a dead man's grave!' He didn't want to let me see the suffering that answer caused him; but he turned pale, and his features, in a moment, appeared worn out. Suffering was worse for him than for others: because, until those last years of his existence, he had never known it. His life, before, had been all fun and games. He had never known that one can suffer on account of another person. Well, just like that, I taught him!

"What tortured him most was the fear that, one day or other, out of impatience, I would quit Procida. If I was a little later than usual, he immediately suspected that I had gone without telling him and was perhaps already far from the coast. But I never left the island during those two years that he was still alive: until one night, while I was sleeping, as usual, down at your grandfather's house, he died unexpectedly, here, alone, unable even to say goodbye to me. It was strange for me, the next day.

"At the moment I wanted to convince myself, by force, that he had only fainted; and I even began to rail at the doctor, yelling that he was a worthless provincial doctor, an idiot, and that was why he was saying there was nothing to be done! His duty was to find a cure right away! A medicine, an injection! It was his duty! I ordered him! I insisted, in other words, that the doctor revive him without delay: I was beside myself. And then when the doctor left and I found myself alone with that dead man, it was a terrible shock to my nerves (I was still a boy), and I began to sob. Crying made me furious, and I insulted the dead man, calling him coward, clown, stinker, because he had died without even saying goodbye to me. That seemed the worst thing, the most unacceptable: I don't know what unique, fatal importance I gave that goodbye. And I was angry, thinking again of all the times that—because of some impatience in my character, or just to be arrogant, even though I had nothing else in particular to do—I had deliberately left the Amalfitano here alone, waiting in vain for my visit, for entire days! In fact, I had done well: It's better not to spoil your neighbor too much, to tell him to go to hell every so often, otherwise it would be the end! Our life would go forward heavily, like a boat loaded with ballast, and would carry us to the bottom to suffocate . . . But at that moment my nerves wouldn't listen to reason: and all the hours and days that I had spent roaming far from the Amalfitano's house, to make him sigh and fret, seemed to me absolute treasures, squandered without any satisfaction to me!"

(At this point in his recollection, my father looked up at the photograph of the Amalfitano, with an expression of tender friendship; but right afterward he broke out into an irreverent, histrionic laugh, as if to mock the dead man.)

"Now it seemed to me that nothing, no person, was worth the trouble of spending one's time with, compared with Romeo the Amalfitano; and I felt convinced and sure that I would never meet a being so fascinating, so marvelous: a being so handsome! Yes, it seemed to me undeniable, irrefutable, that he alone possessed every advantage of true beauty! If at that moment the Queen of Sheba, or the god Mars in person, or the goddess Venus had been introduced to me, I would have considered them vulgar types, café or postcard beauties compared with him! Who else possessed that slightly feverish, sly, delicate smile and, so tall, such small hands, gesticulating at every word, especially when he was talking nonsense? And those eyes which conferred his most terrible charm—because they were hurt, and their expression seemed lost, lifeless, without judgment, different from a human gaze?

"And those ways he had! Helpless, insecure, and ashamed (because he was bitterly ashamed of his blindness), but also grand, incurably grand! The grace of the most beautiful dancers, of the angels, was insignificant, inferior, compared with his!

"Even his gray curls, which fell behind his ears like a mane, and his provincial style of dress, with those rather ridiculous tight pants, now seemed to me the height of refinement! And his grace, his elegance, increased my despair! Damned, idiot blind man! If, by chance, Hell truly existed, I hoped he had arrived!

"To think that his company, which until yesterday had been assured, faithful, and at my disposal, had now become impossible! That desperate thought made me so furious that I threw myself on the floor, weeping and biting the iron frame of his bed. I called, Amalfi! Amalfi! and I remembered the injuries I had done him in life. I regretted them, but at the same time I almost felt like laughing, at the memory, for instance, of times when he was talking and telling me his dreams with grand gestures, and I would suddenly move away without a sound and hide in a corner, pretending to disappear like the fog. After a bit, he would notice my absence and, disconcerted, start calling me, and looking for me through the rooms, groping, pointing his stick at the walls. And the dogs, provoked by my nods, instead of helping him made an ineffectual noise, as if they, too, along with me, enjoyed agitating him. They, too, must have felt some remorse later, which may explain their suicide, if it's true, as it seems, that they had that tragic end.

"And now it was he who let me call without answering. If he had awakened, just for an hour, he would have heard from me marvelous things, all truths without the shadow of a lie, and he would have had reason to be proud! He would neither hear nor see anyone anymore, until the end of eternity, and I knew it; but still, at all costs I must give him a proof, a pledge, that would save our friendship from death.

"So, placing my palm on his stiff hand, full of rings, like a sultan's, I swore to him that, however many friends I had in the future, I would always ban them from Procida! On this island, which had been inhabited for me only by our friendship, his memory would forever be my only friend. That I swore to him. And so here to Procida, where the joined names of Wilhelm and Romeo are written even in the stones, even in the air, I will never bring other friends. If I did, I would stain myself with betrayal and perjury and would condemn our friendship to death!"

## The Amalfitano's Dream

After that solemn statement, my father eyed the portrait of the Amalfitano maliciously, as if to say: "Are you content, dead man, with this homage to your capricious folly?"

And then he sighed.

And so on the island my father had always had Romeo beside him, a faithful companion, in the same way that, away from the island, he always had Algerian Dagger beside him! They shared his love, and his secrets; and both, for me, remained unknown and unattainable. Childhood, I thought, sighing, was always the cause of my bitter destiny. The death of Romeo, the adulthood of Algerian Dagger, left it behind, excluded from my father's enchanted realms.

I was silent for a while; then I observed:

"For two years, you never left Procida! Not even once!" (I was thinking: "Happy time! Ah, because I wasn't yet born?")

"Never!" my father confirmed. "What do you think? It was a unique case! Well, it wasn't only the situation, truly, it was also *Amalfi*. He was a wizard, and knew how to keep me on Procida. And, on the other hand, I thought, 'He's old, soon he'll be out of the way, I can grant him some of my time.' Especially since it was useful to me! If nothing else, it served me to inherit this beautiful house!" And my father laughed brutally in the face of the Amalfitano, as if intending to provoke him. But then, perhaps repentant, he looked at him with a disarming, boyish smile and, letting himself be drawn in again by memory, resumed speaking:

"When he named me the heir of the house, he made me a fine speech for the occasion, as in a great novel: 'This palazzo,' he said to me, 'is the dearest object that I possess on the earth, and so I leave it to you. I also leave you some money that I have in the bank in Naples, and so, adding those to your father's property, you'll be almost a gentleman. The thought that you'll be spared work is a great satisfaction to me, because work isn't for men, it's for dunces. An effort, maybe, can sometimes give pleasure, provided it's not work. An idle effort can be useful and pleasant, but work, instead, is a useless thing, and destroys the imagination. In any case, if for some reason the money isn't enough, and you do have to adjust to work, I advise a profession that favors imagination as much as possible, for example a shipping agent. But to live without any profession is best of all: maybe content yourself with eating only bread, provided it's not earned.

" 'This house I leave you was for me the palace of legends, the earthly paradise, and the day I have to abandon it, the thought that it will be your house will console me. To another thought I'm resigned as well: and that is, that you won't live here alone, but with a wife. In fact, it seems strange, but you're one of those who need a wife waiting for them somewhere, or their heart struggles to survive. And that's all right, I don't oppose your fate and your imagination: bring your wife here, to this house. Luckily, I won't be here then: since I would prefer to breathe even my last breath facing the executioner rather than a woman. Blind as I am, the thought of having a woman before my eyes would make even death go wrong: my dying would no longer be dying, it would be dropping dead! Everything, in fact, can be forgiven one's neighbor (at least at the point of death) but ugliness, no! And any ugly thing, at the thought, seems to me pleasing if I compare it to the ugliness of women. Lord, how ugly women are! And where else has there ever been ugliness so painful? so special? that, even if one doesn't look at it and doesn't see it, one feels vexed merely knowing that it exists?

"'Better not to think of it. Enough: you, my Wilhelm, will marry, and you'll bring her here, and start a family: for you it's fated. And as for me, I told you, I will not oppose you on that. It's your business, and doesn't concern me. Another hope would suffice for me: that you reserve for me alone the place of friendship, in this house of yours, at least, and on this island of Procida!

"'But enough: this is therefore your house, and you'll always return to it, I'm sure, because one always returns home; and for you, too, this island of mine is an enchanted garden.

"'You'll always return, yes; but I would add: you'll never stay long. About that, dear little master, I have no illusions. Men like you, who have two different kinds of blood in their veins, never find peace or happiness: when they're there, they want to be here, and as soon as they return here immediately want to flee. You'll go from one place to another, as if you'd escaped from prison, or were in pursuit of someone; but in reality you'll only be following the diverse fates that are mixed in your blood, because your blood is like a hybrid animal, a griffin, or a mermaid. And you'll also find some company to your taste among the many people you'll meet in the world; but, very often, you'll be alone. A mixed-blood is seldom content in company: there's always something that casts a shadow on him, but in reality it's he who casts a shadow, like the thief and the treasure, which cast a shadow on one another.

"'And on this subject I now want to tell you the dream I had last night. I dreamed that I was an elegant, dashing young man. I was sup-posed to become a grand vizier, or something similar: I was wearing a Turkish costume of brightly colored silk, the color (I'll say to give you an idea) of sunflowers; but not even sunflowers! Much more beauti-ful! Impossible to find a fitting comparison! I wore a turban with a tall feather, on my feet dancing slippers, and I was going along humming through fields of roses, in a beautiful place somewhere in Asia, where there was no one else. I was happy, full of life, with a sweet taste in my mouth, and all around I heard sighing. But to me that sigh seemed a natural thing (there's the strangeness of dreams) and, in my brain, I explained to myself the reason for it clearly. That explanation I remember even now, awake, and it really is a logical explanation, a true philosophical concept. (Who knows why I always have such extraordinary dreams?) Listen, if this isn't a fine concept:

" 'So it seems that living souls can have two fates: some are born bees, and some are born roses. What does the swarm of bees do, with the queen? They go and steal honey from all the roses, to carry to the hive, to their rooms. And the rose? The rose has in itself its own honey: rose honey, the most adored, the most precious! The sweetest thing it loves it has already in itself: there's no need to seek elsewhere. But sometimes the roses, those divine beings, sigh for solitude! The ignorant roses don't understand their own mysteries.

" 'The first among all roses is God.

" 'Between the two, the rose and the bee, the more fortunate, in my opinion, is the bee. And so the queen bee has supreme good fortune! I, for example, was born a queen bee. And you, Wilhelm? In my opinion, you, my Wilhelm, were born with the sweetest destiny and the bitterest:

" 'You're the bee and you're the rose.' "

## Arturo's Dream

If I think back today on those conversations with my father, and see again the scenes of that distant time, everything takes on a different meaning. And I remember the fable of that hatter who always wept or laughed at the wrong moment: because he was allowed to see reality only through the images of an enchanted looking glass.

At the time, I couldn't understand anything of my father's speeches (whether comic, or tragic, or playful) except what corresponded to my unquestioned certainty: that is, that he was the incarnation of human perfection and happiness! And perhaps, to tell the truth, he encouraged those boyhood concepts of mine, habitually displaying his own character in an advantageous light. But even if (let's take an unlikely case) he had had the fantasy of vilifying himself by making the blackest confessions and declaring that he was a brazen scoundrel, it would have been the same. For me his words were divorced from every earthly reason and value. I heard them as one hears a sacred liturgy, where the drama recited is no more than a symbol, and the ultimate truth it celebrates is bliss. This last, true meaning is a mystery that only the blessed know: pointless to seek an explanation by human means.

Like the mystics, I wanted not to receive explanations from him but to dedicate my faith to him. What I expected was a reward for my faith; and this sighed-for paradise seemed to me still so distant that (I don't say this as a figure of speech) I couldn't reach it even in dreams.

Often, especially when he was absent, I dreamed about my father, but never the type of dream that would, so to speak, compensate for reality (or only deceive) with false triumphs. They were always cruel dreams, taunting me with the bitterness of my condition and retracting, without ceremony, the promises I might have believed by day. And in those dreams I had a sharp, precise feeling of suffering, which (because of my natural ignorance as a boy) I still hadn't experienced in reality.

One of those dreams stayed in my mind:

My father and I are going down a deserted street; he is very tall, covered from head to toe in shining armor, and I, a boy who scarcely come up to his hip, am a recruit, with the cloth strips wrapped around my calves and a uniform of gray-green material too big for me. He walks with long strides, and I eagerly try to keep up. Without even looking at me, he orders brusquely: Go buy me some cigarettes. Proud of receiving his commands, I run back to the tobacco shop and, in secret from him, kiss the pack of cigarettes before giving it to him.

Although he hasn't seen me kiss the pack, as soon as he touches it and looks at it, he notices something that merits his scorn. And in a lashing tone he scolds me: "You sappy kid!"


## Final Events


So Arturo's childhood passed. When I was about to turn fourteen, Immacolatella, who was eight, found a boyfriend. He was a curly-haired black dog, with passionate eyes, who lived quite a distance away, in the direction of Vivara, and he came from there every evening, just like a fiancé, to visit her. He had learned our habits and, so that he would find us at home, came at dinnertime. If he saw that the kitchen window was still dark, he waited patiently; and if he saw it lighted he announced himself by barking from a distance, and scraped at the door to get us to open it. As soon as he entered, he greeted us with a loud exclamation, in a ringing tone, which seemed like the announcement of royal trumpeters, and then he galloped three or four times around the kitchen, like a champion at the start of a tournament. He could behave with great prowess and gallantry: he watched us eat, wagging his tail, without begging, to let us know that the only reason for his visits was sentiment; and if I threw him a bone he wouldn't touch it, waiting for Immacolatella to take it. He must have been a cross with some sort of greyhound: he always carried his head high and had a bold character, and Immacolatella was content. I sent her out under the starry sky to play with him, and stood aside; but after a while she left him and returned to me, to lick my hands, as if to say: "You are my life."

When the time for love arrived, Immacolatella became pregnant, for the first time in her life. But maybe she was too old, or had always been unfit because of some genetic malformation: she died giving birth to her puppies.

There were five: three white and two black. I hoped at least to save them, and sent Costante around the island in search of a bitch who could nurse them. Only after many hours did he return with a thin, red-haired bitch, who looked like a fox; but maybe it was too late, the puppies wouldn't suck. I also thought of feeding them goat's milk, as Silvestro had done with me, but I didn't have time to try. They were weak, and born before their time: they were buried with their mother in the garden, under the carob tree.

I decided that I would never have another dog in place of her: I preferred to be alone, and to remember her, rather than put another in her place. It was hateful to meet that black dog, who went around light-hearted, as if he had never met any Immacolatella on the island. Whenever he came near me, insistent on fun and games with me as before, I chased him away.

When, some time afterward, my father returned to Procida and asked the usual question—"What news?"—I turned my face without answering. It wasn't possible for me to say those words: "Immacolatella died."

Costante told him; and my father was unhappy at the news, because he loved animals and was very fond of Immacolatella.

That time, he stayed on Procida barely an afternoon and a night: he had come only to get certain documents from the Town Hall. He remained absent about a month, and then reappeared, and left again the following day, after obtaining from the tenant farmer a sum of money. But as he said goodbye he informed me, for the first time in our lives, of his destination and the date of his return.

He explained to me that for several months he had been engaged to a Neapolitan woman, and was going to Naples to get married. The wedding was fixed for Thursday of that week, and right afterward he would return to Procida, with his bride.

So, he told me, I was to go and wait for them at the dock the following Thursday; they would arrive on the three-o'clock steamer.

CHAPTER 2

# A Winter Afternoon

*A Winter Afternoon*

It was winter, and that Thursday a cold rain clouded Procida and the bay. On such days, so rare for us, the island looks like a fleet that has furled its countless painted sails and is traveling soundlessly with the currents, toward the land of the Hyperboreans. The smoke from the steamers making their usual daily rounds, and their long whistles through the air, seem like signals of mysterious routes, outside your fate: the journeys of smugglers, whale hunters, Eskimo fishermen—treasures and migrations! Those signals bring the joy of adventure or sometimes, instead, dismay, as if they were mournful farewells.

I had recently turned fourteen; only a few days earlier I had learned that starting today, with the arrival of the three-o'clock steamer, my existence would change. And, waiting for three o'clock, torn between impatience and revulsion, I wandered around the harbor.

In announcing to me that he was marrying that unknown Neapolitan woman, my father, in a dutiful tone (which was so unusual for him that it seemed artificial), had said: "This way, you'll have a new mother." And, for the first time in my life, I had a feeling of revolt against him.

No woman could call herself my mother, and I didn't want to call any-body by that name, except one, who was dead! Now in this foggy air I looked for her, my only mother, my Oriental queen, my siren; but she didn't answer. Maybe, because of the arrival of the intruder, she was hiding or had fled.

I didn't try to imagine what my father's new wife might look like or what sort of character she might have. I resisted all curiosity. Whether that woman was like this or like that was the same to me. To me, she meant only: duty. My father had chosen her, and I must not judge her.

According to the books I had read, a stepmother could be only a perverse, hostile creature, an object of hatred. But, as my father's wife, she was for me a sacred person!

At the appearance of the steamer, I approached the dock lazily. I tried to distract myself by observing the maneuvers of the landing; but the first passengers I saw were the two of them, standing at the top of the stairway, waiting for the gangplank to be lowered.

My father carried his usual suitcase, and she another, about the same size. While my father, who hadn't yet seen me, looked for the tickets for the guard, I, first of all, went up to her and without explanation took the bag from her hand: I knew my duty. But I felt, for an instant, that she resisted me, as if she had taken me for a suitcase thief. Then, immedi-ately, recognizing a sign in my gesture, she looked at me with animation. And, summoning my father with a light tug on his jacket, asked:

"*Vilèlm*, is that Arturo?"

"Oh, you're here," said my father. She blushed, for having thought me a thief, and gave me a small greeting, intimate but also modest.

Fortunately, it didn't occur to her to embrace me, as is customary when relatives greet one another. I would have pushed her away, because, really, you can't adapt to the idea that someone is your relative just like that, in an instant.

After picking up her suitcase, I saw that she was also carrying a shabby purse, so stuffed with objects that it wouldn't close. I moved to take that weight from her, too; but, at my gesture, she hugged the purse more tightly, unwilling to give it up, and held the clasp together with her hands, as if she were defending a treasure.

The three of us walked along the pier, toward the harbor square. Although hindered by the suitcases, my father and I moved more quickly. She walked clumsily in her high heels, which she seemed unused to, and kept stumbling.

I would have preferred to go barefoot, I thought, rather than adapt to ladies' shoes like that.

Apart from those high heels, though, and the new shoes, the wife had nothing ladylike about her, or rare! What might I have imagined? To see arriving beside my father some marvelous being, who attested to the existence of the famous female species described in books? That Neapolitan girl, in her worn, shapeless clothes, didn't look very different from the regular fishwives and common women of Procida. And a first glance was enough, right away, to see that she was ugly, like all other women.

Like them, she was bundled up, she had a full, white face, dark eyes, and hair (the shawl that was wrapped around her head left the part slightly uncovered) as black as raven's feathers. And one wouldn't even have said that she was a wife: her body seemed a grown woman's, but not her face, from which, although I had no experience of female ages, I recognized, with an instant intuition, that she was still almost a girl, not much older than me. Now, it's true that a woman at fifteen or sixteen (because she must have been about that) is already grown up and mature, while a male of fourteen is still considered a boy. But my father's claim made me increasingly indignant: that, apart from any other reasons, I could accept as a mother a person who was barely a couple of years older than me, if not less!

She was fairly tall, for a woman; and I felt, in fact, shame and vexation in realizing that she was much taller than me. (That didn't last long. It took me only a few months to catch up to her. And when, in the end, I left the island, she came barely to my chin.)

With a wave, my father summoned the carriage, and it came toward us. The bride meanwhile looked wide-eyed at the harbor square, and at the people, because it was the first time she'd been to the island.

In the carriage, I hoisted myself up to the box, beside the driver, but with my face turned to the two of them, who sat next to each other on the velvet seat. The driver had raised the hood, to protect the travelers from the rain, and the bride, as soon as she was sitting in shelter, hastened to clean her shoes with the hem of her dress. Those shoes (of shiny black leather, with gilt buckles) were, it should be noted, the most elegant I had ever seen; but she treated them as if, for her, they were sacred objects!

My father, glancing at her stealthily just then, had a faint smile, it wasn't clear if of enjoyment or of superiority. But, bent over her shoes, she didn't notice; otherwise, I think, she would have blushed.

It was easy to see that she was in awe of my father. Even when she used with him certain familiar manners that were spontaneous (as earlier, when she gave a little tug on his jacket), she had a hesitant and slightly fearful air. And although my father, for his part, seemed content to be bringing that woman home, he gave no sign of intimacy. I didn't see them whisper, or embrace, or kiss, as lovers are said to do, or newlyweds on their honeymoon. That pleased me. He had his usual expression of arrogant detachment: and she sat composedly, a little apart from him, holding on her lap her precious purse, and clutching its clasp with all ten fingers. Her hands were small and rough, reddened by chilblains, and I noticed that on her left hand she wore a gold ring: my father's wedding ring. My father, however, wore no ring.

None of us spoke. She was utterly intent on observing the town. From her expression, she seemed to imagine that she was entering some historic city, Baghdad or Istanbul, not the island of Procida, which isn't very far from Naples! Every so often I gave her a sidelong glance and saw again her large eyes, shining in astonishment, the lashes rayed like the points of a star. In the half-light of the carriage, her face, with those big, wide-open eyes, seemed jeweled. Her thick eyebrows, irregular in shape, and joined on her brow, reminded me of portraits of barbarian girls and women I'd seen in books.

At the intersection of the main street, passing a niche where, behind a grate, there was a portrait of the Virgin Mary, she raised her right hand, and, with a serious and concentrated air, made the sign of the cross, then kissed the tips of her fingers. Seeing that, I immediately looked at my father, sure of meeting at least a mocking or a pitying smile; but, slouched back in the seat, he was paying no attention to her.

When we reached the square, we could see the great curve of a rainbow rising from the sea and passing through the vault of the sky almost to the center. In the brightening air, amid the countless reflections of the storm, the ancient structures of the fortress appeared, very close, almost above us. Seeing them, the bride made a gesture of extraordinary admiration, and nudged my father with her elbow, asking, in a knowing tone:

"Is that . . . our house?"

I laughed loudly. My father shrugged one shoulder and said to her: "Oh, no!" Then he explained, turning to me, stressing his words:

"*I told her that we live in a magnificent castle*," and he smiled at me, with an astonishing expression of almost childish and rascally complicity, which left me doubtful. The possibility that my father had given the bride to understand some exaggerations or even nonsense had never occurred to me; on the other hand, I had never presumed till today that the Casa dei Guaglioni was a castle!

My stepmother blushed. My father, raising his eyebrows, with a half-indulgent, half-sarcastic look, said to her:

"You know what that is, that beautiful villa up there? It's the prison!"

"The prison!"

"Yes! The prison of Procida!"

"There is the prison!" she exclaimed dreamily, looking at those walls with different eyes. "Ah, you told me about it! That not even in Rome is there such a big and important prison! And criminals are brought there from everywhere! *Madonna!* One can't look! It seems an insult, to think that we pass here below in a carriage, and up there, those poor youths . . ."

But having said this, she pulled herself together and, assuming a severe expression, as if to force her own feelings to a superior morality, concluded:

"Yet! It's justice! They've done bad things and now they're paying!"

Here I commented by letting out a faint whistle, since such a concept deserved all my contempt: as we know, I was always on the side of the outlaws. But she didn't seem to understand my evident disapproval; completely absorbed, perhaps she hadn't even heard me. Probably it wasn't worth the trouble of wasting a whistle, to point out a mature idea to a dull, primitive being like her.

When we turned the corner, toward the bay, the full extent of the prison was visible in the distance, from the ancient fortress to the new buildings; and the bride's eyes returned for an instant in that direction, full of bewilderment and compassion, but, still, with obvious respect for the established authority! Then, without looking again at that enormous house of punishment, she burrowed into the back of the carriage.

## The Three of Us Arrive

During the last stretch of the journey, a subtle interest began to prick at me: in fact, this was the first time in many years that the Casa dei Guaglioni had received a woman, and my incredulity was toying with a certain curious anticipation. What would happen when, very soon, we crossed the threshold with her? I almost began to expect some mysterious warning sign, the walls shaking violently . . . but really nothing happened. As usual, I found under a rock, where I had placed it before going out, the key to the entrance door, which opened obediently; and, a little damp from the drive in the open air, we entered the quiet *castle* of the Geraces. The house was deserted (as usual, Costante had returned to his farm at midday), and my father preceded us through the icy, silent rooms, opening doors and windows as always upon arrival. Some doors banged, shut by the north wind, which had risen and cleared the sky to infinity.

The bride advanced through the rooms as if she were visiting a church: I think that, in her existence, she had never seen a dwelling as imposing as ours. More than all the rest, however, the kitchen impressed her. It seemed that such a large room, equipped with so many burners, and used only for cooking, was an extraordinary marvel to her. Yet she wanted to let us know that a lady, an acquaintance of her sister, also had a kitchen in her house, where she went only to cook and to eat: of course, however, it wasn't as big as ours. At that speech, my father laughed in the bride's face, and, speaking to me, explained that in her girlhood home in Naples, where she lived with her whole family, the kitchen was only a burner on a tripod, which in winter was lighted inside, on the floor, and in summer in the street, in front of the door. They even made the pasta in the bedroom, and hung it to dry on the bars of the bed.

The bride, listening to my father's explanations, gazed at us with her big eyes and said nothing. "And she," he continued in the same tone of mockery and pity, "knows how to do only these three things: make pasta, take head lice out of her mother's hair, and say the Hail Mary and the Our Father."

Here she appeared confused, and gave my father a little nudge with her elbow, as if to ask him not to continue, because she was ashamed.

My father eyed her as if she had no importance, with a repressed laugh. "Starting today, though," he added, with an air of boasting, "she's a great lady: Signora Gerace, the mistress of all Procida." Then, taking me by surprise, he asked me an unexpected question:

"By the way, *moro*, you, when you speak to her, to this bride, what are you going to call her? You have to come to some agreement." (*Moro*, dark-haired kid, was what he called me.)

I stayed on guard, and kept my mouth shut, frowning and proud. She looked at me timidly, finally smiled, and with much blushing, lowering her eyes, answered my father in my place:

"He never knew his mother, poor boy. I feel like a mother to him. Tell him he can call me Ma and I'll be happy."

This was really the boldest, most insulting provocation that the two of them could make! My face must have expressed a revolt so savage that I impressed even my father. He said in an indifferent, almost lightly mocking tone:

"Nothing to do about it. He doesn't want to call you Ma. Well, kid, call her what you like, call her by her name, Nunziata, or Nunziatella."

(Instead, not only that day but later, too, I avoided calling her by her name. If I wanted to speak to her, or get her attention, I'd say, *listen, say, you*, or even whistled. But that name, *Nunziata, Nunziatella*, I had no wish to utter.)

At my father's words, the bride raised her eyelids. Little by little, the blush receded from her face, leaving her, it seemed to me, paler than before, and so intimidated that I seemed to see her tremble. And yet she had displayed a certain audacity in proposing that I call her Ma. Haughty and contemptuous, I stared at her: wrapped in the large black shawl, with those big eyes, she looked like an owl, who never sees the sun; she had a face of wax, like the moon! And who knows what important secrets she kept in that purse of torn, mangy leather: since I'd seen her arrive on the dock, until now, she hadn't let go of it for a second, and she held it closed with her fingers, as if fearing an attack by bandits!

While I considered her in this way, the bride said nothing, seeming to lack even the courage to breathe. Then, suddenly, realizing that I was looking at her, she answered my stormy gaze with a spontaneous smile, which again brought a fleeting color to her cheeks. And as if to consecrate, from that moment, our family, she said with a kind of solemnity, pointing to one after the other, with her red, rough little hand:

"Then this is Vilèlm, this is Arturo, and this is Nunziata."

⁂

My father had leaned against the marble edge of the sink, and was almost sitting there, one foot dangling and the other on the floor, in an indolent, distracted position. His half-lowered eyelids allowed a glimpse of the dark blue of his eyes, like the color of water muddied by winter, in certain hidden caves where no boat can enter. His thin hands, with the long, neglected nails, were clasped idly. And his hair, at that moment of the light, was all mixed with gold.

The bride seemed to wonder if now, here in the kitchen, we could consider that we had arrived at our house and her honeymoon was over. At first she interrogated my father with her eyes; but since just then he was paying no attention to her, she made up her mind and resolutely took off the high-heeled shoes. Evidently, she couldn't wait to be free of them. With great respect she placed them on a chair, and I never again saw them on her. She kept them hidden, like sacred treasures, along with other ornaments from her trousseau that she never used.

I was pleased to see her become shorter, without those high heels: now the difference in our height, which was so humiliating to me, seemed almost negligible. Over her long silk stockings she wore short, dark wool socks, much darned; her feet were small, but stubby and not very shapely; her ankles were rather thick, and her legs still had an almost childish roughness.

After the shoes, she took off the shawl, which was wrapped around her head and fastened under her chin by a pin, and her hair appeared, pulled up, and bound with a quantity of combs, barrettes, and hairpins. This revived my father's attention, and he began to laugh. "What have you done!" he said to her. "You've put up your hair! It was your mamma! No, I don't like it. Anyway, it's obvious just the same that you're not a grown woman. Come here, I want to make you pretty again, the way I like you."

She looked at us, submissive but hesitant, and because of this hesitation my father's desire became stronger. With unexpected, violent animation, he called her over again. Then I could see the enormous fear she had of him: it was as if she had to face an armed bandit, and she stood there, struggling between obedience and disobedience, unable to decide which of the two frightened her more. In one step my father reached her and grabbed her: she trembled, with a wild expression, as if he had seized her in order to beat her.


## In Western Light


Meanwhile, my father, laughing, tore off clips and combs, and mussed up her hair with both hands, as the little combs and hairpins fell everywhere. A grand black head of hair, all natural curls and ringlets, like the fur of a wild animal, fell in disarray around her face, down to her shoulders. Her face became shadowy and almost arrogant, and her eyes were alight with bright tears. But she didn't dare escape from my father; only, when he had finished messing up her hair, she shook her head hard, in an action you sometimes see in horses, or even cats.

I looked curiously at all those curls, partly because I remembered a certain remark made a few minutes earlier by my father, but he guessed my suspicion and said:

"What do you imagine, Arturo? No, no: they deloused her thoroughly for her wedding."

He held her by the skirt, but she didn't even try to flee. With one hand she clasped her precious purse, hiding it slightly behind her hip, to protect it from my father's violence, and she remained docile, between the two of us, in front of the glass door. Now her irises, which in the shadowy light were so black, revealed various streaks, like rooster feathers, whereas the circle that outlined the irises was really as black as a mulberry, like velvet trim. And around it the white of the eye preserved a violet-blue tint, as in small creatures.

Her cheeks were full and round, as in those faces that haven't yet assumed the precise shape of youth. And her lips, slightly cracked by the cold, resembled some small red fruits (always slightly gnawed by the squirrels or the wild rabbits) that grow on Vivara.

Now, when I saw her for the first time in brighter light, her face looked even younger than it had earlier, on the dock. If her body, which was tall and developed, hadn't denied it, one would have thought, seeing her, that she was still a child. Her skin was clear, pure, and smooth, as if even the towel with which she dried her face had been careful not to damage it. Being a woman, she had surely spent her whole life shut up inside: even on her forehead, and around the eyes, where the rest of us, accustomed to the sun, always have some wrinkles or spots, she had no mark. Her temples were of an almost transparent whiteness: and in the hollows under the eyes the smooth, untouched white skin resembled those delicate petals that, once opened, do not last even a day, and darken as soon as you pick the flower.

Her neck, under that great head of hair, seemed very thin, but from the throat to the chin there was a broad, tender curve. There the skin was of an even whiter color than her face; and now, nearby, a black curl had fallen. Two longer curling locks touched one shoulder, and behind the nape, almost under her ear, some short curls sprouted, like a goat's. Big heavy curls covered her forehead to the eyebrows; while on her temple she had a light, fine short curl that moved at every breath.

Her hair seemed to have grown capriciously, following fancy. For me, who had never seen such curls and ringlets before, it was entertainment to observe them; but for her, used to them since she was a child, they must have seemed ordinary, something natural. She wrapped one around a finger, to hide the extreme agitation into which my father had thrown her; and soon afterward, ashamed of being so disheveled, with her hand she casually pushed the hair away from her face. Then her ears were exposed, which were small and shapely, and had a rosy tint that distinguished them from the whiteness of her face and neck. As is customary among women, the lobes were pierced; and in them she wore two small circles of gold, the kind that girls receive as a gift from their godmother when they're baptized.

While instinctively she smoothed her hair, she still couldn't free herself from her mysterious fear, and, near my father, she had an uneasy expression of alarm. My father violently shook the edge of the skirt he was holding, and let it go. In a petulant, hostile tone, he declared, "I chose a curly-haired fiancée, and I want a curly-haired wife." She answered, in a meek and trembling voice:

"But I'm not angry, if you took my hair down. Tell me your wish, and I'll do what you want."

"And what are you hiding there?" my father said to her. "Come on, show us your jewels."

And with an aggressive laugh he snatched the famous purse from her hands, spilling out onto the table everything it contained. It really was jewels! A pile of bracelets, pins, necklaces, almost all given to her by my father during the engagement. I didn't know much about such things, and thought, at first, that they were real gold, real topazes, rubies, pearls, and diamonds. Instead they were fake trinkets, bought at fairs or from peddlers' carts. My father had won her with pieces of glass, like a savage.

The only objects of value in that pile were some branches of coral and a small silver ring, with a Madonna engraved on it, which her godmother had given her at her confirmation, and which no longer fit.

(She never wore any of this jewelry: she kept it hidden in the wardrobe, with religious adoration. She never wore anything but the earrings from her godmother, a silver medallion with the Sacred Heart, which hung on a thin string, and her wedding ring: but these for her weren't even jewels, they were part of her body, like the curls.)

For a while my father amused himself by playing idly with the jewels, then he got tired of it, and left the bride in peace. Drawn by the fine weather that had returned, he told us to wait for him, and he went out toward the edge of the yard to look at the sea. Then the bride, who was standing apart, in a corner, came over again to the table where the jewelry was, like a defenseless wild beast who, as soon as the threat grows distant, comes out of her forest lair.

The glass door was open: and the grand sunset over the sea, cleared by the wind, lighted up the whole kitchen with the last colors of the sun: even the waves of the high sea, down below, threw back on the whitewashed wall their quivering reflection, which gradually faded. Still alarmed, and standing motionless near the jewelry with a jealous expression, she seemed like a swallow or a dove hovering near its nest of little eggs. In the end, making up her mind, she almost furiously piled up all the jewels and put them back in the purse, with a sigh of comfort. Then she got down on the floor and, moving here and there on her knees like an animal, with the hair falling in her face, began to gather in her lap the combs and hairpins. My duty, as a man, should have been to help her: I wasn't ignorant, and I knew it. But recalling that on the dock, not long before, she hadn't trusted me to carry the purse, I remained scornfully in my place.

When she finished, she stood up again, and dumped combs and hairpins on the chair, near the high-heeled shoes. Then she shook her hair back and gave me a small smile of friendship. I looked at her harshly. And she stopped smiling, but didn't seem offended. Her lashes were still wet with those earlier childish, mysterious tears: but in her eyes the wetness of the tears didn't seem bitter and burning, as with the rest of us: it seemed like a suspended vapor that sparkles as it plays with irises and pupils. And her gaze, submissive but very frank, and full of dignity, and always illumined by joy and a kind of prayerfulness, reminded me of someone . . . that's who! Immacolatella! She had a similar gaze, as if she could always see the miraculous God.

I sat on the doorstep to wait for my father. That part of the house was sheltered from the north wind, and the sun lingered there before setting, affording some warmth. Soon afterward, she, too, came and sat on the step next to me, and began to untangle her hair as well as she could with one of those toothless little combs she had picked up. You could hear the sea pounding on my beach and every so often the whistle of the north wind over the island. I was mute. She said:

"Not anymore, but as a girl my mother had hair like mine. My sister, on the other hand, doesn't have a lot of hair."

Then, having finished combing her hair, she exclaimed:

"*Madonna!* How red the sky is tonight!"

And she added, sighing, in a grave and enchanted tone, but not bitter, as if, obedient, she recognized the laws of marriage in her own destiny:

"Think! This is the first time I've been away from home!"

My father returned from the yard; and before it got dark we carried upstairs the suitcases, which we had left in the front hall. As we had at the pier, my father carried his and I the bride's. She followed behind us, carrying, bundled up in the shawl, the combs, the shoes, and the purse with the jewelry.

## Upstairs

The bride's suitcase was fairly light, but, although it couldn't contain much, it made me curious. This was the first time I had lived in the same house with a woman and witnessed her life from up close; and I had no idea about the habits of women, about the clothing of those bundled creatures, and if, even shut up within the walls, even when they sleep, they always appear so shapeless and mysterious. The bride still hadn't taken off her coat from the journey, a faded ill-fitting garment, which was too short for her, so that the wide skirt of her dress, of a shiny but very worn velvet, hung down from it quite a bit. Undoubtedly, in appearance this woman was a common beggar; but after the surprise of the jewels I might expect her to be hiding in the suitcase perhaps the costumes of an Oriental sultan.

For now, she took out of it only a pair of shabby old shoes, without heels, and adapted to use as slippers; and she began wearing them immediately, with satisfaction, although they were too large for her. She had to shuffle when she walked, and every so often they came off her feet.

My father, putting down his own suitcase, had told me to put the bride's in another room, opposite his, where there was a wardrobe and an iron bedstead; and he himself, soon afterward, carried in a mattress and blankets. But the bride, who at first seemed very pleased to have a room just for her things, became frightened when she realized that that room was intended for her to sleep in as well; and, in spite of her awe of my father, she began to repeat obstinately that it was impossible, that she was afraid of spending the night in a room by herself, that she wanted to sleep with everyone else. My father listened to her in annoyance, because he was not accustomed to sharing his room with anyone; but, seeing that she really had gone pale with fear, he turned to me, without even deigning to answer her, and said impatiently: "All right! I'll keep her in my room with me. Come on, *moro*, help me lift this bed." And he and I together carried the bride's bed into his room.

She followed us happily. The new bed wouldn't fit next to my father's big bed, which occupied almost the whole back wall; and we put it cross-wise, with the head against the longest wall, so that it was almost at the foot of my father's bed. As soon as she saw things arranged in that way, the bride, who wanted to make a show of helping us, began to beat and turn the dusty mattresses and pillows energetically, starting with the big bed. And amid those exertions, she asked my father, in all naturalness:

"So now from tonight I'll sleep in the big bed with you, instead of Arturo? And he'll sleep here in the little bed?" Her conviction was, evidently, that I didn't have my own room to sleep in at night, but was accustomed to sleeping with my father, in his bed!

At that new sign of her ignorance, I confined myself to laughing; but my father, who was already annoyed by carrying the bed, scornfully shrugged one shoulder and said to her, curling his lips in an expression of mockery and mimicking her:

"No, signora. When I want to sleep, *you* will sleep in the small bed. *I* will sleep in my big bed, where I've always slept. And Arturo will sleep in his bed, in his room, where he has always slept!"

Then, feigning anger, he shouted at her:

"Remember, girl, that here you are not among the riffraff or in some tribe, here you are in the CASTLE OF THE GERACES! And if you utter another disgraceful word, I'll send you up there to sleep, in that other castle, with the guards and the prisoners!"

It was clear that she didn't understand why she deserved such a rebuke; but still she blushed with the shame of having uttered something disgraceful. And she looked at me, questioningly, as if asking what harm there would be in a bride sleeping in the same room as me, a boy.

Finally, she made me angry; and I said to her, in a tone of lively contempt:

"I sleep alone, in my room! I don't need other people near me. If you think they're all afraid like you, you're wrong. I would sleep alone even in the Rocky Mountains or the steppes of Central Asia!"

At those words, the bride looked at me with sincere admiration, but, eyes wide, she gazed all around the room, as if the idea of sleeping alone with my father frightened her. Yet between those two fears, sleeping utterly alone in a room and sleeping alone with my father, she chose the second rather than the first.

Maybe to comfort herself, she resumed beating the big mattress even more vigorously, so that the dust reached my father, who had flopped lazily onto the small bed. He jumped up and spit in one direction; then, this time with real anger, grabbed her hands in the air and, his face darkening, exclaimed:

"Hey! Will you stop it with these mattresses? What's got into you? When did you ever get such a frenzy for cleaning that you'll ruin the mattresses?"

She murmured in bewilderment: "At my house . . . we do . . ."

"Oh, yes! at your house! When in the world! At your house! They beat the mattresses!"

"Always, every year, for Holy Easter . . . and sometimes more often . . . more often during the year . . ."

He lowered the bride's wrists suddenly, letting go of them with such brutality that it was as if he wanted to sever them; and his angry voice was tinged with scorn:

"Well," he said, "you're not at your house anymore now, here we are in the Castle of Procida, this is my marriage bed, and no one ordered you to do Easter cleaning today."

And, having said that, he spit again, and went to pick up his suitcase from a corner; he carried it to the middle of the room and began to undo the rope tied around it. I had never before seen him attack someone with such intensity and rancor: the times he had had some reason to reprimand me, he scolded me brusquely, scowling and almost distracted, with a few trifling words. This scene with the bride showed me a new form of his moods, as mysterious to me as his mysterious and unquestionable justice; and in witnessing it I felt my nerves contract, as if this time I, too, shared the bride's fear. At the end, when he had let go of her wrists and moved away from her, I had the feeling of an obscure liberation.

Having opened the suitcase, he half knelt on the floor and began to empty it in a disorderly fashion, as he always did. The bride meanwhile remained unmoving near the bed, looking around the room. We were all three silent for a while; then she broke the silence, asking, curious, why the room had so many doors in a row.

My father, having no wish to get into a lot of lengthy explanations, immediately gave this answer, without even raising his head from the suitcase:

"Because in this house, as in all castles, every room is guarded at night by armed sentinels, each one standing watch in front of a door. To prove that they never sleep, every hour, all night long, they play a fanfare on the trumpet together."

She didn't dare to contradict my father, but, uncertain whether to really believe him or not, at that fantastic explanation she looked at me, as if to read a confirmation in my face. I couldn't contain my laughter, and so she, too, her face coloring slightly, laughed full-throatedly. By then my father had finished unpacking, and he quickly got up off the floor. Paying no more attention to us, he placed the pile of stuff on the chest of drawers, and kicked the suitcase into the corner; then, listening intently to the sound of the bell, which could be heard ringing in the distance, he compared the time on his watch Amicus. The story of the doors and the sentinels, which the bride and I were still laughing about, had already vanished from his mind.

He returned to the small bed, where he'd been lying a few minutes earlier, and sat across it, on the edge of the pillow, leaning his back against the bars. Distracted, a little sleepy, his hair falling over his eyes, he stretched out one foot, wiping his spit off the floor with the sole of his shoe. At that moment the bride observed the portrait of the Amalfitano, and asked: "Who is it?" Yawning, he answered:

"It's a holy image, which protects the castle." And he added slyly, lying on the bed:

"As in all castles, here, too, there's a dead ancestor who still wanders around. That's his portrait. Be careful that that dead man doesn't come and stab you in the heart while you're sleeping."

At that answer, she looked at my face, as before, but this time she read there neither a confirmation nor a denial. She shrugged one shoulder, smiling, and whispered:

"If one has a good conscience, why should one fear punishment?"

"Because," my father said to her, "he hated all women."

"What! He hated all women!"

"Yes. And if he had been lord of the universe he would have murdered them all."

"But if there are no more women, this world will end."

My father rested his head on his folded arm and, laughing, glanced furtively at the bride with a hostile and crafty expression.

"What did he care," he said, "about the continuation of the world? Since he's dead. What satisfaction does the continuation of the world offer him?"

"He was a Christian, and had those thoughts!" she said, crossing her hands over her chest, as if to arm herself, in the contest between her own timidity and proper feelings. Her face trembled in such a way that, looking at it, I imagined her heart beating like a bird just stolen from its nest, trapped in a fist. She leaned her head slightly toward her shoulder, swaying from one foot to the other; and finally she asked submissively:

"Why did he hate them?"

"Because," my father answered, lowering his head down on the pillow, "he said that women are all ugly."

"All ugly!" she repeated. "What! All of them ugly! Then . . . how . . . all of them! Then even women in the movies are ugly?"

"What do you know about movies?" said my father, stretching, in a lazy, drawling voice. "You've only been once, when I took you, and the film was about Indians!"

At those words I thought, with some dismay, that on this point I was behind her, since there was no movie theater on Procida, and I had never seen a film in my whole life.

The bride answered, insecure:

"My sister has been . . . a relative of ours took her, who's in Nola . . . a good Christian! She saw that other film . . . I don't remember the name, but the ones who were in that one didn't have red skin. And then you can also see the actors painted on the posters . . . you can see them all over Naples . . ."

"Go on, yes, go on discussing those prostitutes!" my father exclaimed mockingly. "That way we'll soon enjoy seeing your tongue fall off! Don't you know, the Devil cuts out the tongue of people who talk about filth and prostitutes? Your mother didn't tell you?"

The bride turned red. My father yawned.

"So, be quiet, what do you know?" he continued. "Stop it, girl. I don't want to talk about beauty with you."

Mortified, she tried, anyway, to offer a more worthy example, which would redeem her from the unsuitable one she had used before.

"And the Queen," she said, "then even the Queen is ugly?"

My father laughed, crushing his mouth against the pillow, with such gusto that it seemed he would bite it; and I, too, laughed. She looked at us in bewilderment, at both of us, perhaps seeking, in her submissive mind, a last line of defense. Finally, her eyes, as they looked at us, turned cloudy, and in a fervent, trembling voice she offered the supreme argument:

"And the Madonna," she said, "even she is ugly? The Mother of God!"

My father closed his eyes:

"That's enough," he said. "I'm sleepy. I want to rest for an hour or two. Go away and leave me alone. I'll see you later."

We silently left his room and closed the door. In the hall, the bride, in a low voice so as not to disturb my father, asked me to keep her company while she took her things out of the suitcase; because she wasn't yet used to the house and was afraid to be alone in a room, now that it was almost dark.

## The Suitcase

We returned to the other room, where the bed had been. In place of the bed a cleaner rectangle of the brick floor was visible; and there I sat down. The room had several lamps; but the only one with a bulb that wasn't burned out was a kind of metal lantern sticking out from the wall, high up. That bulb was so dusty that it shed scarcely any light; and so she climbed up onto the chest of drawers on her knees and unscrewed it. Then, to clean it, she spit on it several times, wiping it with her slip.

The opening of the suitcase was disappointing. There were only some shapeless rags, a pair of ordinary clogs, and a light flowered dress, already shabby, and discolored by sweat. There was a big kerchief, but not so pretty as the ones painted with roses that my father was in the habit of wearing as scarves; and nothing else. The suitcase was already almost empty. All that remained, on the bottom, was a layer of newspaper pages and wastepaper that you could see right away was being used to protect some framed pictures. They were all images of the Madonna, and she took them out with the utmost respect, and, first kissing them, one by one, she placed them on the chest of drawers.

She believed not just in a single Madonna but in many: the Madonna di Pompei, the Virgin of the Rosary, the Madonna del Carmine, and I don't know what others, and she recognized them by their dress, by their crown, and by their pose, as if they were so many different queens. One, I remember, was wrapped in stiff bands of gold, like the sacred mummies of Egypt, and, like her child, also swaddled in gold, bore on her head an enormous, many-pointed crown. Another, all jeweled, was black, like an African idol, and held up a son who looked like an ebony doll, and he, too, was covered with dazzling gems. Another, instead, had no crown: she was ringed only by a delicate halo, and, if one excluded this unique sign of who she was, she resembled a pretty, buxom shepherdess. With her naked baby, she was playing with a lamb, and from beneath the simple dress a plump white foot stuck out.

Another was sitting, in the pose of a lady, on a beautiful inlaid chair; and she was rocking a cradle so sumptuous that not even in the house of a duke could one see its equal! Yet another, similar to a warrior, wore a kind of armor of precious metals, and brandished a sword . . .

(From what I could deduce, I understand that these Virgins had diverse characters. One was rather inhuman, impassive as the goddesses of the ancient East: to honor her was necessary, but it was better not to ask her for favors. Another was a wizard, and knew how to perform every miracle. Still another, Our Lady of Sorrows, was the holy and tragic guardian to whom passions and sufferings are confided. All of them liked celebrations, ceremonies, genuflexions, and kisses; they all loved, too, to receive gifts; and they all had great power; but, it seems, the most extraordinary, most miraculous, and most gracious was the Madonna di Piedigrotta.

(Then, besides all these Virgins and their children, and all the saints, male and female, and Jesus Himself, there was God. From the tone in which my stepmother named him, it was clear that God, for her, wasn't a king, or even the head of the entire Holy Army, or even the lord of Paradise. He was much more: he was a name, unique, solitary, inaccessible; favors are not asked of him, nor is he worshipped. And, in essence, the duty of the whole immense crowd of Virgins and Saints who welcome prayers, vows, and kisses is this: to safeguard the inaccessible solitude of a name. This name is the only singularity that is opposed to the multiplicity of earth and Heaven. He doesn't care about celebrations or miracles or desires or sufferings or even death: he cares only about good and evil.

(This was the religion of my stepmother, or at least that's how I thought I could reconstruct it, from her behavior and her talk, that day and later, throughout our life in common. Of necessity, it's an imperfect reconstruction, partly because my stepmother was always restrained by a kind of modesty when she talked about holy things. And although on some great occasions she was eloquently effusive on the subjects of her faith, she always left certain points in silence and mystery. Thus, for example, it's hard for me to say even now what particular idea she had of the Devil, or if she believed in his existence.)

❧◉֍❧

A number (at least three or four) of the Virgins brought from Naples were propped in a row against the dresser mirror; but there were as many others in the suitcase that the mirror had no room for. They were placed, each with a kiss, on the night table and on the windowsill.

After the jewels, these pictures of the Virgin Mary were without question the bride's most magnificent possessions. Printed in color, in gold and silver, framed and under glass, they were also embellished with various ornaments. The picture of the Madonna di Piedigrotta was ringed with large shells, strips of silk, rooster feathers, and colored glass, which made it look like an emblem of barbarian triumph.

In essence, I thought, that suitcase had been surprising enough after all. But, although dazzled, I made no comments of any kind.

## *Eternal Life*

Having arranged her Virgins, the bride looked at them again, all around the room, and then asked if I thought my father would let her keep one in the bedroom, at the head of the little bed in which she was to sleep. Shrugging my shoulders somewhat skeptically, I answered: "I don't think so." Then I said severely:

"We don't believe in any Madonna."

And I added:

"Or in God."

"But your father is a Christian now," she replied, gravely. (That statement of hers, which at the moment I let go, distractedly, without really considering it, was to appear subsequently, in my memory, as a surprising novelty . . . but I will return to this later.)

From our brief discussion of the domestic images the bride's thoughts seemed to return, in that connection, to the subject of the ancestor, evoked a little earlier by my father. And, perplexed, she decided to ask me if that ghost, hater of women, was truly wandering through the castle! At her question, I again shrugged, with a grimace. Her credulity was wearing me out!

"But why don't you understand?" I burst out. "It's true that that man from Amalfi once lived here, but he's *dead*. You know what *dead* means? In other words, you should know that my father doesn't believe in ghosts, and I don't, either. Ghosts don't exist anywhere. They're romantic legends!"

She moved closer to me and, circumspectly, in a solemn whisper, asserted that, on the contrary, ghosts do exist: she had never seen one, though an acquaintance of her godmother, who was a night nurse at the Hospital for Incurables, had seen hundreds of them. "But," she said finally, "if I see them, what to do? They're not a thing to inspire fear." And she explained to me that they are simply unfortunate souls, sinners in torment, who, like helpless, wretched beggars, go around pleading for prayers for their eternal peace. In appearance, they no longer have the shape of humans, but look like fluttering scraps of cloth. And it's enough to say a requiem for them: then they go away immediately.

I was tempted to reveal to her that the dead, almost certainly, have no more spirit, that in death everything is extinguished and all that survives is glory; but then right away, having second thoughts, I said to myself that it would be pointless to inform her of certain things. In fact, in no case could glory ever be given to her; and so she might as well be left deluded in her opinions.

I contented myself with pointing out to her sarcastically:

"Well, if all you need is a prayer to get rid of them, why are you afraid of being alone at night?"

"It's not them I'm afraid of!" she protested, determined and almost indignant. "I'd be ashamed to be afraid of them. Of them or of any other thing! I'm not like my sister, who's even afraid of cats' eyes at night! For me, even if there's lightning, or criminals, I'm not afraid! Ask my mother if it's not true: that I'm never afraid! Of anything!"

("But," I thought, without saying it, "you are afraid of my father.")

"The only thing I'm frightened of," she resumed, as if making an effort to explain to me something very difficult that she didn't know how to explain to herself, "is this: being alone. But not for some reason! It's just that fact of being alone, without anyone nearby! It's just the fear of being alone, nothing else, that scares me! And then! Why in this world should so many souls exist if not to join together? And not only people! Animals, too: during the day, maybe, they go around separately, but at night they all sleep together!"

"It's not true!" I retorted firmly. "Certain animals know how to be solitary, and they're magnificent and proud, like heroes! The owl almost always perches alone, and the dugong comes out only at night; and the elephant sets off by itself and goes far away when it's time to die!

"But then man has much more heart than all the animals! He's equal to a king, he's equal to a star!

"But that's enough.

"I," I concluded proudly, "have always been alone, my whole life."

"That's the fate of someone who doesn't have a mother," she commented, with such ingenuous compassion that her sour, toneless voice sounded melodious. "Yes," she added, as if she were stating a rare philosophical thought, "the mother is our first companion in this life, and no one ever forgets her . . .

"I, too," she declared suddenly, sadly, "have had an orphan's fate! Because I've been without a father. And without a brother, too: my mother, my sister, and I, just three women, that's how our family was left.

"Before my sister there was a brother, younger than me: he was eight when he died. Yes, it's five years at Christmas since the day of his death. He died with my father in that very famous terrible disaster!"

"What disaster?" I asked, with sudden interest. In fact, from her grand, aristocratic tone I expected that the disaster she mentioned was derived at least from an extraordinary air raid, or some other event of world importance.

"Oh, that famous disaster of the load of cement, which was talked about as far away as Rome. Because four human beings died, and what fine funerals they had! The band came, and the authority, and all paid for by the city: the horses, the crown, and everything.

". . . My father had gone to work: and think! That usually he was on strike, because he was so lazy: he preferred the profession of gentleman, he was like that . . . But that week he'd felt the desire, and had gone to work to unload cement. And my brother brought him some food.

"We had made pasta without sauce, which my brother liked most of all. Because my brother had all kinds of peculiar ideas; for example, sauce! He didn't like it! And my mother said to him: 'First go and take some to your father, and then come back and eat with us.' And he left, grumbling about it, with my father's plate wrapped in a napkin. And that was the last we saw of him. It was the fatality of destiny!"

That story, although tragic and moving, to tell the truth had been somewhat disappointing to me. Still, so as not to offend my guest, I didn't reveal my disappointment, but, rather, to be polite, I sighed deeply. And she, absorbed in the solemnity of her sorrows, exchanged with me a trusting and grateful look; then, sighing in turn, she observed, in the meditative tone of a thinker:

"Yes, for death a big man and a child are the same. For death they're all creatures!"

As she said this, her girlish ignorance seemed to be reclothed in a great old age, full of an indefinable, almost regal wisdom. But meanwhile a childish consolation had already surfaced in her sad funeral lament:

"But in the end," she asserted with conviction, "the day will come when families will be reunited, all together again, in true eternal celebration!" Here she stopped, as if fearful of shadowing, by some female indiscretion, that non-earthly celebration: and she merely hinted, full of mysterious respect, like someone reciting the exotic books of a sacred Sibyl or the Prophet Daniel:

"Yes, those who fear death really are wrong, because death is a disguise, that's all: in this world, purposely, it appears very ugly, like a wolf; but in Paradise it will be seen in its true guise, with the beauty of the Madonna, and there it changes its name, and is called not *Death* but *Eternal Life*. Because in Paradise, truly, to say that word *death*—no one would understand you."

She broke off, swinging her head with a secret, enchanted expression, as if her imagination already anticipated, even if modestly, the splendors of that future, which, however, shouldn't (in proper reverence) be talked about too much . . . Then, finally, resuming, she didn't hesitate to conclude:

"And so on the last day, beautiful *Eternal Life* will appear to us at the gate, laughing beside the Blessed Crowned Virgin, like another mother of all Christians, who has prepared a great, never-ending celebration for them. And there we'll be again with my father and my brother, and with my other brothers and sisters, too, some of whom died at birth, and some as infants . . ."

From her credulous, rapt smile, with its slightly savage fresh joy, it was evident that for her the impassive indifference of eternity had been transformed into a fabulous fair with lights and songs and joyous dances, and infants and children! She let me know (assuming that particular air of noble pomp that she often used with regard to her family) that besides her, Nunziata, the first, her mother had borne nine other children, male and female. Almost every year, in fact, she had given birth, in the twelve years of her marriage, so that her friends said to her: *Viulante, your Nunziatina doesn't need to get herself a doll, you always take care of making a new one for her* . . . But unfortunately the will of God had caused most of those numerous children to fly back up to Heaven even before they had learned to walk on the earth . . .

Luckily, none of them had left without Holy Baptism, and she began to mention them to me by their baptismal names, one by one. There was a Gennaro, two Peppinos, a Sarvatore, an Aurora, a Ciccillo, and a Cristinella . . . Finally her expression became vaguely bewildered:

"If I think again about those siblings," she said, "I have a worry that I won't be able to recognize them, in a tomorrow: I remember them as if they were all the same, from the same mold! . . . But of course there in Paradise we recognize each other without even saying our names, the relationships will be written on our foreheads! And you, too, will find your mother there, and we'll all be together, all one family!"

The vision of Arturo's mother passed through my mind, who, solitary, and disdainful of any mixing, had left the island of Procida in her beautiful Oriental tent, without saying goodbye to him.

I answered harshly:

"For the dead there is no family. In death, we don't recognize anyone."

She looked at me the way a learned man looks at an ignorant, but, still, with profound respect, and didn't dare reply. Only, after a second, wrapping a curl around her fingers, she observed, in a faint, dreamy voice:

"That brother of mine, who I was telling you about, also had special opinions of his own, so people called him the Reasoner, because he was always reasoning; and when he spoke, everyone was silent. His name was Vito."

After that we were silent for a while. Then, looking at me with timid compassion, she resumed:

"And so you've always spent all your time alone!"

"Yes!"

"But . . . your father . . . doesn't he keep you company?"

"Of course!" I answered. "When he's on Procida, he's always with me! From morning to night! . . . But he has to travel! And I'm not old enough yet for traveling. Soon I will be, though, and I'll travel with him."

"And you'll travel together to do what?"

"What do you mean, to do what! Well! First of all to visit the geographic wonders of the world! That's obvious!"

"What wonders?" she asked.


## The Double Oath


The subject that, with her question, she brought up was too fascinating, and had burned too long with no outlet in the closed space of my imagination, for me not to be instantly drawn into an irrepressible eloquence. And so I began citing to her, emphatically, the most pressing among the many spectacular wonders that, scattered throughout the globe, awaited the visit of Wilhelm and Arturo Gerace . . . But although she had so far accepted every one of my words with such modesty, on this new subject she demonstrated a stubborn authority.

It seemed that for her nothing outside Naples and the surrounding area was worth the trouble of exploring, so that as she heard me celebrate those exotic places jealousy of Neapolitan honor made her darken. And every so often she interrupted to tell me, in a glorious and at the same time bitter tone, that in Naples, too, there was this and there was that . . . As if all the magnificent things that existed in the rest of the world were, in essence, second-rate, provincial, and citizens of that paramount metropolis could save themselves the trouble of traveling: for them it was enough to be born, because they could find the supreme example of everything right close by.

I began to boast about the Castle of the Crusaders in Syria, where, in olden times, ten thousand knights lived! And she, ready, announced to me that in Naples there was a castle (fifty times as big as my father's) that was called dell'Ovo, the Egg, because it was all closed, with almost no openings, like an egg; and inside were the kings of the Two Sicilies, the Bourbons . . . I cited the colossal Sphinx of Egypt, which thousands of caravans came from all the continents to see. And in response she named a church in Naples where there was a marble Virgin, as tall as a giantess, who sometimes when you showed her a crucifix (even a small one, the kind that people wear around their neck like a charm) shed real tears. She assured me that many people had witnessed the miracle: not only Neapolitans but Americans, French, and even a duke; and that that statue was visited by thousands of pilgrims, who with offerings of crosses, hearts, and precious chains had transformed the church into a gold mine . . .

I talked to her about the Indian fakirs, and she immediately had to boast of a collection of phenomena no less marvelous, which dwelled in

Naples! In Naples, in the sacristy of a convent, there was a tiny, delicate nun who had been dead for more than seven hundred years; but she was still pretty and fresh as a rose, so that, in her crystal urn, she resembled a doll in a shop window . . . And in Naples, in Piazza San Ferdinando, lived an old man, with a black tongue and lips, who could eat fire. He performed at the cafés, devouring handfuls of fire; meanwhile his grandchildren went around with a bowl, and so that strange old man made a living for the family.

I let her talk, with a generosity not without pity, since for me the city of Naples signified merely a point of departure for my journeys, a negligible atom! While she, because of her inglorious fate, was condemned to know nothing of the world outside Naples and Procida. So I was listening, with an almost dutiful air, to all that Neapolitan stuff, which others must have told her and that she was telling me with perfect credulity, gesticulating with her little hands . . . when suddenly a fantastic hilarity began to tickle my throat, and I broke into such a fit of laughter that I collapsed flat on the floor on my stomach.

It seemed to me that I had never felt such an extraordinary happiness: so that it seemed to belong not only to me but also to her, and to the entire universe! But she, naturally, took it badly. Her Neapolitan boasts suddenly broke off and I heard her voice protesting, resentful and mortified:

"Ask my mother if I'm lying. You can ask all Naples if those facts I was telling you are my invention or are true."

At that I raised my head a little, ready to loyally reassure her, since in reality I didn't doubt her good faith and, oddly, I didn't like to unjustly upset her . . . But as soon as I saw her in front of me again, looking at me sulkily and swaying back and forth, hilarity, like a musical refrain, possessed me again, and instead of speaking I laughed harder than before.

This scene repeated itself two or three times in the space of a minute.

Every so often I stopped laughing, gave her another glance, and began laughing more heartily. So that without any intention on my part she, inevitably, appeared more and more offended. She stuck out her lips in vexation, which now seemed close to overwhelming her, and I began to think, "What will she do?" with the pleasure of a dramatic game, as when I used to provoke Immacolatella.

Finally, I heard her start muttering; and suddenly she took a step toward the center of the room, where she stopped, exclaiming, in the harsh, absolute tones of a prophet:

"I swear it! in front of all the blessed souls of Purgatory! I didn't invent a single lie! They all stand as witnesses of this oath!"

Before the great solemnity of this scene, I instantly became serious again. But, in the present moment, she didn't even look at me. And she ended:

". . . My father hears me, too, and my brothers and sisters! May I fall to the ground here right this minute if I've invented those things about Naples. May I fall down dead!"

Having uttered her oath, she swallowed, and I saw that her chin and mouth were trembling with the emotion of feeling slandered. Without looking at me, perhaps fearful of seeing me laugh again, she said in a faint voice:

"Now you can believe me, that I didn't tell you any lies."

My conscience then roused itself, to reproach my earlier rudeness. And, angry at myself, I rose to my feet with a determined impulse and stood in front of her. Then I exclaimed, in a tone that was more than serious, in fact historical and fateful:

"On my honor! May I be struck dead here if I speak falsely: I swear that I believed in the sincerity of every word you said from the start, and I don't consider you a liar!"

Within my memory, in my life so far, never had a ceremony of such importance taken place. And I felt a great satisfaction in that. As for her, she had already grown cheerful again, and gave me a smile that seemed to thank me and ask, at the same time: "Why, then, such hilarity?" But, in all conscience, I found no better response than this, which I offered hastily:

"I was laughing like that because I felt like laughing," and she was satisfied by that explanation, nor did she ask for another. She gave a brief, grateful sigh, in which all the bitterness she had swallowed a few minutes earlier seemed to relax, unburdening her heart of every weight; and, shaking her head at her own suspicions, she said in a contented voice:

"And I . . . thought you were accusing me of telling lies . . ."

I shrugged. "Well, come on! I know perfectly well that you don't tell lies!" I exclaimed, adding in a tone of bold proclamation: "I know you!"

That phrase, *I know you*, came naturally to me. And as I said it I realized, surprising myself, that, although it was odd, it really was true: all other people (and my father more than anyone!) remained mysterious to me, whereas although I had met her today for the first time, I already seemed to know her by heart. Had that surprising discovery been, basically, the real reason for my laughter? In any case, not knowing what else to say, I sat down again on the floor where I'd been before, and concluded, in a curt tone:

"Well! I swore on my honor! What else do you want? Damn it!"

Her lips made a slight anxious movement, as if she wished to say to me: "But I've forgiven you! My goodness! I've forgiven you!" But then, instead of speaking, she smiled at me, with the air of asking forgiveness for herself. Thus she hastened eagerly toward me, like a little hen that spreads its wings as it walks; and, still smiling, she stopped humbly a few steps away. Then I smiled at her, too, although with a certain condescension, out of one side of my mouth.

A confused impulse, to laugh, to look at her, to not look at her, bewildered me. I felt her eyes, confident and protective, above me, and that gave me a funny and wonderful contentment. After a while she resumed hesitantly, smoothing her hair:

"And so as soon as you're grown up, you'll leave . . ."

"Yes!" I said. And only at that point, in reaffirming my plan so emphatically, did the thought of her come to mind: What part would she have in the future travels of the Geraces, father and son? Resolutely, I decided: "She'll wait alone on Procida!" But she herself didn't seem to consider her fate.

She stood there looking at me, her eyes brimming with intimacy and childish ancientness, and reminding me, at the same time, of starry nights on the island and Immacolatella. And after another concentrated silence, she again observed, as if she were unable to resign herself to such an idea:

"And so you've spent your whole life without a mother!"


## The Ring of Minerva


Raising my head, I said proudly, "When I was one month old, I could already stay on my own! Once Silvestro went to Naples, to see a national championship soccer match, and I stayed alone for a whole day. He had attached the unbreakable bottle with the nipple around my neck, and he put me on the floor, on some rags, so that I wouldn't fall."

"Who was Silvestro?" she asked.

"He was someone from Naples, who stayed here until he was called for military service. A friend of mine! He's the one who gave me milk."

"What! He gave you milk!"

"He raised me on goat's milk."

"Ugh!" she noted with deep indignation. "Goat's milk! it doesn't even have a human taste. And how did you manage to grow up so handsome! In Naples they say that milk from goats and sheep is good only for goatherds and shepherds. If there was sheep cheese on the pasta my brother wouldn't eat it. And that soldier, what sort of Neapolitan could he be! To give you goat's milk. And think! If we'd known it! Some years my mother's chest hurt because of all the milk she had! If we could have known that you were here on Procida with a goat, we would have brought you to our house and you would have grown up with us!

"Oh, at our house we would have taken good care of you! We're so many women there! It takes women to care for a child! But! That Silvestro! So he was a male; but even though a person is male, he could still be less ignorant! Giving you goat's milk!"

When she said *that soldier, that Silvestro*, her voice sounded inexorably hostile, as if (besides deserving her contempt for having given me goat's milk) that unknown nurse of mine, from the first instant, at my mere mention of him, had roused in her a complete antipathy. I resented that tone; I couldn't allow my first and only friend to be insulted with impunity.

"Silvestro," I proclaimed emphatically, ardently, "is one of the best Neapolitans! And meanwhile you should know that he wasn't a *soldier*, he had the rank of corporal in the army; and if he had stayed in he would have become a sergeant. He was one of the leaders of the whole army, and he was also a soccer player, a center forward on a Naples team. He's my faithful follower! It's more than eight years since he left, and we haven't seen each other, but he never forgets me! He's sent me several postcards in that time: last year he sent one from Caserta, which was also signed by his fiancée, and a master sergeant, and the sergeant's sister. And on December fifth, for my birthday, he sent me one in color, with a picture of a rose and a horseshoe. He never forgets to send me good wishes on my birthday every year. I've saved all his postcards."

She listened to me intently, but with some dismay, as if, in spite of her evident admiration for every word of mine, she still couldn't get rid of that unexpected hatred she had conceived against Silvestro.

"And I also got a present from him," I went on, "years ago, when I turned ten. He sent it to me through a fullback from Naples who was coming here on an outing: it's a German cigarette lighter, one of those authentic contraband ones, without the government stamp. Unfortunately, the flint is used up, and here on Procida you can't find a refill.

"Through that same fullback, I sent him a gift of a cameo I'd found on the beach (a foreigner must have lost it), a magnificent stone, engraved with the head of the goddess Minerva. He wrote me a postcard saying that he'd had a ring made, and that he'll always wear it on his finger: so that's another reason he can't ever forget me. Besides, that fullback also told me: 'You can be sure that Silvestro will always remember you. Often, talking about one thing and another, you hear him name *Arturo, Arturo*, as if everyone should already know who he is, this Arturo! And every so often he says: *I wonder how he's grown up. One day I'll have to make a trip to Procida, and go and see him.'*

"But," I continued regretfully, "because of his work it's hard for him to leave Naples. He has a trusted position as a guard at a construction company: a very good job, I think! He lives in a cottage that can be dismantled, and it moves along with the company's jobs, now here, now there. Once, for more than a year, he was in Pozzuoli, where the fields of fire are; and another time he was right opposite the Port of Naples for about six months, where the battleships and the torpedo boats and the transatlantic liners dock. Who knows where he is now! In his last card he just sent good wishes, without any information."

At these concluding lines of my speech, she seemed reconciled with Silvestro, at least for a moment; and, lighting up with childish pleasure, she proposed:

"You know what we'll do? One day we'll take the steamer for Naples, along with your father, and go and look for him. That way you'll see the Port of Naples, and the transatlantic ships; and you can also see Pallonetto, where my house is.

"In Pallonetto," she added grandiosely, "even the little boys are all soccer players! There they have *fubballe* games on all the streets! A sailor friend of ours, who's called Andonio, went traveling all over the world, and he says that nowhere can you see so many boys playing as there!"

Her eyes rested on me with a gaze full of regret. "Yes, it would have been nice," she observed, "if when you were a kid we were already relatives, like now! Then, certainly, we would have known right away, in our family, that you'd had such a fate: to be a newborn without a mother! And then my mother and my godmother and I would have come, with a pretty basket lined with feathers and silk, and we would have carried you off to our house!"

And she explained to me that at her house I would never have been alone, because her house, in Naples, consisted of just one room, and the door opened directly onto the street; so although sometimes you might be alone in the house, the people passing by would keep you company.

As I listened to these failed plans of hers, I wanted to laugh, because I remembered the story Silvestro had told me: about the time my mother's relatives had arrived at the Casa dei Guaglioni, and he, fearing that they would take me away, had hidden me in the pasta-storage chest. Yes: but, I thought, they hadn't arrived with a feather-and-silk-lined basket; if my nurse had seen these other relatives coming with such a noble basket, maybe he would have let me go with them!

## In the Moon's Reflection

While I was thinking that (but without letting any of my thoughts slip out), sitting on the floor, she came and sat on her suitcase, facing me. And so, a little higher than me, with her chest straight and firm, her head leaning toward one shoulder, and her hands laced around her knees, she continued her argument, as if she were telling a story whose very impossibility captivated her. Her voice (by now familiar to me), that of a girl not yet adult, had the sound of a wonderful, brotherly, almost bitter incredulity:

"If you'd lived there with us," she said, "you'd have had a completely different life. I would have taken care of you, and carried you. What do you think? Even as a child I knew how to hold a baby. Of course! Because our house was a factory! And I held them all. I could even jump rope with the baby in my arms!"

"Tell me," I asked at this point, "how old are you?"

"I turned sixteen in October. And you?"

"I turned fourteen in December," I said. And in my mind I calculated: "So she's sixteen and three months. When I was born, she was two. And she claimed that at that age she could carry me in her arms!" But I didn't point out this implausibility, and let her continue, without saying anything.

"You could be one of our family, like another brother. We have a big bed, that can hold as many as six, eight people! You could sleep there, too, with us. And if your father, after traveling on his own, came to see you, and it was late at night, he could sleep at our house, too, if he wanted. Because our bed has two mattresses: one mattress could be put on the floor, for us to sleep on, all together. And the bed, then, could be left entirely for him."

I succumbed to laughter, and she echoed me. But her laughter ended in a childish sigh that was scarcely repressed: as if, in telling her story, she had become fond of it, and had no desire to abandon it. She smiled at me then, with a kind of protective sadness. And meanwhile her eyes, serious, affectionate, and knowing, seemed to apologize by saying to me:

"I have a stupid mind and I'm fantasizing; but, in my consciousness, I never forget reality."

"Ah! At night," she concluded, "my mother and my godmother and I would sing you some lovely songs so you'd go to sleep happy . . . You'd eat with us every day. And the celebrations, the anniversaries, always together . . ."

We were silent. And then the quiet that had fallen over the island at evening (the din of the north wind had subsided almost completely) increased in the room: so that you really seemed to hear the present passing of the minutes, through the fabulous distances of time, like a great calm breath that fell and then rose, in a regular rhythm. She was sitting there on her suitcase, in a tranquil posture, full of peace and innocent majesty; and I, in front of her, half lying on the floor, was listening without thoughts to those beautiful flowing sounds of night. At a certain moment, I heard her voice observe:

"The light from the lamp's gotten lower," and I answered:

"It's the signal that it will go out soon. Every night it goes out for a minute, when the shift changes at the power plant."

She became silent again; and for a while didn't move from that inspired concentration. Only, a second before the light went out, she looked at me, and again broke the silence with a phrase that was a childish observation, lacking even a meaningful logic; but for that very reason, perhaps, it echoed like a mysterious response.

"And to think!" she said. "During that time, when your father every so often mentioned Arturo, Arturo . . . And to think that that Arturo was you!"

When the light went out, a faint lunar reflection appeared in the room, through the dusty windows. I lay down on my back on the floor, lazily. I glimpsed, beyond my stretched-out body, the seated shadow of the bride, like a statue; and, my head upside down, I looked at the opaque window behind me, imagining the thin crescent of the new moon that behind the glass was descending through the sky as if along a thread. The darkness in the room lasted only a few seconds; but in those few seconds I returned, unexpectedly, to relive a memory. It belonged to an existence that I must have lived in very distant times—centuries, millennia before—and that only now rose up again in my mind. Although not completely clear, it was a memory so truthful and sure that for a moment it carried me out of the present!

I was in a place that was very far away; what the town was I don't know. It was a clear night, but the moon wasn't visible in the sky: I was a hero and I was walking along the shore of the sea. I had received an insult or was in mourning: maybe I had lost my dearest friend, it's possible that he had been killed (this I couldn't now remember clearly). I called to someone, and I wept, lying on the sand; and a very large woman appeared, who was sitting on a rock a few steps from me. She was a child, but still her entire person had an imposing maturity; and her mysterious childhood seemed not a human age but, rather, a sign of eternity. And it was she whom I had called, that was certain, but who she was I could no longer remember: whether an oceanic or earthly divinity, or a queen I was related to, or a seer . . .

I wasn't aware of the instant that the light went on again; I was almost asleep. The bride recalled me:

"Artù!" she said. "I wonder what time it is now?"

And so that was the first time she called me by name.

I roused myself and sat up; and immediately returned to the present, and the lighted room, with the bride sitting on the suitcase. I answered:

"It must be around six-thirty, because it's around that time every day that the shift changes for the electricity."

She jumped up from the suitcase:

"Six-thirty!" she exclaimed. "But then we'd better get the fire lighted, for dinner tonight!"

I let her know that, in fact, in our house we never lighted the fire at night: every morning, Costante cooked the evening meal, too, and surely today he had done as usual, leaving dinner ready for us on the sideboard. But in a tone of self-importance and fervor, she insisted that she wanted to light the fire, to warm the food and maybe cook the pasta. So we went down to the kitchen.

## The Great Leaders

For that evening, Costante had left us roasted rabbit and potatoes cooked in oil; but, looking through the other compartments of the sideboard, we found a package of store-bought pasta, a jar of purée, and a piece of cheese, and she declared that with these ingredients we could also have pasta with sauce for dinner. Rummaging in the kitchen, she also found some dry twigs, a bucket of coal, and the matches, and, contented, decided that she would light the fire right away and start the water, waiting for my father before she put the pasta in. Then she repeated the same request she had already made upstairs: that I not leave her alone, in this house that was still unknown to her. And so, after taking from the drawer a book that at that time I was reading in the kitchen while I ate, I lay down there on the bench. But on that unusual evening I didn't have much desire to read; and I leaned idly on my elbows, the book in front of me, and didn't even open it.

The bride, preparing to light the fire, began to sing, and I was startled at hearing her voice, which, in singing, became sharper and wilder. She went back and forth from the woodbox to the hearth, with fierce, impetuous movements; she was frowning, and had assumed a quarrelsome expression. It seemed that, for her, the lighting of the fire was a kind of war, or celebration.

Not finding a bellows in the kitchen, she began to blow on the coals herself, with great energy; and I was reminded of an illustration of the Crusades, in which you saw the north wind, represented as a curly-headed archangel, in the act of blowing on a fleet. Thanks to her blowing, the coals finally lighted; and then, to stir up the flame, she grabbed the front hem of her skirt with both hands and began to wave it furiously, like a fan, in front of the hearth. She raised a great burst of sparks, but she continued to wave her skirt with the violent energy of a gypsy dancer, and meanwhile she sang at the top of her lungs, forgetting all her timidity, as if she were alone, at home in Naples.

She sang not with sentimental abandon but with a bold, childish roughness; certain high notes recalled some bitter animal cry—maybe a stork, or a nomadic desert bird. The coals were now blazing, and, lowering her skirt, she went to the sink and ran water into the pot, still singing. I can remember a line of one of those songs (they were songs in Italian, not in Neapolitan dialect—and completely new to me), which she uttered in the following way:

*Maybe every apache has his dagger drawn.*

Curious, I asked what "apache" meant (I had never heard of the gangsters and molls that I later found in hundreds of other songs), and she replied that in fact she didn't know herself. She then explained that almost all the songs she knew she had learned listening to the radio belonging to a neighbor. This was someone who had made a lot of money in trade, and could afford certain expenditures. But she was a good Christian! Every time she turned on the radio, she raised the volume to the maximum: and that way all the residents of the alley, standing peacefully in their doorways, could hear the songs.

In the midst of these conversations, the bride, having finished her preparations, came and sat on the floor near my bench. She observed the book that, still closed, lay before me, and laboriously, like a half illiterate, she read out the title:

LI-VES OF THE GREAT LEA-DERS.

*"Lives of the Great Leaders!"* she repeated. And she looked at me in awe, as if, by the sole fact of reading such a book, I myself deserved the rank of great leader. So she asked if I liked to read. I answered:

"Yes! Of course! Obviously I like it!"

Then, chagrined, but still with a sort of fatalistic resignation (like someone who recognizes a fact for which there is no hope or remedy), she confessed to me that she, instead, disliked reading: so much that when she was a child and went to school she cried every morning as soon as she saw the book in front of her. In school, she had gone to the end of second grade and then stopped.

In her house in Naples, there were books: there was a big novel, which her godmother had given her, and also the schoolbooks of her sister, who was in third grade. But, ever since she was a child, she had concluded that reading books was only a penance, with no advantage. To her it seemed that in books there was only a confusion of words. What was the value of all those words written there on a page, dead and confused? Besides the words, she didn't understand anything else in a book. That was all she managed to understand: some words!

"You," I said, "talk like Hamlet."

I had read, in Italian translation, the tragedy of Hamlet (in addition to those of Othello, Julius Caesar, and King Lear), and I absolutely did not approve of the behavior of that character.

"Who is Hamlet?" she asked.

With a contemptuous expression I answered, "A clown," and at my response she broke into a gale of nervous laughter. I didn't immediately understand why she was laughing so hard: but I quickly realized that the designation clown, which I had given Hamlet, she, as a natural consequence of my speech, had also applied to herself. At that idea, I, too, started laughing. Then I became serious again and explained:

"Hamlet was a clown, and I know the reason. But you have nothing to do with him: you understand? He was the Prince of Denmark!"

I saw that, at that revelation, her face expressed an extreme deference; and so I exclaimed firmly:

"Don't make that servile face! Almost all kings and princes are clowns."

This was one of my more recent conclusions; and I realized that I couldn't announce it to my ignorant listener without adding some suitable explanation:

"Possessing a throne is not enough to merit the title of king!" I said. "A king should be the bravest of all his people. For example: Alexander the Great! He was a real king! He," I added with a certain envy, "was foremost among all his people, not only in valor but also in beauty. He had a divine beauty! He had curly blond hair that looked like a beautiful golden helmet!"

She listened to me, as usual, with profound attention and respect. In awe, she observed: "You're more a kid than me and you understand so many things!" I went on, irritated by the word *kid* she'd used:

"But there aren't many kings like him! And those who accept the title of king but aren't as valorous—you know what they are? They're scum and dishonorable, usurpers of power!"

"Of course, the ones in command should do more good than others," she agreed humbly, in a timid voice, "because if those at the top don't set an example, how can this world continue?"

Then, after some thought, she added:

"But so it goes! Even the person at the top doesn't always remember to pay his debt to the Lord. Even the powerful make mistakes, not only the wretched. Yes, there aren't many souls who have an honest conscience. That's why the Son of God, up in Heaven, still walks with a crown of thorns; and who knows when his passion will end!"

As she spoke she sighed, like a fantastic young nun, at the millennial sufferings of that unhappy God (her curls swung in time to her laments). And without remembering that she was talking to an atheist, she looked at me with confident and affectionate eyes, as if her Absolute Certainties matched mine!

In response, however, I confined myself to looking at her with a tolerant expression, and I resumed, continuing my interrupted argument:

"It's also the fault of the populace! It's very clear, if you read world history, and also look at certain countries, that the mass of people don't recognize the only hope in life, and don't understand the feelings of true kings. That's why you can see that even the best and bravest are isolated, like fierce pirates. No one goes with them, except their faithful escort, or maybe a single friend, who is always there and defends them with his life: he alone knows their heart! The rest of the people are divided from them, like a herd of abject slaves thrown into the hold of the splendid ship!

"The *splendid ship*," I informed her at this point, "is a phrase I've said to make a poetic symbol. It's not a concrete object. The ship signifies: the honor of life!"

Amid these explanations, I had sat up and was astride the bench. It was the first time I had revealed to any person the results of my solitary meditations. Her expression was solemn, almost religious. I was silent for a while, every so often giving her a brief glance, before I made up my mind to keep talking; and finally I said:

"The ideal of all world history is this: that true kings should join up with a population that shares their feeling. Then they could carry out any magnificent action, they could even begin to conquer the future!

"The satisfaction in being a brave man isn't enough if others aren't his equal and he can't form friendships. The day every man has a brave, honorable heart, like a true king, all hatreds will be thrown into the sea. And then people will no longer know what to do with kings. Because every man will be king of himself!"

This last idea—highfalutin and grandiose—sounded new to my ears, since it had come to me at that precise moment, just like that, as I was talking, without my ever having thought it before; and I was happy about it, inside, as if it were a true philosophical discovery, worthy of an important thinker! At a glance, I could see that the face of my listener, like a devout mirror, had also lighted up with radiant admiration. And so, inspired by a new ardor, I proclaimed, boldly and confidently:

"I want to read all the books of science, of true beauty: I'll become as well educated as a great poet! And then, when it comes to strength, I'm ready for that: I can do any exercise, I've been training since I was seven or eight months old. A few more summers, and I want to see who could beat me: even if an international champion showed up! Then, as soon as I can, I have to learn how to use weapons, and practice fighting. As soon as I'm old enough, I'm going wherever there's fighting, to prove myself. I want to perform glorious deeds, and make my name known to all! The name *Arturo Gerace* will be renowned throughout the world!"

She began to laugh, a faint enchanted girlish laugh, as she gazed at me in admiration, with absolute faith: as if I were one of her brothers who had come down to tell her about the brave acts of the Archangel Michael in Paradise.

So I no longer hesitated to tell her as well about my most jealously guarded and ambitious plans: and not only the ones I still believed in, in my conscience, as feasible, but also those fantastical ones which I had contemplated as a boy, and which could never come true. Now, at my age, I was aware that some of my old plans were fairy tales; but I told her about them just the same, knowing that she, anyway, would believe me.

"Well, then," I began, "when I become the valorous leader, just like a true king, you know what I'll do? I'll go with my faithful followers to conquer peoples, and teach everyone true bravery! And honor! I'll make all those miserable, shameless people understand how ignorant they are. A lot of them get scared as soon as they're born, and they keep that fear forever! I want to explain to everyone the beauty of valor, which vanquishes wretched cowardice!

"And one of my undertakings will be this. Soon, as I told you, my father and I will go far away together, for a long time, until one day we'll land here on Procida at the head of a proud fleet. All the people will acclaim us, and the Procidans, with our example, will become the greatest heroes of all the nations, like the Macedonians, and very proud, and noble, as if they were my father's brothers. They'll be our followers, and support us in our actions. First, we'll attack the prison and free all the prisoners; and at the top of the fort we'll raise a flag with a star that will be seen over the surrounding sea!

"The island of Procida will be all decked with flags, like a beautiful ship: it will be better than Rome!"

Here, with an air of challenge, I stared her in the face. On this point, as a result of the opinion she had expressed in the carriage, a few hours earlier, about prisoners and jails, there was still an unanswered question between the two of us! But on her face now my gaze found only an exultant solidarity, as if she were already impatient to see my flag waving over the island's fortress, and already promising a great celebration of songs and dancing! Then, to conclude my speech, I resumed, pounding the cover of *Great Leaders* with the back of my hand:

"This, here, is not a book of made-up stories, it's true history, it's knowledge! The leaders of history, even the most famous, like Alexander the Great, weren't fairy-tale people (fairy-tale people are mythical); they were people like other people, in every way, except in their thoughts! In order to be like them, and even better than them, you have first to keep in mind certain true great thoughts . . . and I know these thoughts!"

"What thoughts . . . ?" she asked intently.

"Well," I confided, after some hesitation, frowning, "the first thought, the most important of all, is this: *One mustn't care about death!*"

So now I had revealed to her even the famous reticence of my famous Code: the boldest, that is, and the most difficult of my Absolute Certainties (and also my supreme, most secret uncertainty!). She assented, in a serious tone:

"That's the first truth." And she added:

"Which God, too, teaches."

But at that point I was barely listening to her. I had such a strong sense of satisfaction that I no longer had the patience to go on talking.

I snorted. Suddenly the kitchen seemed to me a prison. I would have liked to be in midsummer, in the morning, on the beach, climbing up the rocks, diving, flipping over in the water; I was seized by an impatient desire to play, to perform bold acts. Suddenly I turned to her impulsively. "Watch!" I cried. And, taking off my shoes, I took a rapid run-up from the wall opposite the window grate, which was perhaps two meters from the ground. In a single leap I gripped one of the middle bars with my hands; and almost at the same instant, with a violent push of my legs and my whole body, I hoisted myself up, with my feet between the two higher bars, letting my neck fall back. From this position I could see her, amid all her curls, clapping enthusiastically.

I had a feeling of extreme happiness. Having performed a kind of somersault, I hung by my hands from the grate, and enjoyed showing off, whirling and swinging; then I exclaimed:

"Look! the flag!"

And, grabbing the bars with one hand, I exerted my arm muscles until my body was stretched out like a banner. I held that pose for a few seconds, like a virtuoso holding a note; finally, I dropped to the floor, and from there I took off in a huge, running leap, as if across an aerial bridge, and landed upright, feet joined, on the table, three or four meters away.

She looked at me as if I had leaped not onto a kitchen table but onto the main deck of a conquered ship; and, carried away by my momentum, I now felt like a mythical cabin boy, flying with fantastic skill from the quarterdeck to the towers to the lookouts! So I demonstrated various similar exercises, all of which she greatly admired.

Finally I went back to where she was, and sat on the floor. I had bare feet, because socks were among those garments my father and I often did without. My shoes were on the floor a little distance from me; stretching out my foot, I grabbed one between the big toe and the middle, and said proudly:

"Look, I have a prehensile foot."

She admired this capacity of mine no less than the preceding skills; and I explained to her that I had acquired this skill only a short time ago, with practice. Here on Procida, I added, since I was born, I had led the life of a real sailor. And a sailor, according to a sentence I'd read in a book of adventures, has to possess *the agility of a monkey, the eye of an eagle, and the courage of a lion*!

I then told her a story I'd read as a boy about a pirate who had lost both hands in combat and, ever since, in place of the missing limbs, had worn two loaded pistols, tightly fastened to the stumps. He had learned to shoot his pistols by pulling the trigger with his foot, and had developed infallible aim, so that in the novel he was always called the Fiendish Amputee or the Terminator of the Pacific.

"You know so many things!" she observed, with devout humility; then, raising her head as if she were singing, she exclaimed with a happy, impulsive smile: "When you become the equal of a king, we'll all come to honor you. I'll bring my mother and my sister! I want to bring all of Pallonetto! And all Chiaia! And all Naples!"

She sat daydreaming for a moment, and added, as if in secret: "Do you believe it, Artú? when you tell me your idea, that you want to become like a king, I seem to see you as if it were already true and natural: dressed magnificently, in a beautiful silk shirt, with gold buttons, and the mantle, and the crown of gold, and so many beautiful precious rings—"

"Hey!" I interrupted her, with proud indifference. "What are you thinking? The crown and the mantle and so on! I say this word, *king*, and right away you think of titled kings. The kings I mean are special kings, who don't go around dressed like clowns the way you say."

"And how are they dressed?" she asked, bewildered but still curious.

"They dress carelessly, however they like," I declared. Then right away, without having to think about it too much, I explained: "In summer, a pair of pants and an ordinary shirt, maybe even torn and without buttons . . . and . . . like that . . . a flowered kerchief around their neck . . . And in winter an ordinary jacket, maybe checked . . . in other words, relaxed!"

She seemed a little disappointed; but after a moment her eyes regarded me again with innocent devotion, and she said, with conviction, shaking her head:

"Yes, you, anyway, you dress like a beggar, but you look like a prince just the same . . ."

I didn't answer, keeping my lips pressed together, to display indifference; when all of a sudden, on the spot, I started laughing, that compliment gave me such pleasure.

Soon afterward we heard my father's steps coming down the stairs; and *the most mysterious of all* reappeared.

⋞◎◈⋟

We saw then that the water in the pot, which had been boiling for a while, had half evaporated, without the two of us noticing; and the coals were almost spent. That fact delayed dinner and, during the wait, my father began to drink some Ischian wine, which was his favorite. He had gotten up from his nap rested and in a smiling mood, and he seemed content, as if it were a game, for the three of us to have dinner together, in the Castle of the Geraces. This gaiety of his elated us all: and the evening took on the air of a great celebration.

## At Supper

The bride had finally taken off her coat from the journey: over the velvet skirt, she wore a red wool sweater that, like the coat, was short and tight on her; in this outfit, the shape of her body could be seen better. Even to my inexperienced eye, it appeared already very developed for her age, but there was, in those womanly shapes, a kind of roughness and childish ignorance, as if she herself were not aware of being grown up. Her bosom seemed too heavy for that immature bust, with its thin shoulders and small waist: and it inspired a strange and even delicate sense of compassion; and the heaviness of her broad, rather ill-proportioned hips gave her figure a character not of strength but of awkward and helpless naïveté. The sleeves of the sweater left her arms bare almost to the elbow: and you could see the division between the white skin of her arms and the blistered, winter-reddened skin of her hands. This, too, roused a feeling of compassion. And looking at her wrists, which were not delicate, one felt that, precisely because they were thick, they had, inexplicably, an expression of tender innocence.

Proud of cooking the pasta, she seemed even to forget the fear that my father instilled in her, and that earlier, in the afternoon, had made her tremble so. But his current mood didn't seem threatening; he wasn't giving her troubling orders now, or mussing her hair; and in fact he wasn't even near her, and wasn't concerned with her.

At the table, he ate a lot and drank more Ischian wine; and as usual the wine, without making him drunk, provoked unpredictable behavior, making him even more mysterious to me. The wine could have different and even opposing effects; at times, it made him more expansive, at times sleepy and somber. And on some occasions it filled him with regrets, with yearning, or with a peculiar violence, in search of objects at which to vent. (He never vented at me except to become harsher in manner; evidently he considered me too small a personage, not worthy of punishment.)

That night the wine matched his carefree mood, making him more talkative and fanciful. His stern gaze yielded, every minute, to a kind of gracious contentment that seemed to cause him to be charmed by whatever he saw, even a crust of bread or a glass. He said, with satisfaction, that upstairs he had had a good sleep, he had slept more than two hours; then he glanced at the bride, with a duplicitous expression, as if, unknown to her, he were plotting some boyish crime, and added:

"And you know who I dreamed about? That ancestor of mine, in the portrait: the ghost of the castle."

"Oh, him," she murmured.

"Yes, him! He was wearing a dressing gown embroidered with stars and half-moons, like a wizard. And he told me: You'll see what happens when you bring a woman into my house. Tonight I'll come with my knights and throw her out."

The bride laughed, with an incredulous expression, but still hesitant.

"You laugh: well, you'll soon stop laughing. The moment has come, I believe, to reveal to you something I've been silent about until now. You approve, Arturo? It's right to inform her, now that she's Signora Gerace? Know, then, girl: There's a mystery in our family! The whole town is aware of it: this castle is visited by spirits. That ancestor of mine, in fact, is a great man, and continues to host theater productions and dancing parties for the best young men, as when he was alive: the only difference, of course, is that now his guests are all ghosts—in fact, SOME-THING WORSE. Naturally, he doesn't invite the spirits of females, because, as you know, he hates women. His guests are all male, boys and young men who died in the flower of youth; and all, if you want to know, DAMNED SOULS! These are young men chosen from among the worst scoundrels, who were transformed into devils when they died! And this gang arrives here every night from all parts of Hell, entering through the windows or from underground by the hundreds. You can vouch for it, right, Arturo?"

I said nothing in response, but smiled at him in a sign of under-standing and (since it was my duty) complicity; but this smile of mine, it seems, served as encouragement to her. She had, in turn, the faint smile of a wise and experienced person, and, shaking her head, she said to my father:

"Well, now you want to tease me, you treat me as if I were ignorant. But I understand about certain things better than you!"

"What? Be careful how you speak, you: better than me!"

"No . . . better than you, no! that word came out by accident, it really doesn't mean anything. I meant that you are seriously treating me as ignorant now if you think you can tease me, and you think that I don't know certain things, and the truth of them! Well! As if it weren't a known fact: that boy devils can't exist! Because if a person dies as a boy, he can't be a big sinner. Even if, in that short life of his, he did some deed like, maybe: steal! Or even maybe: kill Christian souls! Well, it doesn't count. That's not infamy! For him all sins count as venial sins. Boys, at most, can get twenty, twenty-five years of Purgatory; and afterward the littlest boys all become cherubim angels, and the bigger ones sera-phim. That's why people go and console their mothers saying: *Be con-tent, signora: that child has had the greatest good fortune! God has chosen him, to become another angel.* You can't make a devil with a boy. To make devils, it necessarily takes older people."

That argument, which in itself might have sounded rather comical, was delivered with such gravity that to laugh would have been too crude an insult. And so we remained quite serious; even my father was content to laugh just a little.

"And so now," he said to her, "with this wonderful opinion of yours, you feel safe here! Convinced that those knights are angels in Heaven! And you don't even believe what my ancestor told me in my dream, that tonight he'll come with them to harm you!"

"Well, who can believe the words of that fellow, who was saying that all women are ugly?"

"Aha!" my father exclaimed, getting up proudly. "That's the latest novelty, which does me honor. And I have to listen to it with my own ears! So here someone would dare to state that an ancestor of mine tells lies!"

"Nooo . . . I didn't mean that . . . about your relative . . . no, I was wrong . . . But he . . . he really said that all women are ugly? That's what he said?"

My father stretched out in the chair, laughing hard:

"Yes," he declared, "that's just what he said: they're all ugly."

She looked at me, as if seeking confirmation of this curious case. "You really want to know what he said?" my father resumed. And right away he began to declaim, imitating the Amalfitano:

"'Ugh, how ugly they are, better not to think about it, my dear Wilhelm, about how ugly they are. And they come out everywhere, all over the world; they multiply by the thousands, the millions, those insults of nature. I wonder if they also exist on the other planets, on the moon? And the more perfectly they're made (so to speak), the uglier they are! They're petty, it's the stamp of their race, which is bitter! But why? How can it be explained? Everything in creation is so well made, even the things of no importance: A strand of seaweed! A brook! A minnow! An aphid on the roses! A grass-pea flower! A chicory leaf! All things have something alluring, agreeable that makes you say: Ah, wonder of the universe! How beautiful it is! What a pleasure to live! Even when you happen to meet a person who's a bit lame, a poor fellow rejected by the draft, a cripple, a dwarf, and at first sight you think: He's really ugly; yes, indeed, and then, even in this case, if you look closely you always find something that lets you say: But after all he's not entirely displeasing. Oh, yes, in a scorpion fish, in a spider, if you observe it carefully, you recognize that sign of the artistic and enchanted hand that created all things in the universe. Except that for one single species, women, there was no mercy. They got ugliness and nothing else. They must be of another make, that's the only possible explanation.'"

At that speech, declaimed in a comic tone, the two of us burst into laughter. Then my father lazily threw me an orange peel, and said to me:

"You, *moro*: instead of laughing so much, it would be better if you'd tell us your ideas on the beauty of women. For example, what do you think of this bride? Does she seem pretty to you, or ugly?"

I felt my face blaze up, because I wasn't prepared for such a question, and the truth was that I didn't even know, precisely, what I thought of the bride. Before giving my opinion I glanced at her, as if to evaluate her on the spot. But then, at that very moment, I realized that looking at her was of no use, that, unbeknownst to myself, I already had in mind, from before, my idea about her. And here's what it was:

About the ugliness of women in general, as far as I knew and saw it, the Amalfitano seemed to me more right than wrong: and this woman in particular couldn't be said to be less ugly than others. But still, regarding this woman, in spite of her undeniable ugly features, I, according to my taste, considered her supremely pretty!

But this opinion of mine seemed too personal and unmotivated, and I was embarrassed to offer it; on the other hand, I didn't want to lie. And so, disdaining to look at either her or my father, I lowered my eyelids and, with a frowning, almost fierce expression, answered:

"She doesn't seem ugly to me."

"Ha, go on!" my father exclaimed, shrugging his shoulders. "You want to play the gentleman, full of compliments. She doesn't seem ugly to you, come on! What in the world do you find beautiful there?"

She laughed, in sweet confusion, not at all resentful at being considered ugly. I looked at my father boldly and proclaimed with determination:

"She has beautiful eyes!"

"Eh, what do you mean? They're saucer eyes, too big! But go on, what are you telling me, *moro?*"

At that moment she looked at me, and her eyes, alive with timidity and joy and gratitude for the praise they had received, were so marvelous that her forehead was as if adorned with a diadem.

I laughed and was silent.

And my father, turning to her with a haughty motion of his chin, said:

"You needn't pride yourself, Signora Gerace, since we know you're an ugly little thing, a slattern . . . Tonight the dark-haired kid wants to be courteous to you, he wants to play lord of the castle, the ladies' man!

"Rather, madame: instead of acting the beauty, with your saucer eyes, you, too, tell us what you understand about beauty. For example, how does he look to you, this dark kid? Huh? What does he seem like to you?"

She was embarrassed to give a response aloud; she got close to my father's ear and, with a conscientious and solemn expression, said to him softly (but I heard it, too, anyway):

"To me he seems handsome."

I turned my head in another direction, with an expression of indifference. My father laughed and said:

"Well, this time I agree. It's true, he's a good-looking boy: yes, not for nothing is he my son!"

I pretended not to notice, as if I didn't know they were talking about me. To provoke me he gave me a light kick under the table, and continued to laugh almost sweetly, looking at me; and so I, too, began to laugh, with him.

He poured himself some more wine; and for perhaps two minutes while he drank we all sat there without speaking. We heard again the sound of the waves, down below, in the small bays: and at that sound I saw in my mind the shape of the island lying on the sea, with its lights; and the Casa dei Guaglioni, almost sheer above the point, doors and windows closed in the great winter night. Like an enchanted forest, the island concealed the fantastic creatures of summer, buried in hibernation. In undiscoverable dens underground, or in cracks in the walls and the rocks, the snakes and turtles and families of moles and blue lizards were at rest. The delicate bodies of the crickets and cicadas had crumbled to dust, to be reborn later by the thousands, singing and jumping. And the migrating birds, scattered in the zones of the tropics, thought with regret of these beautiful gardens.

We were the lords of the forest: and this kitchen lighted in the night was our marvelous lair. Winter, which until now had seemed to me a land of boredom, tonight suddenly became a magnificent domain.

## Night

A shadow of that earlier sweet hilarity was still playing on my father's mouth; and I thought I could hear his breathing, continuous and reassuring as the sea. The present seemed to me an eternal epoch, like a fairy celebration.

Dinner had been over for a while, although we lingered at the table. My father still had some wine in his glass, and continued to joke a little with us, but soon he tired of it. Every so often he stretched his arms, or sighed, which in him was a sign not of sadness but, on the contrary, of a profound and almost bitter pleasure in existence. At a certain point, he made as if to reach an arm toward the bride, to draw her to him. She rose hastily and moved away, saying that she had to clear the table; and I saw reappear on her features that fear, which had left her for a while.

With a frightened and conscientious expression, she piled two plates one on top of the other, and started to go to the sink with them; but my father, without rising from his chair, grabbed her around the waist and, imprisoning her with his arm, held her close to him.

"Where are you going? Clearing the table!" he said. "Tomorrow morning our servant will take care of cleaning up. You are Signora Gerace, remember! And now our wedding night is about to begin."

Not daring to struggle, she stared at my father with helpless eyes. She was trembling visibly and, with all her hair, looked like a wild beast with black fur, caught in a trap unawares.

"You're afraid, eh? You're afraid of your wedding night!" my father exclaimed, breaking into a fresh, free, and pitiless laugh. "Stay here. Don't move." And he clasped her more tightly to his hip, enjoying her fear. "You're right to be afraid: you know, yes, what happens to girls on their wedding night! But the worst, then, Nunzià, is that you very seldom meet a husband as mean as I am. Husbands are usually meek little men . . . No, it's pointless to try to escape now; you can't save yourself, it's over!"

Instinctively she had begun to struggle weakly, as if indeed under the illusion that she could escape. And that desperate attempt made my father laugh even harder. "It's over!" he repeated, with childish sharpness, holding her easily with just one arm, as if in a vise. "Those days are over when you ran away and hid so you wouldn't have to see me: don't think I've forgotten, girl! I'll make you pay for them all tonight!"

And in a threatening, offhand way he began to play with her curls. His face shone, yet betrayed an intimate, jubilant malice. "Yes," he declared, "she rejected me! She refused to marry a man like me, this flea-bitten girl! She even got it from her mother, because she refused such a suitor, the owner of a castle, among other things!"

Stating these facts, he had assumed the air of a tribune, as if the whole population, summoned for the fatal punishment of the bride, were there at the table, listening to him.

Disoriented, she said, in a faint, weeping voice: "I . . . wanted to be a nun!"

"Liar! Confess things as they are! You wanted to be a nun *because* you didn't want to marry me. You decided to marry me only in obedience to Mamma. You said you were afraid of me! And if I'm not wrong, someone even heard you say that I'm ugly! Is it true or not, that you find me ugly?" He laughed, with an arrogant, inexpressible grace; and she stared at him with her big eyes, which in their distress seemed to become blacker—as if she really did find him ugly.

"And now get ready to pay me back for all of them, Signora Gerace." The hours could be heard striking in the bell tower, and he looked at the watch on his wrist: "Ah, it's ten! Time to go to sleep . . . it's night. I'm sleepy, Nunziatè, I'm sleepy . . . Nunziatè!" And he pressed her to his heart, without, however, caressing her, or kissing her, but, on the contrary, almost maltreating her, and mussing her hair. Then fear, which had been lying in wait for her all day, seemed to descend, like an enormous cloud. She said, "Before I go up . . . I . . . have to close the shutters of the door."

"All right, close them," said my father, and unexpectedly let her go. And, as if he intended to give her a respite, he lighted a cigarette, inhaling a first drag. But this respite was, it seems, a false one, which he was using for the fun of playing, like a cat. She was about to lift the heavy bolt of the door with her agitated hands when he put the cigarette he'd just lighted down on the plate and, getting up from his chair, said to her harshly:

"That's enough. Don't concern yourself with the door! Leave it!"

Just then I seemed to hear a rhythmic din, as if a cavalry were approaching from somewhere; and I was amazed to realize that it was my heart beating. My father, with a kind of angry happiness, moved toward the bride and, taking her by the wrist, with the gesture of a dancer spun her halfway around. His eyes sought hers, with an even harder look than usual; but at the same time there was in them a kind of violent, enchanting, innocent statement. Maybe regretful, or maybe to rouse her pity, he said, making his voice gentle: "Don't you see how tired I am? It's night: let's go to sleep." She raised her defenseless eyes to him. "Let's go! Walk!" he ordered her harshly; and she, obedient, followed. Before crossing the threshold, she turned her head back, to look in my direction; but, gripped by a strange feeling of hatred and rage, I immediately looked away.

I was standing in front of the table. When I looked again at the doorway, they had already disappeared from the hall, and I heard their steps going up the stairs together. Then I lowered my eyes and, seeing the plates and glasses from dinner, the remains of the food and the wine, felt a sudden disgust.

I stood there, near the table, without moving, without thinking, and it seemed to me that a very long time passed; but in fact when I moved to go up to bed, the cigarette left lighted by my father was still burning on the plate, among the orange peels. So it had been barely a minute! And that day, and that evening just ended, seemed instead, who knows why, years distant. Only I, Arturo, remained as I had been, a boy of fourteen; and I had still to wait many seasons before becoming a man.

When I passed my father's room, I heard from behind the closed door an excited whispering. I was almost running when I reached my room: I suddenly had the sharp, incomprehensible sensation that I had received from someone (whom I couldn't yet recognize) an inhuman insult, impossible to avenge. I undressed quickly and, as I threw myself into bed, wrapping myself in the covers up to my head, a cry from her reached me through the walls: tender, strangely fierce, and childlike.

cᴓᎶᴑ

By the way, I realize something here: that not only could I not call her by name when I spoke to her, but talking about her now as well (I don't know the reason) I don't know how to refer to her by name. There is a mysterious difficulty that keeps me from those simple syllables: *Nunziata, Nunziatella.* And so here, too, I'll have to go on calling her *she* or *her* or *the bride* or *the stepmother.* If later, as a matter of style, it's sometimes necessary to name her, perhaps, in place of her full name, I can write *N.,* or maybe even *Nunz.* (This last sound I like pretty well; it makes me think of an animal that is half wild and half domesticated: for example a cat, or a goat.)

# CHAPTER 3

# Family Life

*Family Life*

The next day, I woke at dawn. My father and the bride were still sleeping; the weather was beautiful. I went out, and when I returned it was late morning.

I walked around the house, to the kitchen side; and through the panes of the French door I saw that she was in the kitchen, alone, intent on making pasta on a cleared space on the table. She had dumped egg yolks into the middle of a mound of flour and was beating them energetically with her fingers. She hadn't noticed me, and I stopped behind the panes, astonished to see how much her appearance had changed since the night before.

How, in an interval so brief, could such a strange transformation occur! She had the same red sweater as the day before, the same skirt, the same old shoes; but she had become unrecognizable to me. Everything that yesterday had made her beautiful in my eyes had vanished.

Today, too, obeying my father's whim, she wore her hair loose, but her untidy curls, which yesterday were a fabulous garland, today gave her a slovenly, common look; and their blackness, contrasting with the pallor of her face, added something bleak. That heavy, slack pallor had banished the pure white color of yesterday from her cheeks; and the sockets under her eyes, whose untouched delicacy had made me think of the petals of a flower, were marked by a dark halo, ruined. Every so often, as she worked the dough, she pushed the hair off her forehead with her arm; in that act, she raised her eyelids slightly, and her gaze, which I remembered as so beautiful, appeared veiled, animal-like, and pitiful.

Seeing her again now, I was ashamed that the day before I'd been so intimate with her, going so far as to tell her my secrets! On the bench, forgotten, was my book of *Great Leaders*: and that sight increased my shame. Angrily I opened the French door, and then finally she saw me. A light of contentment and friendship illuminated her face and with a sweet smile she said:

"Artú?"

But without responding to her greeting I looked at her sternly, as when a stranger, and an inferior, takes some liberties that we haven't agreed to. Immediately her face lost its confident and happy expression. Her smile vanished and I saw her look at me with a strange expression: disappointed, questioning, and savage but not humiliated, and without the shadow of a prayer. I didn't say a word to her; and, taking my book from the bench, I left.

During that day and those which followed, I avoided her presence, giving up even the company of my father rather than share it with her. I spoke to her only if I was really forced to, and on those rare occasions my manner was cold and off-putting, to make her understand clearly that to me she was less than a stranger. Wounded by my behavior, whose motivation she couldn't know, she responded in a rapid, unsociable manner, looking at me reluctantly, with shadowy glances. But sometimes, mostly in the evening, when all our family was gathered, she offered timid propitiatory smiles, or seemed to ask humbly with her eyes what had caused her to lose my friendship. At those moments, I felt real disgust for her body. Her mouth especially repulsed me, which, like the rest of her face, wasn't the same as on the first day. It had become a lifeless pink color, and opened slightly when she breathed, with a weak, stupid expression.

In those days, my father always took her around the island, and they were together all the time; I never went with them on their walks and avoided being with them. The weather stayed fine and, continuing the habits of my solitary life, I usually went out in the morning, with a big piece of bread and cheese, and didn't return until dark. I also carried a book, and when I was tired of wandering I went to the café at the port, the one kept by the widow who made Turkish coffee in the enameled coffeepot.

In fact in that period I had money (an extraordinary novelty), because my father had given me fifty lire before leaving for his wedding, the morning he collected the money from the farmer. With that unaccustomed capital, for me an enormous sum, in my pocket, I peremptorily ordered a coffee with anise from the widow; and, throwing the money on the bar in advance, without condescending to any conversation, I went to sit in a corner, where I remained reading as long as I felt like it. At that hour, the only customer in the café was me; and the old woman either napped or devoted herself to long games of solitaire. Every so often, with the threatening, scornful air of an outlaw, I took out Silvestro's famous illegal lighter, and, although unfortunately it lacked a flint and wouldn't light, I clicked it ostentatiously. Reading, then, I always had displayed on the table a pack of cheap cigarettes, which I had recently bought but left untouched: in fact, in the past I had occasionally taken a few drags on my father's butts, and I considered tobacco nauseating.

As night fell, the widow lighted a small lamp on the bar and, in that light, continued her solitaire. The flame of the squat candle, burning in front of the portrait of her dead husband, glowed with an almost sinister effect in the murky shadows of the place; and then I felt truly

proud. It seemed to me that I really was a pirate of the seas, in a dubious tavern of adventurers: maybe in some Pacific village, or in the back
alleys of Marseille.

But since the faint light didn't allow me to read, at a certain point I
got bored and, without saying goodbye to anyone, left the café and went
back up in the night to the Casa dei Guaglioni.

As soon as I returned, I went straight to my room and shut myself
in, not caring to look for the newlyweds; and then a feeling of solitude,
of a kind that I had never known in the past, began to invade me. Even
my mother, the beautiful golden canary of fables, who used to appear at
my first call, no longer came to my rescue. And the worst was this: That
it was not because of her unfaithfulness that she had failed me. It was I
myself who had suddenly lost any desire to search for her, denying her
mysterious person. My lack of belief, which had once spared her alone,
now banished her, too, underground, among the other dead who are
nothing and have no answer to give. Although I was sometimes tempted
by a yearning for her, I said to myself immediately, crudely: "What are
you thinking? She's DEAD."

I thus endured some difficult moments. But even in such moments
I preferred to be alone, rather than find myself with the newlyweds. The
only time we were all three together was in the evening, at dinner.

My stepmother had introduced this new custom at our house: every
night we had a hot dinner, and the fire in the kitchen was burning at all
hours of the day. This was, to tell the truth, the only reform she brought
to our domestic order. For the rest, not being a great housewife, she limited herself to pulling up the blankets on the beds and, every so often,
sweeping, in a very summary fashion but with great energy, the kitchen
and the other rooms. And so, fortunately, our house remained, more or
less, the same as before, with its historic grime and its natural disorder.

Our Costante, now that the bride was there, had with much
satisfaction given up his duties as cook and servant, returning to his

farm life. She could take care of our house herself; he showed up once or twice a week, to bring us fruit and other farm products.

At dinnertime, my father called me in a loud voice, and I came down. After that unique, celebratory evening of the first day, our communal dinners now unfolded rather silently. My stepmother was always fearful and uneasy in my father's presence; but, unlike the first day, now, almost involuntarily, she stayed near him every minute, and even ended up sitting huddled next to him. At times, my father let her be, paying no attention to her, and at times, annoyed, he avoided her; but, as I said, in those days he was never apart from her.

After dinner, we all went to bed. Usually I preceded them, getting to my room quickly, where, closing the door, and without even turning on the light, I immediately got under the covers. From there I soon heard their footsteps in the hallway and the sound of a door closing behind them; and instinctively I covered my ears with my fists, for fear of hearing that cry again from their room. I couldn't explain to myself the reason: but I would rather have seen a fierce beast appear before me than hear it again.

## The Head of the Household Gets Bored

After a week of fine weather the rain began again on the island; but I went out just the same every morning, and sometimes returned home soaked. More days of that solitary life of mine passed like that, when, around the middle of the second week, my father began to talk about leaving. Then I couldn't stand the bitterness of losing the remaining hours of his company, and I was driven to try to be near him, unwillingly enduring the presence of my stepmother as well.

It was afternoon; and, as on the day of their arrival, we were all three in my father's room, while he smoked, half lying on the bed, as he usually did. The smoke from the Nazionale cigarettes, which he lighted incessantly starting in the morning, made the air of the room heavy, and beyond the opaque windows the enormous clouds of the sirocco passed by. No one had any desire to talk. My father yawned, constantly changing his position on the bed, like someone with a fever; and his eyes appeared a strange dusty blue. For him boredom seemed to be a bitter and tragic weight, no less than a disaster. And I recognized, in that, the mysterious laws of his that I adored: the same that, more important than any reason, had once, during my childhood, caused him almost to faint before my eyes because of a jellyfish sting.

So even this boredom, which made him languish, became fascinating. I saw that he was eager now to leave the island; and I regretted more bitterly the days just passed, and lost, when he was present here, accessible at every moment, and I avoided him! All this was my stepmother's fault, and an avenging rage against her was kindled in me.

(At the distance of so much time, I'm now trying to understand the feelings that, strangely, were beginning to crowd into my heart in those days; but I'm still unable to distinguish their shapes, which were all jumbled inside me, and not illuminated by any thought. In memory, I perceive a deep, isolated valley on a night of dense clouds: down in the valley a horde of wild creatures, wolves or lions, have started a fight, almost in play, which becomes serious and bloody. And meanwhile the moon proceeds beyond the clouds, in a clear, very distant zone.)

I think that for more than half an hour no word was heard from the three of us: my stepmother sat quietly on a chair, respecting, perhaps with some apprehension, my father's moods. It was he who, finally, broke the silence, exclaiming in an exasperated tone: "Enough. I can't bear this island anymore. I have to make up my mind to get away." And he threw a just-lighted cigarette on the floor with an expression of disgust.

Already for a couple of days he had been talking about travels, as I said, but had left the date of his departure vague. Naturally, it was understood that this time, too, he would go alone: the bride would wait for him on Procida, according to her duty. She knew it well; and at his angry exclamation she looked down, without making any objection. In her huddled-up position, her shoulders, too narrow compared with her buxom chest, gave her, at that moment, a poor and vulnerable aspect. But the black lashes of her sensitive, lowered eyelids seemed to cast on her face the shadow of a mysterious severity; and under her red sweater the tranquil movement of her breath was visible.

My father threw her a glance tinged with anger and, at the same time, a confusing tenderness; as if, wishing to depart, and yet feeling some regret at leaving her, he were accusing her of being the cause, involuntarily perhaps, of his lingering on the island. Then he repeated capriciously, "That's enough! what the devil am I waiting for, to get away?" and she at that moment blinked, and their gazes met. Then she murmured, looking up at him with serious eyes:

"You haven't been married two weeks and already you're leaving home!"

She had spoken in a tone more of submissive lament than of revolt; but the remark had the power to instantly cancel any shadow of friendship from my father's eyes. "Well, what's so strange?" he erupted with contempt. "Can I get rid of the desire to do what I like, even if I've been married for less than two weeks? Are you afraid the ogre will eat you, if you stay on Procida without me?

"Arturo," he added then, proudly, "has stayed on Procida without me countless times, and he's never made a fuss when he sees me leaving. This is what happens, when you get involved with women."

She shook her head and, nervously toying with her curls, said, "But . . . I . . . *Vilèlm*—" "You, who are you? What do you expect?" my father interrupted her. At the sound of that name *Vilèlm*, uttered by her, he had a scowl of impatience, and even that small nervous gesture with the curls seemed to irritate him. "And leave your dirty ringlets alone," he ordered her finally. "Think instead about getting some of your foolish claims out of your mind, if you had any . . . *But I, Vilèlm!* What do you expect, you, just because you've become my signora?"

The stepmother listened to him, mute and sullen; but her eyes, unconsciously, expressed dependence and loyalty.

He flung his feet off the bed and stood in front of her. I saw mounting in him the obscure rancor that only the bride seemed able to provoke and that had already been revealed once, the first day, in that same room. But that time, in my inner self, I had taken her side; today, instead, I was pleased that he mistreated her. In fact I hoped that he would rage against her physically, maybe throw her on the floor and trample her under his feet. It almost seemed to me that in such an assault I would find a sense of repose.

"Remember," he resumed, flaring up with increasing violence at every word, "that, married or not, I am always free to come and go as I please, and I don't have to answer to anyone for myself! For me no obligation or duty exists, I AM A SCANDAL! No, it's not to you, sweetheart, that I have to account for my fancies! The great emperor is still to be born who can keep Wilhelm Gerace in a cage! And if you, poor little flea-bitten doll, think that as a result of marriage I should remain attached to your rags, you'd better disabuse yourself now!"

He turned toward the window his beautiful blue eyes, darkened by the impossible anguish of boredom and a furious nostalgia: "Oh, why," he exclaimed, "are there no more boats tonight? Why must I wait until tomorrow? I want to leave immediately, on the first steamer, and for a long time I will send no news of myself!" His gaze returned to the bride, with an expression of impatience and bitterness. One would have said, at that moment, that, for the sole fact of existing and encumbering the air in front of him, she was committing a crime, she was threatening the right of Wilhelm Gerace. That right was: to feel as free as the angels— and I considered legitimate the youthful persistence with which my father defended it. In fact, that right was, in my eyes, the primary origin of his grace, and of his immortality, I would say.

"I . . . didn't speak of opposing your will . . . it would be a mortal sin! You are my husband . . . I vowed obedience . . . you are the head of the house . . . and you command me . . ." said my stepmother, with conviction. But she was so frightened by his tumultuous behavior that tears began to well up in her eyes. Since I had known her, I had always seen her resist the temptation to cry. This was the first time she had given in.

At the sight of the tears, my father lost the last vestige of compassion or indulgence that he might have had left. "What!" he exclaimed, with a kind of horror. "Have we already reached this point: that you're crying *because I'm leaving?*"

And he looked at her suspiciously, not hating her, but really loathing her. As if she had suddenly taken a mask off her forehead, revealing the face of a demon nymph, who wished to imprison Wilhelm Gerace.

"I order you to answer that question," he commanded her, with a harsh expression, as if he were accusing her of a crime. "You're weeping *because of your grief at my departure?* Eh? You're crying FOR THAT?"

She looked at him with a singular boldness, her eyes sullen and proud, despite the tears; and resolutely answered no.

"I don't want weeping for *love of me*, I don't want *love*," my father warned her, imitating her voice with aversion as he uttered the word *love*, which, in his slightly hybrid language, he pronounced *ammore*, in the Neapolitan style. "Know, girl, that I would never have married you if I hadn't been sure of this: that you *did NOT have any feeling* for me. It was your duty to obey your mother that made you accept the marriage. You didn't love me, fortunately! And I enjoyed seeing your mamma and godmother, who, thinking they were being clever, hid that from me; while for me, instead, it was the ideal! You will do well, wife, *never to have any feeling* for me. I don't know what to do with the feelings of women. I don't want your love."

During this speech, the bride, holding back her tears, looked at my father with eyes that were large but without wonder, as if she were listening to an incomprehensible, barbarian language. Meanwhile, he had begun to march from the bed to the window, giving her aggressive looks:

"My forebear, who is pictured there, in that portrait, said that a woman is like a leper: when she fastens on to you, she wants to eat you entirely, bit by bit, and isolate you from the universe. The love of women is bad luck, women don't know how to love. My forebear, girl, was a saint, who always spoke the truth. Aah!" And suddenly my father took the portrait of the Amalfitano off the wall and hugged it to his heart ostentatiously. And in that tenor's pose he burst out unexpectedly into clear, spontaneous laughter, as if to mock the stepmother and the Amalfitano.

## Against Mothers (and Women in General)

Then suddenly the stepmother shook her hair hard and stuck out her chin in an expression of insubordination and challenge. "That man," she burst out, invaded by a strange spirit of battle, "that wizard, forgot his mother! To speak like that about women! Goodness! But if it wasn't a woman, who made him?" Here she began to rock back and forth, in an attitude of such boasting, and pride, that she appeared almost insolent: "What even the ignorant know, and even the *goats* know," she went on, "how beautiful the mother is! And no one ever forgets her, she is our first love of all! Who even—"

"Shut up, you ugly, slovenly devil," my father interrupted her.

And, collapsing on the bed, he again burst into laughter, but it was trembling and disjointed, very different from the laughter of a moment before. "The mother!" he repeated. "My forebear," he declared triumphantly, turning to the stepmother, "had no mother! He was born of the encounter between a cloud and a thunderclap!"

"Really!" said my stepmother skeptically. "A cloud and a thunderclap."

"Yes, lucky for him! If only each of us could be born like that, from . . . a tree trunk . . . a crater of Vesuvius . . . a flint . . . from anything that doesn't have the womb of a woman!"

"But . . . women . . . sacrifice everything . . . for their children—" the stepmother tried again to object (although she was frightened by those invectives). "Enough, I told you, silence!" my father interrupted her again. "*They sacrifice* . . . You want to know an important eternal verity, you devil, tiger? Learn this: SACRIFICE IS THE ONLY TRUE HUMAN PERVERSION. I don't like sacrifice. And maternal sacrifices . . . Aah! Of the many evil females one can meet in life, the worst of all is one's own mother! That is another eternal verity!"

Here I was so perplexed that I couldn't contain a sigh; but I don't think my father heard it. He had thrown his head back on the pillow and, talking, tossed on the covers with such turbulence that the bed was like a ship in a tempest. Having imposed silence on my stepmother, he continued to deliver a monologue about mothers, no longer interested in who heard him. Now he argued with teeth clenched, now in a thundering voice, breaking out every so often into a laugh or a vulgar exclamation; and in his tone I soon recognized that particular emphasis (sly, contemptuous, and dramatic) with which, for his own amusement, he sometimes seemed to provoke the dead.

Then I saw again in memory that old group photograph in which, amid numerous classmates of the same age, a large buxom girl in a sentimental pose was singled out by a small inked cross . . .

". . . At least," he was saying, continuing his argument, "you can save yourself from other women, discourage their love; but who can save you from a mother? She has the vice of holiness . . . She is never satisfied with expiating the *sin* of having created you, and, as long as she lives, she, with her *love,* won't let you live. And it's understandable: she, poor insignificant girl, possesses nothing but that famous *sin* in her past and her future, you, unfortunate son, you are the only expression of her destiny, she has no other thing to love. Ah, it's hell to be loved by one who loves neither happiness nor life nor herself but only you! And if you have a desire to avoid such an abuse, such a persecution, she calls you Judas! Precisely, you're a traitor, because you feel like wandering through the streets to conquer the universe, while she wants to keep you with her forever, in her dwelling of one room and kitchen!"

I followed that speech with extreme eagerness, mixed, however, with a feeling of apprehension. In fact, it seemed to me, strangely, that, while he was speaking, a mysterious mother, large and buxom, who had descended from unknown northern regions, was there, torturing him in the cruelest way, to punish him for speaking ill of her. And, in spite of the fascination that the subject of mothers always had for me, I hoped that he would stop; but instead he continued, intensely and at length. As if, to while away the boredom of that day, he were recounting to himself an unpleasant fable:

"And while you grow up, and become handsome, she fades . . . Everyone knows fortune can't meddle with misery, that's the law of nature! But she doesn't understand that law: and wants you, I suppose, to be more wretched than she is—old, ugly, maybe mutilated or paralyzed—just to have you nearby. She's not free by nature, and wants you to be a slave along with her. That is her *mother love*!

"Unable to be your servant, meanwhile, she contents herself with her romance of the martyr mother and the *heartless* son. You, naturally, have no taste for a story like that, and you laugh at it: you like other stories, other hearts . . . She weeps, becomes increasingly boring, senile, grim! Everything around her is infested with tears. And you, of course, wish more and more to avoid her. As soon as she sees you reappear, she accuses you . . . Her insults are supreme, biblical. The least she can call you is *vile murderer*; and not a day passes that she doesn't recite that litany! Maybe, with her accusations, she'd like to inspire in you self-hatred, and deprive you of yourself, so that she can replace your pride and your boasts, appropriating you, like a grim queen.

"And no matter where you flee, far from her, in the city, you can't save yourself from her *love*, from that eternal parasite. In fact, if, for example, you hear thunder in the sky or it starts raining, you can swear that at that precise instant she, down in your hovel, is in despair at the idea: *Now he'll get soaked in this rain, he'll get a cold, he'll sneeze . . .* And if instead the sky clears, you can be certain that she is complaining: *Alas, with this fine weather the murderer will not set foot in the house before night . . .*

"No phenomenon of the cosmos, no event of history, exists for her except in relation to you. In this way, creation is in danger of becoming a cage. She would be content, because her *love* dreams of nothing else. She would like to keep you a prisoner forever, as when she was pregnant. And when you escape, she tries to entrap you from a distance, to give her form to your entire universe, so that you will never forget the humiliation of having been conceived by a woman!"

✦

(Both my stepmother and I had listened to this great outburst from my father without breathing; but, although I was silent about my doubts, I felt somewhat dismayed. Not only had my father's arguments not cured me of my inborn and unhappy love for mothers; on the contrary, more than once, listening, I had surprised myself thinking involuntarily: "Damn! You would say that someone who has good luck doesn't know what to do with it; while someone who would appreciate it doesn't have it . . ."

(In fact, the reasons cited by our chief to demonstrate the wrongs of mothers were, at least in large part, precisely the same for which I, instead, had always resented being an orphan! The idea of a person who loved only Arturo Gerace, to the exclusion of any other human indi-

vidual, and for whom Arturo Gerace represented the sun, the center of
the universe—it was an idea that did not at all offend my taste. So, too,
I did not find the idea that a person would weep and sigh for me at all
disgusting. In fact, it seemed to me that, if you thought about it, certain actions already fascinating in themselves, like, for example, heading
fearless into a storm—or even marching onto the battlefield!—would
acquire a much more exquisite flavor, if, meanwhile, someone were in
despair over me.

(As for the insults my father complained about, I was convinced that
certain insults would have seemed to me not poison but sweetness and
light. Further, he reasoned according to his particular experience, and
that is according to his mother, who was a tall, large German; but mine
was a small Italian, from Massa Lubrense. The Massa Lubrensian women,
from time immemorial, have always been well mannered, even too sweet,
with no hint of bitterness. In my opinion, my mother would never have
insulted me even if she had been forced to by a government decree.

(The fact remained of she who fades while her son becomes more
handsome; but this, to me, seemed by all means a guaranteed advantage. For a faded woman, who has lost her own youth, the boy—even if
he is not the perfection of beauty like my father—will always seem the
emperor of beauty on earth. That, precisely, would have been my greatest satisfaction: someone who would consider me marvelous, unsurpass-
able, imperial! For my father, who possessed perfection, evidently such
a thing hadn't much importance. And that made me admire even more
his heedless sovereignty.)

My stepmother sighed and finally summoned the courage to speak;
but her voice sounded wild and remote, like the lament of a cat lost in
the night:

"Then," she murmured, "if those sentiments you've listed are an offense, people shouldn't love anymore, in this world . . ."

My father turned his head toward her. "You shut up," he answered, "you were born yesterday and, besides, you were born stupid! If you say another word I'll kill you. I can do without certain feelings: I leave them to the wretched, who are free only on Sunday. I don't like love stories of any kind. But the love of women is the OPPOSITE of love!"

Here he started again on his monologue; and, between boredom and restlessness, as he spoke he kept yawning, laughing, turning this way and that on the pillow, like a boy tossing and turning in the half sleep of illness:

"The intention of women is to degrade life. This is what the legend of the Jews meant, which recounts the expulsion from the earthly Paradise because of a woman. If it weren't for women, our destiny would not be to be born and die, like the beasts. The race of women hates excessive, undeserved things, it is the enemy of everything that has no limits . . . That ugly race wants drama and sacrifice, it wants time, decay, slaughter, hope . . . it wants death! If it weren't for women, existence would be eternal youth, a garden! Everyone would be beautiful, free, and happy, and to love one another would mean only: *to reveal to one another how beautiful we are.* Love would be a disinterested delight, a perfect glory, like looking at oneself in a mirror; it would be . . . a natural cruelty, without remorse, like a marvelous hunt in a royal wood. True love is like that: it has no purpose and no reason, and submits to no power outside human grace. While the love of women is a slave of destiny, working to continue death and shame. Ploys, blackmail, self-serving demands: that's what its slavish feelings are made of . . . Aah! What time is it? Look at my watch, here, on my wrist: I don't feel like raising my arm."

I looked at the time on his wrist and told him. He glanced at me from between his half-closed eyelids and called me lazily: "Arturo?" Then, after a pause: "Did you hear what I said about women? What do you think, eh? Am I right?"

I decided in my mind that it was a good opportunity to humiliate my stepmother. And I answered resolutely: "Yes, without women we'd be much better off. You're right."

"Maybe, on the other hand," he said, in a tone of pained uncertainty, "I'm not right or wrong: I talked about a perpetual, limitless existence . . . as if remaining immortal were good fortune and a delight. But then what if this business of living forever bored us in the end? Maybe death was invented to balance too much boredom . . . eh? Arturo?"

"No. I don't think so. It seems to me that the dead must suffer from terrible boredom," I said, shuddering at the odious thought.

My father laughed. "You like living, do you, *moretto*?" he asked. "But you, do you know anything about boredom? Tell me, are you ever bored?"

I thought an instant. "Actually bored," I answered, "no, never. Sometimes, maybe . . . I'm annoyed."

"Aha. And when, for example . . . ?"

For example, I had been annoyed during the previous days, when I condemned myself to seclusion in my room in order not to encounter him and my stepmother together; but that I had no wish to confess, and was silent. Besides, my father no longer cared about hearing my answer: distracted, he had turned his head to the pillow. And shortly afterward, from his breathing, which had become heavier, we realized that he had gone to sleep.

My stepmother then rose and, taking a woolen blanket from the small bed nearby, covered the sleeper. This movement seemed almost automatic, it was so natural; and it wounded me all the more because of its naturalness. In its fatal simplicity it meant: "He may have spoken badly of women; but nothing can cancel out two laws, now established, one of which gives me the duty to serve him and the other the right to protect him. Those two laws are: *that I, being his wife, belong to him; and that he, being my husband, is mine!*"

I don't mean, of course, that at the time my intelligence could translate that gesture of the bride (in its two meanings) with the same logical clarity as now when I remember it. Rather, I didn't stop to ask myself for what and how many *reasons* that gesture offended me. But the sensation I felt was precise and eloquent: as if a mysterious, double-edged weapon had pierced my heart.

The thrust was so rapid that immediately I forgot it; but it must have been very violent if I remember it today, at such a distance. In truth, unknown to myself, I was subjected to trials more bitter than Othello's! Because at least that wretched black man, in his tragedy, had a marked field to fight on: on this side the beloved, on that the enemy. While the field of Arturo Gerace was an indecipherable dilemma, without the relief of hope or of revenge.

## Alone with Him

Right afterward, whispering that she had to go down and light the fire for dinner, she left.

Until dinnertime, I didn't move from my father's room. I felt that I loved him even more than usual, and I was gripped, at the same time, by an anguish I'd never felt before, which, if I tried to translate it into words, I could perhaps put like this: despair at not knowing my fate. Ignorance of our fate, which is with us all at every moment, was always a cause of adventurous joy for me; but today my spirit oppressed me. I looked at my father sleeping, and felt an almost savage affection; but the eternal impossibility of getting an answer and consolation from him gave me a sense of childish weakness. I longed for him to kiss me and caress me, as other fathers do with their childen.

It was the first time I'd felt that wish. Between him and me there had never been such effusions, typical, rather, of women, evidently, and not manly: the only kiss between us had been the one that, in a dream one night, I had secretly given to his pack of cigarettes, but, as for him, not even in a dream had the idea occurred to me that his mouth could give kisses. Are such things thought about a god? The first kiss I had seen him give anyone, since I was born, was the one he'd given the portrait of the Amalfitano today. And, seeing it, I had been consumed by a kind of envy. Why should the portrait of a dead man get what I didn't?

As far as I could remember, in my whole life I had never even once known what kisses were (apart from Immacolatella's, and she was always kissing me, in the exaggerated way of dogs). Silvestro told me later that during my early childhood, when he fed and took care of me, he often planted big sloppy kisses on my cheeks, as nurses do; and he assured me that I had given him lots of little kisses in return. Of course the facts must be as he says, because Silvestro isn't the type for empty boasts; but I no longer remember them. As far as I remember, I repeat, at the time I'm talking about, I had never kissed or been kissed by anyone.

I would have liked my father to give me a kiss, even without completely waking up, in the confusion of sleep, by mistake; or, at least, I would have liked to give him a kiss; but I didn't dare. Crouching like a cat at his feet, I watched him sleep. Even to hear the soft sound of his breath, or his snoring, seemed precious, since it was still testimony of his fleeting presence on the island: of this stay of his that I had missed—and which now was over, I was sure of it.

## In My Room

The next day, in fact, my father left. My stepmother and I went with him to the steamer. Coming back from the wharf, I separated from her and, taking another road, wandered alone through the countryside.

None of my father's departures in the past, although cruel, had ever distressed me like this one. Although there was no reason to doubt his return (since, sooner or later, he always returned to the island), I felt a desperate and ultimate regret, as if our goodbyes a little earlier, on the pier, had been farewell forever! That goodbye, like all the preceding ones, had been without kisses. The childish wish that had surprised me the day before hadn't been fulfilled. But, besides, that desire today appeared to me vain. An arid solitude invaded me; and from the depths of that solitude I felt rising the unnatural anguish I had experienced the day before for the first time. Of not knowing my fate.

The weather had turned as fine as spring, and I didn't go home until dark. Entering through the French door, I found my stepmother in the kitchen singing, as was her habit, as she lit the fire. And this carefreeness of hers I found unseemly. Until a few hours before, I had been angry at her because she was always near my father, like a dog, stealing him from me. And now, instead, I reproached her bitterly in my heart because she wasn't saddened by the separation from her husband. I felt a dark instinct to punish her; and as she set the table, I reminded her meanly:

"Hey, now that my father's gone, you'll have to learn to sleep alone at night!"

Evidently she hadn't yet fixed her mind on this inevitable ordeal that awaited her. In fact, I saw her change her expression and become frightened, as if my mere words had recalled it to her memory. (This was one of the many signs of childhood that persisted in her: that her imagination, always ready for fairy tales and other childish things, was instead sometimes rather slow about what could bring her pain or adversity. One would have said that she trusted the days and attributed to them a kind of conscientious benevolence: as if even time had a Christian heart.)

During dinner, which lasted no more than a few minutes, she didn't speak, she was so thoughtful. I ate quickly, without speaking to her, and right afterward went to bed. I was tired from that restless day, and very sleepy. As often during the cold weather, I didn't waste time getting undressed, taking off only my shoes, and I fell asleep immediately, as soon as I was in bed.

But not even an hour, perhaps, had passed, when I was awakened by small feverish knocks at the door of my room, and by the voice of my stepmother, low and desperate, which behind the door was calling: "Artú! Artú!" I can't say what I was dreaming in that first hour's sleep; but I must have traveled vast distances, and had utterly forgotten about her. Understanding nothing, half asleep, I sat up and turned on the lamp near the bed; at that same moment the door opened and she appeared in the doorway, all upset. "Artú, I'm scared," she said in a faint voice.

She looked as if she had fled from her bed, driven by fear, just as she was: in her slip, and without shoes. On her feet she had only the woolen socks, full of holes, which she usually wore to sleep in, too. And the way she did her hair at night, bound into a single knot on top of her head, reminded me of the crown of curly feathers that ornaments certain tropical birds.

When I returned to reality, I stared at her with scornful, unfriendly eyes. It wasn't the first time I'd seen her like that, in her slip; in the preceding days, I'd caught fleeting glimpses of her crossing the hall or moving around my father's room. And she hadn't covered herself in my presence, but retained tranquil and natural manners: since it didn't seem to her embarrassing to appear in her slip to a boy of fourteen. It was irritating, this behavior of hers!

"I didn't mean to wake you, Artú," she said, explaining with pale lips. "I tried to sleep . . . I recited the prayers of Santa Rita so she would help me fall asleep . . . but I can't . . . I'm too afraid to sleep alone . . . with not another soul in the room . . ."

And, eyeing the dim hall suspiciously, she advanced a little into the halo of my lamp, as if to seek protection against the dark. But I, gruff and contemptuous, didn't invite her to sit or to enter; and she remained standing, leaning against the doorpost like a servant.

The slip left her slender shoulders bare; they were very white, meager and delicate. And her chest, which the material outlined as if it were naked, appeared to me, in its mysterious mature weight, so tender and vulnerable that it inspired a sense of pity. With a bizarre acuteness I pictured to myself the terrible pain she would feel if some cruel person wounded her breast . . . That imagined torture filled my mind for some moments. And it seemed almost incredible that a creature like her, so defenseless, vulnerable, ignorant, stupid, could go through the world without being wounded . . .

"You're over sixteen," I said to her, with an expression of supreme pity, "and you're not able to sleep alone at night. And yet you claim to be a grown woman, as if others were children, next to you! You make me laugh! When a person is a certain age and has certain fears it makes you laugh! yes! Look around, see if others are scared to sleep by themselves!"

"Other women," she apologized, in a lost, humble voice, "sleep with their husbands when they're married . . ."

"*When they're married.* But before they're married? And when their husband leaves on a trip? Who do they sleep with then? No one!"

"What, no, with no one! They sleep with their mother, with their sister! With their brothers and their father! They sleep with their family! Every soul in this world sleeps with his family!"

And she begged me to let her sleep in my room, on the couch, at least for that night. Starting tomorrow, she would learn to sleep alone, but tonight, in there, she felt as if she would faint, because it was the first time in her life that she had been in a room at night without any relative nearby, and she couldn't get used to it all at once. In time, maybe, she would get used to it.

Reluctantly, I had to adjust to taking her in for that night. She went into the other room for a moment to get her covers, and she came back running headlong, dragging the covers on the floor, pale, as if she were fleeing a fire. At the sight of her extraordinary terror, I had a fantastic suspicion; and while, comforted, she went to bed on the couch, I asked her if, in there, the ancestor of the castle and the wicked boys who were his knights had actually appeared to her . . . She shook her head, almost offended that I would come up with such idle talk. "You think I don't know," she said, "that those are fairy tales of your father's? But, of course," she added, with conscientious sincerity, "when you're alone in a room at night you can also be afraid of fairy tales."

I turned out the light, but I didn't fall asleep so quickly. It was curiosity that kept me awake: I wondered if the sleep of women is like that of males, if for example women, too, when they sleep, breathe like men, and snore like them. I had never witnessed the sleep of a woman, while I had seen many men sleep, and they all snored, if in different ways. The snores of my servant Costante, for example, were so loud and lengthy that he resembled a siren. Whereas my father's snoring was a light and pleasurable sound, like the purring of a cat.

Some minutes passed, and still nothing could be heard from the couch, not even the lightest snoring. Maybe she wasn't asleep yet? I called in a low voice: "Hey you, are you asleep?" No answer: so she was asleep.

A moment later I, too, fell asleep, and had a dream.

I seemed to be swimming in a deep, shady grotto. I dove down, to get a beautiful coral branch that I had glimpsed on the bottom; and, as I tore it, I saw with horror the water become stained with blood.

I woke up and, at the very moment I reopened my eyes, instinctively turned on the light, with the confused idea of having to hurry somewhere, to prevent some unknown crime or tragedy . . . In reality, everything was peaceful, and opposite me, on the couch, my stepmother was sunk in a deep sleep, so that the sudden light of the lamp didn't wake her, though it struck her full in the face. At the first instant, her presence in my room seemed to me an enigma, but immediately my memory cleared, and I observed her, curious. She was slightly curled up, to adjust to the size of the couch, wrapped in the covers up to her chin, and her face had an expression of absence and candor. Her silent breaths left a damp and tender freshness on her lips, and the color that tinted her cheeks seemed also to originate in that innocence of her breath. One would have said that she was dreaming of nothing, that in sleep she let the simple thoughts she had when she was awake become even more simple. And she lived no longer with her mind but only with her breathing, like a flower. I recognized on her face that marvelous expression which she had had the day of her arrival, and which the day after had been ruined. The delicate stripes of her eye sockets, which a single day had been enough to damage, were hidden under the long, pitiful lashes. The knot of her curls, on the pillow, seemed the overblown corolla of a big black flower.

She appeared to me prettier than when she was awake. Maybe the famous beauty of women, mentioned in novels and poems, was revealed in sleep, during the night? If you stayed awake until morning, perhaps, would you be able to see the stepmother become beautiful, splendid as a woman in a fable? These speculations of mine naturally weren't serious, I invented them to entertain myself. But still, a little later, as I was falling asleep again, they mingled with a sort of anxiety. I had the sensation that there was a foreigner in my room, subject to strange metamorphoses.

I slept again, without remembering to turn out the light, and it wasn't a full, deep sleep: since, even dreaming, I was in my room, with my stepmother sleeping on the couch, as in reality. In the dream she seemed to me wicked, vile: she had tricked her way into my room, pretending she was a boy like me, dressed in a shirt that fell smoothly over her breast as if underneath she didn't have the figure of a woman. But I had guessed anyway that she was a woman, and I didn't want women with me, in my room. I advanced against the sleeper armed with a dagger, to punish her for her imposture, and I revealed her as a liar by opening the shirt over her chest, so as to expose her white, round breasts . . .

She let out a cry. It wasn't new to my ears, that cry: I had already heard it, I no longer remembered when or where. And I knew no other sound so horrendous, that could so rattle my mind and my nerves.

I woke with a start, hot and sweating as if it were summer. With eyes hurt by the light of the lamp, I caught a glimpse of my guest sleeping peacefully, in the same position as before, and an unrestrained, senseless hatred assailed me. "Wake up!" I shouted suddenly, getting out of bed and shaking her by the shoulders. "You have to get out of my room! Do you understand? Get out of my room!"

I saw her rise from the covers, bewildered, exposing her bare shoulders and the shape of her chest, and I hated her even more angrily. I was possessed by the absurd desire that she should be a boy like me, whom I could fight until my anger was satisfied. Her woman's weakness, which prevented me from taking out my anger on her physically, was what, at that moment, most infuriated me.

"Why don't you cover yourself, you disgusting girl?" I shouted at her. "Why aren't you ashamed of yourself in front of me? I want you to be ashamed of yourself in front of me!"

She stared at me with eyes full of wonder and innocence, then she looked at the neckline of her slip and blushed. And, having nothing there to cover herself with, in embarrassment she crossed her childish arms over her chest.

Her eyes returned to me, confused and uncertain, as if they didn't recognize me. But still—and this exasperated me—in spite of my hatred, and my rudeness, she wasn't afraid of me. In the depths of her eyes there remained (and had remained all through those days) a kind of trusting question: as if my hostility were never sufficient to make her forget a single afternoon when I had been friendly to her; and she still believed *in that Arturo*! Instead, she had to understand that that Arturo, for her, no longer existed; and that that afternoon, for me, was a disgrace. I wanted to eradicate it from time.

A cruel coldheartedness, which longed to sate itself on negations and brutalities, choked my voice: "And I don't want you here in my room, understand?" I repeated. "Get out! You bring me bad dreams and . . . you're dirty and ragged, you're ugly, you have fleas . . ."

She had retreated to the door, which was still open; she had a dark and sullen expression, and I believed that finally an irremediable enmity was in place between us. Then I felt the sharp desire for violence, and its pleasure; and, grabbing her pillow, her covers, I threw them out into the hall and harshly slammed the door on her.

For a moment I could still hear some panting and frightened breaths from behind the door. "She's crying because she's afraid of the dark," I said to myself with bitter satisfaction. Finally every sound ceased. And the next day I discovered that she had gone to sleep in the little room next to mine, where Silvestro used to sleep. Evidently, in that tiny room, not so isolated as my father's room, she felt better protected against solitude and shadows. There she brought all the images of her Madonnas from the room where she had put them the first day, and she arranged them on the pasta chest, the chair, and the windowsill, all around the cot, like bodyguards assigned to watch over her sleep. And, from then on, she retreated there to sleep every night during my father's absences.

## Sleeping Women

Because of her fear, she never dared to shut herself in the room, and always left the door open a crack; and, as she was going to bed, she recited quickly, aloud, all the prayers she knew. From my room I heard the sound of her voice, which seemed to repeat from memory a harsh, melodious lullaby, without meaning. At some points her voice rose, with unexpected emphasis, and a distinct phrase would reach my ears, like, *Queen, our sweetness, our hope . . . Come then, our advocate . . .* So profound was the silence in the house that, at times, one could even hear the ardent smack of the kisses she gave her Virgins after the prayers were over.

I didn't care to know how her solitary days passed in the Casa dei Guaglioni; for the most part I appeared only in the evening, when she called me for dinner. At the table, I always had a book, which I continued to read as I ate, and I let her serve me without deigning to talk or pay her the slightest attention. If I happened to give her a fleeting glance she seemed to turn paler than before, to become melancholy and sad. Her fears of solitude must have caused her to suffer. But I didn't care if she suffered. Didn't I, too, always live alone?

In those days, I had begun to write poems. I remember one that I felt proud of, as of an almost sublime lyric, entitled "Sleeping Women"; it included the following lines:

> *The Beauty of Women appears at night,*
> *like nocturnal flowers, proud owls*
> *fleeing the sun,*
> *and crickets and the Moon, queen of stars.*
> *But Women don't know, for they sleep*
> *like exalted Eagles in their nests,*
> *there, on a cliff, folding their wings*
> *amid silent breaths.*
> *And perhaps no one will ever see*
> *the great Image of their Beauty!*

Whenever I passed the little room, even at the hours when its occupant was downstairs and the space was deserted, I looked scornfully in another direction. But one of those mornings (three or four days after the night when I banished my stepmother from my couch) I happened to wake up very early, when she was still sleeping. Seeing that the weather was beautiful, I immediately opened the windows of my room and, shortly afterward, as I came into the hall, I was followed by a gust of wind that hit the partly closed door of the small room and blew it almost halfway open. So, distractedly, my eye fell on her sleeping peacefully, all wrapped in her covers up to the neck. The sun had just begun to rise, and illumined her face like those spotlights which, in theaters, shine on the dancers so that they stand out to the audience. And I saw that, in sleep, she was smiling with joy, in fact almost laughing, revealing all her little front teeth.

I was surprised by this fact and curious about it, because, the night I had seen her sleeping for the first time, I had imagined, from her expression, that when she slept she didn't dream, and lived only in her breaths, like a vegetable creature. But that smile could certainly have come only from a good dream. What sort of dreams could a creature like her have? That had always been one of my crazy notions: watching others sleep, I often had a tormenting desire to guess their dreams. Hearing a dream recounted later, when the sleeper wakes, doesn't give at all the same satisfaction (even if he doesn't lie).

In some cases, the secrets of sleepers didn't seem to me too obscure. For example, Immacolatella's dreams seemed fairly easy to guess. At most, she could dream, say, that she was a real hunting dog, as the rabbits of Vivara assumed; or that she had learned to climb trees, like a cat; or that a plate of lamb bones was nearby. But undoubtedly the best thing, for her, was when she dreamed about me. It wasn't hard to understand.

And her? Who knows what the dream was that made her smile with joy! Maybe she thought she was at home in Naples, in the same bed as her whole family, and the godmother, too? Or that she was at a great fair in the main square of Paradise, among little carts and lights, in a crowd of boys transformed into cherubim? Or did she imagine that my father would bring her a basket of jewels when he returned form his journey? And who knows if I, too, appeared in these scenes? It annoyed me not to be able to see behind her closed eyes: as if she, so dull and inferior, possessed a domain forbidden to Arturo Gerace. I was tempted to intervene in her dream with a trick. Sometimes, on summer days, when I fell asleep on the beach after a swim, my father, awake himself and bored by watching me sleep, would tickle me for fun with the tip of a piece of seaweed, or blow softly in my ear. And immediately a fish-feather, let's say, made its way into the dream, tickling me with its fins while I was swimming in the depths of the Pacific; or the gangster Al Capone, aiming his deadly air gun in my ear.

I was on the point of entering the room, and repeating with my stepmother the game my father played with me, so as to confuse the thread of her dreams. But was I mad? How could I think of being so intimate with that stupid intruder?

The idea that I had lowered myself to such indulgent fantasies about her continued to annoy me for the entire day; so that later, to give vent to my irritation, I tore up the poem about the "Sleeping Women."

Every time my mind, distracted, or for some other involuntary reason, yielded to less hostile purposes toward her, I became more irascible, as if in revenge.


## Bad Mood


That first absence of my father's was much shorter than I would have predicted. Not even a week had passed since his departure when, to our great surprise, he returned. He arrived unexpectedly, as usual, and I, who happened to be near the gate, was the first to see him; but he barely deigned to say, "Hey, *moro!*" he was so impatient to appear to her. Immediately, with violent anxiety, he asked me where she was; and at my rude answer that she was in the kitchen he went rapidly around the house, setting off toward the French door. I followed him, though unwillingly, and in quite a bad mood: in fact, my happiness at seeing him again was ruined in a moment, by feeling so neglected and unimportant in his eyes.

At his unexpected appearance my stepmother became red in the face with pleasure; and he, noticing that blush, turned radiant. He entered without embracing or greeting her. "My goodness, what a mess your hair is!" he said, glancing at her with an expression of confidence and possession. "Didn't you *do your hair* this morning?" Right away he gave her the gifts he had brought: a wooden bracelet, painted in different colors, and a belt buckle, made of bits of mirror. For me, on the other hand, he had brought nothing; but seeing me sulking in a corner he gave me fifty lire.

Then he asked the usual question, which he repeated at every arrival: "What news?" But unlike the past, when he addressed the same question to me alone, this time he displayed a real curiosity to hear the answers. Still confused by the suddenness of his return, she began to answer: "We're well . . . we've had good weather here . . . and I had a letter from my mother, signed by my sister as well . . . and they write that in Naples they're all well and the weather is good . . ." and he, in the middle of this information, every so often asked: "And did your godmother write? And did you go to Mass?" as if, on a momentary whim, he took a kind of frivolous pleasure in interfering in her affairs.

At the same time, he was going through the kitchen, and he looked around, and recognized the objects with gestures of pleasure and ownership, as if it were ten years since he'd been home! Occasionally she shook her head slightly, with two curls in front that were like bells, and, laughing with her dark mobile eyes, said timidly: "I didn't expect it . . . I didn't at all expect to see you here today . . ."

Then, with casual confidence, like a sovereign, he gave her this response:

"I always do what I like. When I feel like leaving, I go. And when

I feel like coming home, I come back here, and you have to do what suits me."

Soon afterward, he went up the stairs with his suitcase, and we followed. As soon as we were upstairs, right away, first of all, she went to get her covers from Silvestro's room and put them back on the small bed in my father's room.

While he unpacked his suitcase, I stayed there in the room with the two of them: I was lying faceup on the big bed, my arms under my head and knees crossed, and I stared silently at the ceiling with a dark, distracted face. But soon the feeling that my presence was useless made me violently uneasy, and jumping down from the bed I headed toward the door, with the savage attitude and wily step of a tiger. Then my father laughed maliciously and shouted after me: "Hey, Arturo, where are you going? Why so angry? Are we in a bad mood?" But still he didn't trouble to detain me or call me back. I thought: "Well, I'll go out. I've got lots of money, I can go to the café and the tavern, and maybe even get drunk if I want!" But at that moment any place on earth, if I thought about it, seemed to me empty and hopeless. And in the end I stayed downstairs, in the great boys' room, where we almost never sat; and where I remained until dark, sitting on one of those broken couches, without thinking of anything or anyone.

❧

My father stayed on Procida for a couple of days and then left again. After about two weeks, he appeared again, for another day or two. And so, always, in those first months of marriage, he continued to show up at frequent intervals, even if his stays were quite short. But I remained indifferent to his departures and his returns: since it was clear that he didn't come to Procida for me.

Certainly he must have noticed from the start my obvious, ostentatious antipathy toward my stepmother, and in fact on some occasions
one would have said that it amused him; but, like an idle despot, he
left me to my moods and resentments, without too much concern for
me. Only once did he say something about her. It was a moment when
I happened to be alone with him in his room while he was making his
preparations to depart. I was watching him without saying anything,
when, kicking under the bed some old shoes that he didn't need for the
journey, he glanced at me and observed, in a tone of casual arrogance:

"Well, *moro*, you're in quite a bad mood, eh? so it seems?"

Without answering I shrugged one shoulder contemptuously, and
he resumed, with a half smile, looking at me from between his eyelashes:

"Will you tell us why you're so angry with her? Why that poor Nunziata's so irritating to you?"

I frowned, shutting myself in my self. He let out a laugh and then
scowled sarcastically, as his eyes clouded mysteriously:

"Hey, come on, *moro*," he exclaimed, "you can be sure the dangerous
rival who steals my heart from you certainly won't be poor Nunziatina!"
As he uttered that phrase, his voice, and his features, had something
brutal about them; then he smiled, almost to himself, with his mouth
closed and the corners of his lips lifted. And I recognized that fabulous
goat-like smile that I recalled having seen on his face other times.

Uncertain, I looked at him, still without understanding clearly
what conclusion he was aiming at with this speech. "It doesn't matter
at all to me!" I answered randomly, childishly. He let out another laugh,
foolish, insolent. "Oh, it doesn't matter to you . . ." he said, looking
down at me from above, frowning, "and yet *I* formed a different opinion, sorry, O my fine Spanish grandee . . . Do you want me to tell you
what my opinion was? Don't worry, I'll tell only you, I won't talk about
it to anyone. My opinion was that YOU ARE JEALOUS . . . you're

jealous of her, of Nunziatella, because before, here on the island, you could keep me all for yourself, and now she replaces you! Well, what do you think of that, *moro*?"

I blushed as if he had discovered a terrible secret. "It's not true!" I exclaimed angrily. At that point, she came in, and I made as if to leave. But he, grabbing me by the wrist with a hostile, fierce quickness as if we were play-fighting, ordered me through his teeth: "Where are you going? Where are you going? Stay here!" And, keeping his hold on my wrist, while encircling the bride with his free hand, he began playing ostentatiously with her curls. "What beautiful curls," he said, while she looked at us seriously, not understanding the meaning of this scene, "too bad Arturo doesn't have such fine curls!" As he spoke, he glanced at me and laughed to himself, for the pleasure of provoking my jealousy; but finally, seeing the violence with which I was trying to get away from him, he said, bored, "Well, go on." And I left the room without even looking him in the face, in the grip of a furious anger.

That word of his, *jealous*, had offended me extremely. I didn't want to know about such a slur; and it didn't even occur to me to ask myself whether it might be true or not—whether that feeling which since my father's marriage had caused me to live like a hunted animal might perhaps be called jealousy! At that time, although I was good at thinking about ancient history, fate, and Absolute Certainties, I wasn't used to looking into the depths of myself. Some problems were strangers to my imagination. I knew that I was offended, and that was all. And I resented the offense so much that, at the moment, I thought of getting on a ship, leaving the island forever, and never seeing my father or stepmother again. But I had scarcely considered that plan when, at the instant chill and fury of revolt that possessed me, I realized that I wouldn't really be able to carry it out. In fact, the thought that *the two of them* would remain alone on the island, together, without me was unbearable!

My fury, having no outlet, then became so painful that I began to moan angrily, like a wounded person. And certainly I thought that that bitter rage was provoked by the insult, not by something else; but it may be that, in my ignorance, I was already lamenting the impossible demands of my heart. And the opposing and intertwined jealousies, the many-sided passions, that were to mark my destiny.

## Pasta

As far as I can assume, my father kept his word: he didn't let anyone know his opinion (that I was jealous). Besides, as far as my stepmother was concerned, it's plausible that he would never have deigned to confide in her something so serious and important, and about a Gerace! With me, then, his malicious talk of that day had no consequence; he returned immediately to his habitual carelessness, no longer concerning himself with my affairs. And so the memory of the insult was soon buried.

My antipathy toward my stepmother, meanwhile, didn't diminish but became fiercer every day. And as a result the life she led with me during my father's absences from the island was certainly not very happy. I never spoke to her except to give her orders. If I was outside and wanted to summon her to the window to give her some command, or warn her of my arrival, I used to simply whistle. Similarly, even in the house, when I had to call her, I whistled, or at most, if we were in the same room, I would say to her: "Hey, you, listen!" When I spoke to her, I looked in another direction with a show of insult, as if to signify that she was a contemptible object, and unworthy of a glance. And when I passed the little room I turned my eyes away from that half-open door, as if a ghost lived there, or a monster.

I hated that woman so much that, even when I was out of the house, knowing that she was there, in our rooms, which had become her dwelling, was often torture, and I made an effort to forget her existence, to pretend to myself that she was nothing, less than a shadow. The time before she came to the island now seemed to me, thinking back, a kind of blessed limbo. Ah, why had she come? Why had my father brought her here?

The days were lengthening, and starting to get warm. Those beautiful starry evenings were no longer too cold, and often, between the sea, the streets, and the widow's squalid café, I let the dinner hour go by without appearing at the Casa dei Guaglioni. But, however late I came home, I always saw, from the road below, the light on in the kitchen window, and I knew I would find her there, having not yet had dinner and waiting for me before she cooked the pasta. I was already very late and was very hungry; but still, sometimes, seeing that lighted window, I was seized by the cruel wish to prolong her wait. Such cruelty was new to my character. I advanced noiselessly, like a thief, as far as the glass door of the kitchen; and outside, unseen by her, I delayed as long as I liked. Positioned in a dark corner, I could see her, through the panes of glass, falling asleep; at the slightest rustling from outside, she cast a hopeful glance at the door, and every so often she yawned, the way cats yawn (opening their mouth to the jaws, so that they look like tigers and make you laugh), or her chest rose slightly in a sigh. Finally, I would enter in a rush, like a beast hurtling into its den, so that I made her start with fear. And immediately I took my book from the sideboard and waited, with a dark face, for her to serve me.

Once, arriving, I saw through the windows that she was writing on a piece of paper, with a profoundly meditative and inspired expression, like a writer. After dinner, she went upstairs before me, leaving the page on the sideboard, where my eyes fell on it. It was a letter to her mother, and said, more or less:

*Dearest Mother*

*I'm writing you this Leter. With Hope for your good health. And of my beeloved sister Rosa as for me I can give you newss that here we are all well and pleaze send greetings to my dearest Godmother and if she thinks of me and also helo to my dearest freind Irma and Carulina and beloved Angiulina and if they think of me and please give my greetings to Father Severino and Mother Conzilia and if dearest San Giuvani still has that feever but that must be old age and please also dearest mother say helo to my friend Maria and Filumena and to my dearest Aurora you can tel her that the dress is good and my other beloved companyons if they think of me who maybe have already forgoten Nunziata who doesn't forget them either day or night and so too Sufia and the other Nunziata, Ferdinando's daughter, if she thinks of me. And I can say to you dearest Mother! Here on Procida we eat without paying because the land brings everything even oil potatoes and greens and at the shops we pay the acount at the end of the year. And now dearest mother receive a thousand dear kisses from your dearest daughter Nunziatella and also for Rosa a thousand kisses from her sister Nunziatella and I urge you also to my beloved Godmother with a thousand kisses and pleaze many kisses to my other friends who I've already named who for me my Heart thinks of always and I end the Leter.*

*Nunziatella*

Another evening, coming home around ten, I found her asleep, sitting at the kitchen table waiting for me. One arm was folded on the table, and her cheek rested on her hand as if on a little pillow; the harsh shadow of the curls on her forehead protected her from the light of the lamp, and this time, in sleep, her face had a strange, grave, and mysterious expression. I began to pound on the glass, and sing in a loud voice, to give her an immediate, brutal awakening.

Two or three times, arriving home later than usual, I happened to run into her waiting for me outside the gate. "What are you doing out here, at the gate?" I said rudely. And she answered that she was there to get some air.

Besides, she couldn't reproach me. I certainly hadn't asked her to wait. But evidently, in comparison to her dull and solitary days, those dinners in the company of a mute must have seemed to her a kind of important event or evening celebration, something like going dancing or to the movies for ladies. Every morning with great energy she started the preparations for the pasta, which she made fresh every day, and which, just rolled out, she spread to dry on some beams in front of the doorway, like a flag. One morning early, when I had come down to the kitchen feeling irritable and saw her intent on the usual preparations, I announced brusquely that if she was making that pasta every day for me, it was a mistake: in fact, I didn't like pasta and never had.

I said that to humiliate her, not because it was true; in reality, I liked pasta, no less than any other food. It might be said that I ate with equal pleasure all foods that were edible for humans: the only thing I cared about was the quantity, because I always had a ravenous appetite.

"What!" she said in a faint voice, as if she couldn't believe what she was hearing. "You don't like pasta!"

"No."

"What do you like?"

I sought in my mind the worst answer, which could most upset her. And, remembering the disdain she had once shown toward goat's milk, on the spot I invented:

"Goat meat!"

"GOAT meat!" she exclaimed, astonished. But, still, a moment later,

a kind of pleased and yielding fervor emerged from that first astonishment: as if, just to satisfy my tastes, she were already pondering how she
would get goat parts, and prepare goat-meat dishes . . .

At this scene, I was seized by an irresistible desire to laugh and
quickly hid my face in my hands. But instantly I had the thought: "If
I let her see me laughing now, she'll assume we're friends again . . .
like . . . that afternoon . . ." and, shuddering, I rejected that possibility.
But although I tried to suffocate my laughter, I felt it bursting out of my
chest; and, finding no other remedy at the moment for hiding my mirth,
I fell to the floor on my knees, with my face in my arms, and pretended
to cry and sob.

I realized then that if I wanted to I could become a great actor!
She approached, hesitant, solicitous; from under the arm with which I
hid my forehead, I saw her small, short feet, in their house slippers . . .
And since the very play that I was performing naturally increased my
hilarity, my fake sobs became more desperate, lacerating. They were
a perfect imitation. She murmured, disconcerted: "Artú . . . ?" And a
moment later she again repeated: "Artú . . ." I felt her breath on me, tender, almost animal. Then, no longer resisting, her voice, moved, came
out with these words:

"Artú! . . . Something is upsetting you! . . . What's wrong? Tell
Nunziata!"

Along with compassion, there was a kind of mature presumption
in her voice as she uttered that sentence; one could hear, almost, the
importance of the older sister, who has held all her younger siblings
in her arms . . . Hearing her speak to me like that, I was immediately
gripped by revolt and contempt. How could she dare? I jumped to my
feet, furious:

"I'm not crying, I'm laughing!" I exclaimed. She stared at my hard
face, my dry, burning eyes, filled with dismay, as if she had seen a dragon
rise from the earth. "I'm not someone who cries!" I continued, in a tone

of threatening pride. "And you, you mustn't ever dare speak to me in that manner! You're not my relative, you understand? You're nothing to me, nothing, I'm not related to you or friends with you, understand?"

She lowered her eyes onto her pasta, proud and angry; and her lips pouted, as if they were preparing some bitter response. But she remained silent and resumed piling up the dough and working it with fierce movements, as if she meant to abuse it. Then unwillingly she began to spread it; and at the last moment, as I started toward the door, still chewing my breakfast, she gave me an uncertain, clouded look:

"So?" she asked. "If you don't want pasta . . . what do you want to eat tonight for dinner?"

I half turned, and with a grimace of indifference on my lips, I said, as rudely as possible:

"I? Come on, who cares what you make for dinner! You could seriously believe what I told you about pasta! You have to learn that I don't care about eating one thing or another, I can live on biscuits and salted meat, for instance! And even if you cooked, say, ostrich wings, shark fins, or hippopotamus tongues, I wouldn't even notice, because the food you make always has the same taste! For me, you can go on making pasta every day, or whatever you like! I really couldn't care less. And besides, my tastes don't concern you!"

The fact was that I didn't want care or attention from her. I gave her orders for the satisfaction of humiliating her, treating her like an automaton, an object; but her gentle attentions (as if she really presumed herself a relative of mine, my mother!) were intolerable to me. On more than one occasion I repeated to her: "Between us there is no relationship. You are nothing to me," until, once, turning slightly pale, and throwing back her hair, she responded:

"It's not true that I am nothing to you. I am your stepmother and you are my stepson!" And she said it in an arrogant and impassioned manner, as if claiming a kind of ownership!

I laughed in her face with contemptuous fury. "Stepmother!" I exclaimed. "Stepmother is less than nothing! Anyone who says *step-mother* is uttering the most hateful word." And after that dialogue, that very evening, I informed her harshly that I didn't want her to wait for me, for dinner. If I was late, she should eat at the usual time, on her own, and then leave the kitchen, putting aside my food. In fact, I said to her, those dinners in her company bored me; seeing her every evening irritated me; and in short I was the master of eating alone!

## Solitary Song

She was upset by this speech, even more offended and dejected than I had expected; but she made no response and didn't oppose my will. From then on, I got in the habit of coming home very late every night, purposely in order not to be with her. If when I arrived I saw the kitchen light still on, I kept walking around outside the gate (I no longer peeked in through the French door; in fact, I kept my distance) until the lamp was turned off, announcing, like a signal, that my stepmother had gone upstairs. Then, finally, I made up my mind to enter the kitchen. And the dinner she had left for me, kept warm on the coals, I ate alone.

My stepmother did not protest or complain to me, although in those days I represented her entire family and society. Still a foreigner among our distrustful population, she had neither acquaintances nor friendships: and she spent the hours shut up in the kitchen, or in her room, with no one even to converse with. Often, from my boat, seeing up there the walls of our *castle*, which appeared uninhabited, I would begin to suspect that she was only a dream of mine, and that, in reality, no one, besides me, lived between those walls. But then, at whatever hour of the day I might stop by the house, I soon heard again, on the stairs or in the hallways, the known sound of her famous slippers.

Toward me she had assumed a sullen, confused, and fierce attitude; and, proud, she didn't beg for my friendship, which I so cruelly refused her. Still, when our gazes met, there emerged in the depths of her stormy eyes always, like a star, that eternal, irremediable question: *Artú, what did I do to you? What did I do?*

Sometimes from a window I saw her, in her solitude and need for friendship, embrace the bitter-orange tree in the garden, or maybe a pillar of the gate, as if those inanimate objects had been replaced by a sister, a dear companion. Or she began to cuddle one of those mean, mangy cats that came by in search of leftovers, hugging it to her heart and covering it with kisses. I also heard her, occasionally, express to herself, in joyful or rapt phrases, her voice sweet with humming, some thought that was addressed to no one. For example, looking out into the yard one moonlit night she observed: "Waxing moon: boats on the sea, fishing for squid . . ." Or, alone on the doorstep, tasting some sea urchins from a basket, she repeated: "Oh, how good this sea urchin is: like a pomegranate . . ." Or, combing her hair, she got mad at the tangles, and insulted the hair, amid violent tugs of the comb, grumbling: "Oh, you vile things, oh, *dreadfuls!*"

By her nature she preferred the enclosed space of the rooms to open places and streets: like a canary that loves the cage more than the free air. And although the Casa dei Guaglioni was so inhospitable to her, she rarely left it. At times, early in the morning, I saw her go to Mass, quickly, all wrapped in her black shawl, as if she were escaping secretly; and other times I happened to meet her down among the alleys, with the shopping basket on her arm, her curls pushed back under a kerchief, and a worn wallet clutched in her fist. When I saw her bustling among the shops, with her awkward gait, and negotiating for her purchases with those unfriendly merchants, she seemed a poor gypsy girl, in the service of some mysterious abbess or bewitched lady. She had, in fact, a forlorn and somber but also belligerent expression: like someone who shares the secrets of a fascinating master disliked by all. (She must somehow have learned of the malicious stories and gossip that circulated about the Gerace house.)

In that isolation, it seemed to me, I saw her fading more every day. Sometimes I heard her singing in the rooms: she always repeated the songs she'd learned in Naples from the neighbor's radio, that one about the apache, or one whose refrain went, *Tango, you're like a lasso around my heart*, and she also often repeated a church hymn that went: *Let us adore you, divine Host, let us adore you, Host of love.* Her coarse, strident notes were drawn out and full of melancholy, as if all the songs she sang had a sad subject. But I don't think she had thoughts, or was even aware of not being happy. A chrysanthemum or a rosebush, even if its lot is to be in a corner of the window, in a pot, rather than in a garden, doesn't start thinking: *I could have another fate.* And that's what she was like, equally simple.

When I heard her sing, I remembered those famous Neapolitan verses that I had learned as a child, and that I often heard sung by some musician, down at the port: *You're the canary . . . you're sick and you sing . . . you alone, alone die . . .* In truth, seeing her suffering face, with those big black eyes that seemed to burn it, one might suppose that she was about to get sick; I almost began to suspect that the fatal curse of the Amalfitano was a reality, and would cause her to die.

But my heart, armed against her, denied her any compassion: on the contrary, it persisted in its cruelty. One thing above all exasperated me more and more as the days passed: and that is that she, so afraid of my father, never showed any fear of me! When I offended and insulted her, she never replied, yet she stood before me unafraid as a lioness. That attitude of hers was another obvious proof that she considered me a boy, who can't make himself feared by a matron like her. And yet already the difference between our heights appeared to have shrunk since the time of her arrival; and her audacity was a slap in the face. To satisfy my pride, I would have liked to inspire fear in her, like my father, in whose presence she trembled if only a shadow passed over his face. And often, forgetting all my other ambitions, I got absorbed in the plan of becoming a bandit when I grew up, a frightening gang leader, so that she would fall into a faint at the mere sight of me. Even at night, sometimes, I woke with this thought: *I want to make her afraid,* and I imagined using unprecedented cruelties, every sort of barbarism, in the desire to make her hate me as I hated her.

When I gave her orders, and was served by her, I acted like a fierce emperor addressing a simple soldier. And she was always docile and ready to serve me, but that obedience showed no sign of being dictated by fear. Rather, in doing things for me, she grew animated and even assumed a pompous demeanor. And her pale, ugly face became fresh as a jasmine. Maybe she hoped that my commanding her, and being served by her, signified the beginning of a reconciliation? There was no way of making her understand how pitiless my heart was.

CHAPTER 4

# Queen of Women

## *The Hairstyle*

My father had been quite attentive in the early days of his marriage, but as the months passed his visits began to be less frequent. All spring, we saw him maybe a couple of times, and always in a hurry, like a guest passing through: on those occasions, he sometimes resumed the habit of wandering around the island in my company. My stepmother, who had been pregnant since early spring, waited at home for us.

The month of June passed without news of my father; but, once July arrived, I began to expect him, since the middle of summer was always a season of nostalgia for him and, wherever he was, made him long for Procida.

In fact, in the early days of August, he reappeared and, as usual, spent almost the entire month on the island. The morning of his arrival, he sailed with me from the little beach in the *Torpedo Boat of the Antilles*, and from then on we resumed our old summer life, on the beaches and the sea: I became again the sole companion of his hours, while my stepmother, in her heavy, languid state, wandered through the shady rooms of the Casa dei Guaglioni.

The summer days followed one another, all the same and all festive, like radiant stars. My father and I never talked about her; and in
those happy hours the Casa dei Guaglioni, with its single inhabitant
denied lightness and play, seemed like a burned-out planet, outside the
earthly orbit. But in fact I no longer found with my father the childish happiness of other summers: the existence of my stepmother inter-
posed itself between him and me. Precisely because she was condemned
to that obscure slavery, she often seemed more present than if she had
been there, playing with us, not a woman but a fortunate, light creature
equal to my father and me. It was as if there were a great mysterious idol
hidden in a room of the Casa dei Guaglioni, without will or splendor,
but still, by its magic power, able to change the course and the light
of summer.

The pregnancy, which disfigured her body, had also altered her face,
giving her an almost mature expression. Her features were relaxed, her
nose sharpened, and her cheeks were marked by a grave pallor, as if a
disease were consuming her blood. In her slow movements, she bent her
thin, delicate neck, like beasts when they labor, and her gaze was veiled
by a meek, peaceful shadow, with no question, no anxiety.

Suddenly I thought I recognized in her some strange resemblances
to my mother. For months now I had avoided looking at that small portrait, which I kept jealously hidden in my room, forgotten by everyone
except me. And now, at the sight of my stepmother, the small portrait
with its accustomed piety came continually to my mind. I had an aloof,
uncertain feeling about it, which changed my hatred for this woman
into a kind of jealous question; and, more than ever, as one recoils from
a hopeless temptation, I recoiled from looking at the adored portrait.

One day in early summer, before my father arrived, I heard my stepmother complaining that her great crown of curls, in the hot weather,
was bothersome to her. A kind of irresistible whim drove me to suggest
that she gather her hair into two braids, and then pin them up in two

separate knots, just above her ears. (It was the hairstyle my mother had in the photograph, but she, naturally, didn't know this, nor did I tell her.) She remained confused and grateful, at this unusual involvement of mine in something that concerned her; she made some slight objection having to do with the length of her hair, but I insisted, almost violently, and making no other objection she followed my advice, adopting the new style. So, with that same hairstyle (the only difference was that some of her shorter curls always dangled on her forehead and her nape), she and the figure in the picture seemed to me even more alike.

I had sometimes a strange feeling of consolation, of forgiveness, and almost of repose at seeing the small part that the hair made above the nape, between the two braids; and a new way she had of smiling (with her lips slightly apart from her pale jaws) inspired a sense of truce with my bitterness of before. Maybe the person in the picture, the queen of all women, also smiled like that?

She was worried about what my father would say at not seeing the curls on her shoulders, as he liked; but my father, on his return, didn't seem to notice that she had changed her hairstyle, as if he didn't even remember that, at one time, she had been curly-haired. For some time now, he had not interfered in her doings, and was even less concerned with her than, in the past, he had been with me or Immacolatella. He didn't treat her well or badly; any idea of joking with her, of giving her presents or teasing her, had left him. Sometimes he seemed even to have forgotten her, like a presence that has been there for centuries, inevitable, the same, so that now you don't even see it anymore. And sometimes, on the contrary, he looked at her with an uncertain, wondering, and at the same time sleepy expression: as if asking himself who was this strange being, and what had she in common with him, and why was she in our house.

Every so often, in speaking to her, instead of calling her by name, he improvised some slightly mocking nickname that alluded to the present disfigurement of her body. But, although these names sounded vulgar, he uttered them not maliciously but with a kind of boyish detachment, and almost affectionately, because it was natural for him to call others by some characteristic of their person: as when he called me *moro*, or Romeo Amalfi.

After his August sojourn, we didn't see him for a long period. The weeks passed without any news, as if he had completely forgotten that the island of Procida existed on the earth.

## Starry Nights

Meanwhile, I continued my life on the sea. (That year the good weather lasted until November.) From dawn to sunset, I was happily occupied on my boat; and, now that my father wasn't around to remind me of her by his presence, during the day my stepmother, and her isolated kitchen up there, vanished from my memory. Again I had returned to having no thoughts, as in past summers. But, as soon as the sun set, and the colors of the sea began to fade, my mood would suddenly change. It was as if all the joyous spirits of the island, which had kept me company during the day, were descending below the horizon, giving me grand signs of farewell in the sun's rays. The anguish of darkness, which others know from childhood, and then are cured of, I only now became acquainted with! That boundless sea, the roads, and open places seemed to be transformed into a desolate land. And a feeling almost of exile summoned me to the Casa dei Guaglioni, where at that hour the kitchen lamp was lighted.

Sometimes, if twilight surprised me in an out-of-the-way place, or on the open sea, outside the harbor, it seemed to me that the Casa dei Guaglioni, invisible from those places, had fled to a fantastic, inaccessible distance. All the rest of the countryside, with its indifference, offended me, and I felt lost, until that illuminated point at the top of the rock-slide came back in sight. I approached the beach impatiently, and, if it was night, certain childish superstitions pursued me as I ran up the hill. Halfway up the slope, to keep myself company I started singing at the top of my lungs; and, hearing me, above, from the yard, someone came to the kitchen doorway calling in a rhythmic and almost dramatic voice:

"Ar-tu-rooo! Ar-túúú!"

At that hour, she was always busy with the preparations for dinner; I entered with an almost dark, indolent expression, and, waiting for dinner, I stretched out on the bench, resting from my day. Every so often I yawned, with a show of boredom and tiredness; I rarely granted her any sign of attention, nor was there much conversation between the two of us. As she waited for the water to boil, she sat on a low stool, with her hands clasped in her lap and her head slightly bent; and every so often she pushed off her sweaty forehead a curl that had escaped from one of the braids. Her enlarged figure, now lacking any girlishness, seemed to me encircled by sovereignty and repose, like certain figures worshipped by peoples of the Orient to which the sculptor has given a strange, mis-shapen heaviness as a sign of their august power. Even the two gold circles of her earrings, on the sides of her face, lost, in my eyes, their significance as human ornaments and seemed, rather, like votive offerings hanging on a sacred effigy. Sticking out of her slippers were her small feet, which had not played during the summer, like mine, on the beach and in the sea; and the white color of her skin, in a season when all men and boys were always so dark, also appeared a sign of ancient and proprietary nobility. Sometimes I forgot that she and I were almost the same age: she seemed to have been born many years before me, perhaps even before the Casa dei Guaglioni; but, because of the compassion I felt near her, that supreme age seemed a gentle thing.

At times, I dozed a little on the bench, and in that delicate drowsiness the slightest impressions of reality were transformed into images resembling fragments of a fable, which would soothe me like an infant. I saw again the sparkling tremolo of the sea during the day, like the smile of a marvelous being, which at that hour, supine, left to the caressing currents, was resting, too, thinking of me . . . The night air coming through the French door rested on my dark body, as if someone had put a linen shirt on me, cool and clean . . . The night sky was an immense decorated tent, spread over me . . . Or no, it was an immense tree, in whose branches the stars rustled like leaves . . . and among the branches there was a single nest, mine, and in that nest I was falling asleep . . . Down below, meanwhile, the sea waited for me, mine, too . . . If I licked the skin of my arm, I tasted salt . . .

Some evenings, after dinner, drawn by the cool outside air, I stretched out on the doorstep, or on the ground in the yard. The night, which down below an hour before had seemed to me so fierce, here, a step from the lighted French door, became familiar again. Now if I looked at the sky it was a great ocean, scattered with countless islands, and, sharpening my gaze, I sought among the stars those whose names I knew: Arturo, first of all others, and then the Bears, Mars, the Pleiades, Castor and Pollux, Cassiopeia . . . I had always regretted that in modern times there was no longer on the earth some forbidden limit, like the Pillars of Hercules for the ancients, because I would have liked to be the first to go beyond it, challenging the ban with my audacity; and in the same way, now, looking at the starry sky, I envied the future pioneers who would be able to reach the stars. It was humbling to see the sky and think: "There are so many other landscapes, other rainbows of colors, maybe many other seas of unknown hues, forests bigger than the ones in the tropics, other kinds of ferocious and joyful animals, even more loving than those we see . . . other stupendous female creatures who sleep . . . other handsome heroes . . . other faithful followers . . . and I can't get there!"

Then my eyes and my thoughts left the sky in vexation, and came to rest again on the sea, which, as soon as I looked at it, pulsed toward me, like a lover. Spread out there, black and full of allurements, it repeated to me that it, too, no less than the starry sky, was vast and fantastic, and possessed territories that couldn't be counted, all different from one another, like a hundred thousand planets! Soon the longed-for age when I would be not a boy but a man would begin; and the sea, like a companion that had played with me and had grown up with me, would carry me away with it to know the oceans, and all the other lands, and all life!

## Queen of Women

Autumn was already upon us, with its early sunsets: the cruel moment of darkness came earlier every day, driving me away from the sea. Very often, if I got home before nightfall, I would now find visitors. My stepmother had made friends with two or three Procidan women, wives of shopkeepers or boatmen, who came to see her and lingered to talk, offering help and advice while she worked on the layette for my stepbrother who was soon to be born. I don't know how she had been able to induce them to cross the threshold of the Casa dei Guaglioni, and at first their presence surprised me, as an implausible apparition. For the most part, they all sat around the kitchen table, which was littered with pieces of cloth and swaddling clothes, and I noticed that my stepmother, so submissive with my father and me, among those women demonstrated, instead, a kind of matronly authority and almost recognized supremacy, even though she was younger.

All of them were small, and she seemed very tall in comparison. And she sewed with an expression of serious absorption, composed and silent in the circle of chattering, gesturing women.

Their animated voices muffled the sound of my footsteps as I came in from outside; but, at my entrance, they immediately fell silent, shy and distrustful; and a few minutes later they all dispersed, because in Procida women customarily withdraw into their own houses when darkness descends.

Sometimes, coming up from the sea a little earlier than usual, and lingering outside to enjoy the sunset, I happened to hear their conversations. The subjects were almost always the same: doings of immediate family and other relatives, or matters regarding the various jobs of their husbands, the house, the children, and in particular the coming birth of my stepsibling. On one of those occasions I heard my stepmother's voice reveal to the others the name she had decided on for her firstborn: if it was a girl, she said, she would call her Violante (Violante was her mother's name); and if it was a boy she would call him Carmine Arturo. Actually, she explained, she would have preferred to call him Arturo, because ever since she was a child she had liked that name more than all others; but since there was already an Arturo in the house, and two brothers can't have the same name, she had decided on Carmine for the first name, in honor of the Madonna del Carmine, the protector of Procida. Carmine also sounded all right, she observed, especially if you said Carminiello. Carminiello-Arturo! Further, she intended to add to this double name, on the certificate of baptism, Raffaele and Vito, the names of her father and brother.

Usually, when her friends left, my stepmother went on sewing a little longer, while I rested on the bench. For months, she had been putting aside the little sums given to her occasionally by my father, and had done her best to pick up scraps of material in the shops of Procida, to make these clothes for my stepbrother. It was a matter, in reality, of five or six items, which might all fit in a shoebox; and they seemed of a rather cheap quality, as far as I could understand. But her younger brothers had always been content, for baby clothes, with old rags and women's shawls; and the making of a layette like this assumed, in her eyes, the importance of a solemn princely ceremony. Still, in the rigorous attention she gave the work, you could discern a certain inexperience and lack of skill.

I didn't devote any particular thought to my stepsibling. His birth was now approaching; but he remained unreal, like a character from China, which for us meant nothing. It was strange, the idea that in reality he already existed among us, in our house. My stepmother herself, although she was preparing the layette, never spoke of him, and didn't even stop to think about him, I'm sure. At times, one would have said she lived almost unconscious of carrying him inside her. The cats, the birds, the beasts, too, when the time for a family arrives, are busy preparing their nests, like creatures preoccupied and inspired, without thinking of the one who commands them.

## Autumn. Last News of Algerian Dagger

September had been beautiful but as hot as August; and the first autumnal air, instead of bringing relief to my stepmother, seemed to exhaust her weary blood. Her eyes had become opaque and expressionless, as if the spirit that nourished their splendor were wasting away. And that majesty which a short time before had made her misshapen body almost divine was now becoming a pitiful lethargy. Even her hair had lost its beautiful raven blackness, and looked parched, dusty. She was ugly, terribly ugly; and my mysterious sibling, who made her ugly, was transformed in my thoughts into a kind of monster, or illness, to which she submitted without struggle. Circled by a halo of sadness, with the braids that had come loose from the buns, she moved through the kitchen, and no longer sang as she lit the fire. At brief intervals, she would return to her stool to rest; and maybe, turning on me her opaque, expressionless eyes, she hinted at some topic of conversation: her mother, her sister, her home in Naples . . . Of the time of her engagement, and of her wedding, however, she never said anything; that subject, like God, or my stepbrother, seemed to belong to that mysterious power which can't be translated into words or even thoughts. Only seldom, and fleetingly, did I hear her name Vilèlm, and sometimes I thought that in some unconscious hint of hers I caught a gleam of his mysterious life outside the island . . . But even then my pride wouldn't lower itself to show her that her conversation interested me. I would almost have been tempted to ask her some questions, to explore, through her ignorance, the fascinating secrets that she herself couldn't know . . . But, scornfully, I restrained myself. In fact, I made a show of paying no attention, and even less than to her other subjects. And, as usual, her little voice, discouraged by talking to herself, soon faded.

Once, my heart had a kind of shock: I discovered that she had met Algerian Dagger! In fact—I don't know in what connection—she named a certain Marco, from whom my father had received as a gift the watch he always wore on his wrist; the day she and my father left Naples, he had hurried to say goodbye to my father at the steamer, a moment before the gangplank was raised . . .

I thus discovered that she had seen him! Irresistibly, a question escaped my lips: "What was he like?" "Who?" "That person," I exclaimed brusquely, "what sort of person was he?" "Marco?" she said then. "Really . . . I saw him only for a minute, from the steamer . . . I seem to remember that he was around the age of Vilèlm, but maybe a little younger . . . Slender, small, with freckles on his face . . . light, elongated eyes . . . and an unhappy smile . . . and small teeth, widely spaced . . ." I realized suddenly that that was how, or almost, I had always pictured him! I asked her another peremptory question: "Was he dark or fair?" "I think," she answered uncertainly, "he had black hair . . ." That answer gave me pleasure, almost comfort. So now I had learned his name: Marco! I would have liked to find out still if he was Italian or foreign; if maybe he was a native of Arabia, or, rather, a Jew. (I don't know why, I had always attributed to him an Oriental character, and in particular I liked having him belong to the persecuted wandering race.) . . . And still I yearned to hear many other things about this character, who had inhabited the last happy period of my childhood, more magical and shining than Aladdin! But I wouldn't let myself ask my stepmother other questions. And I shut myself up in my cloudy solitude.

## Foreign Lands

As the evenings got longer, I resumed the habit of reading and studying in the kitchen, to pass the time as I waited for dinner. My preferred book in those days was a large atlas, with a lavish written commentary. The volume contained immense, folded-up colored maps, which I spread out in front of me every evening, kneeling on the floor or on a chair near the table. And it was these maps which excited my stepmother's interest. For several evenings she considered them, baffled, as if they were puzzles; until she dared to ask me, in a shy voice:

"What are you studying there, Artú?"

Without raising my head from the outspread map, on which I was tracing some marks with a piece of charcoal, I answered that I was studying my routes; since, I said with conviction, the time when I would explore the world was now approaching: I intended to leave, at the latest, next year, either with my father or, otherwise, alone!

My stepmother looked at the map without saying anything else, for that evening. But from then on, there was no evening when she did not return to the subject. Whenever I began to study my routes again, I would hear her approach, with her labored, heavy, animal-like steps;

for a while she kept silent, gazing at the map spread out in front of me; finally, amid many hesitations, she would make up her mind and, indicating with her hand the points marked with charcoal, ask in a vaguely anxious tone: "Is this very far from Procida? How far is it?" Rudely, I would throw out an approximate number. "And where does it say," she then resumed, while her eyes wandered uncertainly over the whole page, "the island of Procida?" "What!" she repeated, almost an echo, at my answer. "You can't see it from here! It's in the other hemisphere!"

And she tried to get from me other, more precise details about the abstruse shapes on that map, in a voice that, in overcoming timidity, became harsh. I barely offered curt, impatient answers, always using that sullen, unfriendly tone which now seemed the only one natural when I spoke to her. However, in naming the most desirable and fascinating places on the earth—continents, cities, mountains, seas—my tone had a hint of arrogance and triumph, as if they were all my domains! Sometimes, with an irresistible instinct for affirmation, I also reported on certain undertakings that were to immortalize, at every stage, the passage of Arturo Gerace . . . but I quickly sealed myself off again in my scornful reserve.

My stepmother didn't make many comments on my words; often, in fact, on hearing them she became silent, while her face appeared suddenly aged, strangely wild. I had noticed on other occasions that she nurtured a distrust and antipathy toward foreign places; but now those old feelings of hers seemed to have developed into a fearful aversion, which, with the increase in her geographic knowledge, became more serious instead of diminishing. All towns and cities that weren't Naples and its surroundings were unreal and inhuman, like moons; and if you mentioned even a medium distance, of two or three thousand kilometers, the whites of her eyes became waxen, as if she were facing a dizzy spell, or a ghost. "And so," she resumed, "you'll really go all that distance, alone!" *Alone* in her language meant without my father, without any relative. She looked at the Arctic Circle and observed: "And you want to travel alone through those icy lands!" She looked at the dark reliefs of heights and commented: "And a year from now, you'd like to be traveling all by yourself in the middle of those mountains!"

If you heard her tone, it would seem that journeys were not, as they are, a celebration, a marvelous pleasure, but a bitter, unnatural thing. Thus (to give an example) a swan grows sad far from its lakes, and an Asiatic tiger feels no ambition to visit Europe; and a cat would weep at the idea of leaving its balcony to go on a cruise.

I have the idea, then, that the opinion of foreign lands she got from my information was not very reassuring. My word for her was gospel, it seems; and I could have driven from her mind every disastrous vision and convinced her, maybe, that all foreign lands were a beautiful tranquil garden, but I didn't take the trouble. Rather, I wanted to let her believe the opposite. And I suppose that, through those awkward dialogues of ours, she pictured the earthly globe, outside the confines of Naples, as a series of pampas, steppes, and shadowy forests, traversed by wild beasts, redskins, and cannibals, places that only the bold dared to explore. Every so often she would interrupt my silent, enthralling meditations on maps, asking, for example, with that new roughness: "Over in the equatorial zones can you send mail to Procida?" Or, having sought in vain, with her eyes, the island of Procida in the middle of the Pacific or the Indian Ocean, she objected in a tired voice: "You say you're going, and you'll take command of a ship, that in those countries in Africa it's a thing you can do immediately . . . and doesn't even cost much . . . But then will they be good people? To go out alone with them in a boat! And when you find yourself isolated there in the high seas, with all those older sailors . . . if someday, let's say, they revolt? Claiming you're still not old enough to be the commander? Who will defend you? With no one in the family nearby!"

Finally one night I said to her: "Do me a favor, don't distract me anymore with your talk, when I'm studying," and she became mute. Like a commander in his camp tent, I traced some lines through oceans and continents with the charcoal: from Mozambique to Sumatra, to the Philippines, to the Coral Sea . . . and around this work reigned a great suspended silence. I called it *work*, and maybe it was a game, but for me it was better than writing a poem; since, unlike poems (which have their end in themselves), it was preparation for action, and nothing is more beautiful than that! Those charcoal lines represented for me the sparkling wake of the ship *Arturo*: the certainty of action awaited me, as, after the wonderful dreams of night, day lights up, which is perfect beauty. Prince Tristan was truly mad when he said that night is more beautiful than day! Ever since I was born, I've been waiting for full daylight, the perfection of life: I've always known that the island and my early happiness were only an imperfect night; even the enchanting years with my father—and those evenings there with her!—were still the night of life; in my heart I've known that. And now I know it more than ever; and I'm always waiting for my day to come, like a marvelous brother in whose embrace you can recount the long period of boredom . . .

## The Iridescent Spider Web

But let's return to that evening (when I had said to my stepmother: "Please don't bother me"). She said no more, but sat resting with her hands in her lap, half a step away. Her gaze went back continually to my big blue maps; and her soul, which in those days seemed to me ill and almost brutalized, emerged in her eyes, full of childish questions and ignorant suffering.

Every time I happened to look at them, those eloquent eyes said something different. Once, in a language that seemed to echo the cries of Cassandra, they stared, enlarged, dry, and solitary, at my place, as if already they saw it empty. Another time, they rested here and there on my maps with a playful and, at the same time, desolate fantasy, as if saying: "It would be wonderful for me not to have this body! Not to be a woman but to be a boy like you, and run all around the world with you!"

At a certain point she said aloud: "But I . . . if I were your mother, I wouldn't let you leave!"

I looked up and saw that she had unexpectedly assumed a dark, sly expression. Two aggressive little flames lighted her cheekbones, and her ears became colored vividly pink. Turning away from me sullen and hostile eyes, she repeated: "I wouldn't let you leave! I would chain the door, I would stand in front of it and say to you: 'You're not even twenty-one—to leave the house without permission. If you want to leave, first you have to get past here!' "

"Oh, why don't you be quiet? What are you talking about? When I hear what you're saying, I laugh. *Permission*, come on, really . . . in my opinion, your head is a big muddle. Go make your speeches to some poor devil, because if you talk to me like that you're really ignorant. *Twenty-one!* I'm older than a twenty-one-year-old. And who cares about your opinion! For me when you talk it might as well be a Chinese talking."

I'd gone from a tone of mockery to a surly ill humor. "And you should know that if I feel like it I can command twenty-one-year-olds as if they were boys. And also men of twenty-five and thirty. If you think that I'm not as good as they are because of my age, you're ignorant and you should shut up!"

The old perpetual bitterness (of being still considered a boy) that for the past twelve months had so upset me made me resent her bite, and excited revolts and suspicions. "You," I resumed, scowling, "mustn't concern yourself with my business. You've got to stop bothering me with your nonsense, every time I study the atlas: *And you'll go traveling so far alone! And you'll really go so far, alone!* As if I were still a kid, who didn't know how to defend myself alone, and even without weapons! What's your idea? *Others* go off alone and travel alone, and you don't make a fuss, the way you do for me! What are you thinking? That *others*, because they're older than I am, are braver? Is that your idea?"

She hadn't understood my allusion or grasped that my pride expected an answer. Her silent face was shaken by her agitation at having offended me, which made her forgive every insult; but still between her lashes a ray of strange ferocity persisted, which had earlier driven her to provoke me. And meanwhile inexpressible questions, of which her own mind was ignorant, crossed her anxious gaze, with their varied shadows. They resembled clouds that pass in front of a star, and seem to go very close to it, while the star, instead, moves unaware in another space, clear as a mirror . . .

"Is that your idea?" I repeated in a peremptory tone. Then, facing her, with a determined expression, I decided to speak clearly. "*My father,*" I explained, "always travels alone, and you don't reproach him the way you do me. WHY? Answer!"

She raised to me eyes now devoid of any fierceness, in which only a childish wonder laughed. "Your father!" she murmured. "He's different . . ." And a graceful sweetness arrived to remove every shadow from her face: like a beloved sister who had come to caress her and kiss her, interceding with me.

"Oh, he's different! . . . Why?" I insisted darkly. But luckily she didn't see my fiendish expression. She had lowered her eyes, in a sweet, simple smile. "Because . . ." she said, just shaking her shoulders, "because he's not like you. No, I don't worry about him; his journeys aren't big ones! He, *he's like the goldfinches . . .*"

I didn't immediately understand the meaning of that comment, and so she explained that finches, even when they go away, never go far from their dwelling; they may fly to a neighboring cornice, the roof, another windowsill, but they always stay in the neighborhood.

This unprecedented assertion about my father seemed to me a new, extraordinary confirmation of how slow my stepmother's intellect was . . . When, then, a doubt crept in: that she didn't really believe what she was saying but had, on the spot, invented that unlikely and ridiculous answer in order not to give me her sincere, offensive opinion: and that is, that she considered my father a great man and me a child.

That suspicion was enough to make me uncontrollable, worse than a wild animal. I looked at that mysterious smile, like a saint's . . . I burst out suddenly: "You're not my mother, or relative: you're nothing to me. And you'd better not interfere in my affairs again!"

From then on, in the evenings, she stopped concerning herself with what I did. She no longer came over to ask me questions when I unfolded the atlas, but it was clear that that book had become for her an object of aversion, of distrust, and, at the same time, of hated fascination: she avoided touching it, and, if she merely looked at it from a distance, her eyes became agitated, as if it were the book of the Fates, or a treatise on black magic.

If, for some reason or other, I happened to utter the words *next year*, I would see her pupils staring: like two frightened guests, motionless before a threshold they do not want to cross.

And meanwhile, from day to day, I thought about going away immediately, not waiting for next year. So I would show her without delay if I was a child or if I could depart by myself, and what I was capable of! As I was on the point of leaving the island, however, a desperate spell held me there, as it had done since childhood. The marvelous diversities of continents and oceans that, every night, in the atlas, my imagination worshipped suddenly seemed to await me, beyond the sea of Procida, as an immense landscape of chilling indifference. The same that, as evening fell, drove me out of alien places, the harbor, the streets, calling me back to the Casa dei Guaglioni.

And the thought of going away without first seeing my father, at least once more, was intolerable to me. Still, at certain moments, I seemed almost to hate Wilhelm Gerace; but as soon as I resolved to escape from Procida the memory of him invaded the whole island like an insidious, fascinating multitude. I recognized him in the taste of the seawater, of the fruit; the cry of an owl, or a seagull passed by, and it seemed to be he who was calling: "Hey, *moro!*" The autumn wind tossed spray at me, or gusts of sand; and it seemed that he was provoking me, in fun. Sometimes, going down to the shore, I seemed to have a shadow behind me; and I imagined, almost flattered: "It's a private spy, who follows my steps for him." Then, amid these strange illusions, I would hate him more than ever, because, like an invader, he took possession in this way of my island; but still I knew that I wouldn't have liked the island so much if it hadn't been his, indivisible from his person. The new mysteries I glimpsed, the disquieting, indecipherable messages and the mirages, the farewells of childhood and of my little mother, dead, rejected, returned to be reassembled into the ancient many-sided chimera that enthralled me. That chimera now laughed at me with other eyes, held out other arms, and had different prayers, voices, sighs; but it didn't change its enchanted veil—ambiguity, which imprisoned me on the island like an iridescent spider web.

## Murdered?

It was mid-autumn, and my father still hadn't shown up. My stepmother kept hoping that he would return home for the period when the child was to be born. During the first week of November, she said to me every night: Who knows, maybe your father will arrive tomorrow? Then, as the days passed, she stopped saying anything. But at the hour when the steamer from Naples docked down at the port, she went to sit almost furtively at the window, to see if the well-known carriage would appear at the end of the street.

According to her calculations and those of her friends, my stepbrother was to be born in early December. Instead, it was, unexpectedly, the night of November twenty-second.

The neighbor women, who in those days came more frequently than usual to our house, had left toward evening, as always; and after dinner my stepmother and I had gone upstairs to sleep, with no thought. But late at night (it must have been around one) from Nunz's room a dark moan woke me, more animal than human, broken by cries of such unprecedented anguish that, still half asleep, I rushed to the little room and opened the door. The light was on; and Nunz, all disheveled and half dressed, was lying across the bed. She had thrown off the covers, but, on seeing me, she gathered them convulsively and drew them over herself; then immediately she fell back overwhelmed, with a cry similar to those I'd heard before, in a voice that was unrecognizable. And she began to writhe wildly and wretchedly, while her eyes every so often stared at me without even asking for help, but as if driving me out of the room. "What's wrong? What's wrong?" I shouted at her brutally. Not having a precise idea of the necessary sufferings of women, I stood before that scene as before a mysterious tragedy; and my first sentiment was an impulse of hatred toward that aggressive mystery that was torturing Nunz. She at that point had a moment of respite, and turned to me a small smile full of shame but at the same time of importance. "It's nothing," she tried to explain, "but you . . . you mustn't stay in this room . . . you should . . . call someone . . . call Fortunata . . ." (Fortunata was the midwife of Procida.) Her words broke off in a new cry; and the pain forced the sweet smile from her face, giving it an inhuman severity. In her frenzy of suffering, she tore with her fingers at a woolen shawl, fastened by a safety pin, which she wore over her shoulders at night, and, seeing that gesture at the very moment that I left the room to go in search of help, I had a sudden memory: poor Immacolatella, who, during the ordeal of her death, every so often made the motion of tearing at her body with her teeth . . . Almost two years had passed since that bitter day when Immacolatella was buried; but the sight of her end was impressed in my memory in every detail; and because I had never yet seen any human creature die, it remained my only experience of death. Now, as I rushed down the stairs, I was pierced by a suspicion, in fact by a horrible certainty: it seemed to me that I saw, in my stepmother, many signs of that same extreme anguish that had led Immacolatella to end up underground, near the carob tree; and I believed I understood that the same illness my mother had died of, and Immacolatella, would tonight kill this other woman, too.

Childish impressions took hold of me. I almost expected to encounter the shade of the Amalfitano as he wandered through the hallways, singing his tragic refrains in a melodious bass voice. And I was distressed at having to leave my stepmother alone in the house, with no defense against that murderer.

As I hurried through the narrow sleeping streets, I seemed to be in a tumultuous theater, in which many voices were shouting that odious word: *Death! Death!* I stopped first at the doctor's house, which was near the little square, and began to pound on the door like a bandit; but finally a woman's voice, from behind a shutter, told me rudely that the doctor had left for Naples. And so I could only continue on to the neighborhood of Cottimo, around three kilometers away, where Fortunata the midwife lived.

I had some ancient reasons for aversion and suspicion toward that woman, and the necessity of resorting to her annoyed me, as an evil sign; still, since there was no other choice, I ran madly toward her house, fearing that every instant of delay could be fatal to the life of Nunz.

## The Midwife

This Fortunata had practiced her profession of midwife on Procida for more than thirty years; among the women in labor assisted by her was my mother. I blamed her for not having saved my mother for me, and I despised the opinion of the Procidans, among whom she enjoyed a reputation of great mastery in her art. Her enormous, dark hands seemed to me the hands of a murderer; and the knowledge that she had brought me into the light, and had, further, with timely instructions, guided my nurse Silvestro at first, wasn't enough to reconcile me to her. She, among all the women of the island, was perhaps the only one who had never deigned to give any credence to the popular rumors, facing without fear the evil curse of the Gerace house. But not even that seemed to me a special proof of merit, because, although she wore women's clothes, she couldn't be properly numbered among women. To see her cross the town with her professional bag under her arm, with her long, wide-legged stride, military and yet slovenly, you would have said she was some petty soldier of the Turkish fleet, reincarnated as a midwife. Her figure was so tall and large (in some places angular, in others obese) that she had trouble getting through the small door of her house, and, near other women, she seemed a giantess. Her skin was quite dark; over her lip grew a small mustache, and on her chin some beard hairs. She had enormous feet and hands, long, irregular teeth, and an unpleasant voice, dark and rather hoarse. She wore glasses, and always the same dress of faded fustian, with a large flower pattern. In winter she covered this dress with a soot-colored duster coat. And on Sunday she wore on her head an embroidered veil, behind which she seemed even uglier.

Because of her ugliness, she had never found anyone to marry, and she lived alone in a one-room cottage. She used a rude, rough, and curt tone with others, always seeming distracted from their conversation, as if her mind were constantly occupied. And when she uttered some opinion of her own, she usually did so speaking not to any of those present but, rather, to herself, or to the air: in a dark, emphatic mumble, as if she were reciting obscure verses. Only with the newborns, or with her cat, did she at times talk more intimately and fondly. I knew the cat by sight: he was celebrated in the whole town as a kind of venerable centenarian, since he was already nineteen years old. And he was always sitting in the window of the cottage, like a sinister guardian. Often, passing by, I tried various ways of insulting him.

I think it didn't take me more than ten minutes to get to Fortunata's house (which usually is a journey of at least half an hour). I began beating on the door with my fists, and kicking, and the midwife was quick to look out the window, with a cloak thrown over her nightgown. "Hurry up," I said in an imperious tone, "there's a woman who's sick at our house . . . she's really sick!" "Hey, kid, you're just one, I thought you were a gang," she muttered in her cavernous voice. "*A woman!* It must be Nunziata who wants to give birth, who else would it be, this woman of yours! All right, wait for me a minute, and I'm coming." "Hurry up!" I commanded again. Then, as she withdrew from the window, I shouted after her, in a tone charged with hatred and threat: "And now, hey, don't get drunk. If you get drunk you'll be in trouble!"

Truly, although it was known that she had a taste for wine, and always kept a flask in her room, no one had ever seen her drunk, and I made that remark only because I longed to express my animosity in some way. She, for her part, didn't resent it, or bother to answer me. In the same way, when we happened to meet on the street, and I deliberately turned my face from her, she gave no sign at all of being offended, or even, in fact, of having noticed. Without a doubt, because she had helped me come into the world, she still considered me a child, whose fancies can be ignored.

I sat on the low wall, waiting for her. And I was almost surprised to observe that it was a beautiful warm night, the air still, with a big moon, just veiled by wisps of fog. The sea and the gardens had a smiling color, as in spring; and not a movement or a voice could be heard. Maybe I expected that all the presences of creation should be stirring around N., filled with emotion, like the court around a queen! But, instead, the agony of a woman in her room is a thing so small that it can't cast a shadow on the great universe.

I stretched out along the wall, pressing my face against the rough limestone, with a feeling of inconsolable wretchedness. The beautiful landscape and the starry sky and my island suddenly seemed to me bitter, bleak, even abhorrent, because they had no thoughts for that room, which one couldn't even see from here, isolated up at the Casa dei Guaglioni, and important only to me. There, every night for almost a year, guarded under the eyelids like precious gems in a jewel box, the two black eyes of a queen had slept, which could express the assurance, and the adoration, and the honor of serving me and being my relative. But now I saw again the anguish that had appeared a little before in those big eyes: so cruel, too vast for their ignorance. And I repeated to myself with horror: "Ah, certainly it's death! It's death!"

All my pleasures, my regrets, were turned upside down in confusion inside me. I had really forgotten Wilhelm, like a dream. It seemed as if only Nunz and I existed on the earth. And of my famous hatred for her, which had been my cross, not a trace remained.

The midwife reappeared at the door, ready, the usual bag under her arm; and I jumped down from the wall. As we set out (after she had directed toward the interior of the cottage, to her cat, a sickly-sweet, ceremonious goodbye), she examined the path of the moon, wrinkling her bespectacled forehead. And she decreed, speaking to herself in her usual fashion: "Good hours, these, for infants, male and female. Boys born after midnight and early in the morning grow up handsome, lucky, and in good health! And girls in good health and virtuous."

Then, with great satisfaction, she began to march in her soundless rope-soled shoes, purposeful and villainous as the figure of an executioner. My eyes, disgusted, fell on her hands, which in the moonlight appeared blacker, enormous; and to spare my sight I ran quite a distance ahead of her, proceeding rapidly alone. Every so often I turned to see that she was following, and hadn't sneaked off, maybe, into the gardens and alleys; and I shouted at her in a threatening tone: "Hey, move!" But when we got to the edge of the town, at the top of the long ascent after the square, my heart had a jolt: in the distance, high up, the Casa dei Guaglioni appeared, its windows on that side all dark; and it seemed an ancient and abandoned vision, as if already not a soul were alive within its walls!

## The Young Cock

Then I started running again, harder than when I left, no longer concerned with the old woman. I didn't care about anything else now, except to return immediately. I wanted to arrive at least in time to say a few last words to N., if she could still hear me for an instant. What words they would be it was impossible for me to predict: maybe I trusted in an extreme inspiration, in a kind of capricious improvisation, so sublime as to redeem, in a single phrase, all the curses and other nonsense I had said to her; and to be sufficient as an explanation between her and me for eternity! I ran, in fact, toward our *castle*, as if, for me and for her, an eternity were at stake: and were guarded precisely in that mysterious, delicate phrase that at all costs I had to say to her, in the face of death. I'm curious to know what I intended to say, because at the time I still didn't understand anything (and do I understand even now?); but I was sure that I would speak, although, on that last stretch of the road, of all the possible words in existence I remembered only one: *Nunziatella*. I repeated to myself that word *Nunziatella* in the same desperate rhythm as my steps. And all the rest was obscured, I neither heard nor saw anything else. I remember that the fields near our house, as I passed, didn't appear to me as they were; rather, I seemed to be crossing a kind of enormous, ruined foreign square. And yet I had the sensation that, if N. were dead, here on the island and also elsewhere, wherever I went, I would find nothing but that wretched square, of mortar, iron, and stones: without heart or thought for me.

The door was open and the light was burning in the hall, as I had left them when I went out. As soon as I was on the stairs I heard from the floor above the wail of a newborn. Her voice couldn't be heard. And, reaching the doorway, the first thing I saw was her, from behind, lying motionless under the covers, and the bed stained with blood. I thought: "It's over!" and I think my face became waxen, I felt my knees buckle. At that moment, the infant's crying, which had covered the sound of my steps, quieted a little, and she must have sensed my presence. She just raised her head, turning it toward me: she was pale but alive! And a smile of secrecy and fabulous joy transfigured her face. "Artú!" she said. "He's born, Carminiello Arturo is born!"

He started crying again; I glanced at him, but she was holding him under the blanket, so I glimpsed only a small fair head. Meanwhile, in a weak, confused, and anxious voice, she sent me away from the bed and the room, and asked me about Fortunata; and I rushed back down to the old woman. "Come on, hurry!" I scolded her fiercely, colliding with her in the entrance. "You're traveling on the slow train!"

Going back up behind her, I was able to see from the hall, where I stopped, that as soon as she entered the room she made as if to pick up the boy from the bed. But Nunz, as if someone were stealing him from her, quickly defended him with her arm and gave her a fierce, jealous look (not very different from the look that had flashed in her eyes the day she arrived, when I wanted to take from her hand the purse with the jewels; or from the look she had given me a few evenings ago, when she declared: *I, however, wouldn't let you leave!*).

"Eh, what are you afraid of?" said the midwife, insistent, with her brusque, military ways, "I won't break him!" Then Nunz laughed, ashamed of herself, and gave him up.

At that point, nauseated by the sight of that newly born creature, who was shrieking with his toothless mouth, I retreated from the hall into my room; but I left the door half open, so I could hear what happened, because I suspected that the old woman, with her executioner's hands, might still do some harm to N., or even kill her. Her powerful, muffled steps reverberated through the house, while she busied herself in the little room, and passed back and forth in the hall, moving with assurance, as if she were still familiar with our *castle*, though it was some fifteen years since she'd been there. A couple of times N.'s voice reached me, giving instructions, but so low and weak that I could barely distinguish the words. As for the midwife, she, as usual, expressed herself only in authoritative mumblings or bombastic utterances. And the only person with whom she deigned to converse was my stepbrother. I understood that, to wash and dress him, she went with him into an unused room, opposite the small room; so that, through the open doors, Nunz from her bed could watch the operation. And while she waited, in the bed, for the moment when she would have him again, the old woman, in attending to him, seemed to have a kind of private conference with him, as if only she could understand him, and the remaining persons of the family were nothing but common upholstery. "You," her large voice said to him, in a ceremonious and fascinated tone, "must certainly weigh more than four kilos. You're very handsome. Really a fine boy." And at these words N.'s faint voice could be heard from the small room, laughing, and pleased.

"And what nice flesh," the midwife went on speaking, in the other room, "you're a colossus, you're a feast of roses and flowers. And you came out all by yourself, with your own cleverness, what a good boy, like a rabbit. You'll learn to walk by yourself, with no help, and the girls will go crazy for you; and you'll sing like the tenor Caruso. What lovely hair, already curling. And lashes around your eyes already! You came out already decked in your own beauty! You're like a rose embroidered with gold. And what fine little thighs. What a fine bottom you have. And what's your name?"

From the other room, the small voice answered for him:

"Carmine Arturo."

"Oh, like that, you've got two names! I also have two names: Fortunata and Emanuella."

"But he," the little voice specified from the other room, with some emphasis, "is also named Raffaele and Vito."

. . . Here I, feeling dead tired, lay down and fell asleep. A couple of times in the night the urgent wailing of the infant wakened me; but, immediately hearing N. whispering in response, I fell asleep content, in the thought that she was alive. That whisper, carried to my half-closed door by the silent air, came very close to me, so that it seemed to be on my pillow. Near dawn, the song of a young cock reached me from a garden outside; and then, without opening my eyes, in a half sleep I imagined the island growing light, starting with the farthest strip of sea, up to the sandy beaches with the piles of cold seaweed. And the different colors of the houses, the beautiful gardens full of oranges, lemons, and dahlias. Since Nunz wasn't dead, I longed to return to run victorious over my lands, like a grand vassal who has recovered his domain!

My body relaxed contentedly into sleep, but my heart waited for the moment of rising with a mixture of joy, comfort, and curiosity. And even then I understood nothing; I couldn't foresee the sorrows, the torment, that the future days were already preparing for me.

## The Sea Urchin

From the moment we awakened, the next day was a happy celebration. The light had risen so clear that it seemed to be April, not November twenty-third; and after sleeping until late morning I ran to the beach and the wharf, coming back up from the direction of the square. The sea, the air, and all the things I encountered on the street shared my happiness, as if the entire universe were my family. The gardens along the street, which, last night, seemed desert mirages, avoiding me, today celebrated me faithfully. And again I was in love with my island, everything I had always liked I liked again, because Nunz hadn't died. As if, since the time when we were children, and I was here on Procida and she in Naples, it was she who instilled in the indifference of things a thought of intimacy for me, and without letting me know, like a great lady.

That very morning, she moved with her infant from the small room into a bigger one: the same that my father had assigned to her the day of her arrival, and where, at the time, she hadn't wanted to sleep. Now, though, with the arrival of the infant, the fear of being alone at night had ended. And as for the nuptial chamber, that remained again the undivided property of my father; since she foresaw that, on his return, he would not endure the child's crying every night and similar discomforts, which mothers don't mind.

And so that notorious room of the first day *is back in the headlines*, as the journalists say. Right away, we carried in a new bed, chosen for the occasion among the many unused in the *castle*. It was a massive wooden double bed, painted with images, such as used to be done in Sorrento (landscapes, boats, the tarantella, and so on), and rather elegant. It was supplied with two mattresses and many pillows, which her woman friends, immediately rushing to visit, carefully beat and plumped. And here, like a queen, she received the congratulations of the others.

She wore her hair bound simply with a band, as she usually had it at night; and on her shoulders was her woolen shawl, fastened with a common safety pin. She appeared proud, and even slightly self-important (but also, basically, confused), to be at the center of so many tributes; and toward her friends she maintained the attitude of a serious, reserved woman. If one of them began to lament, "Poor thing, you had to give birth alone, with no one, not even your husband around—like a cat! Your husband is always leaving you alone, eh, Donna Nunzià!" she responded only with a severe silence, as if warning that busybody to mind her own business.

When her friends picked up the baby to feel his weight and fondle him, a shadow of apprehension immediately veiled her gaze, in the suspicion that they would hurt him. But, still, seeing him there, raised in triumph like a hero, she laughed with joyous yet uncertain pleasure, as if wondering: "Is he really MINE? Is he actually MINE?"

When she nursed him, she took care to cover her breast with the shawl; and if at that moment she happened to see my eyes resting on her, she blushed and covered herself better. (It was no longer now as it had once been, that she felt no embarrassment toward me. Whereas I, now, felt that, even if she weren't embarrassed, I wouldn't be offended.) At intervals during the day I came back to see her, in the new room, and I sat down on the linen chest, and lingered. I think that on that day I would have been happy also to be her servant, if she had had need of it; but there was always at least one of her friends, often several, and I sat apart, sullenly, without speaking. Now that they were used to my presence, her friends weren't intimidated by me and chatted constantly; and it was annoying to listen to their nonsense. As for Carmine Arturo, he seemed so ugly, with that surly face that didn't even know how to laugh, that, in my opinion, he was worth less than nothing.

Yet even with so many people around she never forgot me. Sometimes, amid the conversations of those women, she turned to me alone, sitting silently apart, and, paying no attention to them, said, with a kind of timid intimacy: "Right, Artú . . . ?" Maybe she meant to ask forgiveness for the fright she had given me the night before! She said nothing but this: "Right, Artú . . . ?" Her voice, even now that she was the mother of an infant, had kept the known, slightly harsh, almost toneless flavor of a girl who hasn't yet grown up. And hearing that familiar small voice that said "Artú" when, a few hours earlier, I had believed she was dead, I felt a happiness so violent, and turbulent, that I became even darker in the face. It was my character. I wouldn't have minded saying to her at least these two words: "I'M HAPPY!" Often, during the day, I promised myself I would come into the room and tell her, without hesitation, "I'm happy," even in an indifferent tone. But in the end I had no wish to say even a two-word phrase like that.

The sight of Nunz alive, restored to health and spirits, smiling at me from amid her curls, at me alone, seemed suddenly a miraculous display, as if the island were populated by gods. And, not knowing how to give expression to the capricious joy that invaded my heart, after a while I left that too-enchanting room. Until today, happiness had been a natural companion of my blood, which might not even be noticed, like a carnal sister. But today at certain moments I felt this new thing: the unexpected, almost unhoped-for presence of happiness, which burned my mind; and I felt I was embracing it, and I didn't know how to distract myself with any other thought. Insolently, my joy invaded the light, the space, every corner of the house, even the dustiest storeroom. I decided to go out, to do something; I thought for example of going hunting and I started looking for a gun, which belonged to our servant Costante. I found it and, for fun, although it was unloaded, pretended to take aim against some object in the house, a chair, a shoe. Then, bored by the idea of looking for cartridges, I left the gun and went out, weightless and free. I wandered through the countryside, and climbed the first tree I saw that looked majestic; and from the height of the crown I began singing at the top of my lungs, as if the island were a pirate ship and I, at the top of the mainmast, its captain. I wouldn't have been able to say precisely what, on that day, I could expect from the future; only it seemed that, since Nunz was still living on the earth, tomorrow and every other day to come would be in itself a joyous surprise, and would bring me some mysteries of happiness. I felt grateful, but didn't know to whom, I didn't know whom to thank. And after brief moments of repose I was unsettled and restless again. I even had thoughts of a gallant knight: it occurred to me to bring Nunz some gift that would please her and give her a sweet sign on my part. One thing she loved, of course, was jewelry; but I had long since spent the last fifty lire my father had given me. Now, as I walked unoccupied along the beach, I noticed a sea urchin of a beautiful purple color, attached to a rock near the shore, almost on the surface of the calm, transparent water. And, remembering how much she liked sea urchins, I decided to bring it to her. I quickly took off my shoes, and went to detach it from the rock, with the help of my pocket-knife. Then I wrapped it in a piece of newspaper I found on the beach, and hurried home, eager for her to have my gift.

But, on the point of entering the room, I felt a sudden sense of embarrassment, maybe also of mystery, and I hastily hid the little package under my shirt. For more than a quarter of an hour I stayed there, sitting, as usual, on the old linen chest, without saying a word, amid all the chatter of her friends. I felt the spines of the sea urchin lightly pricking my chest, through the wrapping of newspaper; and that sea urchin bothered me, but on the other hand I couldn't find either the moment or the method of offering it. (Note: It wasn't that I considered it a gift too modest, or ridiculous because of its worthlessness! No, at that time I had strange ideas about the value of things, which didn't correspond to reality. And I had the conviction that that sea urchin was a splendid gift; but it was really the thought itself of offering her a gift that intimidated me: and, even more, in the presence of all those women.)

I recall that at least three or four times later in the afternoon I returned to the famous room or ventured as far as the doorway, or stood outside in the hall, indecisive, always with the intention of finally offering my gift: maybe rushing in, delivering it to her hands without a word of explanation, and running away. But every time I lacked the will to resolve on that step, until, when evening came, and I went to my room to sleep, I found the sea urchin there, wrapped in its piece of newspaper, and in vexation threw it out the window.

## A Surprise

That night, I recall, one of the friends stayed overnight at our house, murmuring with the others that the poor girl couldn't be left alone, the day after she had given birth, with no one, not even her husband, nearby . . . And then the next day we had an unexpected visit. If I think back to that visit, it still makes me laugh, irresistibly.

*Let's begin with the reconstruction of the facts.* A few days earlier, one of N.'s Procidan acquaintances had had to go to Naples for a day; and N., taking advantage of the occasion, had given her her childhood address, with the charge, if she had time, to bring her mother some dried fruits she had saved for her; and to tell her, at the same time, that she was well, sent her infinite kisses, etc. Now, that busybody, going, punctual and solicitous, to the Pallonetto in Santa Lucia, to N.'s mother, hadn't been content to bring her the fruit, the kisses, and the good news from her daughter, in accord with the commission she had been given; but, after a while, chatting, had taken it on herself to reveal the low opinion that our fellow citizens, especially the women, had of my father! As it seems, the Procidans considered my father a terrible husband, and N.'s friends and acquaintances, talking about her behind her back, lamented her fate.

First of all, they accused my father of leaving his wife alone all the time. In Procida, they observed, it's true, many wives were left alone by their husbands for long periods of the year, but those husbands were sailors: if they traveled far from their wives, the reason was their job. My father, however, wasn't a sailor; he was an idler, and if he behaved that way with his wife, it was because he had no conscience, etc., etc.

It's hard to imagine everything that that gossip said to N.'s mother (after at least a dozen oaths, on the part of N.'s mother, that she would never tell her daughter that the friend had been so underhanded!). Certainly the conversation between the two ladies must have been long and impassioned; in fact, I wonder that the woman didn't miss the return boat to Procida. In the following days, detained by her occupations, she didn't show up at N.'s, satisfied with sending word, through others, that her mother was well, sent kisses in return, etc. So N. remained absolutely in the dark regarding this story (and she remained partly in the dark about it forever, because her mother, having sworn so many oaths, would never admit the whole truth).

Neither N. nor I could have predicted anything: when, two days after my stepbrother's birth, in the afternoon, we heard a rather energetic knocking at the street entrance. Just then we were only three in the house: N. with the baby and me. And so it was I who went to the door. And I found myself facing a short woman with that weary, abundant, and immense corpulence that is proper to mothers of families. Her bosom, in particular, astonished me by its vastness.

On her feet she wore cast-off men's shoes, without socks; and the rest of her outfit was, besides shabby, rather slovenly and dirty. But still that unknown visitor was imposing because of an air of sumptuous grandeur, which derived from indignation. It was evident, in fact, that she was possessed at that moment by a passionate indignation: her black gypsy eyes emitted fire, and her attitude was that of a sultan determined to avenge an outrage. She was alone; but following her, outside the gate, I glimpsed a number of Procidan women, who must have accompanied her so far; and who, at my appearance, retreated, hurrying back down the path.

First of all, the mysterious stranger asked who I was: "I am Arturo!" I said. "Arturo, oh! My son-in-law's boy . . ." she said quickly. "And I am Violante, Nunziata's mother!" she declared.

Then, assertively, although with a very faint shadow of apprehension in her voice, she asked about my father; but at the response, that he was still traveling, she displayed a certain relief, and her audacity had no more limits. Vehemently she came through the door, asking in a peremptory tone:

"And my daughter, where is she? Where is my daughter?"

And she started immediately up the stairs, calling: "Nunzià, Nunziàààà!"

Here, although irritated by her manner, I considered it my duty to accompany her, since she was a relative of ours. Thus I resolutely pushed her toward the wall (the stairs were too narrow for two people to go up together) and, preceding her, led her to the second floor, to Nunz's room.

She was lying in bed with the baby, surrounded by four of her Virgins, happy and tranquil. But at first sight her mother shouted, "Nunzià! Nunziatè!" in a tone so tragic that it was as if she had found her bound in chains in the depths of a cellar, eating bread and water, beaten every day, and covered with wounds. Then, having exchanged with her some thirty or forty kisses, she left the bed and announced, with savage resolution:

"I've come to take you home, my darling. Get up right away, bring the baby, and in the nightgown just as you are, you'll come home!"

At this news, N., who at the appearance of her mother had become red with joy, changed her expression:

"Why, Ma? Did something happen? To . . . my sister?"

"No, nothing's happened, your sister is fine."

"Maybe . . . to Vilèlm?" N. then asked in a faint voice.

"Oh, no. Don't give a thought to him. I assure you that he's always fine. Enough, don't say a word, listen to what Mamma tells you. Look, we won't let him catch cold, we'll wrap him in that blanket. Oh, yes, of course," she added, casting her eyes spitefully in my direction, "we'll bring their blanket back later, we don't want to keep it. We'll send it right back tomorrow, with the cabin boy." At this point I whistled with extreme contempt and said to her: "You make me laugh!"

She went over again to N. and, with a domineering expression, kissed her all over her face; but my stepmother, although somewhat seduced by those kisses, didn't return them, and remained very serious, as if defending herself. "Really, Ma, if nothing has happened," she said, in an increasingly suspicious and restless tone, "why do you suddenly come and talk to me about leaving home . . . with this two-day-old creature . . . and unable even to tell my husband . . . ?" Upon hearing my father named, the other stopped kissing her. "Your husband . . ." she repeated with a grim look. Then, straightening up, she added, some sharp notes in her voice: "Oh, your husband! I forgot about him . . . In fact, tell me something! Why is he absent, these days? and where is he? Eh? We'd like to know!"

"Where is he . . . he's traveling . . . what do I know?" N. murmured, confused by this aggression. But, at that response, her mother's face betrayed true ferocity: "*What do I know*, eh?" she uttered. "Look what a fine answer a poor girl has to give, concerning her husband: *What do I know?* So for him the family is garbage, eh, that you leave in the corner! Oh, so they said, but I didn't want to believe it, and I came from Naples on purpose to find out!"

"Oh, Ma," N. exclaimed, rebelling, her lips trembling, and scowling fiercely, "after nearly a year we've been apart, you've come here to tell me these nasty things! And who was it who spoke ill of my husband? . . . It must have been Cristina, that gossip, who doesn't understand a thing!" she judged after a little, dark in the face, guessing readily the true origin of the outrage.

"Cristina . . . who? That friend of yours from Procida? Come on, yes! That poor woman! Who barely had time to say hello, deliver the package of figs, and say goodbye, or else she'd miss the boat! Eh, what do you suspect? She didn't say a thing . . . Now instead Mamma tells you truly, Nunzià, who it is that spoke to me: my heart, that's who spoke to me! I heard like a voice in my breast that said to me: 'Hurry up, Viulante, dig up that three lire fifty for the boat, no matter the sacrifice, and go to your Nunziata, who over on the island of Procida is weeping bitter tears.' And here, now, I get the proof of what my heart told me! When I hear that your husband doesn't even let you know where he is! Not even a postcard!"

"If he doesn't send news it's not to make me suffer, it's because he forgets! A man has so many thoughts, he can't always write to his family!" N. replied, more and more offended at those charges.

"Thoughts! who can understand them, those thoughts of his? Why wouldn't he tell you?"

"Well, he's not a woman, who thinks it's a sin to keep a secret!"

"And why is he always traveling? Maybe he's a sailor, him, that he has to be traveling all the time!"

"Oh, Ma, I can tell from what you're saying who talked to you! Because the people here, the Procidans, hate him, just for that reason: because they're sailors and they have to travel for money! While he doesn't travel to make a living and doesn't obey any government. He travels," she concluded proudly, "because it's fantastic! And to satisfy his whims!"

"Oh! Whims! Eh! So he's even found an advocate, he has! I know you, come on, ever since you were a child you were called *Nunziata, because she doesn't want to be contradicted.* But my name is Viulante, and I say: *Mea culpa!* Because I, I'm the one who gave my daughter to that murderer! You were against it, you had a feeling, and even though you're a child you had better judgment than Mamma! Think of it! It seemed to me I'd found America for you, finding that husband; but now my eyes have been opened, and I see this fine affair we've managed! Look who I married you to, you my own flesh and blood! I married you to a pig, a criminal, who left you to give birth here abandoned and alone, miserably, as if you were some prostitute. And always leaving you alone, without anyone, like you had the plague, while he goes off to have fun!"

At those invectives, N. seemed not only offended but frightened, and a cold pallor descended over her face, as if she were sick. She rose halfway up from the bed, placing one foot on the floor, and in a heavy, violent tone repeated:

"What are you saying? Be quiet, Ma." At the same time her eyes kept moving toward me, worried that I had had to hear that talk; and when her agitated gaze rested on me she let an affectionate smile show through. As if, among other things, she meant to say: "It's not true that I was alone: Arturo was here with me. You're insulting Arturo more than anyone: is he *no one*? Arturo, my dear companion!"

Then, feeling sorry for her, so humiliated by her mother, I responded with a glance that, along with a scornful shrug of the shoulders, meant: "Don't pay any attention to her, she's crazy, she doesn't know who she's talking about."

All this carrying on had agitated my stepbrother, who began to cry desperately. Immediately she turned her trembling, stern head and tried to console him; and, when he wouldn't calm down, she and her mother together began to say to him the usual stupid things that babies like. Finally, to make him happy, she gave him her breast, and while she nursed, the other remained quiet for some moments; then, suddenly, looking at her daughter with eyes of bitter passion, she broke into sobs and went out into the hall with her arms raised, and new tirades against my father.

Although I considered her of no account, I followed her lazily, hands in my pockets, to keep a closer eye on her. After all, since she was so angry at my father, and couldn't vent against him in person, she might, for example, go and tamper with his treasures: the underwater mask, the telescope, the fishing gun, etc., that he had left at home; and she might ruin them! Or maybe, in her fury, she would go and tear up my writings, my poems! But, luckily, she didn't dare so much; she contented herself with going around like an enraged bear, gazing at the walls with tearful eyes. "And this," she commented, "is the famous castle! This cave! Criminal murderer, he deceived me. To listen to him, he was a rich man, a millionaire, with his castle! But to me this looks like a cave. A real cave!" N. had come to the doorway with the infant at her breast, and, proud of her castle, at those words she exclaimed, amid tears of revolt: "Oh, Ma, what are you saying? Now, don't let people hear you, saying this is a cave! It's a valuable castle, partly because of its age, and everybody likes it!" But, looking with curiosity at our dirty, cracking walls, at the curtains that hung like rags, and at the floor that was like a field full of holes, I admitted to myself that, in reality, the comparison to a cave might be right. A cave! Or an enormous hut! (It should be noted that caves and huts, in my opinion, were very seductive places. And, as a result, I confess that even in the midst of such a drama I was happy inside about that interesting dwelling of ours.)

Involuntarily, N., with that last phrase, had provoked her mother to a fatal argument. At the words *everybody likes it*, she turned to her with an expression between rage and pity. "Oh, Nunziatè, don't contradict Mamma," she exclaimed, "when Mamma is here to defend her flesh and blood! Oh, yes, this cave is very fine! But Mamma is ashamed of having sent you here, it's so hideous! And no family would stay here: that's how much it's liked! Well . . . the devils like it, that's who likes it. Full of devils . . . Oh, You, my patience, help me not to overdo it!" she added, raising her eyes to Heaven and then covering her face with her hands.

But shortly afterward she showed her face again, with a different expression, grim and yet crafty: as if, behind the words she was about to say, she wished to imply also, on her account, who knows what other mysterious schemes! And, advancing toward us from the end of the hall, she began in a low, cautious voice: "You know, Nunziatè, you know, for myself there are certain things I believe and I don't believe. I don't say they aren't true—without a doubt, they are truth! Only, I don't always believe them. But surely you know what all the women down in the town say: that this house is cursed, and full of devils! They're evil spirits and as soon as they see a woman they wake up and come running from every direction, and join together; and sooner or later they cause trouble, because they don't want her here. And you know what they told me about your husband: that with all those spirits from Hell he's as happy as Satan, and in fact, some say, he brings wives here just to annoy those devils: because the angrier they get, the more fun he has! But you, my child, now, you listen to Mamma: she does not want to leave you here in this house!" And as she spoke she began sobbing more uncontrollably than before.

N., seeing her mother weep, couldn't restrain her tears; yet she reproached her: "Oh, Ma, in front of this infant, to speak of those things!" And with her fingers she made the sign of the cross on my stepbrother's forehead.

Here I decided it was time to intervene. "Now, come on," I said, contemptuous and haughty, addressing N.'s mother, "when will you be quiet? You make me laugh, and I don't even care to explain to you certain truths, because you wouldn't understand anything. But if all those women believe in devils, they shouldn't be visiting here all the time. They talk a lot of nonsense; and then every day here they are again! One after the other, they come here, to our house!"

N.'s eyes rested on me, moved and vehement, as if to thank me for my alliance; and as if such an alliance inspired her to the supreme retort!

"They come! Yes! To our house!" she repeated, in her most glorious way, a great lady even as she wept. "They come here! And they even have coffee!"

## Lamentations

Our relative stayed with us for four or five days, sleeping at night in N.'s room, where she had brought Silvestro's cot. From the beginning, though, she must have been convinced that N. was absolutely determined not to separate from my father and not to leave our house: on this point, there remained nothing for the mother to do but set her mind at rest. And so, resigned to fate, she returned to Naples, where her other daughter was waiting for her.

In the days she spent with us after that dramatic start, she proved to be more easygoing and even pleasant. She sat for hours in N.'s room, conversing with her about a quantity of Neapolitan people and doings; and N., who was never very talkative with the town women, with her mother, on the other hand, was eager to discuss. She returned willingly to her own life as a girl; and on various occasions she even talked again about Vilèlm. But if her mother hinted at some comment against him, N. immediately darkened, withdrawing into herself. She was like a sensitive plant when it came to anything that might sound insulting to him.

Yet every so often our guest could not help venting her bitterness against my father; and, not daring to insist on that subject with N., she sometimes vented even to me! I certainly didn't give her much satisfaction: at most I might concede a scowl, or some impatient grumbling. But, even if unwillingly, I sat and listened to her, since I was so eager to hear about him! She naturally didn't dare to say too many bad things. But although she tried to be moderate, she always ended by reiterating in every tone her irrevocable opinion that the marriage was an absolute disaster for N.

"Think," she repeated with pained and bitter looks that seemed to forget my person, as if she were speaking more to herself, "think that she, poor girl, was opposed to marrying him, she seemed to understand him, girl though she was: 'Oh, Ma,' she'd say, 'I don't feel I want to marry him!' 'You,' I said, 'speak with no knowledge. What are you looking for, the moon? A landowner, a millionaire, tall, handsome, who's mad about you . . .' 'To me,' she said, 'he really doesn't seem handsome. When I look him in the face, he gives me a sense of fear . . . I'm afraid of him . . . I'm afraid, Ma! I'd be happy not to get married . . . I'd be happy to become a nun . . .' 'You,' I said, 'you want to torture Mammeta, because you're more obstinate than a mule . . .' And so, insisting, I convinced her! And to do good I did evil, poor little girl of mine! Think! With so many fine young men who praised her, and they would have kept her like a rose in their buttonhole! Look, who did I settle her with instead? With that man . . . that man . . ."

Here N.'s mother, remembering that I was listening to her, recovered herself. But her eyes betrayed her hostility. It was evident that she was firmer than ever in her opinion that my father was a terrible husband. And finally, straining with every word to repress her angry scorn, she exclaimed:

"Is my child a cripple, an old woman, to be humiliated like this? Always alone, summer and winter, not even a line in the mail—worse than if she'd married a prisoner! And at least, when he does reappear, her husband should make a little more fuss, to console her. Instead . . . well, now I understand, how it is, this marriage . . . She won't say and she defends him, but, even if she doesn't want to, I can make her speak just the same. When I want to, with her, I've got a way, I know how to get the facts as they are . . .

" . . . Oh, my poor Nunziatella, she didn't deserve to get married with that fate! Because when a woman marries, it isn't enough to be married. A young married woman needs some other satisfaction as well. And the satisfaction is that her husband holds her near his heart, with some nice show of respect and feeling, and compliments her, with pretty words, and caresses, and kisses, even a husband's beatings are like Oriental pearls! And when it's cold and raining, it's like the house has a great heating system! For that affection! Enough! But a husband who doesn't put sugar in the coffee gives his wife a bad name: because a wife is not like a woman from a brothel, who he throws himself on for those two minutes, then turns around and fare-thee-well.

"Well, Violante, you can say it aloud: for that affection your Raffaele (even if he provoked you to resentment) could die with the conscience of the saints: because he kept his wife like a doll, and never made me look bad! Instead my poor Nunziatella—who would have thought?—had to get married for this shame: never some nice little compliment, never a caress, never a kiss: treated like a woman from a brothel.

"Imagine, such a pretty daughter, with that laughing mouth—folk would fall in love with her just saying hello! And when she passed by, the boys on the street, seeing all those curls, started singing, *Curly, curly!*"

The mother stated these great successes of N. with such emphasis and conviction that for an instant I was almost led to consider N. a kind of beautiful diva: and I saw her walking the streets of Naples, greeted by all the people; while a crowd of lovers, flanking her passage, sang serenades in her honor on mandolins and guitars!

## The Conversion

In those days, since I was often present at the conversations of N. and her mother, I got to know various details of their life in Naples: doings, friendships, acquaintances, etc.

But the most extraordinary fact I learned was one concerning Wilhelm Gerace. Although it seemed almost incredible to me, that fact was the plain truth; and in learning it I could explain what N. had meant, the long-ago day of her arrival, by the phrase *but your father is a Christian now*, which I had attached no importance to at the time. It was this: my father, in order to take N. as his wife, had converted to the Catholic religion!

By birth, as I've said, he was Protestant. Here is the story of his conversion, as I could reconstruct it from the conversations I heard.

Already for more than a month my father had been asking N. to marry him, and she, after much uncertainty, had just decided to accept him, to her mother's satisfaction, and was finally about to tell him her decision, when she learned that he wasn't a Catholic and that the marriage would be only at the city hall. At this news she had been so frightened that she no longer wanted even to see her suitor; and when her sister or other friends instructed by her warned that he was coming up from the street corner toward the alley, she immediately left the house, shaking like a madwoman, and took refuge in some other doorway. Her mother tried to restrain her, even rudely, because she was eager not to put off that suitor, the owner of a castle; but she developed the strength of a tiger, to free herself from her mother's hands; and repeated—as she'd already said, once and for all—that it was impossible, she didn't want a non-Christian husband, and rather than marry without the sacrament she would die. But her mother didn't dare tell the man; and when he asked, again and again, "Why isn't your daughter ever here? And may I know when she'll give me her answer?" she tried to appease him with some civilities, without ever explaining. Then he became increasingly impatient and wondered at never finding the girl, exclaiming every time: "What sort of nonsense is this, that your daughter's never home?" And, every time, the mother had to invent a new pretext, which didn't seem very convincing. He would sit there, waiting for his love, and meanwhile the mother, hoping that she would make up her mind to return, and at least greet him, tried to entertain him as well as she could with her conversation. But he sat sullenly, without saying a word, and didn't even look her in the face: he'd stay for half an hour, or even an hour: out in the alley, sitting on the chair in front of the door, kicking cans, or inside, lying on the bed, chasing flies. Finally he left, more sullen than before, and said to the mother: "Goodbye. Tell your daughter to be here tomorrow, at this time, because I'll come to hear her answer."

So much the better! In this way, he himself had given her warning beforehand: and the next day, long before the fixed hour struck, she took care not to be found, running away to hide in some hole-in-the-wall in the alley. "She had to go . . . you must excuse us . . . holy Madonna, no idea how long they'll keep that girl there now . . . She said she'll do her utmost to get back soon . . . but who knows? Circumstances beyond our control! You must excuse us," said the mother. And he decided to wait, sitting there like one who is meditating murder; but the girl didn't come out of her hiding place until one of her trusted friends told her that he'd grown tired of waiting and left.

Finally, one day, arriving without warning, he caught her at the moment she was fleeing, looking to hide in the alley; and he grabbed her and pushed her back into the house and drove the mother in, too. Then he closed the door and said: "You damn bitches: if you don't stop this comedy, the only way you'll leave is on a stretcher or in a coffin."

The girl, already unnerved by so many days of struggle and fear, barely had the strength to answer in a faint voice: "Don't hurt my mother. I'm the one who should die. I'd die rather than go through with this marriage." And then the mother intervened, and, with suitable words, trying not to offend his religion, revealed the truth.

When he heard it, he fell back on the bed, where he was sitting, and broke out into one of those laughs that he sometimes had: like someone watching a comic scene and, at the same time, eating a sour fruit. Then sitting up again he looked at the girl resolutely, with an expression that was tranquil yet threatening and ironic, and asked her:

"So, the whole story is that it's important to you to get married in church, in the Catholic rite?"

The girl nodded.

"I agree. What do I care!" he exclaimed. "As far as I'm concerned we can get married in a mosque or a pagoda, according to Chinese rites. I can become a Jew or convert to the prophet Muhammad. Anyway, I don't believe in any God, and, one or the other, it's all the same to me."

She sighed. He got up.

"Well," he said to her, "then we're agreed."

Trembling, and not daring to look at him, she moved her lips but didn't say a word. Then she sighed again and finally said:

"But maybe you don't know . . . ?"

"Come, what else does he have to know?" the mother interrupted. "He said he'll make you happy, that you can get married in church. Now leave him alone, so he can rest in holy peace! Why are you still bugging him now?"

"Oh, Ma, let me speak," the girl begged, almost in tears. "It's better to say it all right away, and not leave out anything." And in a slightly rough, cracked voice, catching her breath every so often, as if she were running, she resumed: "But you . . . do you know? That to have a true Christian wedding ceremony both spouses have to be Christians of the true Church, of the true family whose head is His Holiness Our Lord. I've been to the priest, here at San Raffaele, to find out all the explanations of the true ceremony, and the priest also told me that. Because for a true marriage it's not enough to be valid in this world, it has to be valid in Heaven as well. Because Holy Matrimony is a sacrament, and the sacraments aren't just written on paper, they're also written in Paradise. There in Paradise only the eternal truths are written, sanctified by divine approval and the approval of the First Apostle. And so the Lord made us this gift of the sacraments in order to assure us that a thing we do down here on earth becomes an eternal verity in Paradise. Two people can't be joined together without the eternal truth: that would be an ugly union. And so they both have to be Christians, with holy Baptism, Christening, and the Eucharist of the true Church presided over by the Holy Father who sits on the throne of Peter. Then a marriage becomes the true Christian sacrament! And if a marriage is not like that, I won't consent to it."

With the conclusion of her speech, the girl appeared to have consumed in the presence of her lover all the reserves of audacity she had left. From then on, in their later encounters, it was much if she sometimes managed to say four words together without trembling.

Briefly: that very day the indomitable suitor also accepted the final condition that she required, and that was to convert from Protestant to Catholic, performing all the duties imposed on novices in the Roman Church, up to the nuptial sacrament . . . And he listened, more curious than concerned, to the information that, with her few remaining breaths, she believed it best to impart: nor did he make any objections, only some slothful comments, as if certain things did not concern his soul and scarcely his body. Among other things, the girl told him that he would have to confess: "What! I have to confess!" "Yes, you have to make a general confession—of all the sins committed in your life . . ." she explained, in a voice hoarse with timidity, "and first you have to examine your conscience . . ." At this, he began to meditate, as if he were undertaking his examination of conscience at that moment; yet from his attitude one would have said that this examination didn't give him much trouble. "Well, of course," he declared then, in the tone of someone announcing a grand enterprise, "I'll make a general confession!"

So they became engaged. Now that she had promised herself to him, she no longer thought of avoiding him, although the mere sight of him, at a distance, could make her freeze with fear. What scared her most was to find herself alone with him; nor could she have said the reason for this, since, when there was no one else around, he treated her in the usual manner, neither paying her much attention nor offering her much intimacy, and he didn't even take her arm when they went out. In that they differed from all other lovers, who went around arm in arm, and close together; maybe, she thought, he was different because he was born in a foreign country, and that was how fiancés behaved in his country. If he sometimes touched her, it was only to hurt her; for example, pull her hair, or shake her by the arm, or other such abuses. They weren't terrible abuses, but enough to make her tremble. And then he'd let her alone and laugh fiercely, saying: "If you're so scared now, when we're barely engaged, what will happen when we're married?"

Meanwhile, she followed him in his apprenticeship as a Catholic, with constant secret apprehensions: since she couldn't forget that he had said he believed in no God.

As he had agreed, he performed all the acts and practices necessary to join the Church, and from his indifferent and enigmatic mood it was impossible to know what he thought about it. With his fiancée, he clothed himself in mystery on the subject; and once when she dared to express to him some worry he assumed a fierce and solemn pose, and reproached her for her doubts, even asserting that his conversion was so holy and conscientious that almost every day now he had visions of angels flying through the air, and other such marvels.

The moment for general confession arrived for him in the afternoon, the day before the wedding. He had her come with him to the church, where at that hour there was no other worshipper; and while he was at the grille of the confessional, she knelt in a pew not far away to wait. Every so often, amid the intense whispering close to the grille, lips concealed behind the hollow of his hand, he absentmindedly spoke a little louder; and then she was afraid of hearing some word of his, which would not be good, because confession is a secret between the priest and the penitent, and no one else should surprise that secret. But luckily the only phrase that reached her distinctly was this: *Word of honor! Word of honor!* Which, at intervals during the confession, the penitent repeated more than once. What, then, he affirmed on his honor only the confessor heard.

Since she knew that no living soul can sin fewer than seven times a day, the girl prepared for a long wait, considering that her fiancé had to recite all the sins committed in the course of an entire life: and given his age! But instead that confession lasted a much shorter time than expected: maybe six or seven minutes had passed, and no more, when he rose from the confessional and joined her, telling her to leave her pew, because he had finished. She obeyed; but on seeing him heading confidently toward the door of the church she whispered in astonishment, "You want to leave right away? And . . . the penance?" "What penance?" he asked. "What! Penance for contrition . . . I mean . . . prayers . . . the priest didn't order you to recite some Our Fathers . . . some Hail Marys . . ." "Oh, yes, it's true," he answered, "he told me in fact to say two Hail Marys, but there's time, before tomorrow: I'll say them later."

They were now outside the church, at the bottom of the steps; and she stood suspended, with one foot on the step, the news of that penance seemed to her so extraordinary. "What!" she exclaimed, confused and surprised. "Two Hail Marys! Only two Hail Marys after a general confession!"

At her wonder, he looked offended. "Well, then, Nunziata," he said, "what are you surprised at? Maybe you expected he'd give me a heavier penance? But that's a sign that you take me for a sinner!"

"No, you mustn't think that . . ." she apologized, "but all Christians, even if they're good, always find some failing in their life . . ."

"You insult me! Comparing me to all others! Remember, girl, that I'm a rare example of perfection on this earth: I deserve compliments, not penances! And in fact my confessor should feel remorse for those two Hail Marys! Apart from some lies and some bad words that I might have said in my life, I have nothing else to confess! And to give me a penance

for a few lies, even big ones, enormous . . . and a few curse words . . ."
Suddenly at that point he was overcome by a spontaneous joy. And sitting down on the step he burst into laughter, so fresh and irresistible that
he couldn't stop, and she herself would have started laughing frivolously
with him, if they hadn't been in front of a church, and in such a solemn
situation.

In the girl's eyes, that laughter, like a mysterious veil, further
obscured the already mysterious person of her fiancé, making him (it
seems strange) even more authoritative to her. "Why are you laughing?"
she finally dared to ask. "Because," he answered, "speaking of lies and
swear words I remembered some that a friend of mine once said . . ."
That very plausible explanation was enough for her; and so the discussion between the two of them ended.

Still, the fact of that laughable penance left her puzzled. She, at all
events, spent part of the night reciting entire rosaries for the intention of
all the sins that her fiancé, maybe because of a poor memory, might have
forgotten to say in confession. And when her mother, whose sleep was
disturbed by that constant murmur, began to protest, she was obliged,
to justify herself, to describe to her the entire scene in the church. (In
fact, it was her mother who then told it to me. And in large part I owe
not only this last scene but also the preceding account of my father's
conversion—along with other, less important scenes, which I'm leaving
out here—to Violante, not to Nunz. Nunz, on that subject, didn't say
much, held back by an extreme reserve, the same that she had, at other
times, for the things of Heaven. And the few words she said were in a
tone of solemn and extreme respect, as if she were recounting a legend
of Sacred History.)

Then one day after Violante's departure, returning to the subject
with N., I couldn't keep from pointing out to her that, in my opinion,
my father's conversion meant nothing. In fact, from what I could grasp,
I seemed to understand that he had converted without changing his

ideas, and almost out of amusement, as if he were playing a meaning-less game or making a bet. And that, in my view, shouldn't satisfy the Church but rather offend it, and also (admitting that he exists) God! At this speech of mine, N. looked at me with a profoundly serious expression (even in its unconscious childishness). And in an absolutist tone, which did not admit response, she answered that she, too, had at first had some similar thoughts; but then she had understood that they were bad thoughts, which would betray the first thought of God. And the first thought of God is the sacraments. It would truly have offended God had my father married without the nuptial sacrament; but he had had the sacrament—that was the important thing! Here, to demonstrate to me the true intention of God in the sacraments, she offered the example of baptism, which is usually given to infants, who understand as much as cats: and yet it saves them! And as for their extreme ignorance, she cited the case of a boy from Capua who was an acquaintance of hers, named Benedetto. He, at the age of one month, was brought to church to be baptized, wearing nothing but a little shirt (because his family was poor) that left his legs free; and the first thing he did, at the moment of the ceremony, was give the priest a kick on the chin! And yet the priest didn't consider himself offended, and baptized him just the same: because although that child, in his simplicity, didn't understand the great intention of the sacrament, the priest did; and God understood it—that was the important thing!

# CHAPTER 5

# Tragedies

*Tragedies*

My father reappeared after Christmas, when Carmine Arturo was already more than a month old. Arriving unexpectedly, he found three or four women friends of N.'s, who had come to see her. One might have thought that he would be surprised, or maybe even irritated, by that novelty; but instead he found nothing to criticize in the presence of those women and seemed barely to notice them. Although Carmine Arturo didn't know him and had never seen him before, he welcomed him with joyful laughter: more than anything, I think, because, having just learned to laugh, he laughed at any excuse, thinking that he was performing some great feat! But my father didn't even bother to pick him up, in order to appreciate his weight, as N.'s friends eagerly urged him to do; and while they, in chorus, praised that new son, his attention was dull and distracted, that of an unsociable boy who has grown up outside the family, and whose younger sisters are showing him their doll. That behavior toward the child consoled me a little, since I had expected new sufferings from an encounter between the two, and for one reason above all: that C.A. was blond! But, luckily, not even that remarkable characteristic of my stepbrother seemed to merit any particular regard on the part of my father.

It was, unfortunately, the only satisfaction I had on his return. In fact, this time he had disembarked on the island in a mood so preoccupied and dark that he was indifferent not only to Carmine but also to the rest of the family and every other thing. He seemed estranged from all the objects around him, as if he didn't even recognize them; and he himself (if I thought of how he was when I'd said goodbye to him, on his last departure, in the month of August) seemed unrecognizable. In the course of my life, I had grown used to seeing him vary frequently, like the clouds; but this time anyone who had looked at him with faithful eyes would have seen that he concealed in himself some absolutely new fantasy. During this last long absence, an unusual change had taken place in his expression. A kind of inert mask, as rigid as death, had descended over his face.

Not that he was ugly; rather, he was perhaps more handsome than usual! But that inner vain satisfaction that returns every so often to smile on the face of the beautiful was suddenly lost! When he said *I*, his mouth was slightly contorted, as if he were naming a person who scarcely concerned him. He was thinner and dirty; around his neck he still wore the pretty bright-colored kerchief he had acquired the previous summer, but it was all twisted like a rope, reduced to a rag; and his clothes were so wrinkled you would think that he'd slept in them for days.

He spent the rest of the afternoon and part of the evening lying on the sofa in his room, without even bothering to turn on the light. And when, seeking his company, I decided to go and see him, and turned the light switch, he looked at me distraught, as if the light, or my presence, offended him. His suitcase had remained in the kitchen, still closed, and I asked if he wanted to unpack it; but, in a tone of desperate impatience, he answered no, it wasn't worth the trouble, since he would be leaving again right away. And meanwhile I discerned a flicker of tears in his oblique, glittering pupils.

At dinner, he barely touched his food, and afterward he sat near the heat of the coals, without saying a word. Crouching there, like an animal, with the kerchief knotted at his neck, he seemed frozen and lost. It was clear that a single, uninterrupted thought, inscrutable to us, occupied his mind, without relief. His face was fixed, ashen; and every so often he drew weary, long breaths, as if he were suffocating. Sometimes a passionate, inexpressibly sorrowful shadow appeared in his eyes, softening his pride. But he immediately hid them with his fists, as if he were jealously protective of that shadow, and considered us unworthy of seeing it.

With the start of the new year (I didn't know that it was to be the last year I spent on the island!), he began to show up again fairly often. But never in the past had his visits been so futile! As soon as he arrived at home, he seemed sorry to be there, to the point of despair: so he hurried to leave again, and then, at the moment of farewell, parted from Procida unwillingly and, two or three days later, might reappear among us again! It seemed that he sought our company and, at the same time, couldn't bear it. One thing was certain: we had all become dull and insignificant for him (and most of all N., whom he now treated like an ancient relative of no account who has grown old in the house, and whom it's natural to forget). Mostly, he seemed to regard us from an anguished isolation, or not to notice us at all, but sometimes you might have said that he could scarcely forgive us for being alive, and that, by merely speaking or moving about freely, we were committing a breach of discipline and an offense. At such moments, a cry from Carminiello or the voice of N. singing in other rooms was enough to make him break out in mad invectives, in which he elaborated a dark fantasy!

On some days, though, finding no other outlet for his solitude, he could spend hours and hours in the kitchen, in the midst of the family, perhaps along with N.'s acquaintances. He sat apart, shut up in himself, and, with his unshaved beard, which grew over his whole face, he resembled an exile or a deserter. He neglected to shave for entire weeks; and when finally he decided to do it, he used the razor with such brutality that he always ended up with small cuts. He appeared almost to take pleasure in doing violence to himself, in making himself bleed: he who had once nearly fainted after colliding with a jellyfish!

When he didn't come down, he stayed in his room in a kind of lethargy. He remembered me only to send me to buy cigarettes, which he never had enough of and which he nevertheless insisted were bad. In his room there was a suffocating stench of smoke and stale air; yet he appeared to enjoy that, and sometimes closed the shutters so as not to see the light of day. What extraordinary events, after his departure of last summer, had affected him, reducing him to this suffering? What was the mysterious unchanging thought that for months had given him no rest?

One day, passing through the hall, I saw him, through the half-open door, sobbing hysterically and biting the bars of the bed. I got away quickly, on tiptoe, afraid that he would be offended if he knew I'd seen him sobbing like a woman. I recall, too, that I found him, perhaps more than once, lying on his back like a dead man, with one arm folded over his eyes, and smiling to himself. His lips moving in the smile seemed to sketch an absurd, sublime dialogue; but at the same time the smile had a bitter, sick twist: as if, in that dialogue, his questions received only refusal for an answer.

Later, I was to reflect on these things a great deal; but in those first months of the fateful year they were forgotten right away, passing, in their abstruseness, for lesser mysteries. I saw my father leave, return, as one sees a ghost; because, in that period, he wasn't worth much more than a ghost! The sufferings of Wilhelm Gerace had become secondary for me: I was too bound to my own sufferings to be interested in his!

My principal character was no longer Wilhelm Gerace. Now that was certain (or at least it seemed to me).

## Golden Locks

I wrote "my sufferings," but I should rather have written: "my suffering," because in fact the suffering, which had assailed me some time earlier, was one, and could be given only one name: JEALOUSY!

On another occasion, I had driven out as a wicked insult the suspicion, hinted at by someone, that I was jealous. But this time I had to yield to the evidence. Naturally, I would have died rather than confess it to others, but to myself I couldn't deny it: I was sick with jealousy, because of a rival. Now, as I'm about to say who my rival was, I don't know whether to be ashamed or to laugh.

It happened this way: as the weeks and months passed, Carmine Arturo, my stepbrother, who at first had seemed so ugly, was turning out to be beautiful: more beautiful than I was, I fear! His hair was not only blond but curly, and grew naturally in tiny tufts on his head, which perfectly imitated a little crown of gold. That gave him a look of valor and aristocracy, as if a title like Highness, or something similar, were due him, because of his curls. As for his eyes, they were mulberry-black, perfectly Neapolitan; but all around the irises they were infused by a deep, enchanted blue, so that his looks seemed to have a blue-black color. His complexion was fair and he was healthy and plump. His feet and hands, even in their diminutiveness, were shapely, with slender fingers and toes, and around his wrists and ankles were little sort of bracelets.

According to N.'s women friends, those small natural rings of flesh were a sure sign that he was born lucky. In fact, according to them, the good fortune of an infant could be guessed from the beauty and perfection of those bracelets, which most newborns have, since they're usually fat. His were really perfect, and if you added up the ones he had at each wrist and ankle it came out to three, which is the king of numbers! That meant that he would grow up to be a great man, courageous and daring, and the victor in any undertaking. That he would defend the unfortunate with his fist and charm even his enemies. That he would live to the age of ninety, always as handsome as a youth, and those fine golden curls wouldn't even go white. And he would travel over land and sea, under a rain of flowers, celebrated by all.

While N.'s friends contentedly counted and recounted his bracelets to confirm that exalted oracle, he was quiet, looking at them with a certain seriousness, as if he understood that this concerned his destiny. He seemed convinced that those women were a race of stupendous fairies, because they were friends of N., and he laughed when, seeing them again, he recognized them: as if yearning to fly he reached out from her arms toward them. But if, for some reason, she had to go somewhere, leaving him even for a single minute, he immediately burst into a desperate wail, as if from the most splendid triumph he'd been reduced to a wet rag. And in the arms of someone else he writhed ferociously, in a way that seemed to mean: "As for me, I might as well fall to the ground and die!"

In fact, the only true beauty for him was N. It was the presence of that unique beauty that like a magician made all others, even the ugly, as beautiful as saints; so that he loved the whole world and, being very flirtatious, made many conquests. But even his favorites, in the end, counted almost nothing for him. She was his passion. And, as the weeks and months passed, the more attached to her he became. And she returned that. Thus I saw another with that famous happiness that I had always longed for and never possessed!

He insisted that N. always be near him; without her, he refused even to go to sleep, and before sleeping he clutched a finger in his fist. While he slept, he kept his fists clenched, perhaps imagining that he was still holding on to her; and he stuck out his lips in an indignant yet loving expression, as if to say: "I've got you, I've captured you, and you can never escape!"

Now, when my father returned, it wasn't as before: she didn't immediately rush to bring her covers from the little room to the nuptial chamber! My father, to his satisfaction, slept alone, Silvestro's old room was abandoned forever, and her fear of the night had become a memory. I think that with Carmine she would have slept fearlessly even in a terrifying wilderness: as if that child of a few months were a heroic knight, who could defend her from any attack.

As for the present enigmatic tragedy of Wilhelm Gerace, one would have said that for her that tragedy, like all the other secrets of her husband, took place in a kind of mythic theater, whose signs and symbols were alien to simple reality. For a profane spectator, illiterate like her, it would be not only vain and futile but also disrespectful to attempt any explanation of the obscure legend represented. To intervene in it, then, would be a truly impious outrage. And, finally, it would be childishly insensitive to become seriously distressed for the great protagonist who there, on his unreal stage, plays out his inscrutable and necessary myth.

She was occupied with my father only to serve him and look after him (always, of course, in her rather rudimentary way, since she had never had the qualities of a capable housewife). She didn't question his orders, and flew to his calls; but for the rest she left him to his thoughts, as if he were a tyrannical and solitary lodger. The natural submissiveness that she usually maintained toward him resembled not a human passivity but the trustful ignorance of animals, without doubt or anxiety.

And so the secret affairs of Wilhelm Gerace, who left and returned surrounded by suffering, did not darken her happiness with her Carmine.

## The Attack

Now that she had Carmine, she was so happy that she was singing and laughing from morning to night; when her mouth didn't laugh, her eyes laughed.

In a few weeks she had flowered into an unexpected beauty, which seemed a miracle of happiness. Her old, indoor pallor had disappeared: and yet she lived no less than before inside the rooms. Her skin had assumed a happy, healthy pink coloring; and in her body what had been thin had filled out into a delicate female shapeliness. At the same time, though, she had become taller and more slender than in our first days; and she walked with more grace, light on her small feet.

The humiliation that (perhaps since her impoverished birth) had hindered her movements suddenly disappeared: soft as a cat, she hurried to Carmine's voice. And when she carried him in her arms, she didn't seem to resent that weight; rather, the more he weighed, as he grew, the greater the honor for her. In her proud bearing, her head was thrown back slightly, exulting in the contrast with those other curls, of gold.

She still wore her hair in coils, in the style I had taught her; but they'd come half undone, because of Carmine, who played constantly with her curls. He played with her curls and with her face, with her chain and with her body; and she laughed, with an impulsive, fresh, wild freedom. From early morning, I heard them from my room as, barely awake, they began to play, mingling games and laughter, conversing in their manner. I listened to the words that, better than a poet, she invented to praise him; and as I listened, bitterness ran through my veins. Sometimes that bitterness was so intense that I almost wished not to have been born.

It was the injustice, more than anything else, that upset me: for in all my life I had never had the satisfaction of feeling so adored by someone. And yet—although I was dark, and not fair like him—I wasn't ugly. My father himself had said so more than once, for example, on that distant evening when he had said, in her presence: *He's a good-looking boy—not for nothing is he my son!* And similarly on several other occasions in the past. At most, however, his remarks had been: *Eh, come on, you know perfectly well you're not ugly*, or, *Let's see how handsome you've*

*grown in my absence. Well, not bad,* and that was all. Nothing compa-
rable to the fabulous praise that she showered on my stepbrother, and
which even if it sounded incoherent seemed, maybe for that reason, even
sweeter. Now more than ever I understood what pleasure it is, for a man,
to have a mother.

Not only was she constantly praising and caressing him; but, very
often, she talked to him seriously, as if he, who understood nothing,
could understand her, and his tiny inarticulate responses were enough
for her. Now she had this new company, and needed no other. Content to be with him, she forgot about any other person. Ever since the
weather had begun to get warmer, she carried him in her arms wherever
she went, even in the morning when she did the shopping, although she
already had the burden of the shopping bag; and he was delighted as if
he were traveling in a carriage amid exciting unknown marvels: maybe
realms or ports along the seacoasts, bazaars of jewels and gold!

Sometimes, talking to him in the usual way, she pretended purposely to scorn him. "You're so ugly and toothless," she would say to
him, "what am I going to do with you? You know what I'll do? I'll carry
you down to the square and sell you." Then I tried to imagine, like a
dream, the impossible case that she really didn't want anything more
to do with him, and sold him like goods, threw him away, handed him
over to a pirate ship! Merely picturing this dream in my mind I felt some
satisfaction, and some semblance of relief.

                                                 ఌఌ

I thought back to how offended I was the day she had proposed that I
call her *Ma*; and I still recognized that I was right to be offended. And it
didn't seem just to me that, while I didn't have a mother, she had a son.
But I haven't yet named my most intolerable source of envy. It was this:
That she gave him kisses. Too many kisses.

I didn't know there could be so many kisses in the world: and to think that I had never given or received any! I looked at those two kissing each other as someone on a solitary boat at sea might look at an unapproachable, mysterious, and enchanting land, bursting with leaves and flowers. At times she gave in to the same mad games that small animals play with their siblings: grabbing him, squeezing him, tumbling him over, without ever doing him the least harm; and it all ended in innumerable kisses. She said to him, "I'm hungry! I'm going to eat you!" pretending the ferocity of a tiger, and instead she kissed him. And, seeing her pretty mouth stick out in those pure, blessed little kisses, I repeated to myself that this world is an abomination where one has so much, and another, nothing; and I was filled with envy, raptures, and melancholy.

I went out, and it seemed to me that everyone on earth was doing nothing but kissing. The boats, tied up next to one another along the edge of the beach, were kissing. The movement of the sea, flowing toward the island, was a kiss; the grazing sheep kissed the earth; the air amid the leaves and grass was a lament of kisses. Even the clouds in the sky were kissing each other! Among the people out on the streets there was no one who did not know that taste: women, fishermen, beggars, children. I alone did not; and I had such a yearning to feel it that night and day I thought of almost nothing else. I started kissing, as a test, maybe my boat; or an orange I was eating, or the mattress I was lying on. I kissed the trunks of trees, the water coming up from the sea, I kissed the cats I met on the street. And I realized that, though no one had taught me, I could give very sweet, really lovely kisses. But when I felt against my lips nothing but cold vegetable pulp, or rough bark, or a salty bitterness; or saw myself next to the protruding muzzle of an animal, which purred and then suddenly took off, on a whim, unable to say anything to me—then I was more and more embittered by the comparison with that holy, laughing mouth, which, besides kissing, could say the gentlest human words!

I said to myself: "Some day or other, I, too, will kiss a human being. But who will it be? When? Who will I choose, the first time?" And I began to think of various women I'd seen on the island, or of my father, or of some ideal future friend. But when I imagined such kisses they all seemed to me insipid, worthless. To the point that, as a kind of good-luck charm, though I hoped for the best, I rejected them all, even in my thoughts. It seemed to me that one could never know the true happiness of kisses if the first, most gracious, heavenly kisses were missing: *the mother's*. And then, to find some consolation and repose, I pictured in my mind the scene of a mother kissing a child with almost divine affection. And that child was me. But the mother, even without my willing it, did not look like my real mother, the dead woman of the portrait: she looked like N. That impossible scene repeated many times in my imagination, as if in a marvelous theater that belonged to me. I delighted in it, almost to the point of deluding myself; and when, in reality, I saw N. again kissing my stepbrother, he seemed to me an intruder, who had taken my place, and she a traitor. I felt an angry instinct to insult them, to brutally interrupt their idyll; and only pride prevented me, while in vain my reason repeated: "What right would you have?" Out of pride I appeared indifferent, I made an effort not to look at them, I kept away from them; but soon a mysterious will called me back. Along with jealousy, I felt a bitter curiosity to look again at the grace of her kisses. And at the sight of those kisses, I imagined, until I felt it on my lips, a strange and delightful taste, which was like no other taste on earth but was miraculously like N. Not only her mouth but also her habits, her character, her whole person.

One day, entering her room when she wasn't there, I was tempted to kiss one of her garments. The usual pride prevented me: as if she were a lady and I a poor boy who received alms from her! Another day, however, overcome by a new temptation, I took from the kitchen table a piece of bread she had bitten, and ate it secretly. I had a taste of stolen sweetness and, at the same time, of many wounds: as when one plunders a beehive.

If that other boy, who got so many envied kisses, had at least been ugly, defective, I could have been somehow comforted, comparing him to myself. Instead I felt more and more discouraged by that comparison, because the more he grew, the more beautiful he became. He had taken, one might say, not only all the handsome features of my father but also those few of his mother; and as for ugly features, although you might wish to find some, he had none. The particular beauties of the two of them, then, were not reproduced in him as in a copy; but combined in an unexpected way, which seemed a new, original, imaginative invention. To be sincere, as far as I could see then and later, even in Naples and in all the other places I traveled, I never saw a boy who was handsomer than my brother.

And his beauty was my persecution: even when I was alone, during all the hours of my day, I thought I saw him waving before my eyes, like a flag, white and blue, blue and gold, whose intention was to provoke me. One day (while N. was upstairs, and he was sleeping in his basket in the kitchen), I felt such a thirst for revenge that I was tempted to kill him. Among the few mementos of past epochs that remained in the house was, in the great room, an antiquated pistol, now useless and rusty, of the type you load with wadding. I got the idea of using the heavy butt of that weapon to strike my enemy in the middle of his forehead, precisely and violently, taking away his life with a single blow; and with the pistol under my arm I approached the basket where he was sleeping. But it didn't seem fair to kill him unaware, as he slept; and so I decided to wake him first, and I lightly tickled the palm of his hand. He, at this tickle, moved his lips into a funny expression, which made me laugh; so that the wish to play with him overcame the wish to kill him. And as I tickled him on the palm of his hand, in his ears, and on his neck, I imitated with my voice the sound of some exotic feline animal; until, perhaps hoping to find a small leopard or some such creature in the kitchen when he awoke, he began to laugh in his sleep. So it all ended in fun, and my murder went up in smoke.

Now these facts seem so ridiculous that I can't even be serious while I'm recounting them, as if I were telling some extraordinary jokes, and not realities. But think: how angry I was at the time.

## The Great Jealousy

It was torture to see how his simplest actions—for example, offering a bread crumb to a rooster, or shaking a rattle enthusiastically—to her seemed splendid feats. And whenever he, who had never seen or known anything, discovered something new, like the existence of rabbits or that fire burns, she honored him like a great pioneer. If there was something beautiful to see, she became impatient to show it to him; the moon rose and immediately she rushed to pick him up and carry him to the window, saying, "Carminiè, look! Look at the moon!" A boat went by on the sea and immediately she rejoiced, knowing that he liked to see the boats move. And as soon as it seemed (according to her, at least, and those other female adorers) that, in his way, he had learned to distinguish an object by name, for example a chair, the chorus of all those women, along with her, began exclaiming, "Good for you, the chair, yes! Beautiful, the chair! Beautiful! Beautiful!" in a bombastic and obsequious tone. As if that chair, owing to the fact (presumed by them, however!) that he recognized it by name, had suddenly become a distinguished lady. But if, let's suppose, he happened to bump into that same chair and hurt himself, it descended to a low category of delinquent, and was proclaimed ugly, and ill treated and beaten without mercy.

I began to turn up more often in the kitchen, where N. spent with Carmine the greater part of her days. I'd arrive, and to force her to notice me I'd walk up and down with an almost threatening air, or collapse on the floor, yawning, or sit close to her for long periods, dark and proud like a living reproof. Yet one might have said that for her I had become an invisible body, or less. Many times, on those evenings, I made a show of unfolding on the table the famous maps from the atlas, drawing firm pencil lines on them, far and wide; but to no effect. She sat near Carmine's basket, singing softly to him, without concern for my affairs. Often, I picked up the book of *Great Leaders* again, pretending to read it (since I wasn't really in the mood for reading). Every so often, I purposely chose some surprising passage, and read it aloud, commenting with noisy, emphatic exclamations! But she, distracted, barely asked, "What are you studying, Artú?" and returned to Carmine, to observe him anxiously, thinking she'd heard him cry in his sleep.

One day, seizing a moment when her eyes had come to rest on me, I made up my mind and ran at the bars of the window, doing a *flag* and other exercises; and the result was that she exclaimed, "Carmine! Look how wonderful! Look what Arturo is doing!" as if I were an acrobat for Carmine's enjoyment! So I immediately jumped down and left the kitchen, trembling with hidden rage.

This time, I almost swore to leave that wretched woman with her Carmine, and to consider her, too, an invisible being, absolutely forgotten. But, unfortunately, I couldn't resign myself to such an idea: if for no other reason than that I had to punish her. Inside, I accused her of being vile, just like the typical stepmother, who, as soon as she has her own children, throws her stepchildren aside. And I would have liked to imitate the rejected stepchildren of novels, leaving the inhuman stepmother, and trusting to luck. But alas, how could I? Now that I knew she was faithless, I was sure that if I left I would be canceled from her memory: I would no longer be even a stepchild for her, or even a distant relative. To that I couldn't adjust; and so I planned to carry out some grandiose action, so that even from a distance she would be forced to admire me, take an interest in me. For example, join an aerial expedition leaving for the Pole . . . or write a poem so sublime that I became famous as far away as America, and the Neapolitans would decide to erect a monument to me in the harbor square . . . When, at the peak of my triumph, I saw her on her knees before me in admiration, I vowed I would say to her, "Go to your Carmine now. Farewell."

But such plans were too uncertain and remote to console me, in the impatience of my daily disappointments. Besides, those very disappointments, and their cruelty, kept me chained to the island. Because she was on the island, and I couldn't help staying near her, if only to bear witness, by my presence, to our betrayed past and her unfaithfulness.

Now I learned that many poets speak the truth when they affirm the inconstancy of women. And they don't lie about the beauty of women, either; but among all the famous women celebrated by poets none appeared to me worthy of competing, in beauty, with N. In fact, I thought, it doesn't take much to appear beautiful when, like those women, you not only are endowed by nature with locks of gold, and eyes of periwinkle, and a statuesque body but also have garments of brocade, garlands, and diadems! To have, instead, a body with no beautiful aspect, in fact ill-proportioned, with meager, shapeless features, and black hair and eyes; to have broken shoes on your feet and ragged clothes—and, with all that, to be as beautiful as a goddess, as a rose! That is a supreme boast of true beauty! And such beauty can't be described in a poem, because words are inadequate; or painted in a portrait, because it's not a thing that holds still. Maybe music would serve better; and I wonder if, instead of a great commander or a poet, I wouldn't prefer to become a musician. Unfortunately, I've never studied notes, and although I have a good singing voice, all I know are a few Neapolitan songs . . .

Even her irredeemably ugly features now appeared to me unique, incomparable charms; in fact, I was convinced that if by a future miracle those ugly features were to be replaced by perfect ones, her beauty wouldn't gain from it: but the opposite—and I would always regret her the way she looked now. I considered her so beautiful! And it didn't seem possible that all others didn't share my opinion: since even the simplest greeting, the most common words addressed to her, seemed to me reverent tributes, signs of adoration!

And if I thought back even a few months earlier, when that beautiful mother had treated me as one of her dearest relations, considering my orders an honor, sighing for my company—I rebelled at the vile reversals of fate! I felt I could never have peace if she didn't return to being, toward me, at least, the same as she had been before the fatal arrival of my stepbrother; and yet at no cost did I want to betray that longing to her. So I looked desperately for a means that, without wounding my pride, would force her to be concerned with me, or to manifest, once and for all, her irremediable indifference toward Arturo Gerace.

## Suicide

One morning, coming up from the harbor, I met her running down the hill with Carmine held tight in her arms, to give him a thrill. Running, she sang the Neapolitan refrain *Vola vola palummella mia* (Fly, fly my little dove), in a loud voice, like the gypsies. And though she passed close by, she didn't even notice me.

I arrived at home alone and so despondent that my heart was aching. I felt that I could no longer endure this abject state of abandonment she'd left me in. And at the idea of seeing her return, as if nothing were the matter, happy with her Carmine and as usual indifferent to me, my will rebelled, almost exulting in the desire to break this bitter monotony. I decided that I had at all costs to punish that woman and, at the same time, force her to be interested in me, instead of in my stepbrother, for at least a day, an hour! And I suddenly decided on an extreme stratagem, which had flashed through my mind many times during these miserable days.

It now seemed my last remaining recourse, and consisted in this: my death! Maybe the sight of my lifeless body could still make an impression on her. Naturally I didn't intend to actually die but to feign death, planning a scene of terrible verisimilitude, so that she would surely fall for the deception.

I thought again of that time when I was laughing but had pretended to be crying; and she (who until a moment before had been resentful) had become suddenly alarmed and moved, saying in a voice of compassion: "Artú! Why are you crying? What's wrong? Tell Nunziata!" At the memory of that success, the present, and quite different, performance seemed more tempting than ever. And with supreme determination, estimating that because of her errands she would be down in the town for about an hour, I quickly prepared to carry out my plan before her return.

My father in those days was traveling; and I went up to his room, knowing that I would find what I needed there. He had been suffering from insomnia, and often used sleeping pills, and when he departed he had left on his dresser an almost untouched package. I knew the powers of those pills from conversations I'd happened to overhear: in the dose used by my father (one, or two at most) they were a mild remedy, but if you increased the dose they would become a poison. If you took, for example, twenty, they could even cause death.

I dumped the pills from the package into my palm and counted them: there were nine, just the number I needed, according to my calculations. In fact, as far as I knew, that couldn't kill a man but would certainly be enough to cause a collapse that appeared tragic. What sort of collapse it would be I couldn't, in my ignorance, predict, except imprecisely; but I trusted in a fairly spectacular effect.

And, taking all the pills, I went to the kitchen and wrote the following message on a piece of paper, which I left unfolded and in plain sight on the table:

MY LAST WILL
I WANT MY REMAINS TO BE BURIED AT SEA
FAREWELL
ARTURO GERACE

N.B. DESTROY THIS PAGE AFTER READING
SECRECY! SILENCE!!!
ARTURO

Then I poured some wine in a glass, thinking that the wretched drug might have a bad taste and the wine would improve it. And I went out into the yard, since the kitchen didn't seem a fitting place for a suicide.

The yard seemed the ideal setting: since N., on her return from shopping, always came home from this direction. I wondered what she would feel when, soon, passing through here, she came upon my body; and I deplored the action of the sleeping pill, which, in all probability, would prevent me from judging my success. I would have liked to have a double, to be present at the scene; and I was tempted for a moment to throw out the poison and pretend to be a corpse, trusting uniquely to my theatrical talent. But in that case I saw that at the critical point of the tragedy I would be unable to keep from laughing, and would ruin everything; and so I discarded that idea.

## The Pillars of Hercules

I placed the glass on the doorstep and sat nearby on the grass, holding the pills in my fist. On the point of carrying out this strange act, I hesitated, between the decision made and an instinctive dismay. I considered it certain, it's true, that my imminent suicide would not in fact be mortal: what I knew, regarding the specific dose of this poison, had been affirmed by my father, too. It was science, and left no doubts. But still I looked at the pills in my hand as if they were barbarian coins, a toll to be paid for crossing a final, obscure border.

The fact was that I had no experience of drugs, of illnesses, or of poisons, and the laws of science, which I had never studied, seemed to me full of almost religious mysteries, like the laws of magic to a savage. In my imagination, the line that separated the evil sleep of this poison from death was confused. What I was about to confront I pictured as a kind of foray into the territory of death. Then, like an explorer, I would turn back. But death had always been so odious to me that the suspicion that I was advancing even within the compass of its shadow horrified me.

A sentimental weakness surprised me: a longing that some friend, at least, should be nearby, to say goodbye to me at this false suicide. A male friend, not a woman, since women are a faithless race, and I would never be in love with one. The only woman I would have liked to have near was my mother. A living mother, however, not the old one, who was once conveyed through the air of the island in her Oriental tent. Today I felt sympathy for my old illusion: I had since learned that death has a harsh will, never merciful. That beautiful childhood countryside was not suitable to the harshness of the dead.

The first Signora Gerace, like poor Immacolatella, shunned this shining morning. The March equinox, which on Procida practically announces summer, had passed several days earlier. And the air and the water were both so clear that the shape of Ischia, vivid there across the water with its cottages and the lighthouse, was doubled in its own marine reflection. Everything appeared sharp, precise, and isolated in itself, but the countless points of things also mingled in a divine, joyous color, green, blue, and gold. In a moment, that color will be different: imperceptible variations, like a whirl of marvelous insects, spin without pause in the light. Even the grim prison, up at the top of the hill, is a rainbow of a thousand changeable colors from morning to night. Now from the bay the screech of a waterbird is heard, from the harbor behind it the whistle of a ship, then from the town a pealing of bells . . . Even the enclosed spaces in the prison hear these notes, even the owls who don't see by day, even the dumb anchovies dying in the net . . . The happy sounds and iridescences of reality are an enchanted theater that captivates every last living heart.

I was curious to know if the sleeping pill would give me dreams. And do the dead, too, have dreams? So that clown Hamlet supposed; but I'm not a clown like him and I understand the truth clearly: that in death there is nothing. Neither repose nor wakefulness, nor air space, nor sea, nor any voice. I closed my eyes, and tried for a moment to imagine myself deaf and blind, contained in my body and unable to move, cut off from every thought . . . But no, it's not enough: life remains, there in the background, like a point of light, multiplied by a thousand mirrors! My imagination will never be able to conceive the restriction of death. Compared to this lowest measure, not just the existence of a wretched prisoner in a cell but even that of a sea urchin attached to a rock, even that of a moth, becomes a boundless domain. Death is a senseless unreality, which signifies nothing and would muddy the marvelous clarity of reality.

And it seemed to me, as it must have to the sailors of antiquity at the Pillars of Hercules, that I would soon be sailing on a murky current that would drag me away from my beloved countryside toward some shadowy grave.

I wondered, meanwhile, will that poison have a very bitter taste? You would think so, from the expression of annoyance that my father always has when he drinks it; but he confines himself to the prescribed dose, while today I intend to go far beyond the boundary of the forbidden! My superiority filled me with pride. Suddenly the mastery I would demonstrate, the infraction, and the pleasure of the attempt became the most important motivations for this willful act, almost canceling out my original purpose and even the memory of N.! Like King Ulysses, when he rounded the Sirens' cliff, I felt free and alone before a choice: either the attempt or the surrender! And I was invaded by a mysterious and unprecedented taste for play, for an audacious challenge: as if I were a bold officer who, after the fires have gone out, and while the sentinels sleep, makes a raid into the enemy camp, alone, with no escort, trusting in the safety of a moonless night!

I still have the taste of the first of those pills on my tongue: it was faint, a little salty, and very slightly bitter. I swallowed it, with a sip of wine, and everything around remained the same: it seemed to me only that as far as the line of the horizon a fascinated silence had fallen, as at the circus, when the valiant trapeze artist hurls himself into the double somersault. I continued, impatient and careless, swallowing with the wine two or three pills at a time; I think the action of the wine preceded that of the sleeping pills, since I quickly felt drunk. I began to hear a distant buzz, and I supposed that thousands of sawfish were sawing the island at its root. I expected that the entire landscape would be ruined, and such an event seemed to me almost quieting. In fact, the beautiful morning, which pleased me before, now had become repulsive and tedious. The immense dust cloud of the sun, sluggish and sulfurous as a plague, hurt my nerves. I had the desire to throw up there on the grass the wine and all the rest; but I restrained myself; and with the absurd idea of going to rest in the shade, I managed to get to my feet. I think I took a few steps; but I felt a helmet of heavy metal on my head, pushed down over my eyebrows, which could never be taken off, its brim darkening my sight. This was the last thing I was conscious of. I didn't even notice that I fell; and from that moment the universe disappeared. I no longer was aware of anything, I didn't remember, or think, or feel anything else!

## From the Other World

I learned later that my total absence lasted around eighteen hours; but for me it could have lasted five hundred years: it would have been the same. Although I searched my mind subsequently, too, for some trace of those eighteen hours (packed with movements, voices, and noises, of which I was the center!), I could find nothing. That interval isn't even a dream, or a confused shadow: it's zero. And from the point when I tried to move out of the sun in the yard until I came to at dawn the following morning, less than an instant passed for me.

The first impression I had, after what appeared to me an instant, was not that I had returned to life, as I had in reality; but, on the contrary, that I had fainted and died. I didn't know where I was, or the circumstances of my end: I had no consciousness of anything but that end. I felt a terrible nausea, all my senses were spent, in silence and in blindness; and I felt only the agony of my breaths, which separated painfully from my heart, gradually losing the strength to get to my mouth. I said to myself: "I would never have believed that my fate was to die today, and yet here's death, now I'm ending, I'm dying," and, in that feeling, I became inanimate again for another long period. Of this second period, however, a semblance of memory remained, as of a wire along which my consciousness advanced, wavering, like a tightrope walker. I realized that I was lying with my eyes closed, and that seemed natural, since I considered myself dead. Snatches of voices, lost in a monotonous din, perhaps of the sea, reached me. "See, I'm no longer in life," I thought dreamily, "and yet I *hear*. So one doesn't end, with death," and even within the illness that gripped me, I felt, deep down, a tremulous, very faint sense of adventure: "Let's see now what there is in death. I wonder if you really do meet the others again? Maybe I'll see my mother, Immacolatella, Romeo . . ." Among the other vague voices, a high small woman's voice could be distinguished, which cried, sobbing, "Artú, what have you done?" and I understood lucidly that I answered aloud: "Is that you, Ma?"

Every so often I fell back into a dull torpor; and then I heard that tearful voice again. A confused notion formed in my mind: maybe the eternal struggle of the dead was to go around groping for one another, without being able to meet. Every means of orientation has been taken away from them. My beloved mother heard that I was nearby, and called me, and I answered her; but our voices resounded in vain, like mindless echoes, without direction.

More than once it seemed to me that I cried, "Oh, Ma, oh, Maa!" when, unexpectedly, the well-known voice that continued to repeat, "Artú, what have you done?" sounded clear and concrete, next to my ear. "Finally, look, she's here," I said to myself, and reopened my eyes. Then I had again, for a moment, the consciousness of present reality. I was alive, that woman who was invoking "Artú" was not my mother but my step-mother. And the supreme motivation of my existence was: to kiss her.

A rapid and decisive impulse said to me secretly: *Now or never!* And although I still felt almost lifeless I raised my arms and hugged her. I felt, on my face, her curls, her tears, a soft and marvelous springlike fresh-ness. And, like a deep breath, a profound joy went through me: "Now," I said to myself, "even if I were to die from this suicide, I could die happy."

And I stuck out my lips; but, too weak, in that gesture I fell back half fainting on the pillow, without having kissed her.


## Silly Little Kisses


My illness lasted a few more days; as far as I understood later, it seems that the dose of sleeping pills I had ingested, insufficient, according to the information I had, *to kill a man*, might very well have been enough to kill someone of my age—that is, still more a boy, in spite of my claim. So, without intending to, I really had risked death; and I had been saved thanks to my good physical constitution. I was sick in bed, however, for almost half a week, something that had never happened to me before, as far as I could remember. I suffered from a headache, from a weary sleepiness, and every so often from dizziness and nausea, because of which my bed seemed to roll like the hull of a ship. If I wanted to get up and walk, an absolutely new phenomenon surprised me: my body no longer obeyed me. My knees buckled, I swayed, and my heart pounded. I no longer seemed to be Arturo Gerace, with an armor of muscles at his command, but like a girl, wan and indolent, with joints as delicate as stems.

From time to time, I felt my strength return; but, although I had always considered being sick a huge bore, I almost would have liked to prolong this illness. Because N. was always near me, watching over me, and attended to nothing else. To say that she was an exemplary nurse would be a lie, as far as I can understand these things: by her nature, in fact, she didn't possess the special gifts (even the practical) required of a nurse; it wasn't her fault. But the intention was there; and, besides (here is the most important fact), it was clear, from her looks and her behavior toward me, that in those days her entire soul, with a kind of sublime intensity, aimed at a single purpose: the beloved, precious existence of her stepson Arturo! To safeguard my cure, she had taken care to hang one of her Madonnas at the head of my bed: in fact the most magical, the infallible: the Madonna di Piedigrotta. And sometimes I could surprise her looking at me, while she thought I was asleep, in the act of whispering, hands clasped, to that famous Virgin, her suppliant eyes wet with tears and made luminous by heavenly superstition. And for whom was she praying? For me! When she wasn't praying, she spent hours sitting on the couch opposite my bed, watching over my breathing and waiting for every sign of life with the same holy expectation with which savage tribes await the rising of the sun. I will always see the angelic grace of her disheveled, bundled-up figure, in the disorder of those days, sitting across from me, her hands lying in her lap in faithful and passionate idleness. Beside her was a big basket containing Carminiello, fast asleep: afraid that his rowdiness would disturb me, she tried as hard as possible when he wasn't sleeping to keep him quiet, in some other room far from us, alone or in the company of those Procidan women. He didn't hesitate, of course, to cry for her, but if just then she happened to be busy caring for and ministering to me, she let him cry without paying attention, even for five or six minutes in a row!

Sometimes, through my drowsiness, I glimpsed her as, unable to leave him, she wandered around me barefoot, carrying him in her arms; or, sitting on the sofa, she held him on her lap and nursed him, or, in a low voice, sang persuasive lullabies to make him sleep. But if he didn't want to hear of it, and uttered his usual funny little cries and laughs, she warned him severely: "Hush, baby, hush, Arturo is ill!" On one of those occasions, she even gave him two little raps on the fingers. She had hit Carmine for me! This, truly, was the greatest of the greatest proofs I could have expected, even in my most ambitious hopes.

Now, when I think back, being jealous of that little boy seems a ridiculous dream. While I lay there quietly in the half-light, I heard every so often the gentle sound of her kissing him, and I wondered if such a fact really had happened in the world: that someone of my age could envy those little kisses. It would be the same as envying a child its toys, its piggybank, its teething ring, and so on. The jealousy that had suggested this false suicide now seemed to me like a final March storm, after which high spring begins, with its wonderful days. And, coming slowly out of my lethal sleep, I felt—as if new senses had been born in me—that the true taste of life must be much more serious and sumptuous than those childish kisses!

## Atlantis

On the fourth day of my illness, the irritating nausea disappeared completely, leaving only an indolent weakness, and I realized immediately, early in the morning, that I felt much better. But I wanted to take advantage of my suicide for at least one more day, and when she asked, "How do you feel, Artú?" I murmured between my teeth, in response: "I'm at the limit . . . Damn! I'm done for!"

And all morning I continued to pretend that I was sunk in an anguished sleep, whereas in fact I was awake; every so often, in a sepulchral voice, I asked, *Water . . . drink . . .* or, raising my head for an instant and then falling back, I pretended to faint, my eyelids half open, for the pleasure of seeing those large eyes bent over my face in alarm.

But around midday I began to get tired of playing the role of a dying man, and, for the first time since the suicide, feeling the return of hunger, I willingly let myself be nourished. (I was so weak and dazed in those days she had to feed me.)

Then I fell asleep, this time in a real sleep, and opened my eyes, in early afternoon, with a delightful feeling of surprise and freshness. Immediately N. came over and, seeing my clear gaze, trembled with gratitude: "You feel better, do you, Artú? Do you need something?" she asked me, in a voice that almost sang.

I answered, stretching, that I felt better, and didn't need anything, I wanted only to rest. Then, in order not to disturb me, she went back to her usual place on the couch, without saying anything else.

Carmine was sleeping in his basket, the shutters were closed so that the light wouldn't bother me, and the afternoon silence was absolute, without voices or church bells. Never, except in my house in Procida, have I enjoyed such fantastic silences. It was as if, outside, the town with its inhabitants no longer existed but only a great deserted estuary on a calm sea, at an hour when even the seagulls and the other water and land animals rest, and no ship passes. Between the shutters, outside the north-facing window (the same where I had once seen an eagle-owl perch), a tiny cloud could be glimpsed that, moving over the deep blue of the sky, in a few seconds took the shape of a shell, then of a small balloon, then of an ice-cream cone, then of an old man's beard, then of a dancer. And in that last shape, stretching and lengthening like a real ballerina, it grew distant. At the passage of that cloud, everything I'd thought and done the morning of my suicide, until the moment I fell down on the grass, returned with precision to my mind. And, without even looking at N., I said suddenly:

"Say, that piece of paper I left, did you tear it up?"

It somewhat surprised me to hear the sound of my voice, after the illness, because of certain rough low notes that hadn't been there before. Her voice, however, was the same.

"Yes, I tore it up . . ."

"Did you read it? It said: *Secrecy! Silence!!!* You didn't say anything?"

"No. I didn't say anything."

"Be careful, no one should know the truth. They should think that I didn't mean it, that it was an accident, that's all."

"That's what they thought . . . But Artú, what did you do?"

"And with my father, you've got to keep quiet. But if he should find out something you have to make him believe the same as other people!"

"Yes, well, him, who does he speak to? He won't find out anything from anyone!"

"But in any case you mustn't ever tell him the truth. He, especially, mustn't ever know!"

"I won't ever tell him the . . . truth. But Artú, what did you do? What did you do?"

At this point I realized that to reward her for her complicity in the secret, I owed her some explanation. Of course, I didn't, at any cost, want to reveal that the suicide was a fraud, and that she was the reason for it all! And on the spot I couldn't think of anything better than to improvise another explanation, just to give her an answer. Imagination spontaneously came to my rescue; and when one of the many thoughts I'd had that fatal morning flashed back to me, I said thoughtfully:

"Well, to you I'll tell the truth: I wanted to go past the Pillars of Hercules!"

"The . . . Pillars of Hercules!"

I turned over toward the pillow, to hide a half smile that came to my lips. Yet my inspiration pleased me. I knew from experience that my stepmother had faith in every invention of mine, even if it was unbelievable; and appearing to be bold never fails, with women. So, boldly and naturally, I followed my inspiration, assuming a fairy-tale and meditative tone, to which my still slightly labored breathing added majesty.

"I say the Pillars of Hercules," I began, "to make a comparison. You know the Strait of Gibraltar? In ancient times that was a point fantastically distant, because in those days you always traveled in a medium-sized boat with oars. And the passage through the strait was between two massive walls of rock, which looked like two gigantic pillars placed at a border. Every ship that sailed between them was lost, with all its crew, down to the last man, and never heard of again. And it was said that as soon as you came out into the open on the other side you were struck by a cloud and sank to the bottom in a stormy whirlpool: because there ended the earthly world and a mysterious eternity began. That was the idea of the first ancient populations; but then they discovered that their idea was a myth, because outside the strait began the great Atlantic; and advancing they found the new West Indies, full of living people, and buildings, mines . . . In other words, if you want to know, my comparison was this: that the fate of eternal death, where everyone ends up, could be another of the many fables. And that if instead of waiting, and getting trapped by fear like a low coward, one decided to explore, one might find the refutation . . . And so I decided. And I did it."

When I started this hoax of a speech, I had the vague idea of carrying it to the ultimate and most brilliant concluding lie. That is, of going so far as to assert that my strange crusade had resulted in a grand discovery, such as Columbus, da Gama, and others would envy. That, as soon as I passed beyond the limit of the tomb, I had found myself, for example, in sight of a kind of Atlantis or something similar, and had disembarked in a thousand-year-old port, crowded with gorgeous girls and ladies, pirates and captains, amid marvelous machines of gold and massive copper, etc., but when I got to the words *I decided*, the will to undertake this second part of my story failed me. After so many hours of illness and silence I had already talked too much, and I felt tired: besides, my voice, with those peculiar harsh notes, sounded out of tune to me and almost foreign. From N., intently listening to me there on her couch, came no questions or comments; maybe, although she was a little stupid, she wasn't so stupid, I thought, as to give credence to such lies; and she hadn't believed me. I felt some shame for my inventions; but, on the other hand, I didn't intend to deny them. And then, almost to take revenge on myself, and answer her mute uncertainties in the cruelest way, I suddenly came out with this unpremeditated conclusion:

"Well, and so I found the confirmation . . . You know what there is, in death: there's NOTHING. Only blackness, with no memory. That's what there is!"

I remembered again the horrible nausea of when I first awakened after falling; and I turned over in the bed with disgust. From the couch came a sigh; and I thought it was a sigh of bitterness. "Maybe," I supposed, "she's preparing to accuse me of blasphemy, and insist on speaking of eternal life and Paradise . . ." But I was wrong: it was a sigh of relief! and not of bitterness. I heard, after a short while, her voice: which, although still marked by anxiety, betrayed an undoubted sense of relief . . .

"So," she said, "now that you know . . ."

She paused for an instant, and in a drawn-out tone I asked: "*Know* . . . what?" She drew another small sigh: this one, I would dare say, as if of perdition. Then, in a hurry, as if breaking, her voice concluded:

"Now that you know, that there's really nothing there, you won't . . . *try again*! No?"

I burst into a laugh so natural and joyous that in two seconds I felt perfectly healthy again. Truly, my luck was almost incredible: N., to safeguard my existence, went so far as to disavow her Paradise! This for me was even better than hitting Carmine. It was a truly extraordinary proof, beyond every hope. For a moment I was tempted to answer: "Well, who knows . . . ?" since an elementary shrewdness suggested that (if I wished, in the future, to take advantage of the success of my suicide) I should leave her in some doubt . . . But the memory of that terrible nausea still encumbered my mind. Death was too hateful: and the idea of treating its repulsive face as an accomplice (even if it was lying) filled me with horror. To pretend, on that subject, was impossible. "Oh, no, never again!" I said, with violent disgust.


## The Catastrophe


That very evening, I wanted to get up for dinner. I was still a little unsteady on my legs, and I went down the stairs with some difficulty, but going up, after dinner, I already felt more solid; and the next morning I rose by myself, at dawn, full of impatience and hunger. My illness was over: only a kind of drunkenness remained, which gave my steps flair and a dancing sonority. The first sounds of day, echoing in

the cool air outside, seemed to respond with a marvelous softness, as
if they were the chords of an orchestra accompanying me. And when I
came outside into the yard that lighthearted sensation was magnified,
passing through the whole arc of the morning landscape! The great theater of my suicide seemed to welcome me with an exalted and gentle
stupor, as if I had there performed a tragic pantomime, after which,
healthy and gallant again, I reappeared on the stage. But then, as the
sun rose, that famous pantomime seemed, gradually, to recede to an
increasingly remote time, as if to a childhood of the world. Carmine's
joyful shrieks could be heard as he came down the stairs in her arms;
and hearing them I didn't even remember that, in prehistoric times, he
had been my rival!

I don't know what sudden whim suggested, at that moment, that I
hide behind the outside corner of the house. She must have been surprised to find the French door open and no one in the kitchen or the
yard: and I heard her go back upstairs, leaving Carmine in the kitchen,
surely to see if I really had gotten out of bed and gone out at that early
hour. After a minute, she returned and came into the yard, uncertain.
She didn't think to look around the corner but went instead toward
the descent to the beach, where she began to call without response:
"Arturo! Artú!"

She was wearing an old red dress, and was barefoot, out of a habit
developed in caring for me in those days. In the yard, at that hour of the
morning, the shadow of the wall was still lengthening: the sun rising
behind the house had reached only the last strip, where she was; and her
bare legs, in that pink light, had an innocent color that oddly inspired
me to laugh. She took a few steps looking here and there, with the worried air of a mother cat, her curls and clothes ruffled by the wind. Then
she began to call me again from the top of the hill. With a sudden run I
came up behind her and said: "I'm here."

In a start of surprise she turned happily and said reproachfully: "Where were you? You're already out!"

Then, perhaps confused by something aggressive in my behavior, she murmured, looking at me: "Artú, in these few days you've gotten taller . . ."

At those words (whether, during my brief illness, I had actually grown a little, or whether, barefoot as she was, she seemed to me smaller than usual) I realized, for the first time, that I was now taller. That appeared to me the sign of an ancient, proud, and joyful power; and meanwhile she was moving imperceptibly away from me: as if to confess that her heart was pounding . . . All of a sudden I embraced her, kissing her on the mouth.

Her lips had a cold, March taste; and my first sensation didn't seem very different from what you'd feel nibbling a blade of grass, or tasting seawater. My thought was: "So now I, too, know what a kiss is like! That is my first kiss!" And that thought, mixed with a slightly curious, surprised, and faintly discontented pride, almost distracted me from her. Although she didn't respond to my kiss, at first she didn't even try to escape, confused and helplessly dazed. I heard her murmur between my lips, "Artú," as if she didn't recognize me, and, strangely, clutch me, as if to ask for help; while I, in a kind of bold affirmation, held her more tightly, pressing my lips to hers.

Around her softened eyelids a weak and astonished pallor appeared. Her lips had gone from cold to burning. And then I felt on my mouth a taste of bloody sweetness that in an instant destroyed all thoughts in my mind. Suddenly my voice said, "Nunziata! Nunziatè!" but at that same moment she tore herself away with ferocious disobedience and began to say no with her head, in a tender, bewildered, feverish way.

For a moment she stood like that, a step from me, as if, in a dream, not yet aware, she were questioning a mystery; but her curly head (which had never appeared of such angelic beauty) persisted in that fierce negation, and her eyes avoided me, full of guilt and fear. My old ambition had been realized: to instill fear, no less than my father! But the difference between the two fears (although still mysterious, because of my ignorance) didn't escape me.

Her fear of my father, which remained in my memory, was an anguish, and seemed to turn her limbs to ice; while her present fear (a strange and new kind, never seen in her) seemed to be contradicted in herself, and to burn in that contradiction. At the very moment that her desperate will rejected my kiss, her body (which suddenly made itself known, as if I had seen it naked) begged me, contrarily, to kiss her again. That quivering and savage prayer traversed all her limbs, from her pink feet to her nipples, which stuck out sharply under the dress. And in her frightened eyes that damp, marvelous gaze seeped in, tinted with a blue vapor, which I had glimpsed just before I kissed her.

I cried again, "Nunziata! Nunziatè!" and was about to run toward her. But she, at her own name called by my voice, answered with a diabolical and brutal cry, full of dismay. Then, covering her face, she exclaimed with pitiless certainty, as if she were uttering a sacred oath:

"No! No, my God!"

And, giving me a look of glassy, in fact unnatural severity, she fled from me, as from an enemy.

## CHAPTER 6

# The Fatal Kiss

I'm seeking a blessing
Outside of myself.
I don't know who has it
I don't know what it is.

—CHERUBINO, *THE MARRIAGE OF FIGARO*

### *The Fatal Kiss*

So, with that kiss, I had again ruined our friendship; and this time irreparably.

After that fatal event, I had only to enter a room where she was (even if I didn't say a word, even if I was there simply on my own business that had nothing to do with her)—it was enough for me to be in her presence!—and right away she lost all assurance and spontaneity. The natural pride of her behavior, which was combined so delicately with meekness, suddenly fell, overcome by a strange fear. That fear, I repeat, seemed of an unusual type, not the same she had displayed in the past, for example, in the presence of my father. If I had to invent an image for that new fear I could compare it only to a flame, which suddenly attacked her with its treacherous rosy light, and licked her limbs; and which she tried to flee in confused, reckless ways. A sudden blush, then her face turned pale; she walked around the kitchen, with trembling fingers picking up and putting down this or that object, to no purpose; then she sat down again near Carmine, and began singing her usual songs, in a timid, cold voice, as if she herself weren't listening to the words. And those songs were a pretext, or even a small magic charm, to distract her from her own fear, and the burden of my presence. At times one would have said she was taking refuge behind Carmine's basket, or holding him in her arms, to defend herself from a frightening intruder. And that was me, the intruder! But the strangest fact, which I still haven't said, is this: that I myself, in her presence, was afraid!

I say *afraid* because at the time I wouldn't have known a truer word to describe my distress. Although I had read books and novels, even about love, I was really still a half-barbaric boy; and maybe, too, my heart, unknown to me, took advantage of my immaturity and ignorance, to protect me from the truth? If I think back now on my whole history with N., from the beginning, I learn that the heart, in its competition with conscience, is as capricious, shrewd, and imaginative as a master costume designer. To create its masks, it needs almost nothing; some- times, to disguise things, it simply replaces one word with another . . . And in that bizarre game conscience wanders around like a stranger at a masked ball, amid the fumes of the wine.

Since I'd kissed her, I couldn't see her without a mortal pounding of my heart (which began as soon as the Casa dei Guaglioni came into view at the end of the street—closer at every step). Then, in her presence, that anxiety became anguish, a kind of bitterness at the injustice, and rage. The fact was this: that of all the innumerable minutes that made up our common past, I, seeing her, remembered only one: the one when I had kissed her. It seemed to me that my kiss had left a visitble mark on her whole body, ringing it with a kind of halo that was complicit, radiant, soft, sweet, and mine! And I wished to return there to take shelter, as if to my nest. As if she were now the enchanted prisoner of my kiss, and I had been summoned to share that loving prison with her. Now I couldn't see her without feeling the vehement, irresistible need to embrace her and kiss her again. But how could I impose that necessary claim, in fact that right of mine, if she had become hostile to me precisely because of my kiss? And that single kiss of ours, which to me seemed a presence so luminous, for her had become, instead, a figure of threat and fear? I had the sensation that (so great was her fear) if I embraced and kissed her again I would kill her! One day, when she was cutting bread, and I was staring at her with the usual pounding heart, I met her gaze; and believed I read in her sweet, trembling face just these words: "Watch out, if you come near me I'll stab myself with this knife and fall down dead here."

Thus her fear became also my fear. And she and I, together in the same room, moved in confusion, as if through a surging roar that collided with us, brought us near, and separated us, forbidding us ever to meet. After a while, I went out without saying a word, incapable of expressing my bitter anguish and my revolt. Her rejection of my kisses seemed to me nothing other than a denial of our friendship and relationship: a condemnation, which would relegate me unjustly to solitude.

That injustice of which I accused my stepmother nevertheless shackled my will with a grave power and a mysterious prestige; but no scruple or awareness of guilt visited my mind. In my feelings toward her I saw no prohibition. And not even in my kiss! Kissing her, I had obeyed an impulse of happiness and glory, carefree and without remorse. Among my Absolute Certainties there was none that said: *It's a crime to kiss friends and relatives.*

Of course, I wasn't ignorant of the fact that not all kisses are the same. I had read, for example, the canto of Paolo and Francesca. Not to mention the dozens of songs I knew, which all talked about caresses and kisses of love. Also, I had had occasion, down at the port, to look at some illustrated movie magazines, with photographs of couples kissing (from the captions, I even learned the names of some of the stars) . . . But until then I had been too used to being considered a boy to put myself suddenly in the place of Paolo, the damned soul of a circle of Hell, or of the hero Clark Gable (who, among other things, was antipathetic to me, because he had a squashed face and, besides, was dark-haired). The love extolled in songs, books, and illustrated magazines remained a remote and mythical thing to me, outside of real life. As we know, the only woman in my thoughts had always been my mother: and if I had dreamed of kisses, they had always been the holy kisses of a mother for her son.

So now that N., precisely because of her fear of me, did me the greatest honor, the honor I had always longed for (treating me like a man, and not like a boy), I was unable to acknowledge that honor!

## Forbidden

Yes! Now I'm good at asking myself if it wasn't perhaps the cunning of my heart, which pretended not to recognize the obvious evidence, in order to exempt me from punishment. Now I can speculate and investigate better than a philosopher. And I say and I suppose: maybe, if I had manfully interrogated my conscience (which was not completely barbaric, however immature), it would have responded: "Don't play tricks! You're a liar and a seducer." But in the clear calm days of that Procidan spring a kind of sparkling cloud had descended around me, infused with new, strange lights and obscure shapes, in which I lived enveloped like an outlaw, so I didn't even remember that conscience existed, and at times was no longer even aware of being myself.

It may be that everyone at that time of life has felt something not very different.

I was again spending entire days out of the house, encountering N. as little as possible. And in those hours of separation, my mind itself, without any intervention of my will, broke away from the image of her. I never thought about her face or, still less, her body; one would have said that thought shunned the sight of my stepmother. But, even without looking at her, thought, like a blindfolded pilgrim, returned to her.

Here's how. I should say (since I haven't yet) that in the meantime the fatal kiss, in my capricious memory, had become more innocent than it really was (like music of which one remembers only the melody). Some of the bizarre, fierce violence I had felt in that kiss had been almost eliminated from recollection (and so the less likely it became that I might acknowledge my guilt in giving a kiss!). Another thing, however, I couldn't forget: and that is that on that one occasion I had, for the first time, called N. by name (instead of saying as I usually did: *Hey, you,* or something similar). Owing to I don't know what imaginary decree, it had the flavor of an infraction: that single thing! And now that flavor returned often to tempt me.

I don't know how many times a day, even without thinking of her, I surprised myself repeating in a low voice, *Nunziata, Nunziatella,* savoring a delightful but audacious lightness, as if I were confiding a secret to a fellow traitor. Or I traced that name with my finger on a window, or on the sand, and right afterward erased it, as a criminal does the clues that might point to him. But suddenly the roar of the waves, the whistle of the steamers, all the sounds of the island and the sky seemed to cry together: *Nunziata! Nunziatella!* It was like an immense, intoxicating revolt against the notorious prohibition (which in truth I had invented myself) that had always denied me that name. And, at the same time, a profound condemnation of my transgression, which nearly overwhelmed me.

The name *Nunziata, Nunziatella* was transformed for me into a kind of abstract catchphrase: like a watchword among conspirators, which, adopted for devious plots, is stripped of its original meaning. Thus not even the sound of the name—now the symbol of an obscure, broken law!—led my mind to her face, to her physical person. Outside her presence, her person seemed to be hidden from me in a cloud; then, as soon as I returned to her presence, the cloud ripped apart to show me the harsh face of denial.

N. was absent even from my dreams. Or at least I don't remember that she ever visited them, at the time.

I recall that, in that period, I had dreams from the *Arabian Nights*. I dreamed of flying! I dreamed of being a magnificent lord, who threw innumerable coins to the crowd. Or a great Arab king, who crossed a burning desert on horseback, and, as he passed, the coolest springs gushed up to the sky!

In reality, however, I seemed to have suddenly become the armed enemy of all things in existence.

## *The Palace of Midas*

I said that it was a strange time. The conflict between my stepmother and me was only one of the aspects of the great war that, rapidly, with the flowering of spring, seemed to have been unleashed between Arturo Gerace and all the rest of creation. The fact was that the return of summer that year was for me accompanied by what is called in good families the ungrateful age. I had never before felt myself so ugly: in my body, and in all that I did, I noticed a strange clumsiness, which began with my voice. My voice had become odious, neither soprano (as it had been before) nor, yet, tenor (as it was later): it seemed an out-of-tune instrument. And the rest was like my voice. My face was still quite round and smooth, but my body wasn't. My clothes no longer fit, so that N., although hostile, had to adjust to my size some sailor pants that a shopkeeper friend of hers gave her on credit. And meanwhile I had the impression that I was growing without grace, in an ungainly way. My legs, for example, in a few weeks had become so long that they got in my way, and my hands were too big in comparison with my body, which was still lean and slender. When I closed them, I seemed to have the fists of an adult bandit, which I was not. And I didn't know what to do with those murderer's fists: I always felt like punching with them, anywhere, so that if pride hadn't hindered me I would have quarreled with the first person I met, maybe with a goatherd, or a laborer, with anyone. Instead, I started neither conversation nor quarrel with anyone; and in fact, even more than before, if possible, I stayed away from people. Really, I felt like a character so out of place and cursed that I almost would have liked to shut myself up in some den, where I could be left to grow in peace until the day when, as I had been quite a good-looking boy, I would become quite a good-looking youth. But: to go and shut myself up! Yes! Easy to say! But how could I have endured being shut up, when I seemed to have in me a hellish spirit, which transformed me into a kind of wild animal, all day hunting some unknown prey? The gentleness of the season made my mood bitter: I would have been happier in winter storms. The springtime beauties of the island, which in other years I had so loved, inspired almost an angry mockery, while I climbed up and down those cliffs and fields with my long legs, like a chamois or a wolf, in a constant turmoil that found no outlet. Sometimes the triumphant joy of nature overpowered me, leading me to extraordinary exaltations. The fantastic flowers of the volcanoes, which invaded every piece of uncultivated land, seemed to spread out before me for the first time gorgeous patterns of form and color, inviting me to a joyous, changing celebration . . . But the usual desolate anger immediately possessed me again, intensified by shame at my futile rapture. I wasn't a goat, or a sheep, to be satisfied with grass and flowers! And in revenge I destroyed the meadow, tearing up flowers, trampling them fiercely under my feet.

My desperation resembled hunger and thirst, although it was a different thing. And, after having so longed to reach an older age, I almost regretted my earlier age: What did I lack then? Nothing. I had a wish to eat: and I ate. I had a desire to drink: and I drank. I wanted to enjoy myself: I went out in the *Torpedo Boat of the Antilles*. And the island, for me, what had it been up to now? A land of adventure, a blessed garden! No, now it was a bewitched and sensual dwelling, in which, like wretched King Midas, I found nothing to satisfy me.

A desire for destruction took hold of me. I would have liked to be able to practice a brutal profession, for example stone breaker, to occupy my body from morning till night in a vain and violent action that would distract me in some way. All the pleasures of summer, which had once been enough for me, appeared insufficient, laughable; and there was nothing I did without a desire for aggression and ferocity. I dove into the sea belligerently, like a savage rushing at an adversary with a knife in his teeth; and, swimming, I would have liked to break, to devastate the sea! Then I jumped into my boat, rowing wildly toward the open water; and there, in the high sea, I began singing desperately in my tuneless voice, as if I were cursing.

Upon returning, I stretched out on the sunny sand, whose carnal warmth was like a beautiful silken body. I relaxed, as if rocked, into the light weariness of midday; and I would have liked to embrace the entire beach. At times, I spoke endearments to things, as if they were people. I began to say, for instance: "Oh, my lovely sand! My beach! My light!" and other more complicated endearments, really demented. But it was impossible to embrace the great body of the beach, whose countless glassy grains of sand slid between my fingers. Nearby, a pile of seaweed, soaked in the spring salt, gave out a sweet, fermenting odor, as of mold on grapes; and, like a cat, I took pleasure in biting the seaweed, furiously scattering it. Too great was my wish to play: with anyone, even the air! And I eyed the sky, blinking my eyelids hard. The pure blue spread over me seemed to approach, embroidered with stars like a firmament, igniting into a single great fire and then becoming as black as Hell . . . I turned over on the sand, laughing. The futility of these games embittered me.

I was seized by an almost fraternal pity for myself. I traced on the sand the name ARTURO GERACE, adding, IS ALONE, and then, afterward, ALWAYS ALONE.

And later, as I went back up toward the house with the certainty of finding there only an enemy, infernal desires often assailed me. I would grab my stepmother by the hair, throw her to the ground, and beat her with my big fists, shouting: "That's enough of that goddamn behavior of yours! You'd better stop it!" But in her presence my sinister purposes vanished. I felt embarrassment and shame, as if there were no longer a place for me in that kitchen. The well-known bench, where once I loved to stretch out, had become too short for my height. My long legs, my unnatural voice, my hands got in the way more than ever. And a terrible, depressing sensation invaded me: that my present ugliness, and nothing else, was the reason that N. avoided me.

Later, when we're old, I know, such tragedies are, more than anything, comic; and, if I like, now, at a distance, I, too, can laugh. But we should recognize that it's not easy to cross the last frontiers of that terrible *ungrateful age* without having anyone to confide in: neither a friend nor a relative! Then, for the first time in my life, I truly felt the bitterness of being alone. I began to long desperately for my father. (He had now been gone for around two and a half months: an unexpectedly long interval after that period when, as I said, he was often on the island.) In my yearning I created a romantic portrait of him, which was not too lifelike, I should say. I absolutely forgot that between us there had never been any intimacy. And that certain things, to him especially, I couldn't and wouldn't ever have confided and wouldn't have known how. I even forgot his behavior of recent times, which was certainly not encouraging to conversation.

I imagined W.G. as a sort of great affectionate angel, my only friend on earth: to him I could confess, perhaps, all my anguish, all that was unconfessable, and he would understand me, explain what I didn't understand! Gradually, as that traitorous spring wore on in confusion and torment (and it was to be the last spring I spent on Procida!), I clung to the angelic vision of my father as the only refuge to be hoped for. Everything that made such a dream unlikely, utopian, I now hid from myself. Hope, at times, weakens awareness, like a defect.

And I began again to wait for Wilhelm Gerace every day, as when I was a boy, although for different reasons. I was faithfully, stubbornly on the dock, at the arrival of every steamer from Naples: until, as was inevitable, one fine day he returned. He arrived on the second afternoon boat, which entered the port around six. It was the middle of May, the days were now long, and, at six, there was still full sun.

## On the Dock

When I saw him appear on the upper deck, lanky and solitary, standing slightly behind the small group of arriving passengers, I began to call him from below, with uncontrollable joy. But I immediately realized, from his expression, that he was almost annoyed at finding me there. And when he got close he neglected to greet me but right away asked me to go home without him, he had to stay here and would come later, on his own. "I'll see you soon, at home," he said. Then, eyeing me, although distracted, he added: "Eh, what have you done, Arturo? How you've grown in these months!" In fact, as I stood facing him, I didn't have to raise my eyes to look at him, as I used to; and in his surprise there was a note of coldness, as if I were so changed he didn't recognize me.

That cold, hurried phrase was, in any case, the only sign of attention he gave me. At that moment his pupils seemed barely to see me. "So," he repeated, "see you later." And his disoriented, slightly feverish manner betrayed only impatience to be free of me.

Such a thing had never happened in similar circumstances in the past. Usually he was happy to have me go with him to the departing steamer, and even more content if he had the surprise of finding me on his arrival. That new, inexplicable wish of his struck me harder than a blow. In my wonder and chagrin, I was almost on the point of asking him, as a favor, to give me his suitcase to carry to the house; but immediately I was ashamed to the depths of my soul of such a servile temptation. I hadn't come here to be his errand boy! And, without asking for an explanation of his behavior, without saying a word, I separated from him with an expression of indifference, a kind of sneer on my lips.

But I didn't obey his order to go home: as if in defiance, I wanted, rather, to stay on the dock. And, having taken a few idle steps, I stopped a short distance away, near a pile of goods, which I leaned against sideways, in the attitude that delinquents have in certain comics about criminal life. At no cost did I want to show him my bitter humiliation. But, satisfied that he had been left alone, he didn't bother to check if I had obeyed or not. He stayed near the gangplank, his suitcase at his feet, as if waiting for someone who was to disembark from the same steamer; and meanwhile he kept his eyelids disdainfully lowered, paying no attention to me or to anything around. Who, then, could be the delaying passenger he was waiting for? Maybe, this time, he hadn't arrived on the island alone? Among these speculations, in a sign of arrogance, I kept my eyes on him; and I noticed how thin he had gotten. His jacket, still the same as in winter, was twice as large as he. Underneath, the unbuttoned shirt exposed his white skin: evidently, despite the beautiful warm season, he hadn't been out in the sun yet this year.

He lighted a cigarette and immediately tossed it away. I realized then that his hands were trembling; and that the impassiveness of his bearing betrayed, in spite of himself, a strenuous resolution to drive out an extreme, disastrous, and childish anxiety. It was clear that the mysterious person who at this moment he was waiting for exercised a rare sovereignty over his thoughts. But, with a last claim of pride, he wanted to pretend to himself that his vigilant attention wasn't too involved in this faithful and absorbing wait; and so he lowered his eyes to the ground, turning them fiercely away from that deck, from that gangplank, toward which his anxious nerves most yearned.

But who was he waiting for? By now, according to all evidence, the few passengers whose destination was Procida had disembarked, while those who were departing had already boarded; only the signal to cast off the moorings and set out was needed. "Maybe," I thought sarcastically, "he's waiting for some prisoner?" In fact, the last shift to disembark was reserved for the new guests of the penitentiary: after the movement of arrivals and departures ceased, and the small crowd on the dock had dispersed.

## Sinister Individual

I had thought, "He must be waiting for a prisoner," only out of a sarcastic deduction, never expecting that I was guessing the truth. I saw, at that point, that the truck from the prison, which I hadn't noticed before, stood at the entrance to the square, and that a guard in a gray-green uniform, bayonet over his shoulder, was walking back and forth near the steamer. Sure signs, these, that on board there was some guest of the castle of Procida, still shut up in the security cabin near the hold, waiting for the two guards assigned to his escort to lead him out. Another brief wait followed, maybe a minute, during which my father, making an extreme demand on his will, seemed to achieve a cold and motionless apathy, as if he no longer cared about what was to happen, or any other human event. He was still looking down, when suddenly I saw him start, and his eyes, full of light, childish, blue, rose instinctively toward the upper deck of the boat. At that very instant the expected trio, now familiar to the inhabitants of the island, appeared on the deck, heading toward the gangplank. Then an unfamiliar, hellish, and terrible feeling surprised me.

Usually when such a trio made its appearance at the port, my heart went out immediately to the condemned man. He could even have an abject, atrocious appearance; it didn't count. He was a prisoner: and therefore angelic. When I first saw him, I dreamed of brotherhood, of escapes; and while I averted my eyes as a sign of respect, I would have liked to shout my complicity. This time, instead, after barely a glimpse of the new prisoner, I felt a savage antipathy, which did not allow me to see his features clearly, and I immediately judged them to be horrendously ugly (a judgment contrary to the truth!). I can say, in other words, that from that first instant I vowed absolute hatred. Maliciously, I almost wished that prison regulations would order the guards—who escorted him, in fact, with an air of protectiveness—to drag him rudely along the dock instead, abusing him with the cruelest tortures.

What I was able to notice, with my hostile eyes, during his rapid passage, was, above all, that he was an extremely young condemned man: he seemed even younger than the minimum age that was surely required for a prisoner. On his face, and on his manacled hands, the almost gray pallor that dark skin acquires in prison stood out in the light; but not even that grim color could age him. Rather, it hardened the character of youthful plebeian brutality—common, but in him ostentatious—that was chiseled in his face, especially in the curve of his lips and the part of his black hair. That dark vitality, which was worse than impudence, and which to me appeared truly sinister, suddenly became, in my eyes, the very shape of him. The image was oblique and, because of his darkness, mysterious: inspiring in me, from the start, angry, contradictory feelings.

His face was bent toward his chest, in severe remorse, which in him, however, seemed merely an expression for the occasion, or maybe ironic. In fact the look on his face was contradicted by his body, which in movement and gait betrayed a fresh, aggressive, and playful adolescence. He was of medium height; but, much more vigorous than my father, he could seem, at first sight, as tall as him. And for the journey he had put on his best civilian clothes (well cut, brand-new, flashy): as sometimes in such circumstances, out of a kind of affectation, certain condemned men do, especially young, inexperienced ones; but in that awkward outfit his body moved as if it were in a puppet's costume, with an untamable, vain, and happy freedom.

In his heart he seemed to be setting out on his sentence as if it were a boast, uniting the two most envied types of audacity: affirmation of oneself, and adventure. (Later I was able to come up with profane reasons to explain that bearing of his: since his flaunted conviction was to turn out to be somewhat laughable. And so his crime must be, too, I imagine . . . But at the time I considered that immature youth a murderer, a true condemned man! And I happened to attribute Promethean causes to his arrogance, as I will describe.)

In addition to certain transfigurations of romantic origin, in the very brief time that that scene lasted I was endowed with a sensitivity close to clairvoyance, which is found at times in women, or in animals. For example, I perceived immediately, with certainty, that my father knew that prisoner, not from today but from before; and the look he gave him will never be erased from my heart. His eyes (always the most beautiful in the world, to me), like two mirrors at the passing of a celestial body, had turned a clear and fabulous deep blue, with no trace of their usual murky shadow. And their expression might mean a faithful greeting, an imaginary understanding, a poor and desperate welcome;

but above all it meant an entreaty. It seemed that Wilhelm Gerace was asking for an act of charity. But what in the world could he ask from that wretched man, to whom he wasn't allowed even to say a word, to make a sign? A look, in response to his look of adoring friendship, was all that he could ask. And that unique pleaded-for thing, which the prisoner could have given to my father, he denied him. In fact, perhaps in spite of himself, having glanced at him deliberately as he passed close by, he composed his boyish face in an expression of boredom, impatience, the most insulting contempt for Wilhelm Gerace. And his extremely black eyes were turned elsewhere. All this lasted barely a few seconds: the time necessary for that unlucky trio to reach the prison truck. I saw my father leave his place and try, almost unconsciously, to follow the three, to be immediately repulsed by the policeman on guard. Only when he heard the door of the truck slam was he allowed to pass; and the truck was already in gear when he reached it. I saw him stop for an instant, as if uncertain, then run a few steps in the direction of the truck, with confused gestures, almost comic in their uselessness. Such as grief-stricken mothers have, when, finally, tearing themselves from the arms of those who are holding them back, with a cry of denial they run down the stairs and into the street. Where already the coffin bearers, with their small burden on their shoulders, have left the doorway and are hurrying away.

Then he stopped, standing there for a moment in an idle attitude, without remembering his suitcase, abandoned near the boat landing. A boy from the port came and tugged on his jacket, reminding him of what he had forgotten; and then with mechanical movements he went back to get the suitcase. He didn't notice me, standing opposite, up against those crates of goods; and probably he hadn't noticed me the whole time. I saw him walking with his suitcase through the square, alone, his shoulders slack and slightly bent. A few minutes later, with a feeling of laziness and inertia, I left the dock.

## *Assunta*

As far back as I could remember, this was my father's longest sojourn on the island: he arrived, as I said, around the middle of May, and didn't leave again until winter. During that interval, a steady, stupendous summer reigned, while in the Casa dei Guaglioni time wore on, obscure and inconstant, toward the final tempest . . . I will begin with the first important event that made that season memorable for me: it happened a few days after my father's arrival, maybe in the third week of May.

✂✐✐✂

Among N.'s acquaintances, there was one named Assunta, a widow of twenty-one. Although I saw her often, I had never noticed that she was prettier than the other neighbors who frequented our house: the only characteristic that had made me notice her among the others, and on account of which I was perhaps less rude to her, was that as a result of an illness she'd had as a girl she walked with a slight limp. To my skeptical, surly eyes that defect seemed, rather, an attraction: all the more since, with the vanity of a simple creature, she often liked to sit in the poses of a melancholy invalid, although now her body was flourishing with health and the vitality of youth. Her relatives, friends, and so on, to console her for the illness she'd suffered and then her widowhood, had always spoiled her with special kindnesses and caresses: and she had grown up with soft, defenseless ways, like the Oriental languors of a favorite cat.

Although she was short and small-boned, her body was well made, quite shapely; but of this, I repeat, I wasn't aware. To me she looked like a bundle, just the same as the other women.

She had dark, rather olive skin, and long smooth black hair.

If you looked out the window of our kitchen toward the sloping countryside, a long, downhill lane could be seen that meandered like a river: and at the bottom the cottage where she lived with her relatives was visible. They were landowning farmers, and went to work every day on one of their properties on the other side of the island; but, because of her past illness, she was dismissed from the work in the fields, and so, not having children, she spent a great part of her time alone in the cottage, especially during the spring and summer. If I happened to pass by there, I would often see her sitting outside the door, picking over the greens for the family soup or combing her hair in front of a small mirror, wetting the comb in a basin. On seeing me she ducked behind her hair, smiling almost hesitantly, and tilted her head slightly toward her shoulder, as she waved farewell with her hand. Sometimes I responded with a hurried hello and other times I didn't respond at all.

She had always been among N.'s friends; but, that spring, she went much more often to the Casa dei Guaglioni, where she was warmly welcomed, both by N. and by Carmine, who often played in her arms while N. took care of the kitchen. Almost every day, at around three or four in the afternoon, when I went home to get something to eat, I found her there; and when I entered she greeted me with her usual shy smile, which was faintly drawn on her closed, full lips, and put a velvety shadow in her almond-shaped black eyes. But I paid no attention to her smiles or to her; I had other things on my mind. As spring advanced, when I again began to desert the house for the entire day, my occasions for meeting this woman were very rare.

❦

One afternoon a few days after my father's arrival, I was wandering through the countryside in the grip of that wretched mood that had been tormenting me like a curse. Never had any summer declared itself so desolate and miserable; and my father's presence on the island, instead of consoling me as I had dreamed, intensified even more the strange sensation that I had become a sort of graceless animal, hated by the universe. Wilhelm Gerace, on his return to Procida, persistently avoided my company, as he had never done in summers past. And, from the evening of his arrival, and my disappointment when he got off the boat, I suspected that his rejection might also be due to the changed aspect (for the worse) of my body. Every time his gaze rested on me I thought I read a critical, amazed, and negative judgment, as if he no longer recognized his son Arturo in such an ugly youth. And it seemed to me that his eyes, like two freezing ponds, reflected my ungainly features, describing them one by one: so that, unlike Narcissus, I fell out of love with myself in a furious manner. In the end I longed to return to the time when W.G. was pleased to say, at least: "Well, he's not bad. Yes, not for nothing is he my son!" And after yearning for so many years to be as tall as he was, now, instead, near him, I felt my height as a hindrance, a shame. I had the impression that he considered it a kind of strange abuse, to be regarded with antipathy or distrust. And I would have liked to be a child again.

Of course, I didn't relinquish my pride. I returned his coldness with coldness. And, preferring to avoid the insult of his looks voluntarily—or at least without leaving him the initiative—I behaved as if I avoided his company no less than he mine.

Here, then, is what my life was reduced to: that my father rejected me, my stepmother kept me distant as if I were more dangerous than a snake. Anything is better than pity: and I didn't want to be pitied by anyone. At night, I returned home with an air of mystery and delinquency, as if I'd spent the day commanding gangs of thieves, pirate ships. Sometimes I would have liked to be a true monster of ugliness: for example, I imagined myself disguised as an albino, with fangs instead of teeth, and one eye concealed under a black patch. In this way, merely by appearing, I would horrify and strike fear into everyone.

It was an afternoon on one of these days when I was passing Assuntina's house. I saw her as she greeted me from behind a window, and I think that I didn't even respond; but as I was going off, I heard her small limping steps hurrying toward me, and her voice calling:

"Gerace! Gerace! Arturo!"

## The Corals

I turned. "Hello," she began, "what ever are you doing around here? I haven't seen you for a long time . . ."

"Hello," I answered. And, not knowing what else to say, I gave her a look from head to toe, with the dark, disdainful expression of a tiger who encounters a family of young lions in the jungle.

Her bare feet, on the dry dust of the earth, were muddy, as if they'd been walking in muck. And she immediately explained that she was intending to wash her feet, when she had seen me pass; and to reach me she had run out without drying them. As she explained, she lowered her gaze to her tiny feet, in an eloquent manner that was intended to signify: "Be indulgent toward that mud, in fact please accept it as a sign of my haste to reach you."

Then her eyes, still half lowered, looked at me with a shy expression, between reproach and servitude. "I was getting ready to go up to your house . . ." she resumed, "but since I knew you're never there, at this hour . . . In the past, at this hour I might happen to see you there sometimes, and now, instead, never! Not this hour or any other!"

Her singsong voice, in saying those words, seemed almost to be lamenting. And, with its notes of sweet frailty, it recalled sounds that bitches make, or small female donkeys, when they complain of wrongs you don't understand.

"In my opinion," she added after a silence, "you must have some girl, down in the town, who keeps you out of the house all day!"

"I don't have any girl!" I declared, with surly pride.

"Really! You really don't have a girl! . . . But I—I might not believe that . . ."

She dared to contradict me! Yet from a woman such an insult didn't bring dishonor as it would from a man; and I confined myself to picking up a rock and throwing it, threateningly, without deigning to give her any other response.

"And if you really don't have a girl, why do you stay away all day? A hundred times a person comes to your house, and a hundred times you're not there. Not in the morning, or in the afternoon!"

"So what does it matter to you?"

"To me . . . well, now, you mustn't be offended. If you're offended, I'm ashamed, and I don't know what else to say. But I don't want to tell you a lie: it matters, yes, it matters a little to me. And the reason is my secret, Assuntina's . . . that Assuntina could tell only to you, she couldn't confide it to anyone else . . . Maybe, if you want to know, I'll tell you this secret now; but if you don't want to know, I won't tell you."

In response I curled my lip, meaning clearly: "Whether you tell me or not, I don't really care. Do as you like."

"And so? Should I speak or not? All right, I'll speak, because I can't stand this thorn in my throat anymore." And she began to speak, lulling herself in her slow soprano voice.

"So here's how it is: when I come to your house, with such pleasure (and I return every day, and I go up there morning and evening—and even with this lame leg!), I don't come for just one reason . . . but for more than one reason. Of course, I come out of friendship for Nunziata; and then out of affection for your little brother, Carminiello. Of course. These are truths that everyone knows, but they're not the principal truth. The principal truth is another (and this is my secret, which I was telling you . . .): that Assuntina comes up to your house principally in the hope of seeing *you!*"

At that my face turned bright red. I would never have believed that a woman could make such a bold declaration so naturally! But she wasn't even blushing! In fact, looking at my cheeks, she broke into a sweet, sensual laugh. And I glimpsed her pink gums, bathed in a wetness that made her teeth shine.

"And so now my secret is yours: and no one else has to know it. Yes, it's already been a while, since before Easter, I swear, that I've had that thought! You've seen that in the afternoon I'm always here alone: and so every day I start thinking to myself . . . and thinking again. You're a man, of course, and you don't think. The only idea of men is to always be going around: they go to the wine shops, to the taverns . . . They don't think. Whereas women, they think!

"And when I saw you hurry by, like today, I always had this idea: 'He could sit down once in a while in my house, and bring a little comfort to Assuntina, who's here all alone!'"

There was a pause. With lowered eyes, she looked at me just fleetingly. "But later," she added finally, "I thought maybe I'd better forget that idea. In fact, I seemed to hear a voice inside, like an old lady, who said to me: 'Well, Assuntí . . . ! Maybe he's running because he's got an appointment with the girl. Who knows how many pretty girls that boy has? You aren't so pretty (even without considering your injured leg). And then compared to him you're practically an old woman.'"

After that, she was silent again, with an air of flaunting her sadness. She kept her eyes lowered, as if virtuously; and meanwhile her small dark hand was playing with a string of coral she wore around her neck.

Not knowing what to say, I exclaimed, with an aggressive, insolent vehemence:

"Those are pretty corals you have!"

"Oh, it's true, yes, they're quite nice," she answered, rather pleased,
but, still, a little sad, "and I don't have just these corals, I also have some
others. Matching this necklace I have earrings, a bracelet, and a pretty
pin, the complete *parure*." (She said just that French word, I remember
it exactly.) "Of course, I can't wear them all together, especially after
mourning," she observed, with some regret.

Then her voice took on a suspended, softened tone. "I keep them
in the house," she informed me, "up in my room . . . Well, if you like
pretty corals, come in, some time or other, sit down, I'll show them to
you . . . When you want, some time or other . . ."

And she peeked at my face. I gave no sign of accepting or refusing
that flattering invitation. Almost furtively she asked me:

"And from here, now, at this hour, where are you going?" and her
face, dark in color, was suffused with a pink that did not resemble modesty or shame: rather, I would say, the opposite.

I didn't know how to answer her question: I really didn't know
where I was going, or, to be precise, I wasn't going anywhere. "Well,
it's hot at this hour," she spoke again, "and everyone's sleeping . . ." So
saying, from under her oblong, thick-lashed eyelids, which seemed to
weigh on her eyes, she gave me a look that spoke clearly: as if she were
an odalisque and I the sultan!

## The Little Bite

And, taking me by the hand, with an important, mysterious smile, she
drew me with her into the cottage. Here, before my eyes, she carefully
finished washing her feet; then she took off the coral necklace, which

she placed on the table near the bed; and then she loosened her smooth, neatly parted hair from the hairpins. (It was as if she were unlacing the ribbons of a jet-black cap.)

So that day I had my first lover. Every so often in the course of that famous hour, my eyes chanced to turn to the coral necklace lying there near the bed; and later the sight of coral always brought to mind my first impression of love, with a taste of blind and joyful violence, of early summer. It doesn't matter if I had that first taste with someone I didn't love. I liked it just the same, and I like it; and every so often at night I dream again about coral.

Toward the end of the afternoon Assunta advised me to leave, because her family would be home soon. Before saying goodbye, she offered me a mirror and a comb so that I could neaten my hair, and, seeing myself in the mirror, I noticed that on my lower lip I had a tiny wound, from which a drop of blood oozed. Then my mind recalled, with a shock, the cause of that new wound; that is, I remembered that a moment before, as I was making love with Assunta, I had had to bite my lip until it bled in order not to cry out another name: Nunziata!

It was as if there, at that moment, before the small mirror, I had received an extraordinary revelation. That is, I believed that I understood only now what, in reality, I wanted from my stepmother: not friendship, not motherhood, but *love*, precisely what men and women do together when they are in love. As a result, I arrived at this great discovery: that, without a doubt, I was in love with N. Thus she really was the *first love* in my life, which is described in novels and poems! I loved Nunz, and surely, without knowing it, I had loved her from the afternoon of her arrival, maybe from the very moment she had appeared at the landing on the dock, with her shawl over her head and her elegant little high-heeled shoes. Now, with that certainty, I went back in memory over all the capricious troubles, conflicts, and sorrows that really had kept me at their mercy from that first distant afternoon until today:

and everything that I hadn't been able to explain before now appeared to be explained. I saw again, then, all those months passed as a mad, directionless crossing, through storms, chaos, and disorientation, until the Polar Star had appeared, to orient me. There, she was that, my Polar Star: she, Nunz, my first love! That discovery filled me with a radiant and unconscious exultation; but immediately I became aware of my desperate fate. Among all the women who existed in the world, if there was one more impossible for me than all others, forbidden to my love by a supreme prohibition, that one was N.: my stepmother, the wife of Wilhelm Gerace! Until a little earlier, when I still didn't know I loved her, I could have dared to hope that I would become close to her again, again deserve her gentle friendship; but now, instead, no hope was permitted. In fact, I should have been grateful to the state of war that N. maintained between herself and me, since at least it avoided any occasion for my criminal temptations to manifest themselves. Not only: but, thanks to the war that divided us, I could, without too many dangers or regrets, stay on Procida, in the same house with my love, avoiding the unbearable punishment of not seeing her face anymore!

## Intrigues of Gallantry

Thus I had again found a way of putting off a farewell that declared itself to me now as a necessary duty; and the summer season, as usual filling my days with richness and activity, helped me in this delay. Every afternoon, I returned to Assuntina's cottage, where she was waiting for me; and there with her, in her room, I found some repose from my restlessness. She wondered that, although I was constantly making love to her, I never kissed her, not even the smallest, simplest kiss that one might give to a sister: and I answered that I didn't like kisses, they seemed sappy. But the truth was different: it was that I could never forget my first, only kiss, given to N.; and it would have seemed to me that I was betraying N. if I kissed that other woman, whom I didn't love.

Now my memory (rethinking some earlier delusions) filled the kiss I'd given N. with all the burning tastes of love: every sensual delight, the most passionate thoughts. It seemed to me that, in the very brief moment when I kissed her, I had known all the promises of paradise that belong to true love alone, and that I couldn't know with Assuntina. Looking at her shameless poses, I thought again of N.'s ways, so modest, so pure, and my heart grieved with regret. Then, seeing my face darken, Assuntina asked me: "Well, what's wrong?" "Leave me alone," I said, "I'm sad." "And I can't console you?" "You can't console me, and nobody else can, either. I'm a truly unhappy soul."

Yet although I didn't love Assuntina I was pleased to have a lover; and, above all, proud, so that I would have liked to let it be known to the entire population (apart from my father; with him I would have been ashamed—I don't know why). Assuntina, naturally, insisted that it should be an absolute secret; and I submitted to that sacrifice, according to the proper rules of honor. But I found a way to let it be understood (with an attitude of fatuous superiority) that in my life there was something . . .

I would have liked one person, in particular, to know . . .

One day, I remember, I got the idea of going to buy (on credit, of course) several meters of lace, for example, or some women's garters, from a shopkeeper friend of N.'s, warning her not to breathe a word of my purchase to anyone, and especially my stepmother: in such a way that the shopkeeper would understand clearly that there was a mysterious woman in my life! But unfortunately when I got to the door of the shop I lost confidence, and turned back without doing anything.

Here I would point out that in considering this failed undertaking, I didn't delude myself about the discretion of the shopkeeper; in fact, I was convinced that she'd be unable to keep quiet with N. I say: *I was convinced*; but I should say: *I counted on it.*

Assuntina, even in her faithful and persistent friendship with Signora Gerace, kept her romance with her stepson Arturo carefully hidden. And so, thanks to her prudence, my stepmother was completely in the dark about it: no less than Carminiello could be. According to the highest moral logic, I should have comforted myself with that; but instead, inside, I was annoyed by it.

The ambition that tempted me—to display to the public my conquest (so that I would happily have printed the facts in the newspapers)—was aimed, I think, precisely at my stepmother. And at the thought that some gossip, for example, would go and whisper in her ear a hint, a tip, I would start laughing to myself involuntarily. Enough: my heart, which had no peace, would have enjoyed a kind of success if, one way or another, she had found out . . .

## The Lane

But why *a success*? What the hell sort of success was it? Undoubtedly, answering those questions would have been a profound problem. But I didn't make many problems for myself when I had such fantasies.

And while I pretended to respect Assuntina's prudence with N., I nurtured a contrary intention. That intention taught me devious and tortuous paths. Every so often, in N.'s presence, I let fall some half-revealing phrase, or cast ardent glances at Assuntina, or gave her small signs of understanding, pretending to believe that my stepmother wasn't looking at us at that moment . . . The sly Assuntina immediately displayed the face of a saint; and later, in the cottage, reproached me: "Watch out, be more careful!" But in response I assured her: "Come on, don't worry, my stepmother doesn't understand anything about anything, she's less intelligent than Carmine. Her thoughts are all Hail Marys and Our Fathers: other things she doesn't see or understand. She, can you believe it?, if she were to look in at the door right now—she might think we're lying here in bed just to sleep in peace, like a brother and sister."

And on this point, at least (that my stepmother was too slow to understand), my words were not lies, in fact they corresponded to my thoughts.

Every day, toward the end of the afternoon, at the hour when I left the cottage, I began to insist, with various pretexts, that Assunta come with me along the lane toward my house. And during the walk, especially on the last stretch, I would suddenly embrace her, holding her tight around the waist. "Watch out, what are you doing!" she protested, trying to get free of me. "Not here, in the street! Someone might see us!" "Well, who would see us," I answered her, "if it's all deserted!" But, a moment before embracing her, I had in fact glimpsed a curly and fleeting shadow in the kitchen window of the Casa dei Guaglioni: which withdrew precipitately behind the grille as soon as the two of us, turning the last corner, emerged at the top of the path, just under the window.

In those days something unusual appeared in my stepmother's behavior, which even a casual observer would surely have noted. She seemed to have fallen into a kind of absentmindedness, which gave her face a sad, almost livid pallor. She performed her tasks, her usual familiar activities, with a heavy inertia and, at times, a distracted confusion, as if her body were moving against her will, divided from her mind: and her meekness had given way to a nervousness, very close to irritability. I heard her scold Carmine; she even responded brusquely to my father; and her friends complained of finding her ill-tempered, contrary to every habit of hers.

One day, looking up, I surprised her staring at me. At the first instant, her gaze, meeting mine, instinctively remained on me, expressing a trembling, crude pain; but immediately it became conscious again, and withdrew beneath pale eyelids.

I don't remember if what follows happened the afternoon of that same day, or another day. I went up the lane in the company of Assuntina, and

every so often, as usual, I glanced furtively toward the window of the
Casa dei Guaglioni; until I saw, not far away, that small familiar shadow
hiding up there, behind the grille.

Then I rushed to embrace Assunta passionately; and all of a sudden,
though I never kissed her, I gave her a big kiss right in the face.


## Scene between Women


At a certain point the next morning, approaching the little beach from
the sea, I had the thought of going home for a moment, I don't know
if to get a new oar for the boat or some other such motive. And as I
entered the yard I was surprised by fierce women's cries coming from the
kitchen, mixed with Carmine's crying. When I got to the French door,
I found myself facing an unusual scene. In the kitchen, besides my stepbrother, who was crying desperately in his basket, were my stepmother
and Assunta; and the first, overcome with fury, was shouting at the second, as if she wanted to tear her to pieces.

Assuntina, who seemed startled and confused, at my entrance burst
into tears, and summoned me as a witness, saying that she didn't understand it. She explained that she had come in a little earlier, to say hello
to Nunziata, as usual; and had picked up Carmine from his basket, to
cuddle him, as she had done many times. But my stepmother, at that
point, had rushed at her like a wild beast, tearing Carmine out of her
arms, and then (since, at that brutal move, the boy had started to cry)
unjustly started to rail against her, Assunta, accusing her of that sin: of
having made the boy cry! And so, still shouting, she had ordered her to
beware of picking him up from now on, because he, that child, hated
her, Assunta, like smoke in his eyes, and would start crying if she merely
touched him! There, just then I had arrived, Assunta concluded between
her tears; and I could take note, as a witness, of that sworn testimony of

hers: that it wasn't her fault if my little brother was wailing! She couldn't understand being treated so rudely: as if it had become a crime to pick up an infant in her arms!

At Assunta's justifications, my stepmother, instead of being soothed, became even angrier, until, in an instant, her face was transfigured, like a Fury's.

Suddenly she burst out, shouting at her friend, "You must never be seen in this house again!"

She shook her head violently, in the atavistic manner of quarreling women in squalid alleys: "I don't want you here! In this house I am the mistress!" she continued, really beside herself. And suddenly she made as if to rush at the other.

Fortunately, I intervened in time to prevent her, and, grabbing her wrists, pushed her forcefully against the wall.

Pinned to the wall, she, out of pride, did not even try to struggle. But, through her wrists, I felt all her muscles tremble, developing a desperate ferocity; and her eyes resembled the fires of two wretched and sublime stars, lost in a storm. Beneath the disheveled curls pasted to her forehead by sweat her face was white, and she twisted it away from me, leaning toward her adversary. "Get out!" she shouted at her, almost transported by hatred. And she added: "Get out, *segnata da Dio*!"

That phrase *segnato da Dio* is a saying of contemptible vulgarity, used in our towns by the cruel to insult cripples, the lame, and other unfortunates. At that spiteful allusion poor Assunta broke into sobs and headed toward the door with her short, limping steps. And I, indignant, left my brutalized stepmother and went out, too, to walk a little distance along the road with her, as it seemed to me was my duty.

Although she was demonstrably grateful for this chivalrous attention, still, as soon as we were alone, she began to reproach me for my carelessness: "If you had been cautious, as I urged you, your stepmother would never have suspected anything, because she's not malicious. And instead, look, here's the result: that she, in my opinion, has discovered everything! In fact, although in front of her I pretended to believe that excuse of Carminiello, I'm not so ignorant that I don't understand it was only an excuse, in order not to speak the truth to my face. Besides, now that I think back, she's been giving me mean looks for several days. The truth is this, if you want to listen to Assunta: that, because of you, because you're so careless, she realized that we two are meeting. And according to her thinking what we do is an evil sin; and a woman, like me, who does it is an immoral woman, without honor. So she, being honest, is disgusted by my friendship, and doesn't want anything to do with it. And all right: let it be as she wants! But she's not right: because I'm not a girl, I'm a widow, and a widow, if she meets with someone, doesn't sin like a girl—much less! Well: I already knew she's hypocriti-cal . . . but I didn't know so bitter! Who would have expected that such a sweet woman, who seemed like a mother hen, could become such a fierce, ugly eagle!"

## Stepmother of Stone

Amid these outbursts from Assunta, we had descended a good way along the path: then, having distinguished at a distance one of her rela-tives heading toward the cottage, she urged me to leave, in order not to encourage new malicious suspicions. And without discussion I separated from her, heading off on another street.

I was grateful for this chance to be alone for a while, and to surren-der without witnesses to my deep, unreasonable exultation.

The truth is I should have felt not exultation but remorse. Assunta couldn't imagine how guilty I was: she accused me of behaving carelessly, unable to guess the worst—and that is that my incautious behavior was not only heedless but also intentional! Yet, although aware of my guilt, in my heart I felt no remorse but, rather, an intimate, triumphant joy, which made me walk as lightly as if my feet weren't touching the ground.

Almost without realizing it, I had taken the road home. It was around midday; in the kitchen Carminiello was sleeping placidly in his basket, and my stepmother was standing at the table. On the table were the usual preparations for the pasta, which had been interrupted by the earlier scene; and her hands were moving weakly on the sheet of dough, as if they were eager to be occupied but hadn't the strength to keep going. Her face was so white, set, and dazed that it made you think of a grave illness.

I asked if my father had come down from his room; and, not finding the energy to speak, she moved her eyelids a little, to answer no; but even that small movement seemed to cost her such an effort that her whole face, and especially her lips, began to tremble.

Then, frightened by her appearance, I asked: "What's wrong? Do you feel ill?" (Ever since she had kept me distant because of that kiss, I had initiated this new thing: to use the more formal *voi* when I spoke to her, rather than *tu*. And I couldn't say if that was intended to imply a deliberate respect or, rather, sulkiness.)

She looked at me, eyes trembling, without answering; but, as if my pity had taken away her last power of resistance, suddenly she fell to her knees, and, hiding her face on a chair, broke into terrible, dry sobs. "What's wrong?" I said. "Tell me what's wrong!" I felt a gentle desire to caress her, to caress at least her hair. But her forehead, her small work-ruined hands, appeared so pale that I didn't dare touch her: I was afraid she would die. Meanwhile, amid those sobs, in an adult, lacerating tone of voice that didn't seem hers, she began to speak: "Oh, I'm damned. I'm damned. God . . . won't forgive me . . . ever . . ."

Phrases of instinctive adoration thronged to my lips: I would have liked to say, "You're my blessed of Paradise! You're my angel," but I understood that I would have frightened her. "At this moment," I thought, "it

will be better if I speak as if I were her father or something like that."
And I said (but in a voice that, in spite of myself, expressed only a joyous,
bold passion, not the severity of a father): "What do you mean, damned?
Come on, stop it, don't be silly!"

Finally those cruel sobs found an outlet in tears; and her voice
became recognizable again, although ravaged by a new torment. "And
how could I," she accused herself, as she wept, "say such a vile word to
that poor woman? It's not her fault, if she has an infirmity. Oh, to say
a word like that is worse than murder! I'm ashamed to exist! And what
can I do now, what can I do? I should go to that woman and ask her to
forgive me, to forget the words I said, to come back here to my house as
before . . . Oh, no, I can't! I can't!" and, as if frightened of herself, she
hid her mouth behind the palms of her hands, while her eyes, at the
thought of Assuntina, grew large with savage hatred.

"Oh, what will I do with myself? What should I do?" she murmured. And with these questions she turned to me a tearful, lost gaze,
which seemed to ask for help, or advice, as if I were God. But her eyes
had become so beautiful at that moment that I paid no more attention
to their suffering: in the depths of their blackness, I seemed to make
out, as within two enchanted mirrors, distant places of light, of absolute
happiness! And I exclaimed impetuously:

"You know what you should do? You should leave Procida, with
me. Then you'll never have to see Assunta, if she's so hateful to you.
We'll run away together, you and I and Carminiello. Anyway," I added
bitterly, "my father doesn't care about us, he won't even notice, he'll
manage, if we leave. We'll go, all three of us together, to live in some
magnificent land, far from Procida, I'll choose it. And there I'll make
sure you live better than a queen."

As I spoke, she made a sudden move to cover her face with her hands;
but still the violent blush that invaded it, to her neck and her bare arms,

was visible. For a moment she couldn't answer me: her irregular breaths, coming through her throat, were transformed into a bitter, wild lament. Finally she said:

"Artú! . . . Since you're still a boy, God will forgive the bad things you say, the evil . . ."

Maybe she was about to say *the evil you do*, but it must have seemed a word too harsh against me, and she didn't say it. And, instead of feeling remorse at her reproach, I was transported with joy, which made me even more thoughtless and mad: in truth, her voice, from behind the mask of her hands, had reached me as a fabulous sound, which betrayed irreparably—even more than the indulgence—the anguish of a renunciation and, at the same time, a kind of restoration of gentle gratitude. I exclaimed, coming close to her:

"Oh, please, look into my face, look into my eyes!" and, armed with sweetness and power, I pushed her palms away. For a second, her troubled face flashed before me still sweet, still pink from the earlier blush; but already she had jumped to her feet, with a pallor that almost disfigured her. And she began to speak, backing up against the wall:

"No! No! What are you doing? Go away . . . Artú . . . don't come any closer, if you don't want me to . . ." And, turning her head slightly, she leaned her forehead against the wall, scowling hard, as if in her weakness, which nearly caused her to slide to the floor, she were collecting all her nerves in a gigantic and desperate act of will.

And without looking at me she again turned her face, now unrecognizable, toward me: furrowed, dull, with the thick black eyebrows joined on her forehead, it seemed the image of some obscure, soulless barbarian goddess, of a truly wicked stepmother.

"Artú," she said in a small, toneless voice, which could have belonged to a woman of forty. "First I loved you . . . like a son. But now . . . I don't love you anymore."

Here her voice had a kind of suffocated convulsion; and then she resumed blindly, with a more acute, jarring, and almost hysterical sound:

"And so the less we see each other, and the less you talk to me, the better it will be. Imagine that I had always remained a stranger to you; because our kinship is forever dead. And I ask you to stay away from me, because when you're near me I feel disgust!"

I suppose that in my place someone more experienced than I would not have doubted that she was lying. And maybe he would have said: "Shame on you, you wicked liar, or at least learn to pretend with more skill! Because you don't have the heart for the outrageous lies you're telling, and you have to lean against the wall, as if you expected to be struck by lightning. And you're shivering so much that I can see, at this distance, how even the skin on your arms is shuddering!"

Instead, listening to her, I had not exactly the certainty but the suspicion that her words were a true representation of her feelings! And this suspicion was enough to hurl me into an icy sadness, as if I'd been condemned to end my existence in a polar night. I was tempted, impulsively, to say, "If what you say is true, swear to it!" but I didn't dare: I was too afraid that she really would swear, thus giving me a conclusive certainty. What hurt me most was that word *disgust*: and I imagined that the palpable shiver, which had made her skin pucker as she spoke, was, precisely, a natural effect of horror toward me. Now I was almost driven to persuade myself that Assuntina wasn't wrong, attributing to a moral contempt the scene she had made! And to think that I'd almost flattered myself at having been present at a scene of jealousy: even feeling a secret satisfaction at the idea that two women had risked fighting for me, right before my eyes! Nothing was sadder than having to give up such sweet, enchanted foolishness for the ugliness of a cold, serious reality.

## The Indian Slave

So painfully did she wound me with those words that, silenced, I didn't reply. It was at that point that, perhaps, Carmine woke up or my father arrived: I no longer remember; certainly our dialogue ended on those words of hers.

And from then on her attitude toward me remained the same, fixed. Never, as the days passed, did she show me any expression except that sort of inanimate, barbarian image, eyes opaque, eyebrows joined to form a dark cross with the line on her forehead. Oh, I would have much preferred if she had treated me like the wickedest stepmother of novels. I would have preferred to see her transformed into a murderous wolf rather than that statue.

✤

Among other things, in the hope of being forgiven, I formed a plan for abandoning Assuntina in a spectacular way (assuming that for N. we shared the same moral failing!). But immediately it occurred to me that, in reality, her hatred for me had begun before I'd been with Assunta: it had begun the morning of that fatal kiss. No, even leaving Assuntina would be of no use to me. There was no remedy: N. abhorred me, without forgiveness.

I felt such a need to open myself to someone, to be consoled, that sometimes I was tempted to confide everything to Assunta: my secret love for N., my despair, and so on. But I always held back in time, mainly out of this fear: that Assunta, sooner or later, would report my confidences to N. Certainly, N.'s horror of me would reach the limits if she learned that I loved her! Such a revelation would confirm the idea that she perhaps already had: and that is that I was a tremendous monster of evil, a true incarnation of Satan. That thought was enough to stifle any desire to confide. And so, luckily, Assunta never learned certain truths.

Following these events, my lover appeared less charming to me: even her lame leg, which before had seemed something so sweet, now sometimes bothered me. The wish to boast about this woman no longer tempted me; and I felt less pleasure in being with her. Yet I continued to see her every day, since that cottage, one might say, was the only refuge that remained to me. Assunta in fact said, with satisfaction, that I had become more passionate than before! Maybe because the desperate flames that I hid in my heart in the end flared up wherever they could.

Besides, even though I didn't love Assunta, sometimes a feeling of pity was kindled toward her that burned almost like love. The mere thought that I didn't love her, and that she wasn't attractive to me, or even that I was bored with her, inspired pity! So small and naked on the corn mattress, with her olive-colored breasts and their geranium-colored nipples, slightly slack and elongated, to make one think of a goat, and with that loose, smooth hair, she seemed to me, at times, a being from another land, maybe an Indian slave. And I was her leader and did with her what I wanted! Then N., up in the Casa dei Guaglioni, appeared to me in the guise of a great white mistress, shining with contempt; and to chase away that captivating, painful image I exploded with Assuntina, practically abusing her with my sudden ardor.

Kisses, however, I never gave Assuntina; my kisses seemed forever consecrated to N. by a kind of holy decree, which couldn't be violated without offending that love.

Later, around sunset, when I left the cottage, I was ashamed of having been with a wretched slave, as of a new indignity toward N. I delayed, solitary, in the nearby fields, over which loomed the massive, crumbling pink-colored walls of the Casa dei Guaglioni, and I no longer looked up at that famous window, knowing already that I would see it deserted. There, behind those walls, amid her grim prohibitions, my chatelaine N. lived, sublime and inaccessible. In the distance her height became greater than it really was; and it seemed to me that all the male and female angels of her imagination, like flocks of shining owls, storks, and seagulls, flew around her, urging her day and night to abhor me.

# CHAPTER 7

# The Terra Murata

*O flots abracadabrantesques*
(O abracadabra-like waves)
—ARTHUR RIMBAUD, "THE STOLEN HEART"

## *Dearer than the Sun*

While I lived under the same roof as N. with the thoughts of a criminal at a heavenly court, another castle had begun to dominate my mind as well, with perhaps an even more fantastic authority. Suddenly that summer the island's penitentiary, which had always been to my eyes the sad dwelling of shadows (scarcely less odious than death), was lit up with a sparkling brightness: as in the metamorphoses of alchemy, where everything is transmuted from black to gold.

The summer, that year, seemed to shine in vain for Wilhelm Gerace. We witnessed an absolutely new event in our history: and that is that my father, at the height of the summer season, dragged out the most luminous hours of the day in the closed space of the rooms, as if time, for him, remained fixed in a perennial winter night. He persistently fled all the pleasurable occupations of the season, which had always been our greatest shared happiness; and the paleness of his skin, in the months of July and August, gave me a mournful and unnatural sensation, as if I were witnessing some sick upheaval of the cosmos.

Especially in the beginning, I often showed up before him, his expression grim and scowling, to insist that he come down to the beach or go out in the boat with me. These invitations were met by scornful rejections, tinged with anguish and drama. His responses seemed to say that this year he had vowed a disgusted, vengeful hatred toward the sun, the sea, and the burning open air, so beloved by him! But that at the same time he intended, with the renunciation of those things, to offer a kind of holy or propitiatory sacrifice. Not unlike a worshipper who mortifies himself to become worthy of a deity.

Finally, although he acted mysterious, he couldn't help betraying himself. (Here I recognized yet again the unearthly grace of his heart, which, even in its most desperate plights, was always somewhat pleased by its own mysteries!) And from certain of his allusions I understood, in the end, without any doubts, his arcane motivation (it was the same, anyway, that I already suspected):

*Someone*, whose friendship was dearer to him than any other, was spending his days enclosed in those four cursed walls. And therefore how could he enjoy a summer, which to him was denied? No, he longed to imitate, hour by hour, the suffering of his friend; and in fact he would have liked, in some way, to deserve, as an honor, an equal sentence, if it were not that, deprived of freedom, he would have lost every last means of communicating with him! Only for this unique thing was his freedom useful to him; and the earth, with summer and the sea, and the sky, with the sun and all the planets, seemed to him skeletons, and inspired in him revulsion.

## Conventional Pearls and Roses

At these exclamations from my father I was tempted to answer that I knew perfectly well to whom he alluded. That I had seen on the dock, at the distance of a few meters, that famous person: and I despised him with all my soul, considering him a foul killer, unworthy not only of friendship but even of being looked at, so odious was his ugliness! But I didn't speak: I glared proudly and turned my back on my father, as if I hadn't even listened to his words, setting off for the beach alone, as always.

After that encounter at the landing, I had avoided returning in my thoughts to the image of the young stranger I had seen passing with the two guards on the dock. The scene of that afternoon, overwhelmed by my other bitter feelings of that time, had been pushed down into the depths of my mind, in the same way that he had been relegated to his prison up there. He was inauspicious for me; and just as I hadn't wanted to observe his features clearly then, so I didn't want to pause to remember him now. If, in spite of myself, my thoughts happened to fall on that criminal, they discerned not a precise human figure but a kind of formless, muddy gray clay, marked by ugliness.

But, at the same time, the insolent, innocent pace at which he set off toward his fate flared before me again, with winged elegance . . . That graceful reappearance, like a sword flashing against my contempt, bit my heart with anguish, startling me. Suddenly, in place of a cursed shade buried in a jail, I saw a fabulous delinquent, distinguished by such marvelous charms that perhaps even the police and the guards were his servants.

Unexpectedly, too, certain romantic prejudices returned from my childhood to adorn him. I mean that the category of *prisoner* was worth as much as a coat of arms according to those boyhood prejudices. And similarly, I would add, according to those of the adult Wilhelm Gerace!

In fact (I now realize), the primitive spark of a conventional seduction was needed to ignite Wilhelm Gerace's faith: and the character of the *Prisoner* well suited his yearnings, which were eternally childish, like those of the universe! In the same way the audience in the theater demands conventional heroines (the Fallen One, the Slave, the Queen) to ignite its faith . . . And so unto eternity every pearl in the sea copies the first pearl, and every rose copies the first rose.

## Metamorphosis

So although I didn't think about it, in reality I had known for some time now toward whom the unusual devotions and sufferings that since the previous autumn had tortured the existence of Wilhelm Gerace were directed; but during the days of that febrile summer that shadowy knowledge had unfolded and ramified hidden beneath my thoughts.

The few allusions I've cited were the only mentions of the subject between my father and me. I stopped inviting him to the beach or elsewhere; and we spoke no more of his secrets. That stubborn and tortuous silence was due not so much to his will as, rather, to mine. The silence was a kind of pledge, made to myself, of contempt for that unnamed man of the dock; and perhaps I thus deluded myself that I was truly crushing his existence under a tombstone, denying his mysterious power. I reached the point where once, with my father, by chance naming the penitentiary, I don't know why, I blushed, disgusted and ashamed of myself.

Every day at a certain hour (usually late afternoon), my father interrupted his tedious seclusion and went out, refusing any company. By now I certainly didn't need to spy on him to know where he was heading; and the towering neighborhood of the fortress, which in the past, owing to a kind of sacred modesty, I had always avoided on my walks, was enclosed by a new, strange, and monstrous ban. It's difficult for me even today to describe that feeling, which, besides, I refused to examine at the time. Perhaps it could be compared to what the tribes of Moses must have felt for the Temple of Baal in Babylon, or something like that!

My father's occasional allusions had confirmed to me that he and the condemned man of the dock already knew each other and were friends before that notorious day when I had seen them disembark on Procida from the same ship. And the obscure favor (it couldn't be chance) that had brought him to the land dear to my father was for me evidence of a sort of magical complicity that existed between the two. The flamboyant behavior of that youth at the dock was not enough to make me think that he didn't return my father's friendship—since insolence seemed a natural habit, like the spotted skin of the leopard.

I didn't know the crime committed by our prisoner. But I had reason to attribute to him a serious crime, because the pentitentiary of Procida rarely housed petty delinquents; and according to my vision, the sentence that seemed most likely was life imprisonment, and so in my thoughts I almost always ended up giving him the title of Lifer.

The idea that he was shut up for life might also be of some consolation; but it was a consolation as poor as it was cruel. I felt, in fact, that the category of lifer, if on the one hand it limited his mastery over my father, on the other magnified him more proudly in his eyes, no less than in mine!

⁀⊙⊙↶

Meanwhile, my childish and superstitious faith in my father's authority (an authority more than human, capable of every miracle) began to operate again. I knew that, by law, the inmates of the penal colony could receive visitors from outsiders only at rare intervals, and for the duration of a few minutes, and always in the presence of the guards. But also, in some unexplored depth of my mind, the opinion was taking root that every day when my father went out he was going to a meeting with the prisoner. Thanks to who knows what obscure powers or devious corruption, in secret subterranean corridors they met and talked together every day. Now, in the usually dormant region of my imagination, as in an opaque fog, those meetings assumed an imprecise but mysteriously horrible shape. The strange image of clay, as murky and fluid as lava, that in my mind inexplicably represented the young convict was transformed, by a foul spell, into the person of my father, softening and being molded into a shapeless, changing, and fantastic statue. And this indecipherable metamorphosis had the occult value of certain dreams that when we wake up appear meaningless but while we're dreaming seem like evil oracles.

In the confusion of horror, that flame of peremptory, incomparable grace was blazing up again, more intense than anything else, returning to transfigure the apparition of the dock. It was as if the young prisoner had tossed me a mocking greeting as he changed again, from a formless monster into a handsome noble character, who cried *fraud* at my scorn. Relentlessly, my childish prejudices returned to adorn him . . . And in a flash the house of punishment was revealed to be similar to the Castle of the Knights of Syria: legendary noble adventurers, dedicated to a bloody vow, crowded that walled palace, in which only my father was welcomed. They dominated the island with their tragic spell: on their gaunt faces slavery and their various crimes became a trick of seduction, like makeup on the faces of women. And they all circled around, protecting with their code of honor that vague underground point where my father met the apparition of the dock.

Although the neighborhood of the fortress was so close, it was now

situated for me in an implacable dimension, outside the human, a kind
of deathly Olympus. I had reached the point of excluding it not only
from my usual routes but, as much as possible, from my sight. In the
boat, I avoided rounding the North Point close up, for behind it the castle, at the top of a foundation of rocks, loomed sharply over the shoreless
sea. And when I passed wide of there I always turned my eyes to the
open water and away from that irregular massive form that, from a distance, resembled an eroded mountain of volcanic rock. In that expanse
of sea, superstition roused in me impressions that I knew were false but
that still became almost hallucinatory. I seemed to hear, from the shape
of rock behind me, some strangely melodious echoes, clamoring in uni-
son. And I was unnerved by the bizarre suspicion that I could distinguish, suddenly, in the chorus, the voice of my father, unreal, like that of
a fetish or a dead man. He was wandering there, in funerary pomp, with
his white emaciated face.

## The End of Summer

It was now the end of September. One day, I delayed so long on the sea
in my boat that without noticing I let the time pass when I usually went
to see Assuntina. When I landed, I judged, from the position of the sun,
that it must be around four in the afternoon; and in fact a little later
I heard quarter after four sound from the bell tower. I decided it was
too late for Assuntina, and I gave her up for that day. After pulling the
boat onshore, I took my ragged shirt and rope-soled shoes from under
the rock where I always left them in the morning and began to climb,
without a precise goal, taking shortcuts through the countryside that led
to the town.

The shadows of trunks and stalks were already long, and the colors
faded and cool. Two months earlier, at the same hour of the afternoon,

the island was still all on fire. The days had shortened since then. Soon summer would be over.

The other days, with Assuntina, I had never paused to consider that reality. It was as if today, taking advantage of my solitude, a sad pale genie, with half-closed eyes, had appeared to me; and he greeted me, running over the grass with an autumnal rustling. His greeting signified *farewell*: as if here today I knew, conclusively, that this was my last summer on the island.

The truth is that in a vague way I had always, in those months, assumed that the end of the present summer would be the end of my time on Procida. But then, thinking *summer*, I saw, in my mind, an indefinite season, with no limits, equal to an entire existence! I deluded myself in the confused faith that, just as this summer would ripen the grapes, the olives, and the other fruits of the gardens, it would, in some way, also ripen the bitterness of my fate, and my sufferings would come to a great consoling resolution. To arrive at the end with those sufferings still bitter: that was the omen I couldn't believe in, and nevertheless saw in the light, and in the delicate breaths of air, like an equivocal and icy farewell. *Question without answer* is what, translated into words, that farewell meant: and nothing and no one said to me another word; not even the eyes of N., which were so beautiful and maternal, and for me made of stone.

Carried along by my distracted mind, I found myself on the steep ascent of the Due Mori, which ends in Piazzetta del Monumento. The square, bordered on the west, in view of the beach, by a simple balustrade, shone at that hour with a calm and brilliant light, between the pink-orange color of its walls and the golden reflection of the water. I've spoken several times of this beautiful square, but maybe I haven't yet said that four streets led out of it. One was the slope of the Due Mori. Another was the one that we had traveled so many times in the carriage, descending toward the area of the harbor, and which then continued on the opposite side of the square, changing its name, into my famous street amid the gardens. The last, on the western side, was the widest and was well paved, and wound upward, like a meandering lookout, toward the height of the fortress. The same balustrade continued from the square along the street's external side, thus leaving it open, at that hour, like the square, to the full sun, which lighted it with a marvelous pink-orange.

## The Terra Murata

That was the only road on the island that led to the gate of the Terra Murata, the walled land (as people call the neighborhood of the prison, in memory of the ancient fortifications). It was along here that the truck carrying the new prisoners up from the port passed. I don't know how long it had been since I'd taken that road, which for me was as if eliminated from the island.

But that day I chose it instinctively, without much hesitation or surprise: noticing only a rapid beating of my heart, as if, in breaking my ban, I were performing a daring and solemn act. The long strip of the road was deserted as far as the last visible turn; and I had a sense of repose going up through that magical calm, whose terrible melancholy seemed to offer me a refuge. The island, whose dolphin shape extended below amid the play of foam, with the smoke from the houses and the din of voices, appeared very distant, and no longer enchanting to me, who sought harsher enchantments! I advanced into an area outside of time, where the end of summer brought neither hope nor farewells. Up in the tragic structures of the Terra Murata, a single hopeless, late season endured forever in its proud devastation, divided from the world of mothers.

Toward the top of the ascent, on the left, opposite the balustrade, were the first buildings of the prison, with the homes of the employees, the offices, and the infirmaries. At the end the ascent broadened into a terrace, which offered on two sides a view of the sea, open to infinity, fresh and blue. Here rose the gigantic entrance of the Terra Murata, with its high stone vault and the sentry towers for the guards dug into the pilasters. An armed guard always walked in front of one of the sentry boxes, but he didn't prohibit free passersby from entering, because, beyond the entrance, beyond the city of the prisons, there existed a populous village, with old churches and convents.

When I reached the terrace, I saw my father, a few meters away; he was half sitting on the balustrade, with his back turned to the view, in a kind of dreamy apathy, letting the western breeze ruffle his hair. Seeing him, I stopped, startled; but he didn't notice me. Against the luminosity of the setting sun, his face, angular because it was so thin, seemed the face of an adolescent, shadowed by the neglected beard that was like a golden down. A moment later, he moved, in his faded blue shirt, unbuttoned over his white chest and here and there flapping in the breeze, and made his way in through the arch of the entrance. Then, I, too, going at a slow pace to keep my distance from him, set off in the same direction. Now it seemed to me that I had already known I had come here to spy on him. And I felt that perhaps since the beginning of the summer I had been preparing myself to follow, sometime or other, the tracks of his mystery.

## The Hunt

From the vaulted passage of the entrance, a gloomy corridor whose plaster was frescoed, from top to bottom, with dusty black crosses, one came out onto the central square of the Terra Murata, which was so immense it seemed like a city square but was always strangely deserted. On the left of this square, at the end of a steep paved dip, a gate barred access to a vast, bare yellow courtyard, surrounded by enormous rectangular buildings. HOUSE OF PUNISHMENT was written over the gate, around a brightly colored relief of Santa Maria della Pietà.

That was the entrance to the penitentiary. From that point, past some low buildings protected by walls, the hill of the prison rose behind the central square, up to the ancient castle that could be seen, on the right, towering above the small village built at its foot. For a second, my heart stopped, as I expected to see my father go confidently down along the slope and immediately disappear, as if by a miracle, from my gaze, behind that forbidden gate. But instead he went to the right; and skirting the square he headed toward the higher area of the Terra, where, on the terraces of the ancient fortress, in a labyrinth of intersections, ascents, and descents, the dwellings of the village had been piling up for centuries.

Unlike the central square, now three-quarters in shadow, that area was still struck by the sun, whose light tinged with red the narrow windows, amid ancient overlapping arches, the uneven roofs, and the loggias flowering with peppers and geraniums. Walking crookedly, as if he were drunk, my father entered those noisy alleys in the sunset. On his feet he wore low sandals with wooden soles that are common on our beaches in summer, and these, echoing on the cobblestones, guided me behind him in the tangle of streets. My steps, instead, because of my rope-soled shoes, were silent; but although I was following him at a short distance, I was no longer afraid that he would discover me. I felt protected by a kind of cynicism and fatality, as if I had swallowed the ring that makes one invisible, and he were an elf, a will-o'-the-wisp substance, and all means of communication between us were cut off. I imagined that the inhabitants scattered about the alleys, or looking out of the loggias, or sitting on the outside staircases, who called and talked to one another, couldn't see us go by.

My mind had become inert; but a dull, almost desolate certainty told me that Wilhelm Gerace was now walking defenseless before me, like an unconscious guide; and that, inevitably, soon, I didn't know how, I would be led into the theater of his mysteries.

I didn't even feel curiosity; rather, a sense of forgetfulness or stillness, such as one has in a dream. At most five or six minutes had passed, and it seemed hours since I had come through the entrance of the Terra Murata.

The goal of W.G. now, in this area, could be only one: the old castle. It was there, evidently, that the prisoner had been assigned his dwelling. He must be in one of those small cells, with the tiny windows like air vents, which faced the sea without seeing it, and toward which travelers on the steamers, looking out curiously from the railings, on the journey to or from Procida, directed their pitying attention. But although that could be my father's only goal, he continued for a while to wander in a disorderly fashion here and there through alleys and side streets, around the single street (called Via del Borgo) that led to the entrances to the castle. I wondered if in fact he might have been drinking. That senseless back-and-forth made one think of nocturnal butterflies madly fluttering around a lamp. Finally he made up his mind and, as I expected, took Via del Borgo. And there, suddenly, I lost track of him.

Via del Borgo was a kind of tunnel excavated into the rocky ground below the inhabited area, with no other pavement than a thick layer of dust. For its entire length (perhaps three hundred meters), between the archway of the entrance and that of the exit toward the castle, the only light it received was from an opening cut out halfway along, which was as wide as a small door, and led to the space above. For long intervals, therefore, this street (which the inhabitants commonly called the

Canalone) stagnated in an eternal darkness; only occasionally, on the sides, a faint light glimmered from some small cavelike entrances at ground level, from which narrow stairways led into the cottages above.

As I entered Via del Borgo, the blue stain of my father's shirt, which preceded me by a few meters, was swallowed up by the shadows. At first I was able to distinguish ahead of me the sound of his wooden clogs, which, although muffled on the dusty ground, echoed faintly under the vault; then nothing. From the town above, voices of girls could be heard calling their brothers in from the street, for the day was ending; and here and there, in the small dark entrances, a boy could be seen playing on the ground near the stairway, among dogs, hens, and sometimes the beating wings of a pigeon. Now my eyes had grown used to that dim light; but, walking faster, I sharpened my gaze in vain, trying to see my prey. I ran along the rest of Via del Borgo, and in a moment was at the exit, in the vast grassy courtyard at the end of which, through a massive doorway dug into a kind of rampart, one approached the dungeons of the nearby castle. But of my father no trace. On that arid field, in front of the barred doorway, there was only the soldier on guard, weapon over his shoulder, who barely glanced at me, more sleepy than suspicious. Apart from him there was no sign of a human presence. I stood there bewildered for a while; and finally, with a shrug, returned, lazily, along Via del Borgo.

It seemed to me pointless to retrace the shadowy Canalone from end to end; and I left it halfway along, emerging through the cut-out opening. It occurred to me that my father, too, might have come out here; and in that way his disappearance could be explained, without too many fantastic tricks. It might be. But, even if that was the exact route, who could say, at that hour, where he might be? And besides, finally, what did W.G. matter to me? What did it matter to discover his secrets? Suddenly, more than the hope, it was the desire to find him that had left me. Climbing up toward the heights of the fortress, I ran into a group of boys who were coming down carrying a kite, and I was tempted to ask if they had seen a tall man dressed in blue; but I decided it wasn't worth the trouble. And I kept going only out of inertia, without a precise plan.

## The Palace

From the cut-out wall of the Canalone, one ascended piles of rock and rubble to an abandoned terrain called the Guarracino, which ran behind the village, along the far edge of the Terra Murata above the highest cliffs on the island. The Guarracino was blocked, at the end, by the immense structure of the old castle; and the last stretch was made up of a mountain of derelict houses (I think from the time of the Turkish pirates), roofless and largely buried under mounds of earth. That mountain of ruins was separated from the castle, erected almost on the edge of the rocks opposite, by a natural, impassable gully, its bottom littered with garbage and stones; and on the right, amid steep thickets of thorns and weeds, it sloped down toward the sea.

Below was the island's North Point, which I had avoided during the past season, like a specter, whenever I had to cross that area of the sea in my boat. Now you could hear the sea, which, sucked into fissures in the cliff, crashed repeatedly with a faint roar; no other sound could be heard. The Guarracino was completely deserted; and climbing up that mangy ravaged mountain I was filled with a desolate sadness.

The voices of the village, not far away, reaching me muffled and softened in the calm air, seemed voices of a childish race, different from mine: and, hearing them, I had the feeling that a grim wandering knight might have as, toward evening, he goes alone through woods and valleys, listening to the dialogues of the birds gathering in the trees to sleep all together. I regretted the days when at this hour I was lounging around the port, sated by having made love with Assuntina all afternoon, and already half asleep; and I felt some remorse toward the Indian slave, who today had waited for me in vain. "At this precise moment," I thought, "she is busy preparing dinner down in her cottage for her relatives returning from the fields. And my stepmother, in the Casa dei Guaglioni, is beside the basket, trying to sing Carmine to sleep. But Carmine isn't sleepy, and wants to keep playing . . ." All were occupied with simple, natural things. I alone was following terrible and extraordinary mysteries, which might not even exist, and which, besides, I no longer wished to know.

Among the ruins of those buried cottages, the remains of taller structures still rose here and there—some pieces of wall, two or three meters high, with crumbled squares in place of the old windows. Unexpectedly, at the foot of one of those walls, I noticed my father's wooden sandals.

I backed up and hid quickly behind the wall: suddenly, after having sought W.G. so intensely, I was afraid of seeing him, even without being seen by him. And I stayed there, suspended, my heart in tumult, without venturing out of my hiding place. Evidently he had taken off his sandals to walk more quickly, barefoot, on that rough terrain: and he couldn't be far, since between the rocky abyss and the sea every path was cut off. But even if I held my breath, I couldn't hear, in the passing of the seconds, any sign of a living presence.

On that side of the mountain, the structure of the castle had neither windows nor doors: nothing but gigantic blank walls, reinforced by columns, buttresses, and blind arches, so that it resembled almost a mass of natural rock, rather than some human place. On one wing alone, jutting out in a semicircle that extended sheer over the sea, a few small vent-like windows could be seen from here, where I was; but through those windows no sound or movement could be perceived. As if the persons in somber white uniforms who lived in the palace were lying in lethargy, locked inside those walls.

Unless you had wings, it was impossible to reach the rooms of the palace from this part of the Terra Murata. And in the abandoned silence that persisted around me, every sort of marvelous vision regarding W.G. surfaced. Stairways, secret passages, fantastic deceptions, or maybe, even, death. I pictured him as, having taken off his wooden sandals, he rushed down the cliff and was smashed to pieces: and it seemed to me that nothing mattered anymore, even if he was dead. Whether he was dead or alive, near or far, had become indifferent to me. I desired suddenly to have already left the island, to be among foreign people, with no return; and I decided that in the future I would let all new acquaintances believe that I was a foundling, with no father or mother or relations. Abandoned in swaddling clothes on a step, and raised in an orphanage, or something like that.

I yawned, to insult the invisible shadow of W.G. But, weary, I stayed there, not knowing what I expected. The sun had almost completely disappeared on the sea. I'm not sure how many minutes had passed, when I heard him, not far away, singing.

## The Wretched Voice and the Signals

His voice, which I recognized immediately, with a jolt, came from the lowest, hidden spurs of the mountain, so that it seemed to be rising from the bottom of the sea cliff. That illusion gave the scene the restless solemnity of dreams; but the strangest thing was this—that he was singing. I almost never heard him sing, and his voice, in fact, wasn't beautiful (it was, one might say, the only ugly thing about him): it had an acid sound, almost female, unmelodious. But precisely because it lacked musicality and grace, that song of his, mysteriously, moved me still more. I think that not even the melody of an archangel could have been so moving.

He sang a verse from one of the most popular Neapolitan songs, which I'd known, more or less, since I learned to sing; and for me it had become common and banal from the many times I had heard it and repeated it on my own. The one that goes:

*I can't find a moment of peace*
*Night becomes day*
*I'm always here waiting*
*Hoping to talk to you!*

But he sang with a bitterness of persuasion so raw and desperate that I listened as if I were learning a great new song, of tragic significance. Those four lines, and their melody, which he sang slowly, drawing it out, and shouting, seemed to be speaking of my own solitude: when I went wandering around, avoided by N., without friendships or happiness or repose. And of today, when I had ended up on this mountain of misery, in this reckless hiding place, in order to understand the ultimate sadness.

Unable to see the person of W.G. from where I was, I climbed up onto a ledge of the wall I was hiding behind. And from up there, spying through an old broken window, I immediately saw my singer. He was alone, half lying on a patch of weedy ground, at the end of the last terraces in the direction of the cliff; and from that narrow sloping flower bed he sang in the direction of the palace, like a wretched toad singing to the moon. His eyes were fixed precisely on one of those small windows that could be discerned even from the ground, set in the wing that extended in a semicircle between the depth of the mountain and the sea. It was an isolated window halfway up, and like its companions it gave no sign of life through the small space open above the vent: nothing but silence and darkness.

Yet it seemed that my father was waiting for some response to his song. Reaching the end of the verse, he remained for a while in an anxious silence, turning over painfully on the ground like a sick man in a hospital bed. Then he started from the beginning, in the same way as before. At that point, fearing that he might see me, I left my look-out and jumped down to the foot of the wall. From there, leaning out sideways slightly, I could, although without seeing him, keep watch on that impassive window of the palace. And in fact I didn't take my eyes off it.

Three or four times more his voice could be heard resuming its song from the bottom of the mountain, with a dark, childish stubbornness. He repeated, from the song I knew, always and only that single verse; and at every repeat his tone expressed a different sorrow: entreaty, command, or tragic, onerous infatuation. But the window remained blind and deaf: as if the prisoner who lived there had deserted his room, or were dead, or, at the least, sunk in a deep sleep.

Finally, the futile song ceased; but soon afterward, in place of the song, I heard some brief rhythmic whistles rising from the hidden slope, in a new attempted call to the window. And at hearing them, I trembled, consumed by jealousy!

I had immediately recognized, in the rhythm of those whistles, a secret language of signals, a kind of Morse code, that my father and I had invented together, in the happy times of my childhood. We used that alphabet of whistles to send messages at a distance, during our beach games in the summer; and even sometimes, by mutual consent, to make fun of certain types of Procidans present and unaware at the harbor or the café on the square.

Now evidently my father must have taught the prisoner that mysterious alphabet, which I thought was the property of us two alone: Wilhelm Gerace and me!

Those invented signals had been so familiar to me for years that, hearing them, I could immediately translate them into words, better than an old telegrapher. The jealous emotion that had surprised me made me miss, however, the first syllables of the message sent by my father. What I heard sounded like this:

. . . NEITHER VISITS NOR LETTERS NOTHING
AT LEAST A WORD
WHAT WOULD IT COST YOU?

A new silent wait on the part of my father followed; but the window persisted in its tomblike indifference. My father repeated:

AT LEAST A WORD

And then, after another silence:

WHAT WOULD IT COST YOU?

Finally, through the small space at the top of the window, where the vent, unfolding like an accordion, left exposed the last section of bars, two hands could be seen, gripping the bars. Certainly my father, too, saw them immediately, and suddenly stood, so that I could see him, from the shoulders up, hurrying toward the edge of the cliff. There he stopped, almost under the palace, from which the void of the sea separated him by only three or four meters; and he remained mute in expectation, as if those pitiful clinging hands were two stars, which had appeared to announce to him his destiny.

A little afterward, the hands left the bars; but the prisoner, certainly, was still standing behind the window, maybe he had climbed on his bunk to reach the vent; and from there he brought two fingers to his lips to send his responding signals louder! His whistles, in fact, were soon heard, very sharp and rhythmic, in a sequence of barbaric monotony. And instantly, with an incredible feeling of certainty, of adolescent pride and contempt, I recognized in them as in a known lashing voice the unique, extreme arrogance of the criminal of the dock!

His message to my father, which I translated to myself immediately, consisted of the following three words:

### GET OUT, PARODY!

Then nothing more. Except, maybe because of a simple auditory hallucination, I seemed to hear all around, from the nearest windows, a chorus of low laughter, like a dark, great mockery of my father. Then again there was a dead silence, which was interrupted soon afterward by the guards on their rounds, beating their clubs against the grates, to check the bars before evening. The sound was gradually approaching, from the invisible windows of the façade that faced the sea; and I saw my father, at that sound, leave where he was and prepare to go back up slowly. Then, in fear that he would catch me, I ran headlong down from the mountain, retracing the return route rapidly.

All the way home, I was repeating to myself, in order not to forget it, the word *parody*, whose meaning I wasn't entirely sure of. And when I got home I went to look it up in an old school dictionary, which had been in my room for years: maybe it belonged to my schoolteacher grandmother, or maybe to the student of Romeo the Amalfitano. At the word *parody* I read:

IMITATION OF THE BEHAVIOR OF ANOTHER, IN WHICH
WHAT IN OTHERS IS SERIOUS BECOMES RIDICULOUS,
OR COMIC, OR GROTESQUE.

Thus Wilhelm Gerace had played on me the ultimate trick. If with full awareness and intention he had examined the most malicious way of getting me back under his spell, he could not have invented a treacherous game equal to this, into which he had drawn me without knowing it. Now, that is, it had become clear to me that in his pilgrimages to the Terra Murata all that awaited him was a shameful solitude; that up there he was mortifed and rejected like the lowest servant. And at that discovery, I don't know why, my affection for him, which I had believed suffocated and almost gone, was rekindled, more bitter, anguished, almost terrible!

# CHAPTER 8

# Farewell

You won't go anymore, amorous butterfly,
Fluttering around inside night and day
Disturbing the sleep of beauties . . .
Among the soldiers, by Bacchus!

—FIGARO, *THE MARRIAGE OF FIGARO*

## *Hated Shadow*

Two more months passed. It was near the end of November. At that time I learned that Assuntina was betraying me.

It's pointless to waste time telling how I found out: I have to hurry now to the end of this memoir. Enough to say that I was informed of it without possibility of doubt; and not with a single lover was she betraying me but with more than one; and even before me she had had these different lovers! The day I learned all that, I purposely passed by her house; and when, seeing that I didn't stop, she ran after me, I turned and pushed her away with such precise insults and such violence that she retreated in fear. I passed by again later: there was no one in front of the cottage, the door was closed. With my penknife I carved into the door a picture of a sow—*troia*, a whore—with the caption: "Farewell forever."

After that, I wandered through the nearby countryside and got lost; finally I collapsed in a field and burst into sobs.

I had never loved Assuntina, that was true; but recently I had even thought of marrying her, so great was my desire to have a woman who was attached to me and was mine. I had decided that, right after marriage, I would kiss her, the way I had once kissed N. and never her. And then—this was the main thing—we would have a child together. I liked immensely the idea of fathering a child, and I amused myself thinking what he would be like, and planned to take him with me on my future travels, like a true friend. Now that plan, too, evaporated, like so many others.

At least if my mother had been alive, I could have told my sorrows to someone! For a moment, I had a vision of N., as she had been with me in other times; but immediately the image of now was superimposed on that: so angry that even her curls seemed to have become fierce. In truth, on that point what the vile Assuntina had said could be recognized as just: and that is that my stepmother, under the appearance of a lamb, hid the untamable toughness of a wild beast.

Enough: now I really was alone. And what, then, attracted me still on that enchanted island? What kept me from abandoning it for eternity, as I had done with my revolting faithless lover?

Answer: Wilhelm Gerace, who in other years had left again on his travels by this time of the autumn, this year still honored Procida with his presence.

Often certain of our affections, which we suppose are magnificent, even superhuman, are, in reality, insipid; only an earthly, even atrocious bitterness can, like salt, awaken the mysterious taste of their profound mixture. For all my childhood and youth, I had thought I loved

W.G.; but maybe I was deceived. Only now, perhaps, was I beginning to love him. Something surprising happened, which certainly in the past I would never have believed, if it had been predicted: I felt pity for W.G.

I'd had a feeling of pity for others in my life. For example, I had felt it for strangers, unknown people, even, occasionally, some passerby. For Immacolatella. For N. Even for Assuntina. In other words, I already knew how incomparably terrible that feeling is. But the people I had felt it for had nevertheless been, even if dear to me, connected to me only by chance, by a choice; they hadn't been relatives by birth. For the first time, now, I knew this inhuman violence: to feel pity for my own blood.

In spite of the winter tedium that already prevailed on the island, W.G. had for some weeks appeared less gloomy and more sociable. Not, certainly, that he was cured of his fixed thought; rather, I would have said that that thought held him, more than ever, in its sovereign power. Only now, shaking him from his anguished half sleep, it appeared to draw him, day by day, toward a new and obscurely joyful impatience. Which made him move restlessly from one room to another, and along the streets of the town and the paths of the countryside as if pursued by a crowd of cruel presentiments and impossible wishes. Sometimes he broke into an exalted, innocent cheerfulness, childishly; but that cheerfulness seemed to tire him desperately; and then, in need of repose, he took refuge in a tremendous melancholy.

I noticed that his pilgrimages to the Terra Murata became less frequent; but that was not enough to deceive me. I constantly recognized in his eyes, in his behavior, the hated shadow that occupied his mind. And so I always showed him a sullen, taciturn face. When, going into the town or for a walk in the country, he sought my company (this had been happening again, for some days), I followed him unwillingly. And if he spoke to me I answered in short sentences, rudely.

Those last weeks, when I think back, seem truly to have "flown by," the fastest of my life. And how long, instead, they must have seemed to him, who surely was counting the days! The dramatic, impatient joy of waiting surrounded him, in the air. And I felt that some new thing was about to happen; but I refused to share the joyful drama with him, and so I didn't even try to explain to myself that wait, or maybe I was pretending to ignore it. Anyway, the explanation soon arrived.

## One Night

One night in early December, I came home very late. Ever since N. had declared her irrevocable aversion, I'd been coming home late, in order not to be at the table with her. Before going to sleep, she always left my dinner warming near the coals; but, then, for some weeks, I had gotten into the habit of eating on my own in the town, at the Osteria del Gallo or the widow's café. I was in fact very wealthy that autumn: my father showered me with money. There was no day, one could say, when he didn't give me a bill of fifty or a hundred lire, and that morning he had given me the crazy sum of five hundred lire. I didn't know what to do with so much wealth; and I left banknotes in the middle of books, amid the rags in the drawer. I always had at least seven or eight piled and creased in my pocket, and I gave grandiose tips, so that perhaps, to find another such case in their history, the Procidans had to go back to the Spanish seventeenth century.

Usually I went to eat at the tavern around seven; but afterward I lingered in the town until ten or later; so that sometimes coming home I was hungry again, and willingly ate the meals that my stepmother left for me. With that intention, I returned home that evening and went to the kitchen. And here I had a surprise: the ashes were still warm but the two small earthenware pots where N. usually left me the dinner were

uncovered and empty nearby. And on the table, unlike every other evening, the plates and silverware that N. set for me were not to be seen.

It was the first time such a thing had happened; I took a piece of
bread from the drawer and went out to eat it in the yard. But I felt that
my hunger had passed, and I threw it away.

It was a dim night, pierced by a damp, cold wind. I had barely
taken a few steps when, behind me, a gust closed the shutters of the
lighted French door, which I had left open. Without lamps or moon,
the yard was so dark that one couldn't see the edge: it didn't seem
inviting, and I soon decided to return to the house, which rose in the
background quiet and sleeping. It was while I was approaching the
house that I noticed, behind the large window of the big room, a pale
reddish glow.

Especially in winter, our family always left that cold enormous room
closed and deserted. The first thing I thought of, even without believing
it, was the spirits: the stories that had left me doubtful as a boy came
to mind—about the ghost of the Amalfitano, about his youths . . .
"Maybe," I thought, "it was the spirits who ate my dinner . . ." And,
reentering, skeptical and puzzled, I went immediately to the big room.

I saw right away that the reddish glow I had noticed from outside
came from the hearth. Someone, wishing to warm that cavernlike space
that was the room, had lighted some pieces of wood in the old monks'
fireplace: and because it hadn't been used for perhaps half a century,
the room was nearly filled with smoke. At my entrance a solitary form
moved on one of the broken couches near the hearth; and at first, in the
dark, it seemed a dog. But it rose: it was a man, and, turning on the light
switch, I recognized him immediately. Even if I hadn't recognized his
features and his outfit (the same Sunday outfit he had worn that day on
the dock), the instant, bitter, and consuming hatred that I felt toward
him would have been enough.

## *In the Big Room*

The faint, dusty ceiling lamp barely illuminated that corner of the room. But even in the poor light, the hospitable, refined, exulting welcome that my father, inexpertly improvising, had prepared for him was immediately evident to my eyes, like a painting in sharp relief: a kind of innocent, disorderly celebration! On the table, which had been moved near the sofa, were the plates with the remains of my dinner, olives, pastries, dates, cigarettes, wine, also an empty bottle of *spumante* and one of liqueur. On the floor, dug out from somewhere or other in the house, a carpet; and on the couch a pillow and my father's wool blanket . . . All that, to my eyes of a wounded savage, assumed the importance of a royal display!

This time (unlike that day on the dock), his features immediately stood out with an extraordinary precision: more clearly than if they'd been illuminated by a floodlight. Right away, on first seeing him again, I realized how mistaken I'd been, on the dock, to judge him ugly. And the instant knowledge that he was handsome pierced me like a blade. Perhaps I wouldn't have so detested his looks if he had been fair-haired; but he was dark, instead, as dark as and even darker than me; and that produced in my feelings, I don't know why, the shock of an intolerable tragedy.

In my memory my conversation with him remains wrapped in a smoky scene, set ablaze by my hatred. The shape of his body inspired hatred: it was tall, well developed, and the muscles, which didn't seem to have suffered in prison, stood out in his movements. And his shoulders. And his strong neck, which proudly supported the head (molded with bold grace, with its prisoner's pallor). And his beautiful dark hair, cut with care, boyishly, the hairline low on his forehead, as in a sculpture . . . There was not a feature, a gesture in him that could induce me to forgiveness.

His eyes, in shadow in the hollow sockets, the eyebrows unkempt, had a scornful, arrogant, and sly manner of looking at his interlocutor not directly but sideways. His mouth was hard and graceful, and his lips didn't part when he smiled but rose slightly on one side, in a sort of allusive brutality, as if a true, kind smile would deny his virility. And on his chin he had a hint of a dimple, which added further determination and daring to his expression.

## Betrayal

"Where's my father?" I said curtly, as soon as I was in the room. My turbulent, aggressive tone was meant to announce that he and I were already sworn enemies. He eyed me, without moving a step from the corner of the hearth.

"And who is he, your father?" he said, with pretended ignorance, in response.

"What! My father! The owner here! I'm Arturo Gerace!"

"Oh! A pleasure . . ." he said with an air of false, lazy formality. "*The owner* went upstairs just now; but he'll be down again before long."

"Then I'll wait here," I declared. And I settled myself on the threshold, standing, my back against the doorpost.

"Please, sit down," he said, with a half-indifferent expression, as if to say that for him my presence or an ant's was the same. Then, stretching out again on the sofa, he added: "By the way, would you turn out the light again? Your father advised me not to leave it on: there's danger in being seen from outside . . ."

I didn't move; and he glanced at me. "Well, what are you waiting for? Turn it off," he said. And at my deliberate disobedience he rose onto his elbow, while an expression of insolence and playful mystery flashed through his eyes. "It's dangerous, I'm telling you," he threatened vaguely, "the police . . ." Then, lowering his voice, with an inspired, sly emphasis, he uttered:

"I AM A FUGITIVE!"

I looked at him, without batting an eye. From his manner, from his accent, I had quickly scented deception; but it was also possible that his words were true—they certainly accorded in an ideal way with the image I had had of him from the first day . . . And that was the only explanation for the presence, tonight, in our house, of a life prisoner, as from the start I had supposed he was . . .

For an instant, in spite of my hatred, I almost let myself be drawn in by that mirage of magnificent complicity that blazed before me, surprising, unexpected: hiding in our house a genuine fugitive—hunted by the police!—was an honor and at the same time a force against him: keeping him at our mercy . . . Yet in my doubt I left the light on: if only so that he wouldn't presume that I seriously believed him. He looked at me:

"What are you waiting for, turn it off!" he repeated again.

I shrugged, with an expression almost of disgust. Then, almost in spite of himself, he let out from behind his arrogantly closed lips a short childish laugh. At the same time, assuming an attitude of sarcasm and superior pride, he arched his eyebrows, so as to wrinkle his forehead:

"Well," he said, "as far as I'm concerned, do what you like. I AM A FUGITIVE is a film title. Did you believe me? *I* am a free citizen, starting tonight, in order with the authorities. I was legally turned out of my house, up there at the villa, at exactly seven o'clock p.m. today, December third, if you want to know!"

So saying, and without getting up from his slouch, he gave me a look that was lazy and impassive but full of malicious understanding.

"You're disappointed, are you?" he said after a pause. "Tell the truth: you swallowed the story of the escape right away, and already you were enjoying the thought . . . of going to report me . . ."

From the moment I planted myself there, facing him as I waited, I had promised myself not to address a word to him, and absolutely not to deal with him, any more than if he had been an animal. But on hearing him utter such a crazy slander I couldn't restrain a loud, haughty cry of derision.

His response, however, was merely a condescending half smile, as if his opinion hadn't changed. "You can spare yourself the inconvenience," he continued, undeterred, settling himself more comfortably on the couch, "and as for the lights, as far as I'm concerned, I assure you, lights on or lights off is all the same to me here, at night. It's your father who, for motives of prudence, thought up that trick, to turn off the lights . . . The police have nothing to do with it. A question of private family matters."

Here he yawned and lighted a cigarette. "Well, just so you know," he explained more clearly, "your father wouldn't be eager to let you others in the house know I'm here. That's why, as you see, he didn't give me a room upstairs. I think, especially, he isn't eager to introduce me to the signora . . ."

His speech had some inflections different from the usual, Neapolitan notes I was used to hearing: less singing and more robust. Yet he didn't speak a dialect but a quite precise Italian. In fact, out of a taste for insults, he seemed to enjoy uttering refined phrases; and his manners, innately plebeian, were offensive with a more provocative pride while he pretended to be respectable. He spoke in a drawl, between drags of the cigarette. And every time he said *your father* he put into it a note of ironic servility and revulsion: as if he were avoiding a pathetic, annoying object and, at the same time, mocking that paternity, which I boasted of!

"And of course," he continued, letting the words fall from his mouth with the expression of an undisputed sultan, as if he considered himself

the chief gangster of the century, "I am not a family type, I'm a dangerous criminal . . . At the trial," he declared, boasting, "they gave me two
years! Yes, then they had to reduce it, because in the meantime these big
international events intervened, and as a result the pardon of H.M. the
King . . . Won't you congratulate me on the lucky coincidence? If not
for the march of history, I wouldn't be here now, in your house, enjoying
this lovely evening!"

Hearing that speech, I gave him a bewildered and almost questioning look, in spite of myself. Not because of the big international events
he had hinted at: of which I knew nothing, and which at that moment
didn't interest me; but for another reason. "Two years only!" I thought,
disconcerted. So this man whom I had considered a genuine life prisoner
was, as it seemed, a petty criminal of no account! But still, I now realized
angrily, even the knowledge that he could be a mere pickpocket or local
troublemaker—rather than a fatal killer or outlaw—wouldn't serve to
diminish his dark, odious magnificence in my eyes.

To indicate that he was of no importance, I twisted my lips into
a sneer of disgust. He, meanwhile, had started yawning exaggeratedly,
as if this lovely evening, just by being named, had provoked in him an
atrocious tedium. But he added no other word.

Some seconds of silence passed. I stood there, straight against the
doorpost, hand in my pocket, in the attitude of a gang leader who is
confronting a hostile gang leader in the middle of the deserted pampas.
Finally I broke the silence, grimly, to find out:

"So? You're sleeping here tonight?"

"Where do you want me to sleep, the Grand Hotel?"

"Why?" he opined, sarcastically, after a moment. "Maybe the idea is
disturbing to you? Maybe—"

I shrugged, with the disdain of a great lord:

"Pff . . . I don't give a damn about you," I answered.

"Yes, I accepted your father's invitation," he resumed, in a tone of tranquil admission, with a kind of insolent generosity, "because, all things considered, this seemed to me the most comfortable inn here on the island, since I had to spend a last night in the place. There weren't any more steamers for the mainland until tomorrow morning . . ." At that point a nostalgic and long-harbored impatience crossed his face, which made him extremely simple, even childish: "But if it hadn't been for your father, who got mixed up in my fate," he burst out all of a sudden, throwing his legs down from the couch, in a tone of outraged counterattack, "I could already be sleeping in Rome tonight, next to my girl. You can get from the prison of Viterbo (where I was) to my house, in Flaminio, in less than an hour by car! He's the one (and he would even deny it!) who, on some pretext or other, brought about my transfer to this fine oasis of Procida: he did it, with his high-up acquaintances . . ."

Oh, like that . . . At that speech I saw again, like a court of veiled and evasive followers, the authoritative, mysterious, and nameless society that already, as a child, I had imagined in the service of my father. And, proudly, I was pleased with my father's prestige, as I'd been as a child. Now it was explained why the famous Terra Murata had housed this petty criminal, condemned to a paltry sentence . . . It had been the will of my father, who had had him dragged into the land of the Geraces, reluctant, arrogant, like a slave . . .

But at that vision, suddenly and only now (and I was surprised at myself for not having thought it before), I remembered, with a real shudder, the famous old promise, sworn by my father to the dead Amalfi, never to bring any other friend to this island and this house, dear forever to a single memory! I had still in my ears the words of Wilhelm Gerace: *If I failed, I would be a traitor and a perjurer.*

So, then, he was!

My face must have revealed my sudden inner bewilderment. And perhaps it was this defenseless expression that momentarily disposed my adversary to a certain courtesy. With a distracted movement of his petulant, dark gaze he nodded in the direction of the set table and, in a tone of almost patrician urbanity, came out with:

"By the way, I haven't yet apologized for eating your dinner . . ." That apology made me tremble with rage; but I didn't want to give him the pleasure; and, displaying a pirate-like scowl, of one accustomed to the sleaziest carousing in the taverns, I said with fierce nonchalance:

"What dinner are you talking about? I always eat out."

"Oh, yes, I didn't think of that . . ." he answered in that same ceremonious way; but, meanwhile, he began to look at me curiously, eyes laughing. "In fact, say, boy," he added, in a different, impertinent tone, full of meaning, "why do you go to bed so late at night? You have a girl?"

"No!" I declared, harshly.

"You don't have a girl," he replied, with a sudden expression of complicity in his cheerful eyes, "because you have at least two or three girls. You know what I found out from your father a little while ago? That you eat out, and go to bed late, because every night you go looking for girls, like a cat. That you go mad for the ladies! And already have lovers!"

I felt myself turning red: so W.G., unknown to me, knew something of my business! In any case, luckily, the man, perhaps, didn't see my boyish blush. He had turned his gaze away from me and suddenly his smiles had disappeared into a black mood. He gave a big, yearning sigh, like a wolf's. And, rising, he proclaimed, in a tone of triumph and threat, as if he were challenging to the death anyone who dared to dispute his word:

"I, too, like women!"

And he repeated, more threatening than before:

"I like women, AND THAT'S ALL!"

Then he began pacing back and forth in the room, with his proud, elastic jockey's gait. He turned angry eyes to the walls painted with fake pergolas, vines, and grapes, to the scribbles of the boys, to the table set for a banquet, to everything, as if he were still in a jail. He complained to me:

"Well, if you know some pretty woman around here, why haven't you brought her up here, so at least we can have some fun tonight?"

And he flung himself down again on the sofa, whose broken skeleton took offense, creaking painfully. The overhead lights, still on in spite of my father, gave no more illumination than as many wax tapers; and every so often, because of the unsteady current, the bulbs flickered, like insects in their death agony.

My father delayed. From moment to moment, I decided to go upstairs; but I don't know what barbaric requirement of my instinct— perhaps a predestination to new bitterness—kept me there instead, in that cursed room, in front of him. This time it was he who interrupted the silence. In an unhappy, sullen voice, and barely turning an eye toward me, he said:

"Hey! Arturo Gerace!"

I muttered a response. Then, without leaving his sleepy supine position, he brought his hands to his mouth in the shape of a megaphone, and began declaiming, with the artificial, exaggerated emphasis of a police show:

"ATTENTION! ATTENTION! Dangerous criminal sought, escaped from Sing Sing! Attention to the description: regular nose, regular mouth, Greek profile . . ."

Then he began laughing softly to himself, with a definite and malicious (although almost affable) allusion to my credulity of before. I was tempted to respond to him with some terrible insult; but he had already fallen back into his languid, bored silence, as if he were dozing on his own account . . . And it was here that suddenly, in the silence, almost without expecting it myself, I let out, with peremptory abruptness, a question that for too long I had held inside:

"Why were you inside? What did you do?"

Although with some delay, he turned to consider me from between his lashes, raising half his lip in a smile of boastful pride, which didn't seem, however, to deny me a response . . . "So you're curious to know!" he observed, as a preamble. And in fact forgetting my antipathy, I looked at him, intent and in suspense, in the adventurous eagerness to hear him. As if I were expecting that his imminent confidence, there, in the big room, were to reveal to me an absolutely unique and extraordinary crime, which I had never in my life heard of, never read in any book: decked out with who knows what marvelous, hateful attractions . . . And that awakened in me a fantastic sensation: as of a funerary initiation or of manly promotion! Full of importance and fascinated repulsion.

Meanwhile, lying there, his eyelids half closed, he slowly stretched, making me wait still longer for his response. Finally he began, staring into the air, in a sly voice:

"So . . . Well: armed robbery. I attacked a stagecoach . . . that was traveling at nine hundred (meters) an hour . . . on the streets of Buffalo . . . in Texas . . ."

But he was quick to retract, resuming, in the same accent:

"Actually, no. I kidnapped and raped . . . a fifty-seven-year-old lady . . . of royal blood!"

Then, after another pause:

"No, in fact, I was wrong . . . I stole . . . the priest's cassock!"

And he concluded:

"Now you can choose."

"Who cares about knowing!" I exclaimed, with a contemptuous sneer. And from that moment on, I decided to remain absolutely mute, as if on the couch, in place of him, there were a corpse, or an Egyptian mummy. However, a little later, as if he were seeking an excuse for making up with me, he offered me a cigarette. I refused. At which he got to his feet, and finally, in a tone of religious seriousness, addressed me:

"You know who I am?"

Without speaking, I raised my chin, in a scornful sign of denial. He then dipped a finger in the wine in the glass, and with his wet finger traced on the wall, among the old drawings and signatures of the boys, the figure of a star:

"I'm Stella—Star. Tonino Stella!" he declared.

And, offended by my obvious indifference, he proclaimed gloriously:

"My name appeared in all the papers!"

He came over to me and, as if to document his identity, pulled up his sleeve slightly and showed me that he had a tiny star tattooed on his wrist.

But even before the tattoo of the star, I happened to see on his wrist something else that, as soon as I noticed it, truly startled me: a watch, too well known and familiar for me not to be able to distinguish it among all the watches of Europe! Besides the mark Amicus, I even recognized small abrasions on the face and some salt stains on the steel band. It was, with no possibility of doubt, the famous watch that my father had received as a gift from Algerian Dagger, as a sacred pledge of their friendship, and from which for years he had never been parted! I recalled that I had seen it on his wrist until that very morning; and for a moment I suspected that Stella had stolen it. But immediately I understood that the truth was different: it was not a theft but a gift, which my father had given to Stella on this, their evening of celebration, without any regard for his faithful old friend.

So in the space of a day W.G. had denied without scruples first Romeo and then Marco, the two most faithful companions of his fate. Doubly a traitor—and perjurer. In honor of this ingrate.

## Parody

I'm almost certain that Stella must have realized instantly that I recognized the watch; but nevertheless he showed neither embarrassment nor remorse. In fact, though without stopping to discuss it boldly, he glanced at that magnificent timepiece, as if in open pleasure at possessing it. And meanwhile he proceeded haughtily:

"But don't you get the newspapers from Rome down here? My photograph was even in some of them, around a year ago, in the days when they were looking for me . . . Ask your father if you want other information! . . . Yes, it was just at that time, it seems to me, while I was hiding here and there, that I had the *honor* of making his acquaintance!

". . . By the way," he observed at this point, "*the Count* is making us wait, tonight . . . It must be more than half an hour since he went up!"

And with a shake of his forearm he made the sleeve go back above his wrist, consulting the watch:

"Exactly," he declared, "twenty-six and a half minutes."

It seemed that he was eager to annoy me with that watch: he rewound it ostentatiously, then put it to his ear. Finally, following the direction of my looks, he noted, with insidious arrogance:

"What? Maybe you think you recognize this watch? Well, then let me inform you that it's become my property: *by right!*"

I shrugged, and, to show how much I didn't care, I gave a kick to a nearby chair. He reconfirmed:

"BY RIGHT, yes, precisely! *Owed* to me by your father. And besides the watch HE OWES ME some naval binoculars, a speargun, and an underwater mask, which he says he already has in the house, stored upstairs. Also, tomorrow HE OWES ME a complete new set of clothes, to be bought at a leading tailor in Naples, and a pair of new shoes, with rubber soles. Then, according to the pledge, he'll owe me some capital: as much as I need to open a garage, in Rome, so that I can get married to my girl!"

He had sat down in a composed way, his back straight against the sofa back, with solemnity and regal assurance. But, at his last words, a frown of perplexity appeared on his forehead:

"By the way," he asked me, "is it true, that your father is so rich?"

A disparaging suspicion was clear in his tone: and, at that, anger, too long masked by nonchalance, began to storm fatally in my chest. But more than ever now I felt that unmasking my indifference would be, for him, a satisfaction too much desired! And I contented myself with letting him hear, in response, only a dull mumbling.

"Because to listen to him," he insisted, curling his lips with barely concealed skepticism, "he can spend what he likes, he's got millions . . . But then to look at him one wouldn't say he's any type of millionaire. He doesn't have the appearance of a gentleman, really . . ."

"Oh, you say so . . ."

"Yes, I say so! But any other self-respecting person even if he doesn't say it thinks it! What sort of gentleman is he? Who goes around dressed in rags, which aren't even patched, and he doesn't shave, and never washes, so he stinks . . ."

"Hey, watch how you speak!"

"Well, sorry."

"Watch how you speak, I'm telling you!"

"I repeat, sorry . . . On the other hand," Stella explained, "if I interest myself in his finances, it's for a matter of business! It's a business matter that your father is proposing to me: he gives me what I told you, in objects and money, and, in exchange, I agree to go on a two-week journey with him . . . But he intends to give me the cash (the money he promised, I mean) only at the end of the two weeks, not before, because if he gives it to me ahead, he says, he loses the only good guarantee that I won't clear out . . . Well, all right! I'll take his word for it! But I would advise him not to cheat: for his health!" Here Stella looked at me, threatening and harsh, as if he took me as witness and guarantor. "Obviously," he concluded, with an expression of disdain, "if instead of going right back to my girl in Rome I go and look at some sunsets with him, I won't be going for his pretty face!"

At that, he seemed to sink into a vexed and demanding meditation, as if the mere idea of that promised journey he was preparing for were a torture to his nerves. As for me, from the moment I heard the word *journey* I remained without color or breath, silenced.

And in the question that, from the deepest childhood regions, came to my lips I barely recognized my voice, so weak and lost did it suddenly sound:

". . . You're going . . . far . . . ?"

Stella raised an eyebrow: "Far . . . what?" he said, with an obtuse expression. "Me, you mean? With your father? Oh, for our journey, you mean! *Re-e-eally far!* . . . Of course! More or less, we'll be around here, through the usual area . . ." His lips formed a bored, skeptical, and mocking half smile. "Your father," he added, like someone stating a well-known fact, "isn't the type to move around too much. He'd be upset, heartbroken. He's one who always travels in the same neighborhoods. You know those old tethered hot-air balloons? Well, he's like that . . ."

Uncertain, I looked up at my interlocutor, as if to question whether he was speaking seriously. It wasn't the first time such an unexpected judgment on my father had struck my ears. I recalled that in the past I had heard another person assert something not very different. And that fact now seemed to me something bewitched (an arcane, intricate allusion to my nature and my destiny): that two witnesses, unknown to each other, and opposite, and distant, should be in agreement in an opinion that I, instead (maybe only I, in the entire world?), still persisted in treating as heresy.

"You," I cried, "don't understand anything about my father!"

"Oh, maybe you understand better . . ."

"You can't even dream the journeys my father's made!" I cried. "His whole life has been to travel through the farthest foreign lands! Always! His whole life!"

Regarding me with a slight, ironic, but rather sincere surprise, Stella arched his eyebrows in his usual way, so that on his forehead many transverse wrinkles formed.

"Oh, seriously!" he observed. "It's a new idea to me . . . And, as far as we know, what would be the main journeys he's made? All right: Germany-Italy forty years ago: that's known. And then . . . ? Well, of course, the trip around Vesuvius: that's a season ticket for him . . ."

"I feel sorry for you!" I declared, blazing with scorn.

"Oh, you feel sorry for me . . . Really! . . . But, getting back to the point, satisfy my curiosity on something else, if it's not too much trouble . . . Why would he devote himself, all his life, to these great cruises? For a touristic purpose? Missionary? . . . Or why?"

I felt my nerves jump, and my blood throb, such was the spirit of revolt and bitter certainty that inflamed me: "*Why!*" I repeated. "*For what purpose!* Well! For his freedom! For true knowledge. That's the purpose. To learn about the entire world, and the nations, with no borders—"

Stella turned to laugh on his own account. "That's enough, now," he interrupted me, raising one palm with an air of being sated, as if he'd had too much. "I led you on . . . Now I have the proof that what he said really is true: that you're crazy about him."

"Who said it?"

"Him. He said: I have two sons, one a little blond and one dark: no one will ever be capable of making better-looking sons than mine. And the dark one, ever since he was born, has been crazy about me."

"It's not true that he said it!"

"Yes. It's true that he said it. And it's true that you're crazy about him."

"It's not true!"

"It's not true that you're crazy about him?"

"No."

"Then if it's not true, how do you explain the fairy tales you're telling me about him? To listen to you, he's a kind of long-distance oceanic flyer . . . of . . ."

He rose solemnly to his feet. ". . . A kind of . . . true *Citizen of Space!*" he continued, in a tone of fierce mockery. ". . . While in fact he's the sheltered type who's never been weaned from his mother's breast, and never will be! And as for journeys, ever since he got himself out of his barbarian lands and found a cradle in this fine volcano, it would be something, as far as I know, if he got as far as Benevento, or Rome-Viterbo!"

Here, for the first time in speaking of my father, Stella had a curious, almost irrepressible laugh, a friendly and ill-concealed indulgence. "Maybe," he resumed, "he's afraid that this sacred treasure island will fall into the sea if he loses sight of it. As soon as he goes three or four stations too far, he starts to get homesick, like an orphan. And, remembering it, he makes a face . . . He's even jealous of it, like it was a woman! So he's called Procida, as a nickname . . ."

This last bit of information (whether truth or lies) I didn't too much mind hearing. And I waited, almost thirsty, for Stella to continue. But he suddenly abandoned the subject. And, sitting down again on the couch, in a kind of brutal and thuggish gaiety, he shook his head, so fiercely that his hair, which he had smoothed and carefully brilliantined, got all mussed. Over his features passed a coarse expression of youthful grace, in which I don't know what reflections, amusements, abandonments, rowdiness, intrigues clashed with the arrogance. It was clear that his mind had suddenly been drawn away to follow a thought from which I, there present, was excluded; but it wasn't clear if this thought attracted or bewildered him. As when you watch a cat chasing a feather, you can't tell if its mood is play or tragedy.

With a bored, impulsive expression he got up and stretched his arms; then he sat down again. But suddenly he came out with a strangely serious, almost dramatic laugh. And he exclaimed:

"Your father is a PARODY!"

This was fatal: sinister, uncontrollable anger overwhelmed me. Clenching my fists, I advanced toward Stella with these words:

"Now I'll spit in your face."

Then a hard, strangely oblique shadow fell over Stella's face. In turn, he moved toward me. And he said, accentuating each syllable:

"Whose face will you spit in?"


## The Final Scene


Beside myself with rage, I was about to charge at him; but at that very moment a hurried, familiar step sounded in the hall; and my father, arriving in the doorway behind me, grabbed me by the arm.

He had just caught Stella's last words and, like an echo, repeated: "Whose face will you spit in?" He gave me a penetrating look, tinged with threat and apprehension, and turned very pale. That tortured pallor disarmed me. Still, it was with abrupt violence that I struggled out of his grip, refusing to give him any explanation. Then I moved sullenly away from Stella, who, in turn, abandoning the fight, had sat down again on the couch, in an indifferent and mocking position. And I paused at the corner of the hearth, a few steps from them.

He had brought from upstairs, in a pile in his arms, sheets, blankets, a pillow. "Like a servant," I thought. At the same time, I noted, with bitter surprise, that he had put on new clothes, which I had never seen before today: striped velvet pants, and a gray knit jacket, and at his neck a blue silk kerchief. He had shaved with care, and even combed his hair, smoothing it back. So clean, elegant, he appeared to me as handsome as a great prince in a novel; yet, as I gazed at him, enchanted, I surprised myself by seeking in him, absurdly, desperately, that comic or grotesque aspect that deserved from Stella the epithet "parody."

I longed to recognize in him something truly ridiculous; but, unfortunately, I saw only grace. His weary thinness, which stood out particularly in that luxurious outfit, made him seem weaker and younger: and Stella's boyish health was offensive, like insolence or vulgarity, next to him.

He again turned his gaze, shadowed by alarm, from Stella to me. But he asked no other questions. Then, immediately and deliberately retreating from our mysterious fight, as if it had been nothing, he approached the couch and, dropping the sheets and blankets beside Stella, announced to him, with open animation:

"So it's all done. I've even packed the suitcase!" Then, to me, in a different voice, tuned to authoritarian pride:

"By the way, Arturo. I looked for you to tell you, but you weren't in your room. I'm leaving tomorrow morning, with the first boat."

Tomorrow morning! Until that last word, I had refused to understand the imminence of that reality, which swept away tomorrow, and all the other days of my future, in a storm of devastation. I stared at my father with lost eyes, after which he informed me, frowning:

"It's as well to say goodbye now, because tomorrow morning I won't have time . . ." My voice broke out, suffocated by revolt:

"You're leaving . . . with him!"

"That doesn't concern you," my father answered.

"You can't do it! No! You can't do it!"

My father gave me a sidelong glance, looming over me in angry splendor:

"I," he answered, "leave with whomever I like. With the kind forbearance *de Usted*."

I felt that he was now displaying his worst arrogance against me partly to shine in Stella's eyes: partly, maybe, to revenge himself on me, with his authority, for the low servitude in which Stella kept him! Stella himself seemed to understand this thing: and looked at him furtively, ironic, with no appreciation. But he was so fierce, with his dramatic fire, that he didn't notice that irony.

"So, Arturo, we're agreed?" he ended, turning halfway toward me, in a curt, conclusive tone, which was meant to be an invitation to take my leave. I was about to answer: "Of course! Goodbye!" and turn my back on him. But an instinct, prouder than any will (similar to what is called *for preservation*), shouted in my ears like a thunderclap that, afterward, between him and me it would be over, and that there, just outside the room, a night without end awaited me. I took a step and (just grazing Stella with a look of disdain, as if his presence were something to be ignored) stood in front of him:

"I'm sixteen!" I exclaimed. "You promised that when I became a man you would travel with me. And now that time has come. I'm old enough, I'm a man!"

"Oh. I'm glad about it," said my father. Then, moving to the end of the hearth and leaning against it, one hand in his pocket, he invited me in a tone of forced calm:

"Come here, Arturo, here in front of me, please." Of course, he was afraid that I would again insult Stella. Contemptuous, I obeyed. And then, staring at me, he said:

"Shall we part politely, Arturo?"

I scowled, without answering. "Well, in that case," he continued, mastering with difficulty his stormy impatience, "please put off the subject to another occasion, and go upstairs, if you don't mind. We're agreed, about the promise you mention: of course, every promise is sacred, between gentlemen . . . But this doesn't seem the best time to discuss it: midnight, when I'm about to leave . . . We'll talk about it more calmly when I return."

I gave a laugh of desperate cynicism. He darkened.

"So, meanwhile," he added, in a grim, altered voice, "you'll have time to grow up a little, I hope. For example, you might learn not to act like such a boor as tonight: since you're just proving that even if you're old enough you're a boy, or, rather, a child . . . Good night!"

I felt myself turn fiery red, then pale as the dead. "Yes," I answered, "I'm going. But your promises—you can keep them, I don't want them . . ."

In confusion I noticed that my voice was starting to shout. It had now become a true male voice, no longer toneless as it had been some months earlier; and hearing it I again had the peculiar sensation that a stranger, a barbarian, was speaking through my mouth. I wasn't thinking about what I said; and I no longer saw anything outside the person of W.G., who looked at me with a kind of curiosity in his cloudy blue eyes. My pupils, avid with bitterness, went to his left wrist, stripped of the watch:

"You have no loyalty," I continued to shout, "to promises or to vows! You even betrayed friendship! I know you now! You're a traitor!"

I seemed to be utterly lost in a real storm, with no support beneath my feet but a horrible rolling motion. I saw W.G. slowly separate from the side of the hearth and come toward me at a slightly weary but deliberate pace; and I expected that he wanted to beat me. It would have been the first time in our lives that he'd beaten me; and even in that instant I had time to think that I certainly wouldn't react. He was my father, and fathers have the right to beat their sons. Although I was now grown, it was still he who had produced me.

But it can't really be said that he beat me. He was satisfied with seizing my arms, near the shoulder joint, and saying, "Hey! *Moro!*" Then he released me with a violent shake, his expression threatening, but at the same time he gave a laugh almost of amusement. And he added: "Oh, so now you know me, eh! You said!

"Well, and if you know me *from now on*," he resumed, taking two or three steps in front of me, "I have known you for quite some time, my little dark-haired boy!"

"No, you don't know me at all," I murmured. "*No one* knows me, not me!"

"Oh, really, my great unknown! But I know you very well, I know you like the back of my hand. And in fact now, here, before witnesses, I intend to tell you what you are!"

"Then say it. Who cares!"

He stopped, a step away from me, in a cruel and pitiless position. And at that moment his face began to display: magnificence, and celebration, and complicity, and supreme judgments, and duplicity, and futility, and slaughter! In other words, all those already known expressions he assumed when you couldn't understand if he was preparing (perhaps) some august and lethal punishment or, rather (perhaps), was plotting a diabolical trick.

"All right," he said, "I therefore here attest, and all the world must know, that you, Arturo, are JEALOUS! Or, more precisely, we'll say that Your Lordship merits the title of Universally Jealous. You in fact, oh great Hidalgo, oh Don Juan, oh king of hearts, suddenly fall in love with everybody. And you go around shooting Your arrows at everyone like the Love child of Venus, and if you don't hit us then you get jealous . . . According to Your claim, the whole world should be the lover of Arturo Gerace. But then, for Your part, Your Lordship doesn't love anyone, given that you are willful and vain and egotistical and sly, taken uniquely by your own beauties. And now go to sleep. Out!"

"I'm going, yes . . ." I said in a low voice. Then in a louder, darker, more desperate voice I repeated: "Yes, I'm going! And I want to forget you! Forever! Listen! This is my last word!"

"Very good," he said, "we're in agreement. It's the last word."

Impetuously I turned toward the doorway; but in that movement I happened to glance at Stella, half lying on the big sofa against the wall. The whole time, without putting in a word, he had witnessed our quarrel in comfort, as if he were at the theater; and during my father's last speech he had let some low laughs be heard. I caught him, in fact, with his mouth still in an attitude of laughter; and that, at that moment, made me lose the last glimmer of reason. I turned back a step and, beside myself, without even knowing what I was doing, grabbed at random a piece of silverware from the table and hurled it at him.

My father remained motionless for several seconds, contained by anger and by astonishment, while Stella, skillfully avoiding the throw, put the article down calmly (I don't think it was a knife, rather a fork, but I couldn't say precisely) on a chair nearby.

Meanwhile, I had stopped halfway between the hearth and the door, and waited, determined. I couldn't, in fact, after such a challenge, leave without something else, at risk of letting them assume, maybe, that I was running away in fear of Stella. But he, without even getting up from the sofa, smiled at me very seriously, and said in a conciliatory tone:

"Well, why are you mad at me now? I'm sorry, but I wasn't laughing at you."

Then, turning to my father, with an expression of gracious and superior patience:

"From the first moment," he said, "immediately, as soon as he set foot in this room, he's been trying in every way possible to quarrel with me."

"Get out of here! Go, and don't come back! Do you understand?" my father repeated, now trembling with a true, terrible anger.

Then my hardened gaze ran around the room, which seemed to rotate in my view like a revolving scene on the point of disappearing forever; and abruptly I left. When I got to my room I didn't even bother to turn on the light. I threw myself on the bed, with my face against the pillow, and remained for several minutes like that, waiting for an apocalypse, or an earthquake, or some cosmic devastation, that would resolve that hateful night. On the one hand, I would have wanted morning never to arrive; on the other, I counted out with fear the interminable hours of the night, certain that I wouldn't be able to sleep.

## The Letter

My intention was to stay awake all night; but at the same time I would have liked to fall into an extreme lethargy, which lasted days, months, and maybe centuries, as in a fairy tale. My eyelids burned, but I wasn't sleepy. After a while, I turned on the light and wrote a letter for my father.

I no longer remember, naturally, the exact text of that letter; but I remember very clearly the concept. It said, briefly, more or less this:

> *Dear Pa, my last word, which I now write to you, is this: that you were wrong tonight if you thought I still wanted to travel with you, as I did when I was young. At that time, maybe it was true that I wanted to, but now that desire is gone. And you are wrong if you think I'm envious of your friends. Maybe it was true that, as a boy, I envied them, but now I've learned that they're monstrous criminals and disgusting creeps. And I hope that some time or other, in the city where you're with them, one of them will kill you. Because I hate you. And I would prefer to have been born without a father. And without a mother and without anyone. Farewell. Arturo.*

I don't know how long I stayed awake, ears straining, to hear if my father went back to his room, because, as soon as I heard his steps, I intended to go out into the hall and deliver my letter, without saying a word. But no step or sound interrupted the silence of the night outside my half-closed door. Still, I could have carried the letter to his room and left it for him, in plain sight, on the suitcase; and I thought of doing that. But the idea of going outside there, into the hall and the big deserted room, disturbed me. It seemed to me that those walls, those familiar objects, tonight had been marked and made ominous by the insults I had received. And that to confront alone their mute presences—that, too—would be a new insult.

So, without having decided to bring that terrible letter to its destination, I threw myself back on the bed, and gradually fell asleep, with the light on. I woke with a start before daylight; and, seeing my letter folded on the table, I took it and hid it under my sweater, which I had left on. Then I went back to bed and, turning out the light, wrapped myself in the blanket, because I felt very cold.

## Farewell

But I didn't fall asleep again. The roosters crowed, and, shortly afterward, the first glow of dawn appeared. Then, through the closed window, a sound of wheels and hooves reached me from the street below. "There's the carriage coming to get them and take them down to the port," I said to myself. I thought also of the letter I had hidden under my sweater, for my father; but now somehow the wish for him to have it disappeared, and I stayed unmoving under the blanket. I strained my ears fitfully to the slightest sounds of the house. Usually, at other departures of my father, the whole family was in movement; but this time instead my stepmother evidently hadn't awakened. The bedrooms and the upstairs hall lay in silence and in stillness. From the street every so often the muttering of the driver could be heard as, alone, he spoke to his horse.

Suddenly along the corridor I heard a sound of long, hurried steps, trying to be quiet. The door was pushed, delicately, without making any noise. And my father entered my room, closing the door behind him.

I quickly locked my eyelids, pretending to be asleep. He shook me a little, making with his lips the usual small whistle he had always used when he wanted to wake me in the morning. Then he called in a low voice: "Arturo . . .

"Arturo . . ." he repeated. I opened my eyes, hard and fixed, without looking at him. "In a few minutes," he said, "in a few minutes I'm leaving . . ."

I didn't blink, or move. Even without looking at him, I glimpsed in the still frozen light of dawn the color of his blue eyes. I felt in him a vague anxiety, which, in the uneasy, nervous joy of departure, kept him suspended over me, dividing his heart. His breath was close to me, with a fresh smell. And it seemed to me that into my small closed room he carried around himself, like a second body made of air, all the icy festive freshness of winter mornings on the dock, amid the animation of departures!

"Hey, are you listening to me, Arturo?" he insisted, still speaking in a low voice. "I'm leaving soon. I've let the others sleep, since I said goodbye to them last night . . . I've come to say goodbye to you."

"All right," I said, "goodbye."

"That friend of mine," he resumed, "went ahead down to the port, on his own. He's waiting for me on the steamer. I'm going alone, in the carriage."

The horse could be heard at the gate, pawing the ground. "The carriage," he continued, "is below, ready . . ." I turned slightly under the blanket, and in that movement I felt, under the sweater, my skin lightly scratched by the letter I'd hidden there. Now was the moment, or never, to give him my letter. But I didn't know how to give it to him.

"Well, so, what will you do, Arturo?" he asked. "You won't get up? You won't come with me as usual down to the port in the carriage?"

"No," I answered.

"You don't want to?" he asked again, in an inviting and irritated tone, of reproach, cheer, and regret. But at the same time you could feel his nerves vibrate with impatience to go, down to the port, to the steamer where Stella was waiting for him!

"No!" I repeated. And I turned over on the pillow, in the tentative gesture of turning my back to him, like a person who is annoyed and wants to be left to sleep. My eyes fleetingly saw him still lingering, disappointment on his forehead, and as he leaned over, some disheveled locks fell over it. And, resting my gaze at that moment on those nearby locks, I saw that mixed with the blond there were some white hairs.

"Then . . . goodbye, see you," he said, appearing indifferent.

"Goodbye, see you," I answered. And as he disappeared from the room I thought: "Goodbye, see you, and yet we won't see each other ever again!"

## December Fifth

When the door closed again behind him, I huddled in the blanket, pulled up to my face, covering my ears with my fists in order not to hear his steps as they grew distant, or his movements for departure in the rooms, or the last rolling of the carriage wheels as it went down the hill. I held out in that deathlike rigidity for an unnatural length of time. When I roused myself and threw off the blanket, the sun had already entered my room, and the house was plunged back into silence.

I opened the window and, leaning out as far as I could, gazed through the grille to the street. The small space beyond the gate and the street were deserted: not even a distant echo of wheels could be heard, or of horses' hooves. Only some voices of strangers, distant and scattered, resounded in the clear cold of the morning. But those real voices were vanquished by an unreal, very high sound, a single sharp note, which it seemed to me I heard from inside my brain: a kind of deafening and incredible exclamation that might perhaps be translated into the words "Goodbye, Wilhelm Gerace!"

I felt a mad temptation to run headlong down into the street, in the hope of reaching the carriage and finding myself next to him, at least for a short distance. But, even with that temptation, which lacerated my heart, I remained immobile, letting the minutes pass, until every hope became impossible.

I began to hear sounds, familiar voices in the rooms: my stepmother and brother had gotten up. Angrily I ran to the door and locked it. I would have liked only, at that moment, to have in my room the company of a dog, who was my friend and would gently lick my hands with its rough tongue, without asking any questions. But every human nearness, and even the sight of the landscape and all the known places, seemed intolerable to me just to think of. I would have liked to transform myself into a statue, in order not to feel anything.

So I stayed shut in my room, as if I were dead. For several hours no one paid attention to me. Then, in the afternoon, there was a knock, and my stepmother, in an uncertain and very faint voice, asked if I didn't want to eat, and if I felt ill, and why didn't I get up. I chased her away, shouting, with cruel words. But a few hours later I heard knocking again, and the same voice, which had become even more uncertain and fainter, told me that, if I wanted it, outside the door, on a chair, was a snack. Almost shouting, I answered that I didn't want anything, either to eat or to drink, only to be left alone.

For the first time in my life, I wasn't hungry, although I wasn't sick. Every so often I fell asleep, but immediately I roused myself with a start, with the sensation of a terrible jolt or a frightening din. And immediately I realized that in reality there had been nothing, neither din nor earthquake; it was suffering, which used those evil artifices to keep me awake and never leave me. It never left me, in fact, for the whole day! This was the first time since I was born that I had truly experienced suffering. Or at least I thought I did!

Now I knew, with utter determination, that these were the last hours I would spend on the island, and that the first step I took beyond the threshold of my room would be to go away. For that reason, perhaps,

I persisted in remaining shut in my room: to put off, at least for a few hours, that irremediable and threatening step!

Meanwhile, I wouldn't have wanted to weep, and I wept. I would have liked to forget W.G. as an insignificant person encountered scarcely once at a café or on a street corner; and instead, as I wept, I surprised myself by calling, "Pa," like a child of two. At some point I took the letter, which I still had under my sweater, and tore it up.

Of course, fasting also weakened me. By thinking of my father, I ended up deluding myself that he, too, in the same way, at that moment, was thinking of me. And that while I was calling, "Pa," he, too, from where he was, was calling inside, "Arturo! My dear *moro*," or something like that. Finally—impossible though it seems—as the hours passed, a last hope surfaced that toward evening managed to convince me almost completely with its seductiveness. It was this: I haven't yet said that the next day was December fifth, and, that is, my birthday. (I would be sixteen exactly.) Out of pride, I hadn't reminded my father of the date the night before. And he, on his own, wasn't used to remembering birthdays and things like that. But this time I began to hope that his memory, prompted by a miracle, would suddenly during his trip alert him to what he had forgotten. And that at that reminder he would immediately decide to return to wish me happy birthday and maybe even spend the day on the island with me. I said to myself that maybe he wasn't very far away yet: maybe he was still in Naples, and from there it would be simple to come back for a day. I thought again of the regretful expression on his face when, a few hours earlier, he had leaned over me, here, in my room; and I would almost have sworn now that that regret (joined to despair that I had not gone with him to the dock) was to bring him back to the island tomorrow. At nightfall, hope, in my imagination, had become certainty. So with that consolation I felt both exalted and tired. I looked outside the door, for the snack left on the chair by my stepmother: there was bread, oranges, and even a square of chocolate (an unusual delicacy in our house). I ate and went to bed and fell asleep.

⋙

I woke up, as I had the day before, around dawn. And so began this second morning, which was to be much worse than the first.

As soon as I was awake, remembering that it was my birthday, I felt a joyful sensation, in the more than ever certain conviction that Wilhelm Gerace would arrive. As I waited, I remained, as I had the previous day, a voluntary prisoner in my room, with the door double-locked. But today this prison was more a good-luck charm than anything else, and I foresaw that my glorious exit was imminent. I had, in fact, a kind of magical confidence that my father would arrive on the first steamer, which landed at Procida at exactly eight.

But when, from my window, where I was on the lookout, I heard nine sound without any news, I passed from certainty that he would arrive to doubt that he would—not on the second boat, at ten, or any boat at all. Yet hope had by now nested in me like a parasite, unwilling to leave its nest. And for two more hours I continued to count all the quarter-hours of the bell tower, constantly moving around, from the bed to the window, now covering my ears purposely, now straining to listen; and thinking and thinking again whether he might not come on some secondary line or private boat; and pacing back and forth in the room; and starting at every sound, whistle, rustling, and so on. In other words, the usual nonsense of someone who is waiting and hoping. Finally, after eleven, I understood conclusively that I had been crazy, and had taken my sentimental fantasies for heavenly omens—that W.G. hadn't even dreamed of returning, and would not arrive.

Then, for the first time in my life, it seemed to me that I truly wished for death.

Midday sounded, with the usual great pealing of bells. All morning, luckily, no one had dared to bother me; but a little after the concert of bells, here again, like the day before, came a knock at the door, with an even lighter beat than yesterday, almost imperceptible. I understood, from what I could hear easily, that behind the door was my stepmother with Carmine. Not daring to do it herself, she had guided the hand of the child to knock. And now she was teaching him, softly, to say to me the phrase *happy birthday*, which he, obedient, repeated to me, shouting in his primitive manner.

Such a family attention, at that moment, revolted me more than an atrocious insult. And with no other answer, I kicked the door, to signify clearly that I didn't want birthday wishes and sent them all to hell.

For another hour and a half or so, no one appeared. It must have been almost two when again I heard that persistent knocking at the door. This time it was she who knocked: and harder, almost brutally. I gave no sign of having heard; and then, in an unsteady voice, almost icy with distress and hesitation, she called: "Artú . . ."

## The Earring

I didn't answer: "Artú . . ." she resumed then, more hurried and breathless, like someone talking while running, "what are you doing? Why don't you get up? I've made *pizza dolce*, like the other year, for your birthday . . ."

Although I had always thought that, basically, she had a stupid brain, never had her stupidity appeared to me as it did this time: immeasurable, worse than infinite! How could she come and talk to me about frivolous things like *pizza dolce* at such a tragic moment? And her very kindnesses, which I had long since become unaccustomed to, and which until a few days earlier would have gladdened my heart, today embittered me. I would have preferred her to be hostile, severe, as usual; and it seemed to me that she should have understood all this: "Get out, stupid, idiot!" I shouted at her. And with desperate ferocity I opened the door with a racket.

She was there, holding the child in her arms, her lips trembling, as white as a dead person. I immediately noted, my sight sharpened by fury, that she had put on the velvet skirt, and had also dressed Carmine for a party: of course, to celebrate the day in a worthy manner. All that, instead of softening me, increased my rancor. Meanwhile, some indefinable impulse of extreme bitterness made me rush first of all to my father's room.

The room was still, more or less, in the disarray of departure. My stepmother, by nature, was never quick to straighten the rooms, and had contented herself with piling in a corner old clothes, shoes, newspapers, books, empty cigarette packs, and so on, which evidently my father, in his haste, had left scattered on the floor. On the bed there was nothing but the mattress, without blankets or pillows. And a rapid glance at the open wardrobe was enough to know irremediably what I had already foreseen: and that is that the place where W.G. usually kept his-our historic treasures (the speargun, the naval binoculars, etc.) was empty.

On the wall near the bed was the portrait of Romeo the Amalfitano, smiling as always, unaware, with its gentle blind eyes.

Feverishly, I moved a little around that deserted room, under the sad, distraught eyes of my stepmother, who had followed me to the doorway. "You know who he left with?" I cried then. "He didn't leave alone, as he made you think! He left with Stella!"

She looked at me, trying, at the same time, with her head, to avoid Carmine, who, agitated by my bizarre behavior, was playing with her curls to comfort himself. I continued, in my vengeful stubbornness, like a real boy:

"He prefers Stella to you!"

Anxiously, she advanced into the room and put Carmine down on the big bed. "Who is Stella? Is she from here?" she asked, her features suddenly upset by a threatening, barbaric ferocity; and it was clear, from her question, that, at the name, which she heard now for the first time, she thought Stella was a woman. But as soon as she had understood from me that it was a man named Tonino Stella her face relaxed, and was tinged with relief.

At the evidence of these changing emotions, I also felt returning another, past jealousy (even if never confessed). "Ah," I shouted, full of grief, overwhelmed by a double jealousy, "but he loves Stella! He LOVES him!"

"He loves him," she repeated; and her voice was inexpressive, like a cold, innocent echo, as she repeated the word. As soon as she had uttered it, however, she broke off, her mouth hesitating, with a jolt of shame. Her eyes rushed to observe me, questioning and suspicious. Then rapidly they turned away.

"Yes, he loves him! HE LOVES HIM! And he cares much more about him than about you . . . and Carmine . . . and me! And everyone!" I resumed, like a lunatic.

She moved her lips to protest; but she was silent, with a weak, painful scowl, which gave her a look of precociously mature childhood. For a moment, escaping me, she seemed to close up in herself, like a sick sparrow that in self-defense huddles in its feathers; then she roused herself and addressed me, almost brutally. "You," she exclaimed with trembling breath, "are not speaking true words . . ." Meanwhile, she peered at Carmine, perhaps fearful that he, with his one-year-old brain, might have understood my terrible words against my father!

". . . That Stella, who left with him," she continued obstinately, frowning, "can't ever be the same as a relative . . . That is a friendship . . ." Suddenly she raised one shoulder slightly: "That is another thing!" she concluded with a curious air of folk skepticism, indulgent and scornful.

At that point, a luminous, almost bombastic maturity seemed to clothe her. And she was silent, proud, and calm, her eyebrows furrowed, as if to let me understand that the subject was closed.

Then, in a mad impulse, I cried: "But you, do you love him?"

I saw her start at that unexpected question, and in a moment grow confused, as if her heart had suddenly failed her. "What . . . I . . . who?" she stammered.

"Him! My father!" I said. "Do you love him?"

Her cheeks devoured by a dark red, like a real burn that was wounding her skin, she stood before me, across the big bed that separated the two of us; and she was so lost that she didn't even pay attention to Carmine. "What do you mean?" she repeated two or three times. "He . . . he's my husband . . ." Maybe she thought I was accusing her of *not* loving my father; and instead it was the opposite that I, wretched me, accused her of!

"I know!" I burst out finally, letting go all my bitterness. "I know! You love him!"

But she didn't take heart at those words; rather, her face quivered abruptly, as if from a shock, and she looked at me with big open defenseless eyes, in a kind of disorderly prayer.

"I know! You love him!" I repeated. "*Why* do you love him?"

"Oh . . . I can't . . . listen to . . . those words . . . I . . . am . . . his wife . . ."

"He's insulted you! He's insulted you!"

"Oh! Artú . . . why do you speak . . . of him that way? He's your father . . ." she broke in. A violent emotion made her face pale, transforming its earlier redness into a feverish, timid pink. "And then," she added, "he is more unfortunate . . . than you."

"My father . . . is unfortunate?"

"Ah, you . . . you're more fortunate . . . than him . . ." she reaffirmed, shaking her head slowly. Automatically, as if without realizing it, she had moved close to Carmine again, and, surely to distract him from our blasphemous words, she let him play with a ribbon that she took out of her hair. "You are more fortunate than he is," she repeated. "Ah, you, who knows how many beautiful women you'll have, in your life . . ."

As she made this prediction, her chin trembled slightly, like a real girl's. And the almost insipid, slightly sour innate innocence of her voice gained (from hidden tears) a resonance, like the imperfect music of certain humble childish instruments. She continued, her head still swaying:

"And he, on the other hand, women don't much want him. He . . . he's too natural . . . he's not tactful . . . with women he doesn't have the imagination to show them off. Well, because many women don't like a man who stays just that bit of time . . . and then forgets them . . . And no little kindness . . . a nice compliment . . . nothing, as if he were dealing with some low woman . . . That fact, a lot of women think it makes them look bad . . ."

These phrases, necessary to demonstrate her conclusion, she drew from her breast with obvious difficulty (between blushes of awkwardness and innocence, and maybe even echoes—barely perceptible in her breath—of involuntary secret sighs . . .), but yet with the gravity of profound experience! And it was with a sense almost of amusement that I recognized, there, in her present demonstration, certain notorious speeches of her mother, Violante.

"So that's why," she concluded, "I say of him, that he's more unfortunate: because with women he can't have much luck!"

"But," I objected, "he's a very handsome man!"

"Yes, very handsome . . . I don't want to say he's ugly, no! So—so . . . then he's old."

"Old!"

"What, isn't he old? You know how old he is?" She counted on her fingers. "Thirty-five, he's in his thirty-sixth year. He already has wrinkles, white hair . . ."

That I had also noticed; but still I hadn't yet thought that my father had now, in effect, reached old age!

"So for that reason," she resumed, "I begged you to remember . . . respect for your father. Because, besides being his son, you, with your fate, compared to his fate, you're like a great lord of wealth! Because in your life who knows how many beautiful girls you'll meet, and brilliant young women, and foreigners who . . . who . . . will love . . . you . . . And who knows what a beautiful bride you'll have . . ."

She swallowed once, twice. Her voice again cracked. But she quickly concluded, lowering her forehead with a meek, gentle, and persuasive seriousness:

"As for him, if he didn't take me, where—now that he really is old— where would he find the affection of another soul? Yes, if there wasn't me, maybe no other woman would get involved with him . . . And since he was born without a family, poor man, he'd be alone and a gypsy for his whole life, like a soldier in the foreign legion . . . Now, in his life, there's only me to take care of him . . ."

She uttered those last sentences not with humility but in fact with the satisfaction of a matronly superiority, in which was mixed an air of somewhat childlike valor. And in that comic mixture, her unattainable beauty appeared to me magnificent, worthy of a true king! I looked at her for a moment; then I burst out:

"You're wrong if you think I'm going to have a wife!"

"Artú! . . . Why . . ."

"You're wrong. There's one woman alone, who could be my wife! I know who it is! And I don't want another! I won't ever marry anyone!"

She stared at me with fear in her face, as if I had shouted a curse at her. But without wanting to, her gaze spoke a winged, smiling gratitude, even in the disbelief that shadowed it: as if she would not be unhappy, in essence, if I remained celibate in honor of that woman.

Then all my love for her seized me again, in a great fire of regrets, demands, and revolt! Like a mad Catherine wheel, all the wonderful compliments I would give her if I were her husband were ignited in me; and the kisses, the caresses I would shower on her; and how every night I would sleep next to her naked body, to feel her bosom near me even in sleep. And of the beautiful clothes I would buy her, I would want her in a silk petticoat, and a shirt of embroidered silk, so I could see them on her when I undressed her. And I would take her to visit her mother, Violante, dressed in furs, with a feathered hat, like one of the finest ladies of Naples! And the journeys I would make would be uniquely in order to send her letters every day, written as beautifully as the poems of a genius. And I would go to America, to farthest Asia, to bring her back jewels such as no other woman had. Not for her to put away somewhere: but to cover her neck, and her ears, and her little hands, as if they were all kisses. So that her friends and acquaintances, seeing her pass by so rich in gold and true precious gems, would have to say: "Lucky her, she has such a grand husband!"

These thoughts (which I'd had more than once, and repressed with difficulty, during the preceding months, since that famous day when I had discovered I loved her) swirled in my mind, I repeat, like a festival of fire. The impossibility, which transformed those joyous thoughts into sorrow, was an unnatural injustice, tormenting me. But as N. stood there before me, breathing and physical, suddenly every impossibility became absurd. In an arrogance of happiness, I ran toward her, on the other side of the big bed, and said:

"I love you!"

It was the first time in my life that I said that word: and it seemed to me that, in hearing me say it, she would have to feel the same emotion as me saying it. Instead, the usual fantastic negation (which at that moment seemed to me more odious than any vile superstition) twisted her face. She cried:

"No! Artú! You mustn't do evil!"

And then, with the rage of one who wants what is his right, I embraced her, holding her tight, and tried to kiss her on the mouth.

But she was ready to avoid my kiss, twisting her head back feverishly, and repeating: "No! No!" in a sort of wild invocation of help: as if there were someone in the room, besides the scared, defenseless Carminiello, who could help her. So she began to defend herself from me, struggling with knees, elbows, fists, even with her nails and teeth. A beast of the wilderness intending to kill me could not have developed such ferocity as she used to deny me a kiss! Then my love turned into hatred; and before I left, without having kissed her, with furious hands I blindly hit her cheeks, her neck, her hair. Until, with wonder and amazement (composed of a strange innocence, rather than remorse), I saw in the mass of her curls a small pink ear stained with drops of blood.

In my reckless rage, I had given a violent tug to her earring, so that the clasp came unhooked and had slightly torn the lobe. And, letting her go, I found in my fingers the poor prey of that small circle of gold. As in a dream I heard the crying of my stepbrother, who surely was convinced that I wanted to murder his mother! And saw her, who, now pale, leaning against the child, held him by his garment so that he wouldn't fall on the floor. It seemed to me that she wasn't even complaining, she was so stunned; and she stared at me with wide eyes that were weak and suffering, as if she expected from me some new horror. I threw the earring at her feet. "You vile murderer!" I shouted at her. "Don't be afraid, I'll never kiss you again." And running out of the room I added: "Goodbye. Forever. It's all over."

## In the Cave

She had remained still, leaning on the bed, without a word; but when I was on the stair landing I heard her calling from the doorway, fearfully: "Artú! Artú! Where are you going?" Then I heard, from inside the room, Carmine's crying grow sharper; and she hurried back to try to calm him. Again, as I crossed the hall, I heard her voice, which from the top of the stairs had resumed calling breathlessly, "Where are you going? Artú!" mingled with the clatter of her clogs as they descended the first steps and the babbling of Carmine in her arms. But a moment later I was in the street; and the voices of the house vanished behind me, with distance, like sounds of another world.

I didn't know precisely where I would flee. I had no friend on the island, and besides, in my fury, I had neglected to take any money, abandoning my entire capital in my room. Aside from that bread and chocolate and fruit of the evening before, I hadn't eaten for a day and a half: and, surely, the bizarre sense of unreality that transported me and lightened my anguish a little was due partly to that. With unalterable determination, I knew that soon the island would belong to the past. There were no more steamers leaving for the mainland that day; but I didn't care about knowing exactly how and when I would leave. What I asked for the moment was only to retreat for a while to some deserted corner of the island where I could hide my lacerating solitude. "And so," I said to myself bitterly, "ends the day of my birthday!"

I crossed the square with the monument of Christ the Fisherman, then the main harbor, leaving the wharf behind; and, although I had no definite goal, seeking only uninhabited and solitary places, I set off to the left, toward the last gray bit of coast that, against a background of earth-covered rocks, formed the edge of the island on that side. On the level space before the Lingua del Faro, cluttered, like a shipyard, with boats in dry dock and under repair, some village girls were playing hopscotch on squares drawn on the ground with chalk. In my brutal course, I almost hit a jumper, but, paying no attention to her protests or those of her companions, I kept going toward the shore.

Several natural caves were dug into the rocks there. Two or three of these—with an entrance no wider than the measure of a door, but spacious and comfortable enough inside—had been appropriated as storehouses for equipment, oars, and so on, by boat owners. They paid rent to the town, and had provided the entrances with strong plank doors, usually tightly locked. But going along the shore I saw that one of those doors was open. Maybe the renter of the cave had left the island, or that space was unused. Inside, in fact, there was nothing but a pile of old rotting ropes and some cans of glue covered with mold.

I had happened onto that shore, one could say, by chance, and chance helped me! The small abandoned room was exactly what I needed. I entered, and pulled the door closed; swelled by bad weather, it fit perfectly into its opening, so that from the outside it appeared unquestionably locked, like the others. To better secure it from the wind, I barricaded it with that pile of ropes, on which I flopped down and stretched out. And there, on that bed, ignored by everyone, I felt free and alone, like a miserable vagabond.

Lack of food, followed by that long run, began to make itself felt, with a light buzzing in my ears and a confused weariness. I gave no thought to my destiny, not even that of the next hours, as if it belonged not to me but to someone else whom I still didn't know, and whom it didn't much matter to me to know. And I no longer hated my father, I no longer loved N. In place of the dramatic sufferings that until a little before had agitated me, I felt an amorphous sadness, with no more feelings for anyone.

## The Goddess

The wind had turned to scirocco and made the weather warm, stormy, and dark. The gaps in the plank door let a glimmer of murky light into the cave, mixed with the heavy salt scent of the air. The small stretch of coast, in that season, was deserted like the farthest reaches of the world; and for some minutes no other sound reached me but the noise of the sea stirred by the African wind. But soon afterward amid that din I heard coming closer through the wind the same voice that at the moment of my flight had pursued me to the door and, hoarse and breathless from the run, continued to cry, "Ar-tuuuro! Ar-tuuú!"

My stepmother had evidently delayed just long enough to put Carmine down safely somewhere, and had immediately run out to look for me. From someone who had seen me go by and, finally, from the girls who were playing hopscotch, she must have found out the direction I had taken. But no one had seen me enter the cave, and, confident of my hiding place, I raised myself from my pile of ropes and, squatting behind the door, peeked out through the gaps between the boards.

An instant later, I saw my stepmother emerge, breathing hard, at the end of the beach; and, from her habits, I seemed to guess with certainty, and not much difficulty, her thought. Hearing in the room my supreme farewell, "Goodbye forever," she must have gotten the suspicion that I wanted to pass the notorious Pillars of Hercules again, this time with no return. (Besides, I confess, perhaps I had even, in a way, intended her to understand something of the sort.) And now, before that desolate empty shore, her suspicion was magnified.

She passed the storehouse caves without stopping, since, clearly, those being private spaces, and properly closed, she didn't consider that I could be there . . . She ran along the beach to the last barrier of rocks, then she turned back, more frantic, and then she retraced the same stretch. And suddenly she began to pound on the doors of the caves with her fists! But surely it was only her violence that found an outlet against that wood, without any real hope: in the mad disorder of her blows, one perceived the certainty that she was pounding in vain. I also seemed to hear her trying, with her little hands, to force the door of the cave next to mine. But she immediately abandoned that undertaking, which must have seemed to her absurd and futile.

And she returned to the shore, back and forth, like a desperate murderer. Maybe, at this moment, she already saw me hurled down into the whirlpools and swept away to an unknown distance. She ran, shouting "Artú!" in all directions, in a new, strange, carnal voice of lacerating sharpness; and letting the wind drag her dress, with no shame. Her black shawl had fallen off her head, uncovering the curls, all disheveled and torn after the struggle she'd had with me; and when she ran into the wind her hair covered her face, went into her mouth, muffling her cries. Every so often her knees buckled and she slowed her pace; and her lips, which had become livid and almost swollen from so much shouting, relaxed in a brutal, inanimate bitterness. In the few minutes since we had left the house, she seemed to have grown into a woman of thirty; and to have exchanged her honest soul for the soul of a sinner. From her present devastated and earthly, old-woman's ugliness emanated a sweet, barbaric splendor. As if her soul, speaking, implored: "Ah, Arturo, don't be dead, have pity on a poor lover. Reappear to me alive, and I, in this very place, down on these rocks, will give you not only kisses but everything you want. I will go to hell for you, my holy love, I will be proud of it!"

But, with a cruel and melancholy hardness, I thought, seeing her: "Go away. It's over now. I have no more love for you or hatred for others. I have no feelings for anyone. Go home, go, I don't even like you."

And I lay down again, with my arms under my head, hoping that she would go away and leave me alone.

I heard her wandering on the beach a little longer, continuing to repeat "Artú," but softly now, in a kind of inconsolable babble. Finally that pathetic voice went away along the road home, toward the town, and the beach was empty again.

Then I really did have the feeling of being without life, down at the bottom of the sea, as she so feared. As soon as she left, the whistle of the three o'clock steamer reached me, through the wind, as it entered the harbor. But that no longer meant anything, I no longer expected anyone. The certainty that my father would not return for my birthday, besides, no longer caused me any sorrow. Worse, I was sure that by now his arrival wouldn't cheer me.

"In an hour or so it will be evening," I thought with satisfaction, "and no one will pass by on this forgotten beach, no one will come to bother me anymore." A night without duration or awareness was, perhaps, the only tolerable conclusion of this day.

As the minutes passed, I felt my muscles grow stiff with lack of movement, and my thoughts became dazed, as if I were being transformed into a gigantic sea turtle, inside its armor of black stone. The second signal of the steamer, which after its brief stop was leaving the harbor, reached me as from centuries of distance, like some incredible news, which I no longer wanted to hear. Near me, at the door of my usurped room, the sounds of the wind and the waves mingled, and that natural chorus, without any human voice, certainly was discussing my destiny, in a language as incomprehensible as death.

And it was at that point (the signal of the boat's departure had faded into the distance) that I heard again, advancing from the end of the beach, a voice—not of a woman, manly this time; and not agitated, but, rather, confident and almost gay—that called the name of Arturo. It was not the timbre of my father's voice; and the rapid, heavy-booted footsteps—which, approaching, echoed on the stones of the beach— were certainly not his.

I got up, as before, to look out between the planks. And there outside, a few meters away, I saw a soldier passing.

He had brown curly hair, was shorter than average, with a round face, a black mustache, and animated dark eyes that were exploring the surroundings.

At the moment, it didn't seem to me that I knew him; still, in his figure I noticed immediately something oddly familiar, which gave me a tremor of surprise and mystery.

From behind my door I shouted: "Hey! What Arturo are you looking for?"

He answered: "Eh, Arturo Gerace!"

So I opened the door. "Arturo Gerace," I said, "is me!" At which he exclaimed, "Arturo!" hurrying toward me with evident pleasure. And without any fuss he kissed me on both cheeks.

"You don't recognize me, I see," he added. And, with an allusive and mysterious smile, he showed me, on the ring finger of his right hand, a silver ring, which had set into it a cameo depicting the head of the goddess Minerva.

## The Enchanted Pin

Perhaps our nature leads us to consider the games of the unexpected more futile and arbitrary than they are—too much so. Thus, for example, when in a story or a poem the unexpected event seems to accord with some secret intention of fate, we willingly charge the writer with novelistic vice. And in life certain unexpected events, in themselves natural and simple, appear to us, because of our mood of the moment, extraordinary or even supernatural.

Let's then suppose that on that fateful birthday my only friend had instinctively felt from afar my despair; and so had hurried . . . Well, even that, according to reason and science, shouldn't seem a miracle: when even the sparrows and their kind, simple migratory creatures, intuit by themselves the moment to depart, and find the path without any instructions!

But the arrival of that unexpected visitor, suddenly surprising me on the beach, had an effect so novelistic that at the moment, rather than a living presence, I believed in a hallucination. At the sight of that cameo, my famous gift to my nurse Silvestro, and a clear document of his person, I was dumbstruck. As if there on the beach, right before my eyes, a Valley of the Kings had been unearthed, or some similar underground wonder.

An instant later, though, recognizing the reality, I murmured, "Silvestro!" and quickly returned his two kisses on the cheeks. With the happy assurance that he, at least, being my legitimate nurse, wouldn't accuse me of damning his soul to hell for that pair of kisses!

And at the very moment when I kissed him, I realized that, in truth, his presence here on Procida on the day of my birthday wasn't—even if new—so strange. If anything, the strangeness (and also the ingratitude) was mine: in the present situation I had completely forgotten him, who never let my birthday pass without showing up in some way, maybe with a simple card bearing good wishes. But in recent times I had been thinking too much of other people to have even a single thought for this one!

He explained that, having been recalled back to the army, he had taken advantage of a leave, and also of the discount for soldiers on the steamships, to make this trip (which he had been promising himself for about ten years) and bring me birthday wishes in person . . . He told me that, crossing the square a little while before, having just got off the boat in Procida, he had heard repeated with great animation, in a group of girls and women, the name of Arturo. And on learning that one of those women was my stepmother, who was looking for me, he had introduced himself. Then he had proposed to return to search the beach himself, while she continued her search around the square. Those girls claimed, in fact, that I could have returned to the square by descending through certain impassable shortcuts above the rocks down there, where the storehouses were . . .

Here Silvestro advised me to let my stepmother know immediately that I had been found, since that poor woman was in a state of such extreme anxiety. She must have, he added, a very nervous character.

"No," I said then, smiling, "she's not naturally nervous. But of course she's really worried. Well! She thinks I'm dead."

"Dead!"

I shrugged one shoulder, judging it best not to explain too much. Anyway, I thought Silvestro's advice was good, and I went with him right away toward the Lingua del Faro. There, seeing from a distance one of the girls from before, whom I knew by sight, and who had lingered to jump on the chalk squares by herself, we gave her a call. She ran over, and I said:

"Go to the square, and look for Signora Gerace. And tell her you saw me here with my friend, and that before, I was up at the top of the rocks, resting behind those bushes . . . Tell her that now my friend and I have some things to talk about; and so she should go back home calmly, we'll join her later . . ."

I managed to get that speech out all in one breath; but once the girl had left on her errand, I collapsed and sat down on the ground. And I begged Silvestro, for pity's sake, before anything else, to go to the store at the corner and buy me something to eat, because I was nearly fainting from hunger. And I added that I would reimburse him for whatever he spent, because I had plenty of money at home.

Right away that perfect nurse got from the store some fresh eggs, fresh cheese, and bread, which had the effect on me of an elixir of life. Then we returned together to my cave, which I had become attached to today as if it were my command tent or some other quarters of bravery and importance. And there we sat on the pile of ropes to talk in comfort.

He told me that he had to depart tomorrow at dawn, on the first boat, because unfortunately his leave was up. I asked him then why he had gone back to the army. "They're starting to call up people," he answered, "in view of the war."

"What war?" I said.

"What? You don't know anything about the war? You haven't heard it on the radio? Read in the papers?"

In fact, I never saw newspapers: my father said they were disgusting, so full of cheap nonsense and idiotic gossip that one felt compelled to use them in the toilet. And as for the radio, it's true that for a while there had been at least one in the town, owned by the same innkeeper who had once had the owl. And sometimes, passing by, I had heard talking and singing; but on those few occasions it was broadcasting pop songs or variety shows, nothing serious.

In substance, I knew history from the time of the ancient Egyptians, and the lives of the great leaders and the battles of all the past centuries. But of the contemporary era I knew nothing. I had barely glimpsed even those few signs of the present that reached the island, and paid them no attention. Current events had never interested me. As if they were all ordinary news from the papers, outside of fantastic history and the Absolute Certainties.

And now, hearing the world news that Silvestro brought, I seemed to have been asleep for sixteen years, like the girl in the fairy tale: in a courtyard overrun by weeds and spider webs, amid owls big and small, with an enchanted pin stuck in my forehead!

He was explaining to me that, in spite of a recent peace agreement signed with grandiose ceremony by the Powers (these, I now understood, must be the famous *international events* that Stella had alluded to, the origin of the amnesty and his freedom), the world war, in reality, was imminent, inevitable. It might erupt any month, maybe any day. And even those who were against it, like him, were in the middle, in that hellish entanglement.

⌒⌒⌒

At this news, I reflected for some instants, closed in my thoughts. And then I revealed to Silvestro my decisions.

I confided to him first of all that for certain very cruel, in fact tragic, secret reasons of my own, I couldn't stay on the island, even just a single day more. So I intended to leave with him on the first boat tomorrow at dawn, possibly not to return to the island ever again! If, I continued, the war really was approaching, I was absolutely determined to volunteer from the first day of our national intervention. I wanted to take part at all costs, even if I had to get to the battlefield clandestinely (in the case that my application was rejected because of my age).

Silvestro listened with profound seriousness to this speech. Discreetly, he avoided asking any questions about the secret reasons that were taking me away from Procida; but, without needing to know them, he understood that the reasons were just and grave. And he welcomed favorably, even gladly, my decision to leave with him the next day. He didn't, on the other hand, seem equally favorable to the second part of my program: and that is, my intention of enlisting as a volunteer in the coming war. Seeing that he was perplexed and skeptical on that point, I said to him then, fervently, that in my opinion a man wasn't a man until he had proved himself in war. And to stay home without fighting, while others fought, for me would be tedium and dishonor.

He listened to me unconvinced, with a dubious expression. At the end he said that my idea might perhaps be valid for ancient wars, but modern wars, in his opinion, were another thing. As far as he understood, he said, modern war was a butchering machine, and a horrendous anthill of devastation, without the merit of authentic valor. Regarding the current war, in his opinion neither of the two sides that were fighting was, generally speaking (that is to say from the point of view of the *true Cause*), right. But between the two the one that was wrong was certainly our side! And to fight in that way, without right, and with wrong, was like singing gratis with a thorn in your throat. A disaster with no reward.

Those sensible words of his made me think a little, but also laugh. In any case, I replied resolutely that I, for now, didn't care much about right and wrong. What I wanted was to fight in order to learn to fight, like an Oriental samurai. The day I was a master sure of my valor, I would choose my cause. But to get to that mastery I had to pass a test. The test that offered itself was this war; and I didn't want to miss it, I didn't care about anything else.

"That," he observed in a tone of bitter uncertainty, "is like saying that you're looking to be killed for nothing." Then he asked, studying me seriously: "Why the hell do you want to get killed for nothing?"

I blushed, as if he were exposing a mysterious, extraordinary scandal that should be kept quiet. But immediately I recovered, with my old ideas. And passionately I explained to him that, ever since I was a child, there had been an undecided challenge between me and death. The way some boys are distrustful of the dark, I was of death: and death alone! That disgust for death poisoned the certainty of life. And until I had learned to be heedless of death I couldn't know if I was truly adult. Worse: if I was brave or a coward.

Here I revealed to him in brief my ideas about life, and also the Absolute Certainties. I had almost forgotten about these in recent months, and it seemed to me that, reviving them with him, I was making up for a betrayal. I became passionate about them again as I talked, and he, listening, became as passionate as I was. Suddenly, with a confused, ingenuous smile, he confided that my ideas agreed wonderfully with his—that is, with the revolution of the people. For he was, he said, a revolutionary; and now he was charmed by hearing that I, by myself, here on Procida, without ever talking to anyone, had invented the same thoughts of the best masters! In making these declarations, Silvestro revealed, in his face and his tone, his great admiration for Arturo Gerace. On the other hand, then, it was evident from his behavior that his admiration for A.G. had not begun just now but must have preexisted, one might say, forever, and had merely been waiting for new occasions to be confirmed. It was devoted to me, unlimited and almost magical! Similar in a certain sense—just to be clear—to what I felt for W.G.

Finally, with my outburst, I convinced Silvestro of everything I liked: even of the moral necessity of fighting, trusting to luck, in the first available war. Who knows, we fantasized, full of hope, whether we might even end up together in the same regiment! (That hope was not fulfilled. I was assigned to a company of youths around my age; and he elsewhere, with the older recalled reservists.)

Last, he took from his pocket the birthday present he had brought me and had forgotten about until that moment, distracted by too many emotions: a red wool scarf, the work of his wife. Right away I put it around my neck, with pleasure. Thus he let me know that he had recently married the woman who had been his girlfriend for years. Now that he was in the army, his wife had moved to her mother's house, in a small town near Naples; and if I wanted, he said, I could be their guest. From that town one could get to Naples in a few minutes on the tram.

⚜

During this conversation, night had fallen; and Silvestro reminded me that it was time, now, to go home, according to the promise I'd made to my stepmother. At that I felt a blush rise to my face; but luckily it was dark now, and Silvestro didn't notice. I felt that my voice would tremble in the speech I was about to make; but still I made it, resolutely.

"Now," I said, "for reasons that I can't confide to anyone, I'd better not go back home. You go alone, and talk to her, and make her believe the following lie: that I already left on the four-thirty steamer, which goes to Ischia. And that tomorrow morning you'll join me on Ischia, and we'll go together to Naples, and from there I'll immediately go abroad. Tell her goodbye from me, because she and I won't meet again for a long time, if we ever do meet again. And she should remember me, and forgive the trouble I caused her. And say goodbye also to my brother Carminiello for me.

"Ask her to give you a suitcase. (Tell her you'll bring it to me tomorrow on Ischia.) And go to my room and get: all the written pages you can find, and all my money—there's a lot, in my room, scattered among the books and in the drawers. Please, get *all* the written pages, don't leave any, they're important, because I'm a writer.

"If you want, tonight, you can sleep at the house, because your room is the same, with the cot and the rest. But before you go to sleep, please bring me some blankets and something for dinner. In fact, until I leave tomorrow, I don't want to go even briefly to the square, because I have too many memories there. And tonight I'll sleep in this cave, where I'll be comfortable enough. Luckily it's not cold. There's the scirocco."

Silvestro promised he would carry out all my requests perfectly: but, he said, since I was sleeping down in the cave, he, too, wanted to sleep in the cave with me, rather than in the house, in order not to leave me alone. After all, for most of his life, as a guard at construction sites, he had slept in huts, and now, as a soldier, he had to prepare to sleep in the trenches. Caves were nothing! A cave like ours was a Vatican palace, compared with the trench.

So I should wait for him, because he would return as quickly as possible, with everything needed.

## Contrary Dreams

Not even two hours later, I saw the wavering glow of a candle lantern advancing from the shadowy end of the beach; and I hurried toward Silvestro as he returned, holding the lantern in front of him, more loaded down than the Befana.* Besides the suitcase full of manuscripts and provisions, and several heavy wool blankets, he also carried a quilted coverlet, and even a bucket of coal to warm the damp air of the cave! Some of these supplies that provident man had procured at the Casa dei Guaglioni; but some he had preferred to get in the town, in order not to make my stepmother suspicious, since she was not to know that I was spending the night on the island.

First of all, as soon as I was near him, I asked: "Did you tell her . . . what I told you?" "Yes," he answered. "And . . . did she believe you?" "Yes," he said, "she believed me." And for the moment I asked nothing else.

We placed the lantern on a rock sticking out in a corner of the cave; we spread the quilt on the pile of ropes, carefully dispersed on the ground; and we sat on this improvised but fairly comfortable bed, preparing for dinner. Among the various foods that Silvestro got out of the suitcase was a large *pizza dolce,* wrapped in thick paper. And he told me that my stepmother had asked him to bring it to me on Ischia, saying that she had made it for my birthday and had no wish now to eat it.

Besides the *pizza dolce,* she sent me as a gift, in case I should find myself in need, all her savings, which Silvestro gave me: around four hundred and fifty lire, knotted in a rather dirty handkerchief. Finally, she entrusted to Silvestro one of a pair of earrings, gold, begging him to tell me that I should keep it in memory of her.

---

* The Befana is an ugly old woman who brings gifts to good children—somewhat in the manner of Santa Claus—on the eve of Epiphany, January 6.

In receiving from Silvestro's hands that little circle of gold, I blushed. Then I threw myself onto the quilt, and, with my face down, in shadow, I asked him to describe to me precisely how the scene with my step-mother had unfolded.

So I learned that, seeing him arrive alone at the Casa dei Guaglioni, she had looked at him uncertainly, but didn't ask about me. Then, as he spoke, "Arturo sends word . . ." she had begun to turn white in the face; but still she had found the strength to murmur, "Why are you standing? Sit down," and had sat down herself on a chair in front of the kitchen table. After which he had quickly finished telling her what he had to. And on hearing that I was already on the sea, and had left Procida, she had looked at him with large, serious, cold eyes, which seemed not to see anymore. Suddenly her pallor became unnatural, green, as of a dead woman; and without having spoken a single word or given an exclamation or a sigh she had fainted, hitting her forehead on the table.

In a few instants, though, she had stood up; in fact, to tell the truth she had urged him not to let me know about that fainting fit, which she spoke of stammering, confusedly, as of something shameful. And she had helped him pack the suitcase to bring me on Ischia, moving here and there like a bloodless shadow.

At that point, still lying down with my face in the dark, I interrupted Silvestro, imploring him, please, not to talk about her, starting now, ever again. I preferred not even to hear her named by anyone, from now on.

When we finished dinner, Silvestro and I stayed awake talking until late. Luckily, he had thought to provide a couple of spare candles for our lantern. We talked about a thousand things, about the past but above all about the future; and about the Absolute Certainties, and revolution, and so on. Silvestro also asked me to read him some of my poems; I naturally chose the best and most effective, and saw that as he listened he had tears running down his face!

The lighted brazier, between us, gave off a pleasant warmth; and in the mysterious light of the glass lantern, sitting there in the cave on a grand orange quilt, we could really imagine that we were in an Arab or Persian tent, and that the distant barking of dogs was the roar of exotic beasts. The wind and the sea had calmed, promising us a tranquil crossing for the next day. Around ten, we put the brazier outside the door, so as not to risk poisoning ourselves with its fumes. We closed the door, extinguished the lantern. And, wrapped in our blankets, we went to sleep.

In contrast with that wonderful evening, I had troubled dreams. N., Carminiello, my father were rushing in confusion. And then the chaos and din of tanks, black flags emblazoned with skulls, fighters in black uniforms, mixed with dark-skinned kings and Indian philosophers and pale, bleeding women. That whole crowd passed with an enormous rumble over a walled trench where I was lying. And I would have liked to get out to go to the battle but there was no exit. I felt around my body a weight of sand that was swallowing me, producing, in the sucking, a kind of horrible human sigh. And I called to all those people who were passing over me, but no one heard me.

I woke with a start in the middle of the night, surprised by a big thunderous sound that echoed through the walls of rock around me. At first I remembered nothing: neither the events of the day before nor why I was in this room of stone. But I quickly gathered my thoughts; and I realized that the noise I was astonished at was simply Silvestro's snoring: which, seriously, was enough for an entire platoon, not just for a single soldier! The discovery exhilarated me. I tried to remember the thousands of times that I must have heard that same symphony, in the times when I slept with Silvestro, as a little child; and I laughed to myself, imagining the thoughts I might have had then, hearing my nurse produce such odd music. I promised myself then, anticipating some fun, to tease him about this skill of his, as soon as we were awake, in the morning.

That grand snoring, which a little earlier, in my dream, had been transformed into fantastic sounds of death, now filled me, on the contrary, in the short period of wakefulness, with a sense of repose and trust. And, as if rocked by its kind and friendly rhythm, I fell asleep again, this time in tranquility.


## The Steamship


I awakened naturally, however, very early. It was still pitch-dark, and by the light of a match I could read on the alarm clock (borrowed by Silvestro in the town) that there was more than half an hour before we had to get up. Still, I had no more desire to sleep; and, taking care not to disturb Silvestro's sleep (he continued to snore, although more modestly), I slipped out of the cave.

I kept the blanket on my shoulders in the Sicilian manner, like a cloak; but in fact it wasn't cold, not even now that the scirocco had died down. It was evident, from the shiny reflection of the rocks, that it had rained during the night. Here and there in the ragged sky the small December stars were visible, and a last crescent of moon spread a pale twilight glow. The sea, flat in the rain without wind, rocked lightly, sleepy and monotonous. And, advancing beside it in that large cloak, I already felt like a kind of pirate, without home or country, a skull embroidered on my uniform.

The roosters could be heard crowing in the countryside. And suddenly a melancholy regret weighed on my heart, at the thought of the morning that would awaken on the island, as it did every day: the shops opening, the goats coming out of the sheds, my stepmother and Carminiello heading down to the kitchen . . . If only, at least, this sickly, faded winter would last forever on the island! But no, summer would return inevitably, as usual. It can't be killed, it's an invulnerable dragon that, with its marvelous youth, is always reborn. And it was a horrible jealousy that pained me, that: to think of the island again inflamed by summer, without me! The sand will be warm again, the colors will be rekindled in the caves, the migratory birds, returning from Africa, will fly through the sky again . . . And in that adored celebration no one, not even some sparrow, or the smallest ant, or the lowest minnow in the sea, will lament this injustice: that summer has returned to the island, without Arturo! In all the immensity of nature around here, not a thought will remain for A.G., as if an Arturo Gerace had never passed through here.

I lay down in my blanket on those livid wet rocks and closed my eyes, pretending for a moment that I had gone back to some lovely past season; and that I was lying on the sand of my little beach; and that that nearby rustling was the cool serene sea below, ready to welcome the *Torpedo Boat of the Antilles*. The fire of that infinite boyhood season rose in my blood, with a terrible passion that almost made me faint. And the only love of those years returned to say goodbye. Aloud, as if he really were near, I said, "Bye, Pa."

Immediately, the memory of him rushed to my mind: not as a precise figure but as a kind of cloud that advanced charged with gold, murky blue; or like a bitter taste, or a sound as of a crowd, but instead it was the countless echoes of his calls and words, which returned from every point of my life. And certain almost negligible features: a shrug of his shoulders, a distracted laugh, or the large, untidy shape of his nails; the joints of his fingers; or a knee scratched on the cliffs . . . They returned in isolation, making my heart pound, almost unique perfect symbols of a many-sided, mysterious, infinite grace . . . And of a suffering that became more bitter to me for this reason: that I felt it was a childish thing; like a convergence of swirling currents, it rushed everything into this present, brief passage of farewell. And afterward I would forget, naturally, betray it. From here I would go on to another age, and I would regard him as a fable.

Now I forgave him everything. Even his departure with another man. And even that hard final speech, in which, in Stella's presence, he had called me, besides everything else, heartbreaker and Don Juan: and which at the moment had offended me not a little.

(Thinking back later, I wondered if, basically, that speech of his wasn't just, at least in part . . . Truthfully, maybe, though I thought I was in love with this or that person, or two or three people together, in reality I loved none of them. The fact is that in general I was too in love with being in love: that was always my true passion!

(It may be, in conscience, that I *never* seriously loved W.G. And as for N., who was, after all, that most famous woman? A poor little Neapolitan with nothing special about her, of the type that Naples is full of!

(Yes, I had the well-founded suspicion that that speech wasn't completely wrong. The suspicion, not really the certainty . . . Thus life has remained a mystery. And I myself am, for me, still the first mystery!

(Now, from this infinite distance, I think again of W.G. I imagine him, perhaps, more aged than ever, disfigured by wrinkles, gray-haired. He leaves and returns, alone, confused, adoring the one who says to him *parody*. Not loved by anyone—since even N., who though she wasn't beautiful loved another . . . And I would like to let him know: It doesn't matter, even if you're old. For me you'll always be the most beautiful.

(. . . Of her, in due time, I had some news, in Naples, through travelers who came from Procida. She was well, healthy, although very much thinner. And she continued her usual life in the Casa dei Guaglioni with Carmine, who every day became more charming. But she no longer called him Carmine, she preferred to call him by his second name, Arturo. As for me, I'm glad that there's another Arturo Gerace on the island, a fair-haired boy, who right now, perhaps, runs free and happy on the beaches . . .)

From the cave, which I had left half open, the trill of the alarm clock reached me. I hurried in, afraid that it was not enough to disturb the sleep of my nurse; but I found him already sitting up amid the blankets, rubbing his eyes in a daze and muttering curses against that irritating trill. Immediately, going over to him, I announced, with triumphant impatience:

"Hey! You know you snore?"

"What?" he said without comprehending, still sleepy. I then shouted in his ear, in a thundering voice, and with a desire to laugh that burst out between my words:

"YOU KNOW THAT YOU SNORE WHEN YOU SLEEP?"

"Eh! You're tickling me with your breath!" he protested, rubbing his ear. "Snore . . . oh, and what of it? Of course," he continued, just start-ing to wake up, "what, should I not snore? We all snore, when we sleep."

"Yes!" I exclaimed, rolling on the ground with laughter. "But there's snoring and snoring! You beat the world champion! You're like a radio orchestra at its loudest!"

"Oh, yes? I get great pleasure from it!" he replied, now completely awake and rather put out. "But why would you, kid, believe that you snore softly? Last night, at a certain hour, I had to go out on the beach to pee, and there, at a distance of ten meters, I could still hear a snoring from the cave like a squadron of planes passing at low altitude!"

That made me happy. In fact, if I snored like that, it was a clear sign that I could now consider myself grown up, mature, and truly a man, in all regards.

We loaded ourselves with bags, blankets, and so on, and headed toward the town, along the shore that was beginning to whiten in the dawn. Along the eastern horizon, a red color, under dark stripes of clouds, announced a day of changeable weather. When we reached the square, Silvestro headed toward the harbor office, which was already open, to deliver to an acquaintance of his the various objects he had borrowed yesterday, to return to their different owners. He also took charge of buying the tickets for our crossing, while I went ahead to the dock.

The first rays of sun, fractured and glittering, lengthened over the almost smooth sea. I thought that soon I would see Naples, the mainland, the cities, unknown multitudes! And a sudden yearning to leave seized me, to be gone from that square and from that dock.

The steamer was already there, waiting. And, looking at it, I felt all the strangeness of my waning childhood. I had seen that boat dock and lift anchor so many times, and had never embarked on the journey! As if, for me, that were not an ordinary scheduled ferry, a kind of tramcar, but an aloof and inaccessible ghost, destined for who knows what desolate glaciers!

Silvestro returned with the tickets; and the sailors prepared the gangplank for boarding. While my nurse talked to them, I, unseen, took from my pocket that circle of gold that N. had sent me the night before. And secretly I kissed it.

As I looked at it, suddenly an intoxicating weakness dimmed my sight. At that moment, the sending of the earring was translated into all its meanings: of farewell, of trust; and of bitter and marvelous coquetry! So now I had learned that she was also a flirt, my dear little love! Unaware of it, certainly, but she was. In fact, what other woman's farewell could ever express a coquettishness more beautiful than hers, in her ignorance? To send me in remembrance not the sign of a caress or a kiss; but of a vile abuse. As if to say: "Even your violence is a thing of love for me."

I felt a furious temptation to race back to the Casa dei Guaglioni. And to get in bed next to her, to say to her: "Let me sleep for a little with you. I'll leave tomorrow. I don't say that we have to make love, if you don't want. But at least let me kiss you here on that ear, where I wounded you."

Already, however, the sailor at the foot of the gangplank was tearing our tickets; already Silvestro was, with me, going up the gangplank. The siren sounded the signal for departure.

When I was on the seat next to Silvestro, I hid my face on my arm, against the seat back. And I said to him: "You know, I don't feel like seeing Procida grow distant and indistinct, become a sort of gray shape . . . I'd rather pretend it didn't exist. So until the moment you can't see it anymore, it'll be better if I don't look. You tell me, at that moment."

And I remained with my face against my arm, as if ill, and without any thought, until Silvestro shook me gently and said: "Arturo, come, you can wake up."

Around our ship the sea was uniform, endless as an ocean. The island could no longer be seen.

# ABOUT THE AUTHOR

Elsa Morante was born in Rome in 1912. She began publishing stories in her twenties, and in 1948 published her first novel, *Lies and Sorcery*, which was a critical success and won a prestigious award. In 1941, she married the novelist Alberto Moravia; they separated in 1962. *Arturo's Island*, her second novel, came out in 1957, also to critical acclaim; it won Italy's most important prize, the Strega. Her third novel, *History* (1974), although not well received critically, is perhaps her most famous: at her insistence it was published as a paperback so that it would reach as many readers as possible. Morante's final novel, *Aracoeli*, was published in 1982. Over the years, she continued to publish stories and poems as well. She lived most of her life in Rome but traveled widely, to India, China, the Soviet Union, and the United States, among other places. She died in 1985.

# ABOUT THE TRANSLATOR

Ann Goldstein is a former editor at *The New Yorker*. She has translated works by, among others, Primo Levi, Pier Paolo Pasolini, Elena Ferrante, Italo Calvino, and Alessandro Baricco, and is the editor of *The Complete Works of Primo Levi* in English. She has been the recipient of a Guggenheim Fellowship and awards from the Italian Ministry of Foreign Affairs and the American Academy of Arts and Letters.